THE BOYS OF BELLE HAVEN

THE BOYS
OF BELLE
HAVEN

A NOVEL

PETER HAAREN
& LISA WOLFE

ISBN: 978-1-937650-92-6

Library of Congress Control Number 2018939127

Designed by Susan Turner

SMALL
BATCH
BOOKS

493 SOUTH PLEASANT ST.
AMHERST, MA 01002
413.230.3943
SMALLBATCHBOOKS.COM

For Mark, Willy, Bud, Sam, Mah D, Jackie r, and Willow

&

Karen, Bevel, and Persy

CONTENTS

The authors would like to acknowledge the gracious
help of family and friends.

THE BOYS OF BELLE HAVEN

PART ONE

. . .

CONNECTICUT

THE ARK

I STARTED, A BODY THROWN INTO SPACE, FLUNG OUT INTO ORBIT, late one snowy January night in the approximate middle of The Last Century (TLC) on this planet of hours. The house where I was cut, first Doctors Hospital, then Mount Sinai, now just a ghost on Manhattan's Upper East Side, across from Gracie Mansion, with its ornate front gate, now just another urban address, conferred on me a certain prestige, perhaps even glamour, for I was part of what was to be a brief, aristocratic tradition: birth at the finest hospital in the capital of the world, New York City, oft dubbed "the Big Apple," great as a great drain is great. My parents lived in Connecticut, in Riverside, an affluent bedroom community, cupped in the state's tiny panhandle, where—like anywhere, I suppose—people pursued their dreams and small, selfish goals. Mr. and Mrs. Howard B. Taine were white, bright, and Protestant, and before I knew I had a face, before I became conscious and capable of having experiences in a safe, comfortable reality dominated by parental presences who saw me and formed me in so many

ways I am beginning just now to realize, I was baptized "Cynthia
Taine," gradually learning, as I became capable and conscious of
having more sustained experiences, that "Cindy," my "other" name,
connected me, by necessary or chance association, to drudgery in
a kitchen amid pans and pots, stooping to a low fire, tending the
hearth, sleeping on a bed of wretched straw, sweeping the floor with
my broom, and then, as if I'd tapped into a Protean Power that gave
me sudden wings, a golden coach, a splendid evening gown to wear,
scintillating sequins, the glow of a night spent dancing, a glass slip-
per lost amid much pandemonium, in the end I met my prince, but
none of that ever happened, for I was already there.

My earliest ME-MORE-ME is of Mom holding my feet, washing them in the prismatic spray of a "sprinkler," a water-driven
mechanism controlled by the force in the garden hose, whirling,
making frantic revolutions on the lush, green grass in back of our
house, its lawn bordered with weeping willows and the yellow forsythia bush, flaring, blinding in the sunlight. Tommy, two years older
than I, would wave his orange water pistol over his head, its plastic
shape glinting with light. I can almost hear him, wildly yelling on
the seat of the swing set on chains inside our jungle gym, a veritable sculpture of metal tubing painted bright primary colors with a
tough, rubbery paint I can still feel, an indelible impression. I still
have a mental map of the house, its flagrant red front door and the
large living room picture window, the distribution of its rooms, the
faux-brick motif of the linoleum floor in the kitchen, the living room
carpet, a purple prairie of fuzziness continuing up the stairway to
the bedrooms, to my room with its access to the attic. I was roused
one night from my vast sleep, and my room was filled with eerie
light; I peeked through the window to see the full moon and hear,
from Tommy's room, music playing on the record player, our first
phonograph, a Christmas gift from Mom and Dad, blue and white,
with a long black cord and plug like a snake's head, the gift that Dad
had shown us how to use, which Tommy kept on a shelf in his room

because he felt entitled to. It was a magic moment, like another time when I was startled awake by what sounded like, by what I thought was, the rich, singing percussion of a cash register, like the sparkling silver one with multicolored buttons at the supermarket where Mom did the grocery shopping twice a week, taking Tommy and me or just one of us in the car with her. There was a Texaco gasoline station down the road from our house, and I can still see the sign with its logo, a large, green *T* inside a red star, which we'd pass while out doing errands.

So the years flew by, and everything changed and, simultaneously, nothing did. I am still here, sustained by the stream of my own warm impermanence, the focus of a point of view, and the chain of actions and events that brought me to Belle Haven, the almost whimsical name for this special place, which plays an integral part in my story, forming its necessary preface. I compose myself, sitting like an assiduous butterfly on a rock, a flower, a piece of wood, seeking to produce effects, settled in the Stone Cottage, here on Connecticut's "Gold Coast," keeping to myself, surrounded by so much costly beauty. Our posh neighborhood is rich with rustling trees, wide lawns, expensive homes and gardens, the cargo of the very successful, the place where I, in so many ways, am coming from, part and parcel of a new, dizzy, digitalized world, fiddling with keys in the here and now, making the motions of my exercise in creative autobiography real. I feel, looking up at the clock, that I'm in a rush, caught up in some sort of contest, connecting and cutting with invisible scissors and glue, hoping to meet a finish line that ends at midnight, tonight. Where are we going with this? Who are these "boys," and what does this address of mine betoken: a parallel, projected world where gravity flattens character, the atmosphere warming, its pools of rotting phosphor aglow? Sometimes my sleep becomes shallow, more fitful, and there are instants when I awaken to this cottage of ours, this quirky piece of real estate, to experience a hollow scene set within walls of bone, an empty skull or cavity, and I'm aware of an almost mystical impatience, perversely poetic, profusely syncretic, the impulse to write what recollections I can, before I start my story.

Flummoxed, I pace the worn stone floor, wondering how to proceed with this portfolio of preludes, psychological snapshots wrought in prose, and the shafts of sunlight out on the lawn, out where the heat grows, mix with the scent of mint, the drops of dew sparkling in the grass and hedges. The sky is now a bright lemon glow, almost a fragrance above the salty Sound, Long Island in the distance, its dark mass stretched out in a long, languid ribbon of ink, as a jet plane way up there, a tiny white moth, delicate and ghostly, goes about its business, directed by forces I don't understand.

The city at first was an abstract place, set to the west, where the train stopped, where the sun fell down and bruised its knees. "It's the place of your father's employment," Mom said one morning, as the train disappeared, after a long kiss, prolonged by Mom, who could be so theatrical, as if she were trying to demonstrate something to Tommy and me, but especially to me. I noticed that Dad wore a hat and carried his light brown coat, even on a warm spring day, sunlight scintillating its furry fabric, his right hand swinging a leather briefcase. He almost floated off into the direction of the train, which, like everything, followed a schedule, as I watched it vanish in a blur, erased by a purplish haze, and I wondered where Dad was going. I conjured a fabulously complicated castle, for I thought in terms of kingdoms then.

Before attending kindergarten at Riverside Elementary, I went to "Mrs. Reinhardt's," the local nursery school, an ordinary brick house on a quiet street, shaded by enormous trees, having nothing special about it except its glass porch and backyard, a playground dominated by a swing set, a large sandbox, and a rudimentary merry-go-round of four metal ponies painted bright colors, their forms set on iron springs that bent. I remember going around and around on it, bouncing up and down, and then going inside, taking off our coats and shoes, walking quickly and quietly into a large room with endlessly fascinating wallpaper, where we stood and sang, where Mrs. Reinhardt played the piano, leading us through one of the first songs I'd know best, a simple melody with a little lyric about Christmas coming, a goose getting fat, and invisible auditors being asked to please put a penny in an old man's hat. Sometimes, at Mrs. Reinhardt's, I smelt the rich aromas of food being cooked, coming from another part of the house, a kitchen somewhere, as if someone were surreptitiously cooking something.

Soon I went to Riverside Elementary, taking, with Tommy, the big, orange school bus, which sometimes barged noisily into our neighborhood, disturbing the morning quiet surrounding us where we stood; I was probably singing a song, waiting for the bus at 16 Pasture Lane, where our driveway began and the mailbox stood out against rosebushes, an intricate background of luscious leaves, a dense, emerald screen hosting crimson bursts against which our mailbox figured on its post, a pert little house with a red metal flag put up in the air, indicating something there, a box of new crayons or chocolates, always mailed in a white cardboard box wrapped with brown paper sealed with masking tape. Dad sometimes sent surprise gifts to us, always postmarked "New York City," but he'd never reveal who had sent them, that he'd indeed sent them, that he was the force behind the magic of the mailbox.

Pasture Lane was a long, winding stream of asphalt punctuated by mailboxes, shrines to a Postal Principle that no sane person in the future I imagine will have much time or use for. Our house, set back on a sometimes shaggy front lawn bordered by birches and pine trees, was a lovely Tudor, its stucco walls and deep brown trim absorbing warmth, even becoming hot, on summer days when Mom would drive us down to the beach in the late afternoon, a golden time and place, down past the yacht club, especially at high tide, bright waves snapping the sand. Pasture Lane was shaped like an elongated bottle, a long neck of pavement and then a small loop wrapped around a teardrop-shaped island full of tall weeds and short, husky trees, the place where I'd retreat to play my radio, sheltered from everyone, inventing little scenarios, and every atom of my being was positively saturated with my play. From my hidden place I could see the roof of our house, the brick chimney, the gleaming TV antennae, perched like an ungainly bird sculpture, a metallic stork standing out against the sky.

Dad made fires using iron tongs and bellows that had belonged to Granddad when he'd lived in Belle Haven, an enclave of exclusive properties just a few miles down the road from us, prime peninsular real estate. The bellows were an antique, a device made of leather and wood, the leather painted a red and black geometric pattern, like a checkerboard, its old, painted surface now cracking and crusty. "Use it gently," Mom would say, so I had to be gentle when I squeezed the wooden handles together to create a thin stream of air.

Riverside Elementary, exactly two miles away, a distance I knew by odometer, learning it one rainy morning when we missed the bus and Mom had to drive us to school, was the place where we, according to the words of our school's spirited anthem, were "filled with joy each day / at work and play." I used to think about how awkward the lyric sounded, how inaccurate the word "each" was, because we obviously didn't go to school every day of the week, and I seldom felt joyful about being there, so the lyric's carelessness made me feel secretly superior to whoever had penned those inept words. Elementary school was where we learned to write thoughts out in lines and sign our names to them, to exercise our autographs, to think of words as SILLY BELLS, to understand denominations of money, the principles of geometry and fractions, all cheerfully illustrated in painstaking, colorful, and optimistic detail in our workbooks. When I think of school, I see the building's grounds and then the long, well-lit hallways, fixed with disinfectant, the walls lined with display cases and photographs of faces, past graduating classes, the waxed linoleum floors shining, the giant gym and auditorium spaces, the clothes we wore at different times of the year, the trees outside performing their colorful changes, the leaves leaving, and the arrival of snowflakes. Tommy called us "STEWED ANTS," and some of my classmates bragged about the supposed excellence of Riverside's school system, saying that it was the second best in the state, surpassed only by Darien's. I have a vivid memory of Mrs. Baker's third-grade classroom, with its views of the big apple tree in the back field, where the window shades mysteriously caught fire one December afternoon, shortly after JFK's assassination, the place where I realized that my mathematical skills were profoundly superficial, "learning" the multiplication table by rote, in lieu of a more conceptual approach, knowing that my understanding of it was based solely on memorization, the sensory, sonic contours of words, on the sounds of the numerals as we recited them, sometimes accompanied by flashcards, seeing the graphic figures without any real grasp of the conceptual content they conveyed.

Anna Limbertone, who frequently babysat for us, was a gregarious, athletic, long-limbed blonde, a lithesome gymnast, an effective cheerleader, an effervescent teenager with an elastic, supple smile and an abundance of good vibrations, always ready and able to invigorate proceedings with a pleasurable push in a new direction, taking us up in her wings. She sometimes rode her ten-speed bicycle over to our house, but she'd usually walk the back path from her house on Nutmeg Lane. She said I was lucky to have an older brother, because he'd introduce me, someday, to all of his handsome friends, and I'd be the belle of the ball. She introduced us to The Beatles, playing her 45s on our phonograph, and she danced, flapping her arms around, twisting and shouting like a big, happy bird to the music, and we joined in, dancing and singing. Anna used to perform—just for us, it seemed—a silly song about invisibility: "I love my chains, my chains of love," she'd sing, and we enjoyed having her as a babysitter because she was so much fun, until one Friday night, late in her career with us, when her boyfriend came over, and Mom and Dad returned home early, and that was the end of that.

There was an electrical outlet on the back porch, screened against insects, where we'd plug in our phonograph, play music, and dance, imitating The Beatles. President Kennedy had just been assassinated, but The Beatles provided diversion from the tragedy, so our back porch became a kind of stage where we, just kids in the neighborhood, made appearances on the *Ed Sullivan Show*s of our imaginations, Tommy playing his plastic guitar, me with my microphone, a xylophone stick, Emily Watts on bongo drums, and her older brother Joey playing an ancient ukulele, the four of us becoming lost in the music on the back porch, carrying on, singing about coming home, going home, getting home to my baby, arriving home in time. Instantiations of the word "home," tokens of a type, occur so frequently in rock pop music (RPM), creating formations of word wheels spinning, the spirit of it dawning deeply within me, like a flow of lava underwater, that I don't know where to begin, having so many things to tell you when I reach home, where lamps are lit at dusk, where smiles match faces shining with puzzling light, the safe space of permanent location, a place that I am gradually beginning to realize is merely a state of mind. And once you start to look for it, it pops up everywhere, like a force in one's knees, proof, perhaps, that thinking is the best way to travel. I don't know how many Beatles, Stones, and Led Zeppelin lyrics deploy the word "home," but I'm certain it's a large number.

Beyond Pasture Lane there were roads and houses everywhere, but that was not familiar territory, not the environment I really knew well, for I knew my neighborhood turf intimately, through the rubber of my own shoes' soles, by my own two feet. Young kids, older kids, and teenagers were everywhere, riding bikes or just running around, bouncing balls, jumping rope, playing tag, shouting, playing basketball or badminton on hot summer afternoons, with that white, plastic, red-rubber-nosed, miniature space capsule, the shuttlecock, pushed back into space with the tap of a racket in just the right place. On warm, comfortable evenings, when twilight seemed to conspire with a pregnant buzzing in the trees, when the orange sun morphed for a short time into the ruby heart of a summer dusk, we played outside after dinner, oblivious to the problem of suffering in this world, although once, at the dinner table, Mom stuck her tongue out at Dad as she passed the salad bowl to him, and I saw something shatter, his calm composure break, like a large, glass cocoon, as a new dynamic showed in her meeting his eyes, and the fissure between Mom and Dad began to open, to unravel through angry adult behavior, shouting matches, and slammed doors. I can still see Mom's frightened expression after an argument, when she shook like a nervous animal. Raccoons rummaged through the trash cans at night when the garage door was left open, and Mom would scold Tommy for forgetting to close it, and once, after she'd been drinking, she made a real scene, yelling at Tommy, who was asleep upstairs, throwing the flashlight beam all around, scaring the animals away. She was volatile and unpredictable; we never knew when she might be provoked by something, erupting into a spontaneous display of negative NRG. She once scolded me because I hadn't seemed sufficiently interested enough in my new Barbie doll, something she'd just bought me, and I wanted to play outside with Tommy and the other boys, running around, getting dirt on my clean blouses, skirts, and dresses. She didn't like it when I played roughly in my Indian Princess costume, soiling its headdress of white feathers and imitation turquoise beads set in dark leather straps, which came out of the basement with me onto the lawn, the hazy sky filled with sunlight so diffuse there were no edges on the shadows things cast.

Dad gave me a transistor radio for my tenth birthday, and I listened to music on it, taking it with me everywhere, puttering around with the dial, pulling in notes from the air, filling up on RPM. I vividly recall tuning in and listening to a song about a fisherman's daughter one afternoon at the yacht club, sitting on a towel on the beach, with the smell of low tide rising, then tuning to another station and hearing The Beatles' "Penny Lane" for the first time, the drift of it filling my ears and eyes, later learning about the pretty nurse stealing poppies from a tray, feeling as if I were in a play, or simply asleep, unconcerned about any future consequences my actions might have because it's all drama and dream. There were lots of kids on Pasture Lane, but Dennis Knowlton, my friend Sally's older brother, had the advantage of being the oldest kid, the first teenager I ever knew, the first real hippie too. We'd go upstairs to his room and play the stereo loudly and listen with such extraordinary curiosity and excitement that I remember those times best. Dennis was a REBEL ONION. He was four years older than Sally, and he had a romantic crush on me; he gave me David Bowie's "Space Oddity" LP for a Christmas present when I was in seventh grade. Mr. Knowlton was an executive at a chemical company that made plastics, elastic stuff, the buttons on my dress, automobile upholstery, the handy bags we brought salty snacks to school in, kitchen bowls, plates and cups, the thick skin of my raincoat, my doll, our combs, the shower curtain, our toothbrushes, containers in the refrigerator, Dad's golf balls, Tommy's water pistol, the garbage bags. Dennis had a fantastic LP collection, and he handled with dexterity and a dustcloth his black, gleaming vinyl discs, pulling one out from its paper sleeve, fastidiously spraying and wiping it off, ceremoniously carrying it away by its edges between his hands, and placing it reverently on the turntable in his upstairs room, the walls festooned with psychedelic posters and shimmering fabrics. Dennis spoke in a feigned, foreign accent, vaguely British, as he cued the needle—the "stylus," he'd say—to its properly empty niche on the rotating disc, its contact with the surface an initial hiss, audible on the gargantuan speakers, introducing some new song to us, us to some new song. I soaked my ideas in an atmosphere positively saturated with RPM, as though an autochthonous force, emanating from below us, were passing through the foundations of the house and up into his room, and I felt I was dancing on air.

Before The Who's "My Generation" filled the whole Knowlton household during a weekend of riotous teenagers partying, drinking beer, and smoking weed, Dennis taking charge while his parents were away, setting those stereo speakers up on the picnic table outside; before the first four songs of Led Zeppelin's debut LP, all featuring the word "home" in some form—"I sure do wish I was at home"; "I can feel it [the need to ramble] calling me home"; "Baby, please come home"; "I work so hard, bringing home my hard-earned pay"—before Donovan sang "Mellow Yellow" and "Season of the Witch"; before Joni Mitchell's *Blue* LP, including within its webby matrix of honeyed melodies many direct and indirect instantiations of *home* (I had a poster of Joni, a kind of ad for the LP that I'd tacked to the wall in my bedroom, later, in New Canaan, and I'd look at it, her body bathed in blue, feeling as if I were swimming too, playing in deep water); but before RPM, before the electromagnetic revolution, before "Paint It Black" and those long lines of cars, before all of that, the city was just an abstraction, a point, set to the west, where my father went to work, a tan man in hat walking from Grand Central Station, where the Pan Am Building hovered like a huge electrical component, a generator of some sort, its dark shadow cast over the depths of Park Avenue on a cold winter morning. He walked through whatever weather to his spacious Midtown office in Rockefeller Center, passing through the revolving glass doors into the Art Deco lobby with its murals, walking toward the gleaming fleet of elevators to rise, swathed in a vaguely mechanical hum, up to the seventeenth floor. I was glad that Dad's office was way up there in that futuristic rocket of a structure, and I'd look down through the window to see people like ants scurrying below amid slow-moving traffic, a veritable syrup of gasoline sculpture: cabs, cars, buses, and trucks slowly moving below me after I'd been whisked so swiftly upstairs in what Dad called "the rising room."

Escalators were "rising steps," and on my first trip to the islands, he put his hand to the window and said, "Cindy, look, we're rising on wings. We're on rising wings." Dad was an executive with Hallmark Hotels, the big conglomerate then extending its empire, building new resorts throughout the Caribbean, and his office was a kind of control booth from which he managed construction operations by remote control, by telephone. He'd frequently fly off to inspect construction sites, so he was busy, sometimes bossy and impatient, but he also had a playful streak and a fairly good singing voice, singing Frank Sinatra's "Summer Wind" to Tommy and me when he took us on unexpected adventures in the car. My image of my father's voice is a bugle or trumpet, some kind of shining horn, its clarion call capable of organizing worldly material, ordering people around, building buildings, getting people to do things for him, getting us to do things for him, getting Tommy and me out of bed early on a sunny Saturday morning, repeating, with the intention of rousing our enthusiasm, "Up and at 'em, up and at 'em," which always sounded like "UP AN ATOM, UP AN ATOM" to me, something to do with NRG jumping, and we'd have a fast breakfast and then go out in the car to do errands.

Sometimes Dad's voice had an annoying urgency about it, an uncanny, adamant pitch, not really his own, all about getting errands "done," shopping on Saturday mornings, then getting chores "done," working on the property around the house, mowing the lawn, raking leaves, weeding the garden, polishing the car, painting furniture, shoveling snow. Mom was always finding something that needed doing. "Go and help your father," she would say, and we'd know we weren't really going to help much, or do any real work, but that Dad, under pressure from Mom, was going to demonstrate for us the importance of completing a task.

Dad had roots in rural Florida, in a remote region of swamps and sinkholes, open marshland, and dense, semitropical forest sandwiched between Lake Okeechobee ("the Big O") and a lesser-known body of water to the north, Lake Kissimmee, its shorelines richly populated with wildlife: deer, bobcats, alligators, eagles, wintering waterfowl, and all kinds of wading birds. There were whooping cranes, spoonbills, herons, and egrets. Away from the shore, in the densely wooded forest, there were wildcats, deer, armadillos, and bears. It was undiscovered, uncultivated, elemental country then, with large tracts of land being claimed, developed, and pressed into the service of cattle and agriculture, specifically citrus fruit. The origin of the fruit-bearing species, from which our modern orange derives, somewhere in Asia, on the other side of the globe, was a place Dad located for us, taking the globe down from the shelf to show Tommy and me places on the planet, the islands of Japan, New Zealand, and Australia. He explained Continental Drift to us, showing how South America and Africa fit together over the wide expanse of the Atlantic Ocean, having already arranged to end with his finger on Florida, to stop there and start to tell us about the plantation.

It is only by a series of actions that anyone becomes what he or she is, and Dad's dad, Grandpa Taine, came originally from Europe, from France, Marseilles, and he'd stowed away as a teenager on a commercial ship bound for Miami, of all places, where he found work, saved money, and eventually moved north, purchasing land where he'd hunt with bow and arrow, where he'd eventually plant orange trees, becoming one of the first suppliers for the vast, growing juice market in the cities to the north. Dad grew up, he liked to say, "on the plantation," the only son of a prosperous orange grove owner and his half-Indian wife, Maud, of whom, standing between trees, her hands on her hips, looking like she was enjoying herself and the camera, Dad kept an early, hand-colored, sepia-toned photograph atop his bedroom bureau, and I'd take it down and study her smile and see a trace of me in it. Grandpa Taine died before I was born, but I met Grandma Maud in a nursing home in Daytona Beach, a cheerful old woman with a dark, leathery face, wild white hair, and a hickory cane. She was overjoyed with our appearance, our improbable, impromptu visit, the one airplane trip the family took together, a surprise for Mom, Tommy, and me that spring break, though Dad would take me alone with him, soon, to the islands. Dad had had, I imagined, all kinds of experiences that he never told us about, though he did talk about working on the plantation, managing the groves, and about the little airplane he flew, spraying acres of orange and grapefruit trees with pesticides from a single-prop, low-flying, airborne contraption, a go-cart capable of flight, that could cover a lot of acreage in very little time. There were lazy afternoons during the growing season when he and his father fished for catfish or hunted deer, and there was, after miles of unpaved road, the tiny hamlet of Yeehaw Junction, where the church and the fairgrounds were, and where a traveling circus stopped each year to set up a tent and play calliope music. Grandma Maud, a religious woman, practiced a variety of "home schooling," as Dad described it, so he was schooled at home by Grandma Maud, and he experienced, I imagine, a certain solitude on the plantation during those early years, playing alone with a ball against a wall. Dad didn't go to public school until ninth grade, when he'd ride his bike to the bus stop and take the long ride on a big, orange school bus into Sebring, where there were lots of other kids his own age, not just the farm kids from Yeehaw Junction. He described classmates who were the sons and daughters of Seminole Indians, people who practiced strange religious rites, handling snakes and talking in tongues. He told us that he'd had a girlfriend who was half-Seminole and that this had upset Grandma Maud. Dad attended high school for two years, helping, in his spare time, Grandpa Taine on the plantation. He became something of an athlete at school, but one day after baseball practice he just decided to leave on a whim, one which he'd been considering, turning over in his mind for some time, and he set out on his own; he hitchhiked to Miami, and when he arrived, he "never looked back," as he put it, working his way up from charter plane pilot, taking pleasure groups on day trips to Key West and the Bahamas, up into hotel management and finally executive ontological work, big business—a real success story.

Christmas was the holiday, the hinge on which the whole year turned, when everyone reached out and seemed to live more intensely, yielding to a spirit of pure hospitality and easy exchange. Tommy and I counted the December days with anticipation, opening tiny paper doors on the Christmas calendar hanging over the kitchen table, revealing precious, painted scenes, like multi-colored postage stamps, scenes depicting Santa with his elves and reindeer, or baby Jesus in a cradle, surrounded by the sleeping animals, or snowflakes and angels, boughs of holly, snowmen, candy canes, and stars. We'd usually celebrate Christmas Eve at Gaga and Granddad's snazzy apartment, with its ornate gate and entrance, on Park Avenue, all lit up with the stop and go of traffic lights, especially coded for Christmas.

Mom's parents, Granddad and Gaga, Mr. and Mrs. Arthur R. Prescott, lived in a commodious duplex at the top of a white building located on the western side of Park Avenue, where cabs raced by, competing for customers, CRUST STRUMMERS, the pavement dipping slightly downhill toward Grand Central, "Pan Am" displayed on its top. Granddad once owned a large house in Greenwich, in Belle Haven, right on the water, where I was photographed as an infant; though I have no memory of that time, there I am on a flagstone terrace, cuddling a long-haired dachshund, Crystal, just a puppy then, the backyard's shady trees and formal garden organized around a reflecting pool, with bright flower beds and a fountain, where the adults would sit in Adirondack chairs, like wooden thrones, chatting, watching sailboats, drinking in the setting sun, watching water birds through binoculars.

Dad called their Park Avenue building "The Ark," because it was dark and cool inside, quiet as a cave in the lobby, and a fountain bubbled from a marble alcove in a corner, making a distinct cheerful dripping sound that echoed through space. There was a large tapestry, depicting many animals: lions, tigers, and bears, in pairs, like married couples, hanging over a fireplace that was never used, and I'd train my eyes on it, finding exotic, long-beaked birds, flamingos, and pelicans embedded in its weave.

Taking the elevator up was exciting because of the bright lights and mirrors inside "the rising room," which the elevator operator, the man in charge of our cube-shaped adventure, called "the lift." He always wore a red suit, with a clean white shirt, and he smiled in a way that turned into a grin. He'd give us orange lollipops, ask us our ages, and then talk with our parents on the way up. Once the elevator stopped, Tommy and I would rush out ahead, racing down the hallway to The Ark's formidable door, where Tommy pushed the buzzer, and we'd hear a slow series of eerie electronic gongs resonate from within. The door slowly opened, and Dennis, the butler, materialized, a tall man, dapperly dressed in a black tie and jacket, with strangely blond hair. He moved slowly, with a kind of lurch, and he spoke in a low, vaguely Teutonic voice, "Welcome, my friends from faraway Riverside. Do come in, please. Let us enter-TAIN you," stressing that second SILLY BELL, as he placed his large hand at my back and ushered us down the long hallway, with its dark paintings of dead ancestors hanging in heavy, lugubrious gold frames. He led us into the living room, where a lively din of music and voices prevailed, ice cubes clinking against glasses, and the snap, crackle, and pop of logs in the fireplace, an acoustical background against which Aunt Pauline's voice in particular figured.

Although there were shadows lurking in corners, The Ark was alive with light, a place to see and be seen. Dressed up one Christmas Eve, I felt extraordinary excitement, wearing my emerald green satin dress, something Mom had worn when she was my age, and when we walked down the hallway, led by Dennis into the big room, Gaga immediately recognized it, swooned. "Oh, Arthur, just look," she said, delighted that Mom had saved it for me to wear. I felt proud, sequins sparkling, feeling my patrician roots. From a crystal decanter, Scotch whisky was being poured; I could smell its pure and peaty scent. I once stole a sip from my mother's drink, and I think I felt a little kick, a moment of bright warmth, setting a small electric motor inside of me whirling, making The Ark the happiest place in the world. "Photograph this; remember this," I thought to myself, tracking my train of impressions, where Gaga laughed and Aunt Mary spilled dip on the carpet, where Mom lit the wrong end of her cigarette, and where Granddad's voice boomed with authority, while everyone seemed happily mixed up.

Aunt Pauline, Granddad's much younger sister, sometimes visited The Ark for Christmas and, I liked to think, to see me exclusively. When most people enter a room where others are and have been for some time, they adhere to its mood and precedence, but Pauline, making her entrance, always created a contrast, in my mind at least, my eyes fixed on her presence. She lit up space like a ball of light, a blaze of sparks, and the conversation around her sparkled with instant invention. Almost everyone, probably, has a home to go to, or to get to, one of these days, but Pauline never seemed to have or even want a place she called "home." Home, for her, was a perpetual unfolding of experience, synonymous with time itself, the ephemeral evanescence of the present, which was wherever she happened to be, a place she was always simultaneously both arriving at and departing from, in rapid oscillation, somewhere to be from and let other people ask about. It was as if she were always on her way, like a personable wave cresting into place, glad to arrive but just as happy to be moving on. It was just her way. She was a wandering spirit with a marvelous voice, a restless soul, and she could go anywhere in the world that she wanted. She was possessed by what Gaga called "nomadic madness," and she thrived on the spur of the moment, taking some interest in musicology, taking a great interest in other people, cultures, and locales, following her fancy and traveling around the world at whim, visiting friends in distant places. Sometimes she stayed in expensive hotels. She'd been on safaris. There was a photograph of her in khaki clothing, pointing her finger at a lion lying down in the shade of a tree the size of a house. She'd seen zebras and aardvarks, and as Aunt Pauline described them to me, I spontaneously generated an image of my grandparents as aardvarks, sprouting hairy aardvark hands clasping crystal goblets of red wine, while relatives and friends gathered for a formal dinner with settings, our places indicated by our names carefully written on white cards. There were elegant, tapered candles, white linen napkins, and heavy, real silverware. Pauline floated in, donning shiny, tiny earrings that looked like little green ants. Not bound by gravity, she moved through the room with ease and intimacy, here, there, and everywhere, which seemed to be the point around which her being revolved. "Oh, darling," she said, "life is short, make fun of it," and she laughed. I loved the way she laughed when Gaga asked her why she hadn't packed any high-heeled shoes for her visit, and she winked at me, saying, "Darling, I'm going to Mexico City, where I'll wear sandals in the sand," but before that, she was stopping to see a friend in Memphis, Tennessee, of all places, and she held out her hands to stretch out her fingers and say, "TEN, I SEE. I see ten. What do you see, Cindy Taine?" She said she was going to see her "friend in Memphis," a mysterious man whom I'd never hear about again, though I now remember that he'd worked in the music business, had had something to do with Sun Records and Elvis Presley, but that was before I was born. But she always went on to Mexico City after Christmas, back before the air there turned bad and they installed oxygen masks in the phone booths, back when the public parks were filled with wild parrots and monkeys, and I'd ask Pauline to please let me sneak into her suitcase to travel with her around the world. She once sang a song about "mobile deeds" becoming "noble seeds." She told me I'd never be able to step into the same river twice, that a subtle fire animated every atom in the universe, that life was essentially strife, and that

I was a flame, alive and victorious. She taught me the Greek name "Aristotle," that it named a great Greek philosopher who was an aristocrat but who wasn't "airy" at all, because he said that experience is the greatest teacher, that totality frees us from all error, and she pointed her right hand's index finger down, down toward some pattern buried in the carpet. She asked me to show her where my thinking took place—a silly question, I thought—and I pointed to my head, and then, placing my hand on my chest, she said, "The heart is the engine of thought, Cindy," and she added with laughter, "That's where the real beat goes on, always aspiring to achieve the condition of music." Walking toward the piano, laughing some more, she reached its closed top and made a mock pounding of her fists in the air. Then she opened it, revealing the keyboard, and she sat down to play, and as Pauline played, she began to sing, improvising, and the elation in her voice inflated a little lyric for a melody, making her lips shine more brightly. She appeared to be utterly beautiful. She didn't wear very much makeup, but her face was a perfect matrix of features, the picture of expressiveness, and she always wore jewelry and dressed in exquisite silks, shimmering ephemeral stuff, but what else is there?

One Christmas Eve, Pauline played a tape she'd made of indigenous tribal music, highly rhythmic, played on drums, recorded somewhere in Africa, played it on Granddad's reel-to-reel Sony tape recorder, and I remember how he cringed, as Pauline was putting the tape on, as if she'd harm his precious property. When the button was pushed and the music played in waves of busy particles, it created an effect far beyond the combination of the instruments and voices, and the synergy, the unshackled rhythms, and the cascading, unexpected notes generated an unheard-of, alluvial, and savage zone of aural attention for about fifteen minutes that evening, puzzling at first, because the music was almost violently percussive, but persuasive, and I came to make sense of the sounds, the recorded performance hanging like a great invisible structure in the air, something you could move around in, maze-like yet open to your participation if you made the effort to figure a way into its flow. Granddad, with a scowl on his face, insisted that the machine be turned off, saying, "Noise, Pauline, noise! Is this what you call music? Is this what you spend your time with?"

Pauline took me to the Plaza Hotel one wintry afternoon, to the Palm Court, where we had formal afternoon tea, poured from a perfectly elegant, rooster-shaped silver teapot into white cups with dainty, gilt-gold handles, and we sat on satin-cushioned chairs, chatting about what, I don't know. On the way there, we had stopped to admire an extravagant diamond necklace on display in a shop window, where Pauline pretended to initiate an imaginary conversation with the necklace, proceeding to interrogate it, and a pair of silver earrings encrusted with colorful gemstones, asking them about their origins, where they had been mined—the strangest thing I'd ever heard—questioning the inert, mute jewels, ripped from the earth, standing on tiny pedestals, like cake decorations—cut and polished for our eyes alone, it seemed—her voice breaking into melodic song about lucky stars. It was as if she had been placed temporarily under a spell, possessed by a spirit that impelled her to pose, absurdly, these geological, geographical questions, and she remarked with felicity to our reflections in the window on how fortunate she was to be standing there in "luxury," wearing a fur coat, with "money to burn." Those were the words she used on that corner across from the Plaza Hotel. Then, as she snapped out of it, returning to reality, she turned to me and said, "Africa. Most of the diamonds and precious gems in the world come from Africa. Did you know that, Cindy? People are exploited, forced to work under deplorable conditions in the mines, for pitiful wages." We stood for a moment, and then we walked on, almost oblivious to the traffic rushing around us, teetering on the pavement's edge, for I was reflecting on what she'd said.

Inside, seated, Pauline lit a cigarette. I glanced around, noticing other people, mostly women, wearing furs and expensive jewelry, sitting at the tables, politely talking, chatting away, creating a hushed, unbroken murmur, a myriad of mirroring pools of speech, and it seemed as if I were already inhabiting a vast, parallel reality that I was somehow a part of, but also far apart from, outside of, the space abuzz with conversation, piano music, and the constant clinking of tea cups, plates, and silver utensils, all of it unfolding like a pageant on another planet. "Smile away, Cindy, and smell the grass in the meadow," Pauline quipped, raising the rim of her cup, and then she laughed with her characteristic gaiety, adding, "because you can't go back to yesterday. Yesterday's gone. It's vanished in the haze." I felt tuned to a present tense spinning with promise, something like what a pianist might feel, really caught up in the articulate duration of the music and the expectations it arouses.

I was, most of the time, an introverted young girl, nurturing a yen for self-containment and the viewpoint of the reticent, accurate observer around adults, a listener, not a talker, but with Pauline, with just the two of us there, I let my usual reserve drop. My reluctance to express myself dissolved like sugar in hot tea, and I found myself stirred into speech, talking, confiding, suddenly finding that the setting was providing me with images and background music I could relate to, the twinkling fountain a goad, the crystal everywhere encouraging, as I explored new possibilities in conversation, enjoying a wider scope as we spoke about what, I don't know. I don't remember. All I retain is the glow, for I'd never spoken with Mom or Aunt Mary or any other adult woman so candidly before. Later, that spring, Pauline took me to the Boat House in Central Park, where, one brilliant afternoon, we rented a metal rowboat and rowed around on a surface like a river, and we talked about what, I don't know. I remember the feel of the wooden oars' handles when we changed positions, and she let me row past the willow trees, pointing out the lady ducks, the magical, blue-violet, velvet ticket tucked under a female's wing. Maybe it was then, looking around at the flowering trees, that she told me about her trip to Africa, producing a vivid tableau, and around Pauline I faced the latent cunning of my nature.

Granddad guarded a not-very-secret resentment toward his much younger sister, for whom he had no empathy, for she was vivacious and free. She lacked what he called "proper focus." She never did anything that he deemed worthwhile, and he harbored deep disapproval of what were, for him, her fatuous, frivolous pursuits. Granddad had to be dragged to church, but he liked to argue that "In God We Trust" was printed on the backs of our paper dollars for a reason, for money gave people purpose, and it helped them aspire to be better, because it gave them something to achieve. Despite their shared patrimony, Arthur treated Pauline as if she were not who she was, tied by blood, and he disparaged her, as if she were the sister from another genetic lineage entirely. He said she wasn't responsible with money, that she didn't know the meaning of the word "work," and that she lived life as if it were a party, where no work ever got done or whatever work got done got done in a kind of dream. Pauline provoked her older brother's ire because she didn't really care about money. She had plenty of it, so she could afford to flaunt an impertinent indifference to the conservative social conventions it bred. She'd inherited a small fortune from her dead husband, long-gone Uncle John, and so she was financially set, though she made some money—just for fun, I think—purchasing paintings, masks, and other items in remote villages in Africa and selling them in New York City through a friend who owned and ran a certain "Tribal Arts Gallery," a downtown venue of dubious distinction, later shut down for fraudulent sales. So she had money—free, it seemed—and Granddad resented that and would mutter, "Work is what you have to tell yourself to do, and I don't think your Aunt Pauline ever told herself to do much."

Granddad's beliefs were purely proprietary, seeded early in TLC, informed by strict adherence to tacitly accepted codes of behavior, class boundaries, and the dynamics of class awareness, all related to the power of money, the scope of its effects played out in time, as the trajectory of his own colossal success in the publishing industry followed from privileged origins. The way things had been was the way things still were and the way things would be, and he could become abnormally affirmative, absolutely adamant in his judgments about "reality." The final arbiter of all value was Capital, the bloodstream of society, the Ideal Measure, "the great I AM," he used to say. It sometimes seemed he lived to make money, as quickly as possible, to accumulate and amass it, to wisely invest it, not waste it like Pauline. Granddad was the rigid exemplar of a type, one for whom number was everything, a participant in a meaningless contest that favored the fit, the luck of the well born, well educated, and well connected, a vicious game, played to benefit the flows of an already fortunate few. He was a fervent proponent of free market capitalism, what Pauline derisively referred to as "the KAPUT A-LIST System," so he and she engaged in vocal political disputes, concluding once with Granddad's refusal to continue conversing with someone who was, as he put it, "so poorly informed." Pauline never read the newspapers, she rarely voted, and she never watched the evening news on television with the other adults, though I remember watching *Gilligan's Island* with her, laughing hysterically as Gilligan danced around with some monkeys on a beach, playing football with a coconut. She said that someday I'd have GILLS AGAIN, that I'd swim through the sea with the fish, and that my days would be alive with love, craft, and industry. She said that the institution of marriage, like Christianity, was "shipwrecked, on the rocks," and, oh, she liked to drink Scotch!

Granddad was already a teenager when Pauline was born, so they belonged to different decades, different styles of dress and speech, different musical tastes, and they moved in different circles. She was flamboyant, in a way that offended him, that struck him as puerile, and his contempt for her independent lifestyle showed in simple unconscious gestures and glances, glaring at her grace.

Pauline, so young in age and spirit, might have been my mother's older sister, and her open, whimsical ways complemented Mom's natural reticence, bringing them into an easy alliance against Granddad. Pauline encouraged Mom's rebellious, fun-loving side. I can see it, the fun they had together, in photographs taken at formal functions, such as weddings, or on the beach, or dressed in sweaters and kilt-like skirts, tartan patterns amid parked cars at a tailgate party before the Princeton-Harvard football game, dancing at parties, drinking, and laughing. Dad had a joke, a silly saying about Aunt Pauline being "a shirt aloft," her direction always random, determined by the whim of the wind, always "taking off like a dirty shirt," while her older brother was "a stiff shirt, a just-laundered, overly starched shirt" still wrapped in its shield of paper and cardboard, still on the counter, sitting there, and that together they were "a strange pair of shirts," which isn't especially funny, but Dad liked the expressions.

Being with Pauline provided me with useful information about a world beyond my own. Granddad liked to read to me from books, but Pauline showed me photographs of places she'd visited on her amazing journeys, places I was just beginning to learn about. "There are too many people in the world," she said, showing me a photo of a huge sea of people flooding the plaza in front of Saint Peter's Basilica in Rome, city of fountains. She joked about Granddad's being "square," his good, grey suits, his conservative musical tastes, his carefully clipped speech. Why was it, she asked, that people who enjoy RPM can also appreciate the classics, such as Bach, Beethoven, and Brahms, while lovers of classical music usually dismiss RPM as so much vulgar noise, incapable of giving it a chance? It seemed like an interesting question then, and I sometimes ponder it now, though I still don't have an answer. I could tell, one Christmas Eve, that Granddad was bothered by the way I was conversing with Pauline, in a whirl without anything to stop her telling me about her friends in Paris—actors, painters, poets, and musicians she knew.

She moved in what were, I guess, "bohemian circles," and she said things for fun, complicating communication with impractical, playful language, making her own distinctive mark through purposeless humor and puns. One time Granddad exploded, "I thought we were having a serious discussion here!" when Pauline made a silly remark about the stock market being like a misguided rocket. I don't know exactly what she said to support the likeness, but I know it derailed his agenda, which I was becoming aware of, for he'd already become a powerful agency in my consciousness, planning to get me "on the right track" and send me off to Princeton or some other Ivy League college, where I'd study hard and excel, studying business, law, medicine, or one of the hard sciences that Granddad and Gaga both had so much respect for. He'd said that I was "the smartest little girl in all of Fairfield County," and I believed him, and he wanted to see his little girl succeed, as he had. He wanted to launch me and see me sail into a world of privilege and prestige, based on accomplishment, the moneyed world he knew, a realm of propriety and power, the world that Pauline disdained and treated as a joke, as if it were all farce, stuffing, a total waste of time, a world which she, in her own way, participated within. Tommy was the blond-haired boy in the blue blazer with gold buttons, but Granddad treated me like the sole male heir, quizzing me on what I thought I knew about whatever, or what he thought I should know, mostly historical figures, dates, vocabulary, and geography. He always acted indifferently toward Tommy, as if Dad and Tommy had so much in common that Tommy was just pure Taine, beyond his control, but I was closely watched, for I was the one person toward whom he felt the least indifferent.

Christmas presents were opened before dinner, an extravaganza of getting and giving, "preprandial," Dad would say with a wink, "because that's the way your mother's family does it." The Prescott family had always celebrated Christmas with great pomp and formality. I could see it in an old photograph, hanging in the hallway, of men dressed in tuxedos and women wearing long evening gowns under the chandeliers in a lofty room bordered with potted palms, and predinner presents were part of the protocol. Rising from his seat at the head of the table, fluted glass in hand, Granddad announced "the opening of the presents." The adults were laughing and drinking Champagne—"the Bubbly," Gaga called it—and everyone laughed as the orgy of exchange began. One Christmas, Gaga gave me a ridiculous white faux-fur hat, a sort of rabbit's helmet that I'd wear around for days in an attempt to raise some bunny ideas. There at The Ark, joining Tommy in his Frankenstein outfit, I hopped around on the carpet in the living room, our antics provoking small applause from the crowd of adults, sitting in chairs, lounging on the sofas, drinking, chatting, watching us perform. Presents were opened with a determined fury. "This is for MY KNEES," Pauline said, laughing as she crouched down to my level. She gently tapped my knees, then she handed her gift to me, a box wrapped in silver paper, from which I took out a smaller box and extracted from it a metal and plastic contraption, a camera, and I lifted it up to my face, like a swimming mask. Peering through the lens, I soon found a new way to see the world, framing things, and so I went rushing around the apartment, pleased with my just-given, newfound power, aiming to photograph a tree festooned with a popcorn garland, Tommy posing with his plastic gun, Pauline laughing and holding up a glass, Uncle Albert smoking a cigar. I still have a photograph of Crystal, the brown long-haired dachshund with spooky eyes that glowed from within, the dog that always appeared at the door, yapping, snapping away at our feet like a dainty, hairy alligator—not dog at all. There was an unearthly component to her comportment, the touch of another planet. Tommy and I followed her around the apartment, into the dark rooms upstairs, keeping low on the rug, pretending we were predators tracking alien prey. I photographed Crystal a lot, the glow of her peepholes like marbles lit by tiny dots of phosphorescence. I photographed red roses, petals reflected in a bowl's silver sheen. I photographed the ornaments on the tree, the electric rainbow of its coat. I photographed Gaga wearing the pearl necklace Granddad had just given her. I photographed Mom and Dad sitting at the piano, she in his lap, laughing together on the black bench. I photographed the dazzle of the candles on the table. I photographed myself photographing myself in the big oval mirror.

Proper, patriarchal, looking this way and that, a bit like an angry eagle, Granddad sat at the head of the table, collecting snapshots, sweeping his lenses through us all, making slow daguerreotypes of who was present. He took his spoon and struck it with impatient elegance against the side of his glass of ice water, nodding ceremoniously to Gaga to indicate that she'd lead "the GULLS" and he'd lead "the BUOYS" in a sing-along, a holiday fugue for voices. He hit his glass again, and that deep voice, coming from a place I never questioned, began singing, so the boys joined in, "For health and strength and daily bread," at which point we, the GULLS, chimed in with a rise in pitch, "For health and strength and daily bread," as the boys' voices finished the verse, "We praise thy name, O Lord," the BUOYS beginning again with "For health and strength," as the girls finished with "We praise thy name, O Lord," to begin again and repeat the lyrics, around and around. Singing that song seemed silly to me, an empty formality, like something we'd do in church or school, and the word "Lord" made me feel hollow, like I was serving someone, like I was someone's slave. Gaga, when suitably provoked, sometimes used the word "Lord" as an expression of surprise, but here it seemed a word without an object, an abstraction, a glittering generality. I never discussed my religious views with anyone until one Christmas when Pauline identified herself as an atheist, having, she declared, "no beliefs in anything." "I don't believe in anything. I believe that things are as they are," she said. She said that she believed that things were the way they were at the present moment; that she really couldn't think beyond the present moment, where what you take is equal to what you make, and that was that, and Granddad said, "Let's agree to let this subject drop," and I dropped my knife on the floor and noticed, for the first time, how big its blade was, how little of the metal I actually used, just the sharp edge, when I used it to cut meat. Pauline identified herself as an atheist again, explaining the word to Tommy and me later, showing us her tarot cards, particularly the Wheel of Fortune, and photographs of places she'd been, things she'd seen, like the statue of the little mermaid girl in Copenhagen, the Eiffel Tower, and the white, sun-drenched ruins of temples on islands in the deep, blue Aegean Sea. I recall thinking how fortunate I was, enjoying my time in The Ark, where I had my camera, where I was Dad's priceless Indian Princess and Granddad's little girl, and I had this wonderful great-aunt who brought music and laughter into the tenebrous Ark. I became so aware of my good fortune that I excused myself from the dinner table and went into the bathroom again to focus on the black pupils of my blue eyes. Outside, the adults were drinking and laughing. Piano music was playing, and I imagined, or I tried to imagine, with my eyes closed, prismatic bits of rainbow brightly beaming from the tree. I walked out of the bathroom, thinking about places in the world I'd visit when I grew up and could be like Pauline.

"Uncle Albert" wasn't really an uncle at all, though he's someone I recall fondly, a friend of Aunt Pauline's, and a boisterous laughter filled the room whenever he told jokes. He had the air of the ruddy mystic about him, and his cheeks shined like polished apples. He once told me that I should become a gypsy because of my blond hair, because that was a good way to see the world and "get around," as he put it, making large circles in the air with his fists, for he was a man who talked with his hands. He laughed loudly and for a long time, telling Tommy and me about how his own mother, not long ago, had had to discipline him, tying him up with rope to a tree because he was always running around like an Indian and getting into trouble. "Pow wow! Pow wow!" Uncle Albert jested with Tommy, putting his fists up for a fight and then falling backward into his chair, to land on the floor and remain there, chattering away about bows, arrows, and hunting bear naked. A pungent amalgam of Scotch and cigarette smoke clung to his jacket as he joked, renewing himself with sips from his drink and bits of psycho-semantic silliness, rapidly making hand movements, pretending he was doing something funny, so unlike our great uncle Edmund, from Gaga's side of the family, the bachelor, a taciturn, retired university professor of mathematics, who'd politely inquire about my teachers at school and nod slowly, stressing his complete and aloof agreement with anything I said. Unlike the other adults, Uncle Edmund never became sloppy when he drank, probably because he didn't drink alcohol. And then there was some small applause: Uncle Albert had just told the joke about Jed, the chicken farmer who sleeps in the nude, and when Jethro, his faithful hound dog, begins barking, waking Jed from his slumber, he immediately hears a commotion in the henhouse outside, so Jed jumps out of bed, fetches his gun, and goes out with Jethro in tow. "Well now," Uncle Albert said, as he slowed down, making a significant pause, creating a sense of suspense, and now his voice, speaking as Jed, dropped into a very low, countrified, rustic register, "Well now, old Jethro here, he done *cold-nosed* me . . . an' AH, AH been plucking chickens ever since"— a joke nicely poised at the threshold of Gaga's tolerance for a certain kind of humorous material.

The flickering flames of the candles on the dining room table, rising on wicks, sometimes made me stare, and I'd focus on the action, using my eyes as a camera, the shapes morphing from blue to orange and yellow tips lit in a dance, crowns tapering off into invisible heat, and I'd disappear, become a particle in a wave ascending on incremental steps to a high place, a suspended state from which I'd survey the scene, the white wax dripping, forming almost invisible dots on the linen tablecloth, white on white, like sugar in milk. Gaga scolded me, telling me to stop staring, because I'd burn my pupils out, so I cut to the green of Pauline's earrings, or the painting behind Granddad's head, or the elegant trio of silver candlestick holders that dominated the table. "You can't beat beets," Uncle Albert said, pointing to the ruby red vegetable glittering in a crystal bowl, putting a spoonful on my plate and then helping himself to some. Pinpoints of light were reflected in the ice cubes in our water glasses, in the silver spoons, knives, and forks, multiplied by the plates on the table in that room where ancestral shadows seemed to gather in the background and hover, watching us, felt but unseen. Mom smoked a cigarette, and everyone had some more Champagne, and when the bell rang to start, we gourmandized on roasted beef and broiled lamb with mint sauce, white potatoes and garlic in butter, and sweet, fluffy yams whipped up with maple syrup and cream, served from a clay tureen, and there were egg noodles in golden cheese and pickled herring and nuts and fresh fruit.

"I am taking my girl to the library," Granddad would announce with funny formality, lifting me up from the dinner table by hand and leading me to the platform of the electric escalator that he'd let me ride upstairs on because I enjoyed riding it so. Granddad's library was a spacious room, one whole wall lined with wooden bookcases anchored to the floor like cargo ships beneath a high ceiling. A large oriental carpet (its edge ending about a foot in front of the bookcases, so that I'd plant my foot there and say to myself, "This is a foot") covered most of the floor with a complicated, abstract pattern, and the wallpapered walls were punctuated with framed photographs. There was a large orange and black banner, which Tommy called the "Halloween Flag," hanging on the wall opposite the bookcases, displayed as if it were a title on a theater marquee, announcing the place and time of Granddad's college graduation, "Princeton 1915."

We'd walk down the long hallway, passing mysterious rooms of unused furniture, some of it covered in drapery, for what seemed like a very long time, as he held my hand in his. He'd flick a switch, and the huge chandelier overhead flashed on like a futuristic space-ship, revealing walls painted a milky avocado green. He'd select a book from the shelf, turn the reading lamp on, and we'd settle into his large leather armchair, the book in his lap like an open road. Tommy didn't have the patience to sit still and be read to. Gaga said he had ants in his pants, but I sat and followed Granddad's voice in its weirdly modulated imitation of Babar, king of the elephants: "I, Cindy, am animate. I suppose you can see these animal tracks," and he'd make his hand imitate an elephant, his middle finger its trunk, make a little elephant out of his hand, and it walked around on me. Granddad's voice was deep and rich, like a bassoon's, as I sat and followed it, leading me down to the words, like so many wheels. He taught me to read each word at a time, pronouncing it fully. Pouncing on one, he'd seize it, then say it again, making each SILLY BELL count as if it were a new word for him and me, and he'd define it with a pedagogue's exactitude.

"Really, Pauline, where does the time go?" Gaga asked, and Pauline, in response, said nothing.

During the last few days before Christmas break, our teachers allowed us to goof off, and one Christmas, Cousin Andy blurted out about how he'd walked on stilts all around the perimeter of his cool new school in Darien, just as the snowstorm began. "Oh, Lord, Andy, you're pulling my leg. I've never heard of such a thing," Gaga responded in the openly amused manner she'd sometimes display. "Kids these days, Mother—they're sure to surprise you," Uncle Steve added, nodding to Andy, who, in a quiet, automatic re-sponse, sat up straight in his chair. Uncle Steve was able, with just a glance, to monitor and control all of his brood, all except sometimes Ernie, excited eyes darting into space, playing with his silver fork and knife, making inarticulate noises, so that Aunt Mary smiled and checked him, gently taking the silverware out of his hands. Ernie had just decided to excuse himself from the table, to get up and go play with his new battery-operated *Star Trek* toy, ignoring table manners, an issue of great importance to Uncle Steve, glancing up with concern, as he excused himself to fetch his son. Cousin Andy smiled slyly at me, silently applauding his younger brother's decision to act on impulse, so I said, "Excuse me," and went to the bathroom to look at myself in the mirror some more.

I remember one Christmas when Aunt Pauline, angry with something Granddad had said, when he'd prattled on about "our angry negroid poor," stood up from the table and shook her knife at him, bringing the bottom of its handle down like a hammer on the table with a force that would have made a bang, were it not for the white linen, muffling the impact.

"What do you say, Cindy?" Granddad asked me frequently, and I sometimes never did know what to say, for he could be intimidating, especially when I was older and learning more about adults.

One Christmas, Granddad gave me a mysterious present in a square cardboard box, wrapped with grey paper, bound with a silver ribbon, and I was surprised by how heavy it was as I lifted it and carried it to the table from its place under the tree. He asked me to guess what was inside, and I couldn't. I attempted to gauge its weight. What could it possibly be, a bowling ball, an astronaut's helmet, an anarchist's black bomb? Someone had given Tommy the new Beatles LP—*Revolver*, I think—so RPM music was playing in the background. "Do you call that music? It's irresponsible to call that music," Granddad complained. Pauline called it "EAR-RESPONSIBLE music," pointing to her ears, which infuriated Granddad. As I undid the ribbon, he was shaking his head, and he growled at Tommy, "Turn that noise down!" I tore at the paper, and I opened a cardboard box to reveal a portable electric typewriter, a new IBM model, secure in its hard metal case. It wasn't something I wanted; I was in fifth grade then, so I didn't need to type any papers for school, and I felt disappointed and disappointing, sensing he'd expected me to be more pleased with the gift.

I never wanted to leave The Ark, because it felt like being on vacation while we were there, its form now a trace from the past, where I bore no responsibility for my actions, so we'd hide, disappearing into the vast coat closet, closing its sliding wooden doors over where Granddad's heavy black cashmere coat hung, hidden amid an assortment of thick furs and fabrics, and I'd wrap myself up in it and believe I was thoroughly safe, insulated from the reality of the long car trip home. It was a game, with Granddad yelling out, "I wonder where those kids are?" and he'd always act as if he couldn't find us, so it was a bit of forced theater, but the heat and the darkness of the closet with the doors closed, the fuzzy texture in my face, began to feel uncomfortable, and I was always a little glad when he discovered us.

2

RIVERSIDE

Riverside, a part of Greenwich, always seemed like its own little town, with a distinct personality and look, especially around Christmas, when the streets and store windows were lit up with decorations, and a festive restlessness reigned. We were always so happy to play in the snow. Mom called Christmas "Yuletide," an expression that harkened back to an ancient stage of history, evoking some epic night of the world, reminding us that Christmas was originally a pagan celebration, becoming geological, of chthonic origin, older than Bethlehem, predating Babylon and Memphis, a result of the planet's tilted rotation around the sun. Mom expressed the Christmas spirit with an enthusiasm bordering the precincts of infectious zeal, accessing the myriad joys of being alive, at home in one's skin, the loving fun that money can't buy, and she wanted everyone to see and hear, to taste and feel, its manifest massage, the phenomenal world around us, just as it is, an enormous gift, an almost edible essence. Mom's generosity, giving so much of herself, finding satisfaction in the act of giving, essentially preparing something for someone else's surprise, a compression of the future into the now, dominated the mood of our house, endowing it with levity, for Eudora adored the holiday season. She made Christmas the peak of the year, an emotional highpoint, always about to happen, and then it happens, and then it's about to happen again, imagery decorating the mantelpiece, festive music playing on the stereo, the piney fragrance from a tree festooned with ornaments wafting through the air. Mom made spectacular cookies with an antique tin cookie cutter that had once belonged to Gaga, deftly carving out angels, stars, and crosses from the dough she'd bake to a crisp, golden brown, then sprinkle with red and green confectionary sugar, making Dad and Tommy grin in one photo I still have of them in the kitchen all aglow and shiny, the three of them there by the open oven, and I think Eudora thought of herself as a character in a movie, the whim of some director's rebarbative imagination. She adorned the front door with a large, lavish wreath she'd made by hand, wrought from her own set of cuttings; she set holiday candles on windowsills. She baked holiday cakes and pies, spiced with nutmeg and cinnamon. I remember overhearing her chatting to herself in the kitchen, bubbling into melody as she prepared a tray of appetizers for the cocktail hour, which began, officially, when Dad arrived.

Eudora poured an abundance of NRG into her holiday decorations and preparations, her flights of fancy, and, just after Thanksgiving, her Christmas cards, an annual writing project that she undertook each year with a pronounced burst of enthusiasm. She pointed out to me that Christmas cards were like postcards because they almost always carried an image on them, a picture of something, but they were not at all like postcards because they were always sent in envelopes, so that all of their secrets arrived guarded, hidden, sealed by paper sleeves. Dad enjoyed the spirit of the season, but he was indifferent to the religious iconography and mythology; "superstitious baggage" he called it, while Mom seemed inspired by the Christmas message, its essence being an awareness of the best thing in us all, our shared humanity, and she became one of its fervent messengers, chosen to convey the good news. Bending her head to paper, she'd compose variations on holiday sentiments, all painted deep blue, as she wrote with a fountain pen, the ink flowing down through a thin, narrow tube to the metal tip of its nib to go on a surface, stay there, and dry, forming loops of intelligible sound, as I followed her curvaceous, expressive handwriting. She always chose the same Renaissance Annunciation painting—"my Dresden Madonna," she called it—and I can still see her elegant cursive letters, proof of a certain control. She'd sit at her desk, working through the late afternoon, a certain slant of light through the window striking her head, a diligence about her, leaning forward, thinking with fingertip to lip, slipping the card into its envelope, adding the address, then licking and sealing it, so that a pile of cards in addressed envelopes arranged in alphabetical order, ready to be taken to the post office, sat on the table in the front hall outside Dad's den for everyone to see.

Riding in the car through Riverside, when I was younger, just as I was learning to write and read, becoming aware of my ABCs, learning that a *u* almost always follows a *q*, that it's always a "me" who says "we" or "you," learning how to wring sounds from words by SILLY BELLS, as I sat in the car and practiced my reading skills, reading the sign for the "Dairy Queen," where we'd very occasionally stop for soft ice cream cones, I could also read the word "WINES" in red neon in the window of the liquor store where we'd stop, usually with Dad, sometimes with Mom. "Candy is dandy, but liquor is quicker," Mom quipped in one of her up moods.

Our eyes are the visible parts of our brains, and I remember how, in the throes of her later addiction, her eyes would swell. One hazy summer evening, when Dad wasn't there, when the alien cackle of cicadas pervaded the sultry air, Mom was sitting on the back porch, talking with me, or to me. She nibbled at her vodka and lime juice like a fish, taking quick, furtive sips of it and becoming her theatrical, other self, coming out of her shell, something the booze helped her do, and she made up a song about the flickering, flying pinpoints of light spiraling around us. She explained to me that the male fireflies were sending out signals, that the patterns made them attractive to bugs of the opposite sex, that the lights were all part of a complicated mating ceremony. Mom put her arm around me, and she began to sing a silly song about the fireflies, inventing the lyric as she went along, celebrating something, but nothing special, just the flow of the alcohol radiating through her, as it rid her of her "demons," the insects' phosphorescent dance lighting up the night sky, sharing it with me, and I remembered Aunt Pauline referring to whiskey as "gasoline" because it empowered people, fueled them, and fooled them with artificial NRG. Granddad had always used the word "hooch" to refer to his Scotch, a powerful amber in a crystal decanter. Gaga said, "O Bubbly," when she lifted a glass of Champagne from a tray, and Dad called the drinks he prepared in the silver cocktail shaker "Martins." When he arrived home from work, he'd smile and say to Mom, "I'll mix us some Martins."

On good days she'd be cheerful, even dancing with Tommy and me to music on the phonograph, and we'd dance and feel fine, but I guess we'd all get carried away, a bit too involved and caught up with our play, reaching a noisy crescendo. Mom, suddenly annoyed, yelling, calling us "spoiled brats," would retreat into an authoritative, organizing silence, as if we'd all been on an emotional splurge and now it was time to repent, and I'd feel like a sermonized sinner, although she never really said much. There were times when she stayed in the house all day, reading or watching television in the bedroom, which at first didn't seem strange, for I didn't have anyone to compare her with, but I eventually discovered her obsessive need for privacy. She'd complain about headaches, about how she was sick and tired of being plagued by "demons." It would be a beautiful day outside, and she was a beautiful woman, but she'd be indoors, sitting in darkness, the curtains drawn, sitting on the edge of her bed, her arms wrapped around her torso in a posture of lamentation, humming softly to herself. She'd always pull herself together in the late afternoon with a grim, determined punctuality, pour a glass of white wine, and begin to prepare dinner. Later, when Dad came home from work, before we all sat down to eat, he'd take off his tie and jacket, put some music on the stereo, and mix drinks, and they'd drink "Martins," Dad pouring the transparent elixir from the silver shaker into fist-sized glasses, topping them off with a twist of lime. I can still see the frosted-glass sides of the oblong-shaped gin bottle he kept in a wooden cabinet amid other bottles of liquor, though Mom and Dad mostly drank gin when they were together. It helped her laugh and joke with Dad, who, at his spontaneous best, could be a lot of fun. So "the cocktail hour" was a celebration of Dad's arrival home, a break from monotony for Mom, a little ritual of Riverside life, when Mom would say, "You children, go and play."

I remember playing with Tommy, running up and down the stairs, in our days as roughhousing ruffians, firmly convinced of some fantasy reality in which we played vital roles, Tommy with his water pistol, me in my bunny hat/helmet, until Mom became upset again, complaining about an imminent nervous breakdown, bringing an end to whatever fun it was we were having, showing that it's possible to play too hard, at least sometimes, but then it all started up again. Dad had a book of illustrated riddles, really childish stuff, such as "Why did the man sit backward on his horse?" "To see where he had been." "What is black and white and red all over?" "The newspaper." Or maybe it was something more abstract, such as the question "What looks like an Indian, has feathers like an Indian, wears moccasins like an Indian, carries a tomahawk like an Indian, wears war paint like an Indian, has a smile like an Indian's, has everything that an Indian has, but isn't an Indian?" Now what could that be? "A picture of an Indian," a simulation, a photograph of one, a duplication.

When I was in the second grade, Mom and Dad went on a vacation—a very memorable one for me, as I suddenly now recall— for what seemed like a very long time, a second honeymoon in Brazil, in Rio de Janeiro, where Dad combined business and plea- sure, where he drove Eudora around in a snazzy black sports car, upholstered with red leather, and somewhere there's a photograph of her standing under the famous statue of Jesus on Corcovado, the steep mountaintop overlooking the city. Anna Limbertone took care of Tommy and me then, for a full two weeks, letting us stay up late to play music, dance, and watch TV with her, so that we lived like, as Anna put it, "Parisian bohemians," and when my parents returned, Mom went through a phase when she seemed obsessed with Latin culture, as if deliberately breaking from her WASPy ways, tearing at her patrician roots, watching episodes of *I Love Lucy* in the bedroom, playing Herb Alpert records on the stereo, dancing alone to the music, sometimes reading, in translation, a novel by a Mexican author she'd discovered, quite by chance, at the library, being initially attracted to the book, as she explained it to me, by its flashy, enticing cover. She was drinking a lot of Tequila then, and she'd mix it with coffee liqueur, concocting the powerful cocktails she called "Tequila Mockingbirds," which she served with plantain chips and avocado dip. She'd cook rice and beans, and all kinds of spicy, tomato-based stews, and she often made flan for dessert, the caramelized, creamy custard, which was bland but smoother and better tasting than rice pudding.

Uncle Steve, my mother's older brother, was, according to Aunt Pauline, "a real straight arrow," which was a happy coincidence, because Uncle Steve and his family, Aunt Mary and the four boys, lived in a gigantic stone house on Salem Straits Road in Darien, the town where, according to my limited comprehension of two basic linguistic bits—one German, one French, "there," *da*, was literally "nothing," *rien*—so I liked to say they lived on "Solemn Straits in THE NOTHING THERE," and Mom said that that wasn't very polite. Outwardly dull and impassive, Uncle Steve had natural numeric abilities that had made him very successful, having majored in mathematics at Princeton, where he honed his innate gifts, and then on to Wharton Business School. He was now vice president of something important at IBM (which made us giggle), which made him piles of money, and that was why the house was so big, the surrounding lawn always green and trim, manicured like a golf course stretching away for what seemed like miles, punctuated by tiny copses of ornamental, flowering fruit trees. Uncle Steve enjoyed looking out and knowing that what he saw he owned, that it was all under his control, for he was, to borrow a phrase from Aunt Pauline, "a control freak," so he objected to other people doing what they wanted to do by, and for, themselves. He was constantly supervising people and ordering them around, barking out commands, telling us what he wanted us to do, especially out on his yacht, the black yawl he'd named *Swift Enterprise*, ordering the crew around. He was always telling Mom what she "ought" to do, and Mom would say, "Don't use that word with me." But he'd just continue pontificating, from simple things, such as how to hold a tennis racket or where to buy fertilizer for the azaleas, to more complex, abstract issues that I couldn't access at the time, but I know that she'd say, "Don't use that word with me," which always made her brother step back. It was entertaining to watch Uncle Steve closely. I sometimes thought that he thought he was on a stage or a movie set, for there was something duplicitous and feigned about his gestures.

The property was impressive; there was a swimming pool and tennis court, a small bowling alley in the basement, an ornamental indoor pool filled with goldfish in the entrance hall, and "the ballroom," an enormous, cavernous space, bound by a mirrored ceiling and walls, designed for Aunt Mary's dancing and the extravagant parties she hosted, with live music and catering, like weddings, but ordinary events for her, with lots of help from hired staff.

Standing on the front lawn as we drove up, Uncle Steve was evidently stooping to investigate some imperfection on the lawn—a stray bit of paper, a chewing gum wrapper, a cigar butt, a bird turd? He straightened up to welcome us, his broad face full of sunlight as he smiled and gave us a wave. "Everything in its place and a place for everything" was a favorite expression of his, and he used it to express himself, congratulating us for being so punctual. The eucalyptus trees were in bloom, but a litter of wilted petals caught Uncle Steve's eye, as a slight breeze came to their aid that day, scattering them away. He was fantastically fastidious, and he had an almost military zest for cleanliness and order, as if in constant preparation to do battle with a mighty adversary.

Aunt Pauline was the first person I knew who used the word "kicks" to signify having a good time, and she told me I shouldn't let other people get my kicks for me, saying that happiness, according to Aristotle, was an activity, something you have to do, to actively aspire to achieve in the constancy of the present moment, then adding that Uncle Steve never seemed able to get any real kicks out of life because he was always thinking of some future goal, something outside the present moment. Uncle Steve was proud of his brood, the four boys. Above a marble fireplace hung a masterfully executed oil painting of the family together, sitting in the formal garden with its reflecting pool, brick walkways, and inky blue hydrangeas. Pauline once said that you can tell a lot about a man by the kind of wristwatch he wears, and Uncle Steve, like many successful men, wore an expensive wristwatch with all sorts of buttons and dials, like something a deep-sea diver or airplane pilot might sport, which he'd consult with a quick, almost aggressive gesture, checking the time, bringing the place on his wrist to his gaze, as if there were always something more important he had to attend to.

Dutifully, we climbed out of our car like trained animals, and Dad said something stupid/funny about the water, the river we'd passed on our way, saying we'd just been "way down upon the Suwannee River" because he'd seen so many white swans gliding on the river, their feathery, white headdresses afloat, flaunting a poised, intelligent indifference, though Uncle Steve was never especially responsive to Dad's wordplay. Whatever it was he was doing, Uncle Steve always seemed to be projecting himself ahead, into the future, which put his mind out of sync with his body, and he became alien to the present, if I can put it that way. He played tennis with Dad, and I remember sensing that his grasp of the game was undermined by an inability to really let go and get into the swing of its unfolding in the present. He seemed to suffer from some kind of chronic inattention, unlike Dad, who was naturally relaxed and flexible, attuned to context, at home in his skin.

Uncle Steve always seemed distracted, torn from the weal of ordinary discourse, as if inhabited by one of those business machines his company fabricated, always working, always thinking about IBM, as it consumed him most of the time, even at home, where he was able to conduct business by telephone. Once or twice during the week he'd drive in his silver Mercedes-Benz, swiftly up into Westchester, to IBM headquarters, but he rarely went into the city, and he virtually never traveled overseas, because he never had to travel overseas, because he was that far up on the corporate ladder. A humorous moment occurred once, between him and Tommy and me. We were driving in his silver Mercedes, out to Oyster Bay, where a friend of the family lived. It was hot, and we were stuck in traffic, late in the afternoon, with shadows on the pavement growing, and he turned to us to announce, with a touch of bravado, "Hey, kids, this is what we call 'the lie,' the L-I-E, the Long Island Expressway. Get it?" Then he smirked, mostly to himself. It seemed like a stupid joke and strange that he'd told it to us, because he was usually so serious.

It was interesting, one summer afternoon, when I snuck into his office and secretly experienced the printed matter inside, as if it were top secret and confidential. Everyone called his office "the Lion's Lair," and that afternoon while everyone was outside playing croquet, I sat in the leather chair where he'd sit and work, reading, writing, opening mail, dictating into the microphone of his tape recorder, talking on the telephone, taking notes, making big decisions. There were many bound volumes stored on shelves behind glass, and glossy business magazines piled in a stack on a table, at one end of which stood a small stone sculpture, an abstract head, like one from Easter Island, but miniaturized and put on a pedestal. Outside his office, beyond its closed door, there was a long hallway, a sort of empty runway of polished wood, its long center covered with a heavy rug—a "runner" one of the boys called it—and we'd race with them through that hallway, running from one end to the other, from the door of the Lion's Lair to the door of Aunt Mary's painting studio, usually closed, shielding from view the place where she found the time to be alone and get things done. Her folkloric watercolors of boating scenes, seagulls, and flowers were amateurish and dull, though she herself was an animated, vibrant woman who worshipped the sun and left red lipstick traces on whatever glass she was drinking from. She wore terrific earrings, and she was, unlike Mom, always wearing a dress. I don't think I ever once saw her in slacks or pants, and she was, like Mom could sometimes be, loquacious and enormous fun when she was drinking, which she was, most of the time I saw her.

Later that evening we had dinner outside by the swimming pool, the table illuminated by flaming torches, and a professional pianist played background music, while waiters served an elaborate meal, which consisted of several courses. Mom made a face when I slurped my soup, so I made an effort to sip it, quietly minding the distinction between sipping and slurping. The table was cleared of spoons and bowls, and then salads were served, and I noticed a small brown stain at my place on the white linen tablecloth, a field of unsullied snow, except for that spot where I'd spilled some soup.

Afterward, we all went inside, finding relief from the heat in the cool, conditioned air of the ballroom, where we danced to music playing on the stereo. It was an unusual evening of revelry, a striking memory. I remember Mom and Aunt Mary both drinking too much, laughing hysterically, as Dad steered Mom toward the car, Aunt Mary pleading with us to stay longer, for the night was still young. So a compromise formation was arrived at, and Tommy and I stayed overnight in one of the many guestrooms, and my parents were able to party until late with abandon. The noise of adult laughter and music mocked me in my effort to sleep, so I wandered down in borrowed pajamas and asked them to be quiet. Uncle Steve's voice could be so loud, and he was proud of the new IBM headquarters, with its many floors and metal doors. He once took Tommy and me to see it, and, pointing to a door, he said, in his deep and serious voice, "You kids own a part of this door. You each own stock in the company, so you each own a part of this door." And then he smirked.

Old McDonald's Farm, a converted barn, a brick ship of a building, was a family-oriented restaurant, offering the best charcoal-broiled hamburgers in the area, its ancient, brick foundation attached to the earth, almost a part of it, set right on the road, at the edge of a large area of land near the border of Darien and Norwalk, then a small city with a busy downtown section and a river that reeked of tar and rotten fish. To reach Old McDonald's Farm, we'd drive east on the Post Road, passing various commercial enterprises, past a car wash and miniature golf course, past Rip Van Winkle's Bowling Lanes, not really very far from the Prescott house on Salem Straits. We'd go there, to "the funny farm," as Dad called it, for dinner with Uncle Steve, Aunt Mary, and the boys, the ten of us all together forming quite a rowdy contingent, as we climbed out of our cars, excited by the change of scene and sense of expectation. The food was always excellent: charcoal-broiled burgers served on savory rolls with melted Swiss cheese. I'd order Russian dressing on my salad, featuring fresh tomatoes, sliced onions, and chewy black olives. The wooden front door was massive and dark, with a small window of diamond-paned glass at its top, like something you'd see in a castle, and an intricate iron handle, the latch requiring extra pressure from my thumb to make it work. Bells jingled when the door, pushed by a shove, swung open, revealing the busy bustle inside, the light, the bodies, the din, the cooking smells. The restaurant felt like a colonial inn, full of warmth and historic detail, a place where George Washington might have stopped, with a big stone fireplace and a thick scattering of sawdust over the wooden floorboards. We'd troop in, and I'd think of our first four presidents, and then of Dolly Madison with her unflagging hospitality. The tables were covered with gingham tablecloths, sporting that familiar, comforting, red-and-white-checkered pattern that I associate with a way of life that's disappearing before my eyes, set with unusually large napkins made from a coarse fabric dyed deep blue, and heavy ceramic plates bordered by antique pewter utensils, and bouquets of seasonal flora, all bathed by the glow of firelight, from the leaping flames in their place of stone to the tiny acts of combustion on our tables, candles charging the air, giving our conversation and gestures an almost animal attraction and intimacy, both for ourselves and for the place where we were, under those low rafters of exposed timber.

Behind the restaurant there was a small farm, featuring a petting zoo with barnyard animals: rabbits, goats, sheep, roosters, and hens. Aunt Mary used to call Old McDonald's Farm "the heart of our town," and she'd lead us through the whimsical sing-along about barnyard animals, making up new lyrics and sounds, as she drove us there in the air-conditioned station wagon, with all or with some of her boys, who lorded over the place as if they owned it, especially Stevie, the eldest, who, under Tommy's influence, liked to "play plantation," pretending he was intimate friends with the elderly black man who operated the merry-go-round, which was why we often walked up on the platform and could choose a horse for a free ride. The old man sang along with the calliope music, conforming his voice to its many modulations on a cloudless, hot day, the sun high in the sky, as I picture us now, seated in our saddles, clutching painted ponies' handles, merrily circling around and around, caught in a field of centrifugal force, heads bobbing up and down. Strangely enough, it's all as clear as a scene seen through glass, our sitting at the picnic table, while the fearless, friendly white ducks approached us, quacking, begging for food, and I'd feed them my crusts of bread. The boys, following Tommy's example, formed pellets of white dough, dense little bullets that they'd throw into the nearby pond, clapping and carrying on as the ducks followed, flapping and splashing into the water, a flurry of feathers and wings in a rush. It was some display! I wondered why the ducks' webbed feet and ankles were so brightly orange, and I felt a bit of Pauline impinge on my consciousness. "Crackers for the quackers," she used to say to the ducks in Central Park. I looked down at the area sprinkled with white feathers, the brown ground almost matching the color of the picnic table, and I relished the smell of hay and dirt in the sunlight. Ernie, being the youngest, was always a bit behind the other boys, and while they ran off, chasing the ducks, he sat with Aunt Mary and me at the wooden table. And that's all I remember, just sitting there with them.

About a mile down the road from Pasture Lane, heading inland, away from the water, at the edge of a field filled with small trees and tall weeds, there was a compact, windowless structure, huddled like a little house, its cinderblock walls painted a bland grey. It had a flat tar roof and a narrow metal door, like a gym locker but heavier, thicker, painted with black enamel, a veritable plank of steel. Tommy called it "the Bunker," maybe because he was watching *Combat!* at that time, the popular TV show about a squad of American soldiers in World War II, and I called it "the Lab," suggesting a clean, well-lit place with tiled walls, running water, and, of course, soap, like the biology lab at New Canaan High, where I'd later work with graph paper, keeping track of observable mutations in fruit flies. From late in the spring and all summer long, the Lab was obscured by a vast screen of riotous foliage, a dense curtain of green, with lots of places to hide things, but around Halloween, as the trees lost their leaves, I'd see it there as we passed in a car, or I alone on my bike, its presence set back from the road, lurking behind the denuded, almost frightened branches of the trees, and I'd wonder what it was there for. It just seemed to be there, silent and mysterious, like a tomb. There were cables, rubberized wires for electrical input and output, leading in and out of the Lab, making it into a kind of black box in a network I imagined of other black boxes, more labs in space, connected by copper wire, like stations in some relay. Like a location in some horror movie, it seemed to be a place where experiments on someone's brain might be conducted, where someone's "grey matter," simmering in a vat of chemicals, might be hooked up to electrodes and monitored, experimented on—a possibility I think I believed in to some extent, more than I'll ever recollect, back when I was popping M&M chocolates into my mouth and listening to Tommy's creepy horror stories. There was an aura of imminent danger, a savage menace about the place, the piles of dirt, holes in the earth, empty oil drums, and rusted mechanical debris. Flocks of black starlings circled in the air above, cackling away, their feathered forms sharing inscrutable motives. Passed on a late, wintry afternoon, seen through a tangled lattice of vines and branches, the Lab had a forbidden presence, the place we'd later ride our bicycles to, where Dennis Knowlton broke down the door, springing the lock open by throwing rocks against it and finding a light switch inside, flicking it, revealing boxes filled with electrical equipment and a metal panel of ominous dials, buttons, and levers.

I don't think I believed her at the time, but I can remember the day Miss Vero, my third-grade science teacher, tried to explain to us that the earth revolves around the sun. It was difficult for me to comprehend this truth, because everything around me seemed stationary. I couldn't feel any motion. Miss Vero, however, provided proof, bringing out from the metal cabinet where important educational tools were kept a small, motorized model of our solar system, an "orrery," she called it, with a big, yellow bowling-ball-sized sun surrounded by the nine planets. She plugged it in, pushed a button, and then they all moved, making a whirring sound. Earth was a blue and green ping-pong ball, with a small, white marble for its moon. Mars was a smaller ping-pong ball, followed by the other planets, some the size of tennis balls, and Pluto, far out, was a purple marble. She explained that the orrery didn't depict the real dimensions of the planets, the vast distances between them, nor the incredible size of the sun. She then pulled down a big chart of our solar system from above the blackboard. She took a piece of chalk from the blackboard's ledge and drew, with swift elegance, a big circle on the blackboard. "So this is the sun, class, and if it's this size, how big do you think Earth is?" Nobody knew what to say, and we all sat there in silence. Miss Vero went back to her desk to pick up her pocketbook, search for her purse, pull it out, open it, and select a shiny, new penny. I remember how bright it was, reflecting the light outside, as she placed it in the center of the circle she had drawn, saying, "There, that's our Earth, and if that's Earth, then the distance from it to the sun...." She looked around the classroom, and then outside, into the parking lot, and she pointed to the big, yellow school bus parked in its usual spot. "If this little penny is Earth, then our sun is that school bus out there," and we looked out in its direction. "That's the real distance between them," she said.

Some people don't like the winter months, the short days, the dusks that fall with a sudden crash, like a glass roof collapsing, light yielding to the cold, dark stasis of a long, icy night, but I've always loved January. My birthday is just a little more than a week after Christmas, so it was the season of presents for me! Gaga and Granddad came out to Riverside on the train for my tenth birthday party, and my grandparents met my grade school friends. We'd all been outside, frolicking in the sunshine and snow, bundled up in warm clothes, boots, and mittens, running around in the backyard, and the living room was hot and radiant. I could see charged particles of dust in the air, heated by a crackling fire, like Christmas Eve but in the middle of the day, and there was a magician there who performed tricks for us. Mom had decorated the room with festive ribbons and balloons. Granddad was wearing a jacket and tie. Gaga was wearing her mink stole, which looked barbaric, its fur sparkling in the January glare, and the adults seemed to be percolating with laughter, drinking Champagne. Mom, already tipsy, had prepared her special caviar dip and was trying to get a friend of mine to try some, when Dad pulled her aside and shook her. I was impressed by how dressed up everyone was. Granddad struck his plate with a knife. "Order, order! It's time for Cindy's presents," he announced, and he produced a white cardboard box wrapped with a red velvet ribbon, like a hatbox but very heavy. He set it on the table, and as I undid the ribbon, the cardboard sides collapsed outward, and thousands of coins emerged: one hundred dollars in new silver quarters, a flowing stream of shining cash. I put my hands into the glittering mound, feeling its metallic warmth run through my fingers, and the next day, a very bright, cold January morning, when the sun made me blink and the snow stood in piles around our driveway, Mom and Dad took me and my re-boxed collection of quarters in the car to the bank in town, next to the post office, an austere building with many steps leading to a revolving glass door, producing a sudden *whoosh* of sound behind us as we entered. We visited a teller's window, and then we went out on the marble floor, carpeted in places, where wooden desks were anchored like boats, and we were safe in some harbor's lap, under a domed ceiling decorated with painted scenes of a mythological reality. Then we walked to a desk, where Dad, with unusual formality, held a chair out for me, and I sat down. Then a tall, serious man in a business suit emerged, and he carried my box full of quarters away.

We sat there in silence, just the three of us, waiting, the desk lit by a beautiful brass lamp with a green glass shade. The tall man returned and shook my hand, saying, "Pleased to have you aboard, Miss Taine," as if we were going off on a voyage somewhere. I signed my name on some paper, and he explained that I now had an official bank account, that my one hundred dollars would grow at a certain rate, a bit each year, and if I were patient and waited, the bank would make my money grow and grow, like an oak tree from its acorn, and I'd be a very wealthy girl. Then he opened a drawer, shuffled around in it with his hand, and produced an elegant, little black book, a moleskin bankbook, where I could keep track of the money in my account. I remember our drive home and how sunlight filled the car, so that Mom put on her dark glasses. Dad turned on the radio, seeking a soundtrack, something to fit the scene. There were electric lights on wires crisscrossing store windows. Christmas had passed, my tenth birthday had just passed, and I was puzzled about how the bank—just another building, really—would make my money grow and grow. It didn't make any sense. By what logic, what magic mechanism, would my money become increasingly more? I just accepted it, without understanding it, like other childhood beliefs I once entertained though soon had reason to abandon, enlightened by the arc of my own experience. A robust sense of causality, that essential adjunct to reality, wasn't a real trait of mine then, nor is it really one now, but I don't understand how I ever could have really believed in Santa Claus, in the causal chain of his actions, how a fat man had squeezed himself though our chimney with a sack full of presents on his back, parking a sleigh and flying reindeer on our roof. Had I really believed that a fluffy, white Easter Bunny delivered chocolate eggs and jelly beans, hopping into the living room and depositing his goodies in our straw baskets, or that the Tooth Fairy, a smiling, radiant, with elegant, white, waving wings had risen from her home in the tall grass behind the willows, approached me in my deep sleep, tampered with my pillow, and left under it a silver coin in exchange for what had been taken from me, restitution for a part of me?

IT WAS SOMETIME during the summer of 1965, probably on a Saturday, when I was ten and Tommy was twelve, that Dad drove us all in the station wagon across the Whitestone Bridge to Long Island, to Flushing, Queens, to the World's Fair. I'd never seen such a huge parking lot, so many white lines and parking meters, over which, to the west, the great globe rose, its steel arcs looming over a sea of cars, continents held in the air, suspended, welded to steel lines of latitude and longitude. I mused to myself, "This is not a picture. This is a sculpture of the world." Inside the fairgrounds, visiting pavilions, sampling foods from all over the world, I'd never seen so many people from different ethnic backgrounds all in one place, collected like marbles, all swirling together in crowds. The Pepsi Generation was coming at us and going strong, pushing its product with that "It's a Small World after All" slogan, summed up in a song, which, insofar as I understood it, all made a lot of sense, shrinking the planet. I remember Dad and Tommy slugging back, in great gulps, the glistening, dark cola and how Mom, around that time, began to bring six-packs of Pepsi home from the market, the red, white, and blue logo gleaming on each bottle's neck. Inside the Pepsi Pavilion, we watched a display, a myriad of mechanized dolls set on a stage in tiers, tier upon tier, representing people from all over the world, singing in unison, "It's a small world after all."

One sultry summer weekend that year, sometime in the dog days of August, Dad, Tommy, and I went for an overnight cruise with Uncle Steve and his boys, setting out on *Swift Enterprise* quite early Saturday morning from the mooring off Long Neck Point. Dad had been on boats before, so he knew a bit about yachting; he could tie knots, throw nautical language around, and maintain a steady course at the helm. I remember having difficulty operating "the head," our toilet at sea, which required the use of a hand pump, and how Uncle Steve exploded when Tommy clogged it full of tissue paper. We sailed across the Sound on a calm, almost windless day, playing cards in the cockpit, listening to RPM on the radio, Dad pointing out that the grey spiky bits of matter on the horizon in that far, southwestern corner of water were very distant buildings of New York City. We anchored in the tiny harbor at Eaton's Neck, where we rowed ashore to the beach and barbecued steaks on a portable grill, not far from the lighthouse. It was a hot evening, and while Dad and Uncle Steve drank beer and smoked cigars, the six of us went off and explored the area. Andy and Tommy set off some firecrackers. The next day there was a fresh, northerly breeze blowing, and I can still feel the spray and the sunshine, sailing back, tacking against the wind. It was a cool Sunday evening when we returned to Noroton Harbor. We had just taken down the sails and tied up at the dock, the sky awash with pink clouds, and I remember being in the rowboat, the dinghy, with Tommy at the oars and a funny red-headed girl who was older than I sitting on the stern thwart. I don't know who she was or what she was doing there, but there she was. While Tommy was rowing, she suddenly shouted out, "Learn me to oar. I want you to learn me to oar!" Her grammatical error made Tommy laugh, but I felt sorry for her, amazed by the poor choice of words, making it clear that grammar isn't everything, that a deeper intentionality, a language of thought, informed by belief and desire and always keyed to present-tense circumstance, operates through us all.

It was sometime around my thirteenth birthday, when winter in its dormancy equaled the stupidity of plans, sealing the yard with a thick, silent carpet of snow, a blue, moody time of the day, when the light was about to be sucked forever, it seemed, from the sky, leaving the long evening ahead after the sun would go down, and there was an immediate sense of dread, when the weakened waves of waning light struck some clumps of snow on the woodpile on the back porch, and I had homework to do, probably something for math class, but I kept continually postponing it, knowing I'd have to eventually apply my "grey matter," as Granddad referred to the substance that is the basis of our cognitions, the substratum of my mental acts, the cool, grey porridge of matter making consciousness possible. He was always telling me to apply my "grey matter." Once it turned dark and I couldn't see anymore, I resigned myself to my task and went upstairs to study math before dinner. I opened my textbook and gazed at the pretty symbols, regarding their abstract world with a weary sense of futility and resignation. When Dad was home, he was a stabilizing influence, and Mom maintained a schedule, serving dinner at seven sharp on weekday evenings, but in his absence Eudora had to wrestle with her "demons" alone. White wine helped her manage them most of the time, but that particular night she lost control and was moved by extravagant impulses, succumbing to outrageous whim, mixing "Martins" on her own, hosting an unplanned, improvised party for her friends—the guests in her head, I guess—turning all the lights in the house on. Tommy had been listening to one of his Beatles LPs on the stereo, and she turned it on, tweaking the dial, turning the volume way up, so that the whole house shook, and my room reverberated with RPM. I remember hearing her singing downstairs, first bellowing out the lyrics to "Yellow Submarine," vocalizing her gin-fueled conception of where we all were, under a sea of green, at the top of her voice like a lunatic bird. The next song's slow melody, "Here, There and Everywhere," made her abruptly silent, as I imagined her listening pensively to its lyrics, sitting on the sofa, running her hands through her hair. It played for its duration, and then I heard her change the record. The next thing I knew, she was singing again, with renewed vigor, singing along with "Penny Lane," her voice reaching a strained, upper register, harmonizing strangely with Paul and John, losing herself in the chorus, full of herself in a boisterous way. She yelled upstairs for us to come down and join the party, which soon devolved into mayhem, with my screaming and Tommy wrestling the bottle from her hands.

So the days went by, and Eudora's drinking played its role in the course of her decline, first becoming a kind of defense, a convenient way to maintain some control over the chaos of her emotions, a way to pacify and soothe, to escape inner tensions and turbulence, the storm and stress—whatever it was all about. I could only observe her behavior and be bewildered, wondering, "Where is Mom?" It was as if she were having a constant argument with the rest of the world, and then she'd obliterate reality with booze, those bouts of inebriation sometimes modulating into an infectious enthusiasm we couldn't resist, while Dad seemed evermore consumed with business, busy with work. He was often away from home. He bought a funny foreign car, the deep purple color of a plum, a Fiat, made in Italy, shaped like a Volkswagen bug but sleeker, more compact, a two-door gasoline sculpture with a stick shift, featuring a curious diagram set in white on its top black knob. The car had dusty insides and, behind a metal door, an engine in its back that made loud, mechanical snorts and squeals, like a baby pig. Later, when Dad bought his snazzy black Jaguar, the engine made a high-pitched, competent buzzing sound, like an amplified bumblebee, and we became a three-car family, but he always drove the purple Fiat to the station, so I rarely rode in it, but when I did, I was in his environment, his virtual office on wheels. He kept his briefcase and tennis racket, screwed into its quadrangular press, in the backseat, along with pens and big pads of yellow legal paper. The glove compartment was full of road maps. The dashboard sported a sticker, a disc of glossy silver set on a larger black circle with the words "Panic Button" printed beneath it. Dad said that he pushed it when things were going wrong, haywire—"when the weather was rough and sailing was tough," he used to say—and that he just touched it and thought about the situation, and then things calmed down.

Mr. Burnham, my seventh-grade math teacher, was a big bear of a man, whose manner exuded an exceptional calm and confidence, whose hairy neck and dark, bushy eyebrows over deeply set, kind eyes reminded me of someone who lived in a cave. Patient with his students, devoted to our instruction, he familiarized us with the necessary, immutable laws of algebra and the process, through a slow, patient application of those laws, of solving problems printed in our textbooks, taking us, step by step, through their solutions on the blackboard. Mr. Burnham moved, despite his bulk, with great agility. He loved mental exercise; a befuddled audience piqued him, stimulating his pedagogic impulse, and with cheerful directness, he'd get up from his desk, smile, and go to the blackboard to elucidate, to demonstrate, to show for us the correct solution to a difficult problem posed in our textbooks. And as he spoke, he made quick marks with the chalk and provided an intelligent soundtrack for the numerals and symbols he'd draw on the blackboard. I just thought of chocolate and how he used CHALK A LOT, and I'd look out the window, wonder, and let my mind wander off. I was never good at math. I never found it interesting. Although I felt perfectly confident that if I really applied myself to it, I'd be able to do it well, I just never applied myself. I didn't have any interest in, or patience for, all the abstraction, the concentration the abstraction required, and when Mr. Burnham, with good intentions, began to speak about the numerals and symbols printed in my book, now on the board for all of us to see, thinking it through, in a collective process of arriving, by logical and self-evident steps, at the correct answer, the only answer to the problem, which had always been out there, waiting for us to discover it, hidden in mathematical space, my eyes would swim, and I'd experience a vague, sinking sensation. I'd relax my mental grasp and turn my divided attention toward the window again, because all that math seemed to be about was following rules, moving the mind to no end in circles, like thinking about the multiplication table. Though I'd follow the steps of a proof, one by one, seeing how they worked together, producing a relation, circular ultimately, between the problem and its solution, and thus understanding, for a moment, mathematical truth or insight, and I'd stand as on an eminence, from which the petty perceptions, opinions, ups and downs, and contingencies of life subject to mass society and gravity are tiny and insignificant, math class was boring—boring because of its irrelevance to my experience. There was always a world outside, a condition of renewed relevance to aspire to, and it didn't seem to have much to do with numbers, and I'd look out into space, the weather, the trees.

Sitting in class, waiting for time to pass, watching the electric clock each minute make its big hand move, it occurred to me that Mr. Burnham bore an uncanny resemblance to one of my favorite cartoon characters, Fred Flintstone. Sometimes the clock made a buzzing, low-decibel noise, just enough to disturb the proceedings, and he'd rise from his chair, slowly, and excuse himself, telling us to sit and be quiet, while he went and fetched our lanky-boned janitor, Mr. Coin, who, because the buzzing couldn't be stopped, would just shut the clock off by yanking the plug from its socket high up on the wall. There was something about the way Mr. Burnham moved to get Mr. Coin: slowly, as if he were now letting his mind slow down, and he'd smile like a man about to go on a vacation. He walked out the door. I remember the buzzing sound, the way the broken clock filled time, which prompted my motionless explorations. I think I was attracted by the numerals on the clock bearing a similarity to the numerals engraved on Fred's tiny stone wristwatch, the one he consulted just before the end of the workday at the gravel pit, and how the bird-operated whistle shrilly blew, announcing the end of work, along with Fred's triumphant "Yabba Dabba Doo," signaling the beginning of evening relaxation, while a cheerful chorus of sunny voices sang on about watching *The Flintstones*, being with the Flintstones, and having a "gay old time." Fred did his trademark dance, referred to in the opening lyric, "Let's ride with the family down the street / Through the courtesy of Fred's two feet," to which he added, with a grin, addressing Wilma, his wife, who wore a bone in her hair, "When you in my arms are in / I quiver just like gelatin," and together they formed a pair, a page "right out of history," "a modern Stone Age family," and I pondered the expression "modern Stone Age," recalling the many animals employed by Stone Age technology in Bedrock: the bird airplane, a pterodactyl with a stone cabin strapped to its back; the alarm clock activated by a small bird sitting on top of some seashells; the hummingbird record player with its pointed beak/stylus; the cat-broom; the crab-lawnmower. Most of the animals spoke English, even the octopus-dishwasher, even the mobile dinosaur–garbage can, while Dino, the Flintstones' "dog," a young, obedient dinosaur, never uttered a word and seemed to be part of a sentient, nonverbal order, like the clams used for coinage in Bedrock.

Mom often referred to Dad as "harebrained," an expression that, at first, didn't make any sense to me, and then she explained it to me, but it didn't seem like a value judgment; it was just a fact of Dad. But then he began to give me bad advice, and Mom said he should "have his head examined." He'd always said that I'd be a "head turner," and he bought me my first miniskirt. He'd always treated me as if I were older than I was, taking me with him on errands to Hauser's Hardware Shop, the liquor store, the post office, particular places where he'd linger and talk. The man at the liquor store gave me orange and green lime-flavored lollipops, and Mr. Hauser took me to the back of his shop, where a mixing machine shook cans of paint at an incredible speed. After running errands, Dad sometimes said, "Never do today what you can delay until tomorrow," and we'd take our time and go for a drive in the car, the purple Fiat, just to observe phenomena, which is a way of making time per se productive, breeding from it whatever is there, like the time we stopped by an open field and watched men working at a distant construction site. There was a hammering or driving machine of some type, a pile driver, working away at a regular, loud pace, and each time its broad hammerhead struck the ground, the sound of impact was delayed by a second or two because of its distance from us, and Dad explained the slowness of sound in contrast to the speed of light.

The Knowltons lived in a sophisticated house, an exemplary work of contemporary architecture set off from the road on a small hill. Its high concrete walls were painted white, and there were big glass windows that sometimes, in the right light and weather, functioned as mirrors for the wooded surround and blue sky above. The house was designed by a famous architect who'd studied with Frank Lloyd Wright, and its roof was a sensationally large plane of what looked like tar paper, angled at a steep pitch. There was a long, skinny metal chimney, like a futuristic totem pole or vertical piece of modern sculpture, polished and gleaming in the sunlight. The house was constructed at the far end of Pasture Lane, where the pavement looped around the little island of weeds and bosky trees. It seemed strange, but finally understandable, that a house like that, so strikingly impressive, set way back on a rolling lawn, would be built there, its well-lit interior spaces projecting an animated aura at night, for the lights always seemed to be on. Everybody in the neighborhood knew that Mr. Knowlton was CEO at Dumont, the plastics company, and almost everybody knew that Dennis, the long-haired, rebellious teenager who once rode a Stingray bicycle with a banana seat around the neighborhood, was his son. Dennis was, according to Sally, his youngest sister, a "black sheep," and he broke all the rules. He was seized by an impetuous imagination, flunking classes and listening to RPM in his room all day, taking the time to teach himself electric guitar. Up on the top floor of the house, which was all his own space, he kept a large aquarium, with bright green parrot fish in it, and he had an enormous, amorphous beanbag chair, where he'd make me sit down, put on headphones, and listen to RPM. I was just a curious sixth-grader, and he was already in high school, but it was totally intimate and innocent. Dennis was a kind of older brother, so very different from my own, and he really just wanted me to appreciate what he was into. I knew he had a girlfriend and that he was taking me under his wing, playing a part, patronizing me a bit, as he sat there, grinning outside the intensity of my own auditory perceptions, knowing that I was at least hearing what he'd heard.

Dennis was a conduit leading into another world, where RPM, and the culture that came with it, mattered enormously. I think I shared my first cigarette with him behind the garage, in a break from a game of kick-the-can. He'd been the first kid in Riverside to wear bellbottom jeans, paisley shirts, and beads, and he'd drawn peace symbols on the sidewalk in chalk, precociously, at eight, and he'd use the word "man" with whomever he happened to be talking. He told me that "Penny Lane" was really about an inexpensive Scotch whisky that was popular in Liverpool at one time; he told me about that Donovan song "Mellow Yellow," explaining that it was all about the hallucinogenic powers of dried banana peel, putting bits of dried banana peel, mixed with saffron, into the tobacco inside of some cigarette paper that he'd roll himself, that we were about to share. Curious, I partook of a quick puff and held the smoke in, but nothing happened. Dennis, however, seemed to be transformed by the experience, transported into fantasy. "I intend to walk right through the wall with you," he said to me, though I didn't know what he was talking about. Being almost five years older, Dennis spoke with authority; he had an enormous breadth of RPM knowledge, extending over a remarkable range of material, and he'd soon introduce me to new music: to Bob Dylan, Janis Joplin, Jimi Hendrix, and Joan Baez; to bands beyond The Beatles, such as The Rolling Stones, Led Zeppelin, Cream, Moby Grape, Ultimate Spinach, The Electric Prunes, The Strawberry Alarm Clock, The Mothers of Invention, The Kinks, The Doors, and more. He introduced me to Joni Mitchell, and I remember listening to her *Clouds* LP in his room, and then comparing the raucous rock version of "Wood-stock" by Crosby, Stills, Nash & Young with Joni's wistful and more subtle performance, where you can really hear the words—not that I thought much about them then. Who'd have thought those songs had such lyrics?

Dennis eventually played rhythm guitar in a band of his own, "The Earth Telephones." They practiced out by the swimming pool on long summer evenings and performed at private parties and high school dances, so he was semiprofessional. He always had his guitar handy, so he'd pick it up and play along with whatever was on the stereo, his head of hair swinging along with the rhythms he'd coax from the strings. Right outside his window there was a birdhouse and feeder, hanging from a birch tree branch, a tiny house, with a small hole/door, set on a wooden platform, usually attracting drab sparrows, and squirrels to the ground below, where they fought with blue jays over scattered sunflower seeds, but sometimes a cardinal, the blood-red bird, appeared, there on the platform, flashing sensational feathers, and Dennis would say, "Wow! Will you look at that!"

It was a warm evening in May and a good way to start the big party, sitting down by the swimming pool, with Dennis at the picnic table strumming a new twelve-string guitar, his long blond hair hanging over his forehead, making him look like a Beach Boy. He observed and spoke about the world around him with child-like wonder, as if whatever it was he'd noticed were of paramount importance, something remarkable to think about, in a detached and lucid voice, sometimes feigning a British accent, as if he were lounging on a sofa, dictating to someone, or just hanging out on a surfboard, waiting for a wave. He began singing that David Bowie song about the man in a space capsule, commencing countdown, blasting off, and soon floating far above the world, singing about planet earth being blue and helpless, later explaining to me that "Major Tom" is an anagram for "Motor Jam," code for our global car culture. Dennis was, I guess, prescient. He was, he said, "waiting to see what happens."

In the evening before the big party, when The Who blasted the air with "My Generation," shaking the whole house with all of its lights on, marijuana smoke filling the air, as teenagers arrived with sleeping bags over their shoulders, Dennis was down by the swimming pool, and I was there. "Come on, Cindy, take the lead. Sing a song, any little song that you know," he said, somehow in conspiracy with the water, its place in space illuminated by electric lights set inside plastic casings on the blue walls of the pool, quivering with invisible aquatic NRG, as Dennis encouraged me to sing something for him before the crowd arrived and he'd be preoccupied with guests his own age, such as Kathy Oppenheim, his petite, pretty girlfriend, lively and almost always laughing around Dennis. She was an accomplished dancer, and she said she'd been at Shea Stadium in 1965, when The Beatles performed there, playing for only twenty action-packed minutes. Kathy was a spoiled rich girl, dancing, with amazing flowers in her hair, showing off her pretty legs and figure, an instantiation of a certain type, the arrogant, silly girl, her head full of boys and hype.

After moving to New Canaan, I still saw Sally Knowlton occasionally, and I was at her house, there in the driveway, one summer afternoon when Dennis appeared, bearded, wearing beads, his hair flowing down to his waist, walking away from a Volkswagen bus that had stopped at the end of the driveway. Kathy got out after him, carrying a bundle of what looked like potatoes in a burlap bag. They nodded to us, and then they walked up to the house.

The third or fourth time Dad took me to the islands, to Jamaica, where a new hotel was being built, he left me alone on a beach by the water while he went off on business, and I had to deal with intrusive male behavior all on my own for the first time in my life, making my adrenaline rise, sunlight bouncing off the crashing waves, the hoods of cars parked at the beach, the surfboards, and brightly colored boating equipment. I was carrying my new Kodak Super 8 movie camera, a gift Aunt Pauline had given to me for my fifteenth birthday, making footage into scenes, and that's where I filmed my first sequence of men walking on a beach, coming toward me, framed by a sparkling sea. Sitting on my blanket in the sun, I aimed the lens, beginning to communicate with the men, to hold my own place in their world and let them into my own world, a little: "Yes, I'm here on holiday." "No, I'm not alone." Our being present to each other on such unequal terms, the questions were mere subterfuge. I was a girl alone. Two groups approached me that afternoon: first, a couple of white guys, close enough to my own age to be harmless, but then there was the group of older, dark-skinned young men, carrying a Styrofoam cooler. When they noticed me and stopped, I hid my camera under my towel and heard a spoken language I did not understand. Soon they were standing right there, and a tall guy opened the cooler, and there was a six-pack of Red Stripe. "Does this young lady desire to 'sheer' a beer with us?" he asked, his use of "this" turning me into an object of attention, his weird accent skewing the word "share," making an implausible rhyme with "beer." I said "No," or maybe just shook my head, but this guy was persistent; he really wanted me to take a beer, and he was grinning, squatting at the edge of the blanket where I was sitting. There was a radio somewhere playing an aggressive in-strumental soundtrack, taunting me with its rhythms, as if the music were on their side. I didn't want to appear rude, so I proceeded to make small, diversionary talk about the weather I'd flown away from, just after Valentine's Day, that we'd departed from Kennedy in the first flakes of what would be a monstrous blizzard, such a contrast to our sunny surroundings. There was a definite tension, a palpable sense of stress, and I could taste a vague threat in the salty heat, just hanging there. Luckily, Dad showed up, which quickly defused the situation, and after they left, he asked me what we'd been talking about. Had I been leading the conversation or just letting them have their way with me with words? Had I been at all afraid?

Later, as we sat in wicker chairs on the terrace, as I sipped my first piña colada, served in a large chilled glass, garnished with crushed ice, shredded coconut, and a pineapple wedge, and as we shared a view of the sun going down into the sea like a ship on a nocturnal voyage, Dad talked about his job; it was deeply satisfying, his working with people, and he knew that he was doing something for the benefit of everyone involved. He said that it felt as if he were part of the entertainment industry. Hotels were proliferating, boosting tourism throughout the Caribbean, providing employment for local people, providing entertainment for the guests he felt he himself personally hosted. I understood my father's excitement, and I enjoyed his candid approach to my young, impressionable character. The sun was sinking like a galleon aflame, with orange and purple cloud formations obscuring its ruby red center, setting a bit of the ocean on fire. I fiddled with my swordfish, conflating present and past, and the moment was perfumed with the fragrance of aromatic, blossoming flowers, and then Dad asked, "Can you tell the difference?" "What?" "The fish. It's fresh." Then he lowered his eyes to his plate. His tone of voice changed abruptly, and he simply said, "Your mom and I. We're breaking up. It's over." Those were his words, a fragment and two short sentences, as the white flesh fell in flakes from my fork. As we walked back along the beach to the hotel, Dad pointed out some lights in the sky; there was commotion nearby, a bunch of young guys playing volleyball in the sand, their bronzed torsos illuminated by torchlight, and I looked in slack-jawed awe for an instant, as one of them smiled at me, but Dad didn't catch that.

Although my early memories of Mom and Dad include the two of them in the kitchen kissing, sometimes dancing in the living room, Dad showing off, shaking the cocktail shaker in a lascivious jig, calling her his "key lime pie," the four of us on vacation, visiting Grandma Maude in Florida, the happy, holiday times at The Ark, there were long, unremarkable stretches of time when I wouldn't

see them together, when they didn't speak to each other, maintaining emotional distance, and the marriage was a disaster. Silence
reigned in the house at Riverside, on Pasture Lane, silences punctuated by stormy outbursts, arguments, and slamming doors. One
night, when I was very young, there was angry shouting, and I think
I heard, from my room upstairs, my father shove my mother against
the kitchen wall. I remember placing both hands on both ears and
looking at my collection of wooden blocks with bright colored letters on them, throwing them all against the wall of my bedroom,
thinking, "Stop!" There was the sudden slamming of a door, and
then the loud voices stopped. Another night, after another violent
shouting match, Dad raced upstairs to my bedroom, where I was
reading, my capacity for sustained attention just beginning to come
into play. His face was very red; he was breathing heavily, as if he'd
been running, and his breath smelled of liquor. There was lipstick
on his shirt, a lilac color that wasn't Mom's. He explained to me
that he had to go away. He said that I'd have to look after Mom,
that Tommy could take care of himself, but that Mom needed to be
looked after. I remember he said that, and it didn't make any sense
to me. He shut the door, and I threw my book against the wall. I had
just begun to enjoy reading alone, out on my own, and the idea of
not having him at home frightened me. He returned, of course, and
my parents sustained an uneasy truce, most of the time, when they
were around us, which was rarely.

When the final fight occurred, the last episode, right in the living room with all the lights on, Dad had some light luggage with
him, and there was a car, a black limousine waiting for him at the
end of the driveway. I guess he'd planned for that last time, and this
time it was for real. Mom ran out in her bare feet on the snowy lawn
after him, screaming, "Howard Taine, Howard Taine, you can't do
this!" She raised her fists to the wintry sky. The car door opened and
Dad slipped in, asking, rhetorically, "Can't I now?"

3

NEW CANAAN

DAD VANISHED, AND WE PREPARED TO LEAVE RIVERSIDE, SUDDENLY packing all of our things up in boxes, leaving most of the furniture there, and I cried to myself with the irrepressible emotion of a young girl in a tragedy, sobs breaking out in the night. We moved because Mom didn't want the large house and wanted to be farther away from her parents, choosing New Canaan for its distance, for its better schools, and because she had a friend in the real estate business there, Barbara Percy, who'd directed us to a modest house, a Cape Cod bungalow on Crozier Place, set near the center of town. We drove up behind the moving truck one bleak March morning, patches of snow on the ground, segments of snow clinging to tree branches twitching in a raw, grey wind. I'd just turned fifteen and was being uprooted, torn from my home. Why we had to leave town so suddenly was an enigma to me. It seemed irrational. Mom was acting on impulse. "We've got to get out of this place," she said to us, announcing her decision. I think the effects of drinking had already begun to tarnish her judgment. Selling the house and moving to New Canaan was a way of reacting to the situation, putting it all behind her, into the past, where it belonged. It was her way of expressing her rage at Dad, although he wasn't there. She was doing something striking, taking us away from Riverside in an act of self-assertion, proof of her self-reliance, bringing us to a new location, and I cried because I realized my family was not conventional.

The drive was dreary, and the anticipated shock of starting midterm at a new school made my stomach feel hollow and rumble inside. When we arrived at the house, I noticed a light brown bed of pine needles beneath the Norwegian pine in the front yard, and it seemed like a place where I might put down a blanket, rest my head, and drift away. I didn't want to deal with the house, an ordinary two-story saltbox, its wooden sides painted a drab greyish green, with windows set off by white shutters, a brick chimney, the front yard dominated by one towering evergreen. The backyard was small and cramped, like a meadow stuffed inside of a shoebox, with a straggly, struggling apple tree in one corner, nothing like our spacious backyard down in Riverside, no willow trees, no birches, pines, and raspberrry bushes at the edge of the property. The four rooms on the first floor—the kitchen, the dining room, the living room, and "the mud room," a sort of walk-in closet with a sink in it and hooks on the walls, where we'd hang our coats, and a big mat for boots and shoes—were all tidy places, because Mom, although she became sloppy in so many ways, always insisted on clean floors and boundaries—"a place for everything, and everything in its place," she'd say, echoing her older brother. At first the house felt like a fortification, a kind of outpost on a frontier. The living room was too small for the rug we'd brought, which had to be rolled up at the edges.

Eudora fled Riverside to forget about Dad, to forget about how he'd plundered her soul, for she believed, for a time, that he'd been practicing voodoo or black magic on her, and she'd formed the notion that he, in secret alliance with malevolent, occult forces, was the cause of her "demons," her chronic moodiness, despondency, and heavy drinking. She felt compelled to put what she'd been through behind her, changing location, mainly in response to Dad, but also as a reaction against her parents, whose daughter had been, from Granddad's perspective especially, an ornery infant, a sullen child, a rebellious adolescent, and an adult incapable of making responsible decisions. The move made Mom manic. For the first few months, she didn't seem troubled by any "demons" at all, and she didn't drink any alcohol, nothing that I can recall. She became autocratic, taking control with a confident air, raising her voice, painting the house, working in the yard, doing some significant interior decorating, preparing the place, her place, for the warm weather ahead, when she'd entertain guests, host garden parties. She had a flagstone terrace built.

She was an attractive, single mother of two, starting out anew. It was fun at first, exploring the town, the antiques shops and clothing stores, especially the Home and Gardening Center, with her being so enthusiastic about decorating and refurbishing the house. I never really thought about where the money was coming from; I took it for granted that we were being financed by some arrangement she'd made with Dad, though she'd eventually work at the real estate office.

An ice storm isn't like any ordinary storm, because it isn't really there, concrete and ready for full presentation, until after the turbulent part is over. During December, just before our first winter there, shortly after a dull Thanksgiving dinner down at Uncle Steve's, I woke on a pristine Saturday morning to see, after a night of pounding sleet and wind, the once-whorled world in a state of icy stillness. "Gelid stasis," I thought, or think that I thought. Every outdoor surface was covered with a thin, transparent film of ice—the wooden picnic table, the birdbath, the intricate branches of dormant trees, the Norwegian pine's already snow-shagged boughs, a chilled world under erasure, all put to sleep—and I went outside with my Super 8 camera, my gift from Aunt Pauline, and sauntered about, filming whatever it was I happened on, capturing some natural fact (icy stones, an icy pinecone) or artifact altered by natural fact (ice on a mailbox, a fire hydrant, a birdbath, the roof of a car) with my camera, scanning phenomena, stealing imagery.

Down in Riverside, I'd often ride my bike to school, ringing my bell, but setting out from Crozier Place, where school was more than a mile away, where there were more roads with more dangerous, speeding vehicles on them, I either had to be driven or took the school bus. New Canaan's impressive new high school, viewed from above, from an aerial perspective, was essentially a huge cross, a colossus of steel, concrete, and glass comprising two long hallways that met at an often-busy intersection. The building featured central heating and air-conditioning, so it was always an ideal or near-perfect temperature inside, sometimes creating a surreal contrast to the world outside. There were large windows with views of the surrounding woods and athletic fields. Inside, I walked on new carpets. There was a new linoleum floor in a gigantic cafeteria with a fleet of working vending machines, and I saw a state-of-the-art auditorium, an Olympic-sized pool, new audio-visual equipment in all of the classrooms, modern equipment in science labs, and spacious lavatories, with plenty of sinks and soap, the stalls spick-and-span. The property surrounding the school was verdant and vast, suggesting a golf course, its borders marked by fuzzy pine trees, which stood out against the leafless deciduous trees that March day, as I stood in the parking lot, marveling at the large, intimidating building, with its constant flow of students, in and out, around and about its entrance. Rabbits and squirrels were killed on the paved access road, caught beneath the wheels of cars, trucks, and buses, so many gasoline sculptures playing roles in the business of education. The structure itself was low to the ground, hunkered down in the landscape like a military base, the concrete foundation forming its cross, its main axis oriented north to south; its center, where the two hallways intersected, was a lively place of bodies moving between classes, a place where bodies bumped, where I was bumped into by a cute, long-haired guy, causing my handheld pile of books to fall, and I saw it all as if I were a camera—him bending down, looking up my legs, grabbing my heavy algebra textbook between the thumb and four fingers of his right hand, putting it into my open hands—so I probably smiled and attempted to say, "Thanks, I'll always remember this."

Now in New Canaan, new to the environment, doing a little reading on my own in the books I'd take home from the high school library, I fell into playing with words, and though my efforts were but facile and airy entertainment, fit for a silly girl's mind, I experienced my fair share of felicitous, free, and fanciful moments when doing things with words made special sense, taking on significance, for me. Somehow simple noun phrases, such as "cellar door," exerted a strange fascination, like cloud formations, and they'd accumulate in a little notebook I kept, along with anagrams and related psycho-semantic bits—don't ask me why—and I'd have to get rid of them somehow, create more litter for a less cluttered mind. Sometime during the end of tenth grade, just after moving to New Canaan, I'd begun to conceptualize the word "feller," so phonetically close in a way to "cellar," as an alternate to "fella," which Dad had often used, talking about a friend or just any guy in a friendly way, which was simply a kind of abbreviated, countrified, or informal way of saying "fellow." I realized that the number of "fellers" or "fellas" filling the hallways and classrooms at New Canaan High with what I thought of as "feelers" was an instantiation of what mathematicians called "the not immediately numerable," I having been introduced by my math teacher to the notion that counting beyond the bounds of one's ten fingers produced "the not immediately numerable," any number that required some sort of "abstracting medium," some sort of "symbolic marking system." As I went walking through the hallways or sat in a classroom in my assigned seat, assigned to discourage friends from sitting together and disrupting the learning process, thinking "feller, fella, feeler," I felt the existence of so many boys.

Rocky the Squirrel, dressed in airplane pilot garb, a comic animal TV icon from TLC, referred to Bullwinkle the Moose as "fella," as in "this fella here," so the expression had an easygoing, cartoonish vibe about it. Mixing "Rocky" and "fella" together might suggest Rockefeller Center and the huge metal sculpture of Atlas carrying planet Earth on his shoulders, which I passed, years ago, when I went to get my passport alone and first noticed, really absorbed, all of the flags surrounding the skating rink, like the flags in front of the United Nations Building, identifying the one that stood for the country I'd soon be flying off to, Jamaica, with its green, black, and striking cross of yellow. But I'm now going back to a much earlier day, sometime near the middle of TLC, when we were driving into the city from Riverside one wintry Saturday afternoon, because Dad planned to take us to see a movie before stopping at The Ark for dinner, *Those Magnificent Men in Their Flying Machines*, a movie he thought Tommy would especially enjoy. I remember that early afternoon, because we parked the car at a midtown garage and walked to a movie theater that was more like a real theater; there was a large lobby with sofas, mirrored walls, potted palms, red carpeting, and an elaborate ceiling with ostentatious chandeliers suspended over our heads. We walked into a dimly lit theater containing more seats than I'd ever seen before in one place; there seemed to be miles of aisles. The screen was enormous, and I sank deeply into the most comfortable cushioned seat I'd ever been in, surrounded by state-of-the-art stereo sound. The movie itself involved the many test flights made in preparation for the 1910 London-to-Paris airplane race, and the duration of the race, re-created with a certain comic flair, was at its center. All of the airplanes were moved by propellers, and that seems relevant to my story, insofar as propellers work with the air, pulling the aircraft through it, somewhat as a swimmer cups water with her hands, pulling herself through the medium, whereas the modern jet engine pushes the aircraft through space. The popcorn was excellent, and as we exited into the dark evening, there were big, widely spaced snowflakes falling, like patches of Arctic lace, bits of angelic clothing attaching themselves to my coat, suggesting the connection between popcorn and snowflakes, instantiations of "the not immediately numerable," the infinite, never numerable number of irregularly shaped popped-corn kernels and equally infinite number of miniscule lattices of ice, each in its complexity, though I can't really see how each and every flake that falls in this universe of ours is a distinct formation, fracturing time in a singular way. The connection between the two domains, the two sets of objects, both "immediately innumerable," made me think of trees on my way to "The Most Famous Christmas Tree in the World," which was, by the time we reached Rockefeller Center, perfectly lit, a real monster, a great big spruce, a colorful multitude cast on its body, glowing in a suit of lights. The exciting points of multicolored light incited me to act, not unlike the luminescent, electrical impulses I imagine certain deepwater fish send and receive. Music was being pumped into the air. There were people moving everywhere, swirling, swimming, caught up in a "pandemonium stomp," Dad's expression, and we stopped to look down and watch the skaters, some with real flair, project their bodies over the ice, through decibels of good vibrations. The Beach Boys were already playing, portentously, on the radio inside of my head for a sunny moment, although it was cold, and the temperature became, the closer we moved to the rink, colder, and the skaters were breathing out icy plumes. A woman, wrapped in a large black cloak, was smoking a cigarette, and when she finished it, she threw it down and stepped on it, and she still exhaled blue smoke. The rink was so far down from where we were standing that it was really like a sunken stage, or cage, lit by overhead lighting, but it was difficult to see how the skaters, the very good ones, could twirl in place with such ease, but there they were, dancers on an icy plane. We stopped at a shop and bought chocolates with coconut cream centers. We took a carriage ride through Central Park, though when I looked at the horse and saw the tremendous capacity for suffering in its eyes, opaque and black, its breathing expressed in long, white plumes, the falling snow now thicker, now sticking to the trees and street, a great place to practice cinematography, when all of these details converged and overwhelmed me at once, I said, "Poor animal. I want to climb out and walk to The Ark," and though I made a keen effort to have my own way prevail, my parents wouldn't let me go, and I felt myself frustrated, striving against limitation.

There was a loud presence in The Ark that night, and I thought, at first, that she was a friend of the family, that this gregarious woman, mouth working away, was someone from what Gaga referred to with a disparaging frown as "the theater crowd," a world with which Arthur R. Prescott mixed on occasion, and my first thought proved, in the course of some time, to be true. The woman was dressed in a little black dress, and her body talked with the spirited confidence of a professional actress. This beautiful, amusing woman was holding her hands out in front of her breasts; she was increasing the distance between her hands as if she were telling the small crowd gathered around her a fish story. It was some sort of joke, because they all laughed when she finished. I was drinking Canada Dry ginger ale with Tommy when she came over to us, a bit tipsy, and introduced herself as "Aunt Alice." She said she was visiting from Montreal, that she had been to The Ark before, back when we were young, practically babies, so we couldn't possibly remember her. She had an incredible mane of shiny golden hair, but then I noticed that the roots of her gorgeous curls were black; she had Latin roots, and I think she understood, almost immediately, that the person behind the camera, the person operating the filming apparatus, was stealing her image, taking it down for future use. There was a studied manner, a strategy, in the way she flipped her head back and went into action, thrown into theatrical time, when she noticed my lenses focused on her hair, notable for its similarity to an important yellow metal. Using her hands a lot as she spoke, Aunt Alice told us there were family secrets that even our mother hadn't shared with us, things that the Prescott family didn't like to talk about. She was laughing in a highly animated way, when her son, "Cousin" Conrad, shocked me, coming up behind me, "Do you want to see something weird?"

"What do you mean?" I asked.

"I mean, do you, persnickety Cousin Cindy, pretty grand-daughter of the influential and powerful Arthur R. Prescott, want to see something weird?" I shot him a questioning look.

"Look, girl, I'm just talking to you," Conrad interjected with sudden force. Conrad liked to pretend to "jive talk," a joke, miming the language of the street, acting tough, like a black kid, a bad boy, a delinquent. I wasn't at all sure what "weird" in this context could signify. I thought I knew all that anyone could possibly know about my grandparents' apartment and its contents. "Cousin" Conrad, dressed in a striking purple shirt and wearing bright white, almost fluorescent, bellbottom pants, a wide black belt with a big brass buckle, and a pair of shiny black leather boots, was not like my other cousins, Uncle Steve's four boys, who were always dressed in a more conservative fashion, in brown leather loafers, or Top-Siders, with corduroy pants and freshly ironed, button-down cotton shirts. Conrad smiled a lot, almost lasciviously. What could this swaggering teenager show me, unless he wanted to go outside? "I don't want to go outside," I said. "No, here, in the apartment. Do you want to see something weird or not?" "See what?" I asked, wondering what it could be. I wasn't going to go, but Conrad pleaded, and I eventually nodded okay, and he led me to the stairway, past the wall of old photographs of now-dead people standing in groups. And I saw the family photograph that Gaga had arranged to have taken, with Uncle Steve and Aunt Mary and the boys, before Dad began cheating on Mom, and she's smiling, though she's obviously forced into bloom for the camera. What is the nature of the smile people showed photographers in TLC? It is a color photograph taken in early May in Riverside, down by the Sound, and beyond an azalea bush, showing its crimson blossoms, behind a group of dark yew trees, a section of pale blue water appears. We are all smiling, though I think my own smile shows a certain skepticism about the whole situation, and I am wearing a cowgirl outfit, a suede skirt, something Heidi might have worn, while Tommy has set his bright orange leather baseball mitt right on the ground, the bright green lawn, down by his right hand. Dad's standing over us, wearing informal summer attire, a white shirt, blue tie, and an eggshell-tinted jacket, its left arm just brushing Mom's exposed skin. Try as I might to visualize what was going on, I feel that I can't, or that I am led to trivialize it, whatever it was. There was a sense that we were breaking rules, going off limits, going into my grandparents' private property without permission, and I sensed that Conrad was intending to force something open, some container that was supposed to remain closed, and that if any adult, relative or not, knew what we were about to do, she or he would condemn our behavior. I suddenly wanted to stay downstairs. I didn't want to see anything weird, but Conrad's determined tug took me upstairs and down the long hallway to an almost empty room, where two beds were, where Granddad apparently stored old magazines in a cardboard box under the bed farthest from the door, a place I'd never been, close to the window, where the curtains were drawn. At this point Cindy Taine, in a sense, split into two parts; one part was looking forward with innocent expectation, while the other disapproved entirely of what we were doing, as Conrad pulled the box out from under the bed and began to dig down into the magazines, like a hungry animal raiding another one's lair, determined to locate the object of his search. I think both of us simultaneously felt a weak, mixed emotion. "Here," he said, producing a glossy magazine and opening it to a photograph of a beautiful naked lady riding a horse. "It's Lady Godiva," Conrad proclaimed, glancing at me, an expression of perverse anticipation playing in his eyes. He flipped the page to another photo of the woman, supine this time, reclining on a mound of hay, the horse in the background, her legs spread open. I'd never seen pornography before, although I'd heard the word, and that's what this was. It frightened me, and I ran out of the room. I ran downstairs and sat down on the sofa with Mom, and Conrad came downstairs and smiled at me as if we were now in cahoots, caught in some sort of conspiracy.

The move to New Canaan was difficult for me at first, while Tommy adapted quickly, being such an outgoing, high-spirited kid who could cut his own figure anywhere, a teenager with curly, dark hair, blue eyes, and an impressive physique, but he was a bit too proud of his athletic abilities, acting as if physical prowess justified an arrogant attitude. It sometimes seemed his life revolved entirely around sports—football, basketball, and, especially, baseball—and soon he was playing baseball, first-string varsity, at New Canaan High. He'd often brag, with a blunt urgency, about some play he'd made, a home run or stolen base, calling attention to himself, but he had a highly developed practical streak, which had made him the athlete he was, which he demonstrated in his new role as man of the house, taking care of the car and lawnmower, fixing things, taking care of Mom as she continued her perilous decline. Tommy was talkative with Mom in a way that I wasn't, and he could engage and involve her in a way that kept the heavy drinking in check, though there were always lost weekends. I'd find hidden bottles of vodka and pour the contents down the sink. Tommy let her have wine with dinner, but after Mom had had a few glasses, before she'd have too much, he'd take the bottle from the table, saying, "Bar's closed. Closing time." "Party pooper," she'd say, pouting, as he put the bottle away. I couldn't believe how quickly Tommy grew up. Dad vanished, and Tommy filled his place.

It's raining now, outside the cottage, rousing me from my account, and the glass panes, struck by wind-driven water, stream, merging like parts of some machine, like Uncle Steve's reel-to-reel Sony tape recorder, time passing more quickly as more experience, more memory, more tape rolls onto the reel that is taking it up from the other, going around with less and less tape, less and less time. Is it possible that there are turning points? I didn't like high school at first, for I didn't feel like making any effort to make new friends, and I didn't enjoy having to take the school bus and being ordered around by those brazen, shrill electric bells, forcing a routine, a schedule, on us. And around that time, for an extended point in that time's space, I think I thought solely of swimming.

I was never a competitive swimmer. I'd learned to swim off the stone pier at Uncle Steve's. Dad had literally thrown me into the harbor water, inaugurating my life in that element, and I was soon comfortable in the demonstration of my innate, amphibious nature, showing off my newly discovered ability, if only for myself. What was it about water that drew me to it so? What was it, a median state between earth and air? There was a swim team at New Canaan High, but I never had the extroverted, competitive streak—not for swimming, at least—and very few students took advantage of the open swim periods, on Tuesday and Thursday afternoons, when anybody could use the pool, so I became a regular in the spanking-new, empty auditorium of heated space with a deep, blue floor of tantalizing water, the aquarium where I dabbled in my medium, conducting my first experiments in assertiveness training, conversations about competition and control, pep talks essentially, doing the distances, using my own lungs and limbs. I'd dive and plunge into the cool, clear substance, and it was as if I had GILLS AGAIN and had become a universal representative of no one in particular, swimming underwater, practicing holding my breath, and I achieved a funny anonymity when I surfaced, coming up for air. My exercise became a kind of rite, ridding me of tedium, so I felt very happy twice a week, during those swimming sessions, the high points of what was soon to become a routine of scheduled classes and after-school activities. I eventually made new friends and soon enjoyed being with them, doing whatever it was we did, but whatever it was, swimming was what I'd rather have been doing.

Just as Mom somehow, despite the drinking, was successfully getting herself off to her job at the real estate office, finding that she could rise to the challenge, no more daytime stupors, probably enjoying the sense of purpose employment gave her, I found myself, one dull afternoon, down in the basement in front of the washing machine, facing its circular window, like a big porthole on a ship at sea, noticing the brief, sudden appearances of clothing, flashes of colored fabric in the suds, like a patch of red, splash against the glass, churning in soapy water until the machine stopped, and the water drained away, and the machine went into a new motion, its internal parts now humming, spinning. And I thought of my thinking and how it was now in spin cycle again, rewinding, going back to Riverside, back before Mom's heavy drinking, before Dad left us, when one of Dad's passions, for sure, was driving his new sports car, the black Jaguar, fast and far on a Sunday morning, off into the landscape. By the time I'd reached the seventh grade, Mom had given up or just forgotten about getting us all together as a family for Sunday morning church, for which we'd made ourselves presentable, dressing up for the morning service at Saint Paul's Episcopal, at nine fifteen sharp, with all the melancholy menace of its bells, where Reverend Holloway addressed us, his flock of mortal forms and hallowed souls, peppering his sermons with biblical citations and extended homilies I could not understand. Saint Paul's was a magnificent stone structure, with a golden cross atop its tall steeple, gleaming above the belltower, the steep slate roofs, the great, elongated gable and stained-glass windows below, set in their narrow casements, gleaming at points like rubies, emeralds, and sapphires. Shady oaks blocked the view of the church for much of the year, but during the winter, the structure stood out like a cathedral, imposing and commodious, behind the stark trees, showing its lines off to anyone who noticed. A new, modern building was connected to the church by a breezeway, a corridor seemingly always flooded with sunlight and heat, even on the coldest Sunday morning in January, when the snow glistened beyond the icy terrace. At a certain point during the main service, after singing the hymn with the choir, after an instrumental interlude played on the organ, just before Reverend Holloway's sermon, the children were led out of church. Up to that point, Tommy and I had stayed obediently in our pew, sitting, standing, kneeling, going through the motions, and I pondered my place, colored light streaming through the windows, flowers blossoming on the altar, the color-coded vestments the clergy wore, the sanctified, perfumed air. We'd rise from our pew, the music playing, to join a herd of children following an older boy holding a brass staff, and like sheep, we'd walk out of the great, resounding cavern and through the narrow corridor into the new building, into immaculate classrooms to sit and be read to, or to read aloud, collectively, from illustrated booklets about the life of Jesus, the miracle of his birth, foretold by John the Baptist, its location presaged by starlight, the signs followed by kings and shepherds, away in a manger, surrounded by sleeping animals. After the reading, we'd sing about Christian soldiers marching, going to do battle in a final event that never happens because it's happening all the time, though I didn't know that then. Later, when I was older and allowed to sit through the entire service and endure Reverend Holloway's sermonizing, his voice raised to an authoritative pitch, I observed how the man in the pulpit glanced up and looked out at some of us in particular, it seemed, as if trying to enroll us in some cause that was ultimately his alone. I resented being expected to listen to what he had to say. Sometimes I felt sympathy for the effort he was making, but I was never very interested, never attentive to the details of his arguments, his admonishments and exhortations, the whole ordeal, about which he was representative and earnest, launching into the Lord's Prayer with gusto. And when he asked Our Father in Heaven to "forgive us our trespasses," I always assumed he was talking about walking on someone's private property, week after week, and when he went into a mild rant about what we were behooved to do or not do, I'd think of playing horseshoes. Shining coins were tossed into a golden bowl, as it passed from person to person, and Reverend Holloway, somehow above it all, aloof, seemed a sort of *Wizard of Oz* figure, a funny moneyman, standing up there in the pulpit, which I'd eye, impressed by the woodwork in the warm glow of the colored light streaming in through the stained glass, its form resembling an upright coffin, featuring decorative interstices, little pyramidal lozenges cut into the sides, or I'd look up at a painted cornice in the ceiling, lit by a beam of electric light, a real piece of sculpture. I looked at my resting hands folded in prayer upon the pew in front of me. Dad was in the same position, head bowed down, probably thinking about getting out, for he never enjoyed church very much. I could tell by the way he'd stay quiet during the drive there, where he'd just go through the motions, the sitting, standing, and kneeling. He never seemed to sing along with the congregation, but he'd let his own voice expand and boom when it was all over, driving home, his left hand hanging outside the window. So, for a time in Riverside, Dad took us off and away in his sports car, in lieu of church on Sunday.

I enjoyed being out on four wheels, playing the radio, becoming familiar with roads north of town. Crossing the state line, driving into Westchester County, we'd pass the Pound Ridge Nursery, an impressive venue for vibrant plants of all kinds, and that was an exclamation mark. Going farther north out of Bedford, up on Route 121, where I didn't know what to expect, there was a swampy area, and one April morning of blue sky and fluffy, white clouds pushed by a gentle, warm breeze, we passed by it. Dad stopped the car, put it into reverse, stopped alongside the swamp, switched off the engine, and lingered, so that we could hear, and listen to, the peepers sing; it was a chorus of myriad tiny frogs. Sunlight played on the still, level water, and the place was suddenly bejeweled, glimmering with emerald fragments, buds on the blossoming trees, ferns exfoliating, tiny green spears popping up from the mud, as I return to where I was then, that first year at New Canaan High, sitting in front of the washing machine, and although I adapted to the new environment, I had my share of social throes.

Michael Tracy was a bold, wayward kid with jet-black hair and a loud, competitive attitude about everything except pleasing his parents and getting good grades. I felt vulnerable just being around him. "Michael the Menace," I'd think when he approached me in the cafeteria or corralled me at my locker between classes. I didn't know why he wouldn't stop following me, teasing me, flirting with me in a hyperactive, provocative way, or did I? Handsome and athletic, he was rumored to be one of the boys who'd "gone all the way," and he spoke with his hands, pulling me toward him once on a bus going somewhere, pushing my long blond hair out of his face. His father was a bigwig executive, maybe even CEO, at Exxon, and the family lived in an incredibly elegant white house, a colonial monster, its many windows wrapped around its great girth, set at the end of an open field where horses grazed. Passing by in a car, I thought of all of those rooms behind all that glass, passed in a blur. The Tracy kids all had a reputation for their achievements and good looks, each one endowed with a healthy competitive streak, domain-specific, the drive to excel and a way to make it show, such as Leslie, who became a successful journalist, or Linda, who joined the air force, or Liza, the scholastic star, who later became president of a small college in Oregon, or Lorraine, who married a famous billionaire. Unlike his siblings, Michael, the youngest of five, the only boy, wasn't competitively inclined at all; he was a slacker, making lewd commentary from the back of a classroom, shoving his cowboy boots on top of his desk in front of him as he leaned back in a chair, threatening belligerence. He was arrogant and didn't show any respect for authority, but he exhibited that self-assurance that is often accompanied by a forceful dexterity, a tender approach, a spontaneous and precocious sexuality, and that one time on the bus, he kissed me, deeply, letting his tongue rest on mine, our mouths stitched together, so that when other boys pursued me, I knew what to expect.

Just before leaving Riverside, I'd begun to notice boys, the way their bare legs moved playing soccer, charging around on the field, the depths of their voices, the shapes they assumed, the determination of their torsos. One crisp afternoon in early October, a lovely admixture of gold and bright blue, the air pungent with the smell of dried leaves, an aroma like cinnamon, I found myself paying attention to some boy or other, as he ran across the playing field. I looked at him as he'd looked at me, expressing a tentative interest, and we shared a certain tension. It was a real NRG shift, echoed later, as I looked at myself in a full-length mirror at Bloomingdale's, trying on a dress for a party, allowing myself to see myself from a different point of view, not mine but the point of view a boy might take, putting us at the center of it all. Being with my girlfriends, I often felt I was by myself, but the presence of boys shifted the order of what was important; I wanted to swing with them, and I didn't want to feel afraid or vulnerable around them in any circumstances, so I practiced acting cool and unmoved, unfazed by things they said, the looks they began to give me, the looks even Tommy gave me.

Tommy brought a stray dog home one spring afternoon, a mutt with a touch of the hound dog in him, with a long muzzle and a faint dark line running down his light-brown back. His floppy ears were flaps of black skin. We tried to locate his owner, but nobody seemed to know the dog or where he came from, like he'd been part of a traveling troop, a K-9 circus act, and he'd just decided to tune in, drop out, and stop in New Canaan, hang out in the high school parking lot for a while for the fun of it, check out the scene, see

what transpires. He became attracted to Tommy. He acted like he'd
already had a lot of real-life experience far away from Crozier Place,
which became, of all places, his home, thanks to Tommy. Mom
had us put him in the basement that first night, where all he did
was howl and whine, but after he was trained and better behaved,
Desmond became the four-legged, four-footed, furry familiar of the
house, hanging out on his mat in the mudroom, sleeping on the
back porch, barking at strangers, chasing squirrels when the spirit
moved him, rushing out the back door to scatter squadrons of unruly
crows that congregated in the backyard. I bought him a beautiful
diamond collar, and Tommy played with him, but Desmond eventually became Mom's dog.

Growing up in Belle Haven, Eudora had a sheepdog named
Molly, for whom she showed unconditional love, the dog and her
being inseparable, so a certain precedent had been set, and she re-
gressed into the time of her childhood around Desmond, living like
she was a girl again, giving him all of her naked heart when she was
with him, which was most of the time. I don't know what she did
at the real estate office. She didn't show people houses; I imagine
she did some light typing, answered the phone, kept papers organized, and kept her friend Barbara Percy company, gabbing away,
though I can't really picture Mom gabbing. But Desmond did give
her something to talk about, like a guiding spirit leading her back
to her pampered childhood, the realm of the petulant princess. Her
father's sheep grazed in the pasture beyond the far edge of the lawn,
and she'd look out on foggy summer mornings when the foghorn on
Great Captain's Island sounded, blowing low decibels out into grey
vapors. She'd see the woolly white animals in the green meadow and
smile, thinking, "Eudora, Eudora, what shall we do?" She'd get up
and walk out of her bedroom, early in the morning, carefully closing the door, everyone else still asleep, and she'd saunter down the
great carpeted stairway into the freedom of the empty living room,
the heart of the house, full of potential and furniture, like being

amid sleeping animals, and there came to her face an expression of flippancy, as she roamed the other rooms, humming to herself, suddenly noticing the paintings, the sofas, the tables and chairs, the clock on the mantel, the cluster of framed photographs on a wall, the extraordinary Persian carpets, revealed in an unusual light as if for the first time, entering an altered, heightened state, neither good nor bad when experienced in the present. Mom was aware, even at an early age, that a certain pressure in the air (a section of her soul, it seemed) released her from mere contingencies—her name, her place and date of birth, her part in a convoluted family tree—and when that something touched her, then she was free, a wild child.

Desmond, I think, played a vital part in her later, adult years, becoming her ally in her struggle against an essentially hostile environment, for she seemed to be always fighting the world. She'd bring Desmond in the car to work with her, and he'd place both paws on the dashboard and look straight ahead, scanning the road ahead intently, already anticipating the mat by her desk, where he'd sit, or the enclosed area outside the building, where he'd be confined but free to move within bounds, connected to an overhead cable by a long metal leash, which made a zinging sound when he ran back and forth. When she was out of the house at night, drinking and having sex with Mr. Van Warner, during those last days of reckless living as I imagine them, she'd return home and find Desmond there, needing to be fed, quietly demanding, with his doelike black eyes, whiskers, and leather button of a nose, giving her his unconditional love. His was the familiar face she'd come home to. At the very end, Desmond's eyesight was poor, but Mom in her stupor alone in the house had him to talk to, muttering sweet nothings, and he'd produce a quiet, affectionate bark, expressing approval, which soothed her troubled soul.

Miss Binder was the only teacher whose class I really enjoyed during those three years at New Canaan High, probably because English was an easy subject for me, and she spoke with confidence and expert ease, as if studious reading and learning to write well were skills of primary importance, actually impacting the way one lived life, giving us the sense that we belonged there, and I admired her for being so pretty, but tough with the rowdy boys. She wore sexy skirts, and she spoke with a slight British inflection, as if she'd been born in England or had gone to school there. She had fine, wispy auburn hair and sparkling green eyes, and she distinguished her eyes with a touch of blue shadow, just a touch, and she effectively managed any crude behavior coming from the boys. "Out of my classroom," she'd command, pointing to the door. Sometimes, in good weather, she'd take the class outside, and we'd sit on a grassy bluff, from which I'd look at the classroom windows, looking away from my book. The passing clouds, reflected in glass, were forms to train my own gaze on, as the white shapes went through mutations, transformations according to my fanciful inclinations, and I paid no attention to what we were supposedly reading and discussing. It was always a marvelous day, with a kind of vibrancy to it, the sky so bright I couldn't help but wonder why—why the clouds were way up there or why I should listen to anyone's words—and I filmed Miss Binder, her body seeking and frequently finding novel ways of making the assigned reading relevant and entertaining, putting her voice into different registers, gesturing with her hands. She used to tell us that we could write about anything we wanted to write about if we really tried to think about it. She frequently compared writing to thinking, that it taught us to see the differences around us, to embody the world we were in, and then she'd say that any one thing is like any other thing if you think about the two of them for long enough. She liked to talk, "to language us," in riddles. She was sometimes outlandish, suggesting provocative ways to interpret the poems and short stories in our anthology, but she always returned to the general idea that language was communicative action. She stressed the importance of knowing who we were writing for, what audience our words were being aimed at, and then she'd quickly

qualify herself, saying that everything we wrote for class would ultimately be for her, as if making a joke, so we should always just give
it our best effort, whatever it was we were writing, as if it weren't a
total waste of time.

So the days went by with their assortments of colors and moods,
sometimes funny, sometimes blue, and Mom began to keep the
curtains closed on bleak days when the sunshine was boring, too
bright outside, and she was just too ill to go to work, but there
weren't too many of those days, or I have purposefully erased them,
deleted forever by me, the blonde with the pretty, rare name. I was
basically out of the house all week, but during the weekends, when
I was there, Mom affected an air of suburban normalcy, doing yard
work outside, cleaning, cooking, taking Desmond on long walks,
taking off in the car for addresses unknown before the sun went
low on the horizon, and I couldn't tell what her eyes were on, Mom
standing at the sink, the rush of water from the faucet mixing with
the clatter of Desmond's paws' claws on the linoleum floor, hitting
it like tiny tacks. Try as I may, I cannot capture her gestures, her
complex relations with the sounds and sights around her in that
environment.

One way to grow up quickly is to be burdened by an alcoholic
parent, and although I was depressed by her failure to stop or even
moderate her drinking, I'd learned to ignore it and just walk away.
Once, when I found a vodka bottle wrapped in a brown paper bag
beneath the bathtub, she denied hiding it there and claimed that it
was Tommy's, and I just said, "Sure, Mom, sure," and I handed it
to her, and that's when she understood that I understood that I was
becoming the indifferent parent, and she knew that I knew what
was happening, so there wasn't much to talk about in the presence
of each other.

Sometimes she felt an excitement so great—so extraordinary, I
guess—that she couldn't hide it, and she'd express herself by preparing an elaborate dinner, something from her French cookbook.

"Let's be pleasant tonight," she'd announce, her voice infected with cheerfulness, putting Chopin on the stereo, lighting candles on the table. She usually prepared something that was both time consuming and really very good, involving pots and pans that I'd later clean. Dinner was rushed through by Tommy, for he was always heading out, leaving me alone to bear her meandering, booze-fueled monologues about nothing, the weather, houses for sale, Barbara Percy's affairs, some decision she'd made in the supermarket, Desmond's enthusiasm for a new brand of dog food, and she capriciously burst into her own idiosyncratic music at points, asking me to sing along. She never asked me about what I was doing or thinking; she'd just continue singing or talking in a tone that suggested confidence but that always felt like, beneath it all, she was about to ask some favor of me, or make a great confession, but it was being avoided. I saw how alienated, how cut off, she was, and I feared for her and at the same time felt repelled, caught in an asymmetrical bind, especially when she began to complain to me, to whimper and cry, making me the adult while she was the helpless child. I'd mutter something about an obligation, get up to let Desmond out, do anything to excuse myself, do the dishes, do homework, make a phone call, do some laundry—anything—and she'd get up and follow me around the house, babbling endlessly, out of control, though some part of her was in control and confident of my attention as she followed me around, prolonging a pointless monologue about nothing, because she wouldn't remember any of it the next day. I'd feign an interest in what she had to say, and I'd smile, but I always maintained my calculated distance, wary of her turmoil. When a booze-related crisis erupted, Uncle Steve, ten miles down the road in Darien, where he sat in his office and worked the telephone, would drive up Mansfield Avenue in his silver Mercedes to his sister's cozy house of craziness on Crozier Place. He was, like his father, a natural pedagogue, and he'd quiz me about current events, exclaiming once, in words I can still hear, "Cindy, you know so little about what's going on in the world!" It was as if I'd never been to the islands, never seen poverty close up, people dressed in rags, living in filth, in shacks within sight of expensive hotels, but I knew, as he droned on in his sere tone of tedious reprimand, that not everyone lived in luxury on the edge of a golf course, or on Salem Straits in Darien, or in Belle Haven, or in a nice house on a quiet, shady street in New Canaan. I knew, as I alone could, by radio, TV, and magazines, something about the terrible war in Vietnam, the ongoing Mideast crisis, the starvation in Biafra and Bangladesh, the vast swaths of suffering humanity born on the dark side of the globe. And I'd be struck by that fact, thinking about whatever it was, whatever packet of misery I had access to, as I peered beyond the bushes of my own backyard, amazed that it was contemporary, simultaneous with my own fortunate happening in TLC.

I blossomed during my senior year into an attractive young woman, without really knowing how it happened. With a little help from my friends, it just happened. Suddenly, I morphed from being a shy girl, a kind of wallflower tomboy, into being part of the cool set, the popular crowd, and I dated boys who played on athletic teams, boys who owned their own cars, golden boys with charmed lives and checking accounts.

On weekend nights I'd leave Mom at home and drive down with friends to a nightclub in Port Chester, across the state border, where we could buy drinks with fake IDs, where we'd dance to loud RPM, good vibrations strained through the soles of my shoes primarily, syncopations registering within the more basic, reptilian parts of my brain. It was fun being young on the dance floor, negotiating a sea of flashing lights, bodies moving, navigating waves of sound, dancing through the decibels, enjoying a sort of parallel world, far out, where all the participants swirl, free as leaves in a breeze, caught in the act of dying. And as I became increasingly glad on my feet that autumn, having the time of my life, Mom's condition deteriorated; she seemed defeated by her demons, pulled by the monstrous lows of her emotions into a lawless nothingness, and when I was at home, I just ignored her drinking and the house ablaze with too much light.

One morning something unusual happened. Billy Jackson came running into homeroom with blood on his shirt. He'd just been in a knife fight with some older kid in the hallway, who was running away with a demoniac laugh. Billy burst through the doorway, fainted, and fell on the floor, his body twitching. We all thought, at first, that he had died. There was blood everywhere. He'd been deeply cut in his chest, and it was striking to see him then breathing there, waiting for the ambulance to arrive, his body writhing like a big, wounded fish, while we tried to stop the blood flow with paper towels. He was in the hospital for a long time after the incident, and I thought I'd never see him again.

During my last two years of high school, I strove to attain pyramidal A grades, though I proved to be a mediocre student. During senior year, I was preparing to apply to Princeton, fulfilling Granddad's expectations, but that never happened. I'd eventually go off to Rowanberry College, ostensibly to participate in its celebrated Environmental Studies Program (ESP), although I knew that I didn't really fully understand all the science, just its nomenclature; that I didn't have a scientific mind; that my limited academic skills were, if anything, literal; that I was most comfortable reaping something tangible from the TOO DIM MOTION ALL space of my books and pads of paper. A positive attitude about the future, an enthusiasm about what you're about and what you're about to do, is probably essential to success, or so we were told, and I'd experience impatience or plain lassitude coming down like the collapse of a plaster ceiling, and I felt crushed, overwhelmed by it all.

Like almost everyone else in TLC, I wrote, predictably, in a diary, or I tried to, but I gave it up, finding the habit of making notes to myself to be a waste of time and paper. I'd noticed how my handwriting, when looked at from an appropriate distance or with deliberately blurred vision, reduced (or was reduced) to a silent alliance, an abstraction of mute marks in space, so that the writing was just stuff, flux, comparable to the fabrics I'd watched through the window of the washing machine in the basement, drenched with the phosphorescence of obsolescence.

There were races along stone walls, running through woods, and a whole slew of little joys I experienced with my first steady and serious boyfriend, Charlie Hartwell, a good-natured, good-looking, slightly dyslexic boy, a jock with beautiful hands, with whom I spent many happy days, sleeping with him for the first time, sharing Cheerios from the same bowl on a camping trip to Mount Marcy, where we really got to know each other. Charlie loved being outdoors. He walked with a natural, almost animal grace, as if the landscape outside were his true muse, though he chose, much to my pleasure, to be with me, and I was pleased to be the girlfriend of the football and hockey star that he was. He was happiest when he'd put his whole heart into something physical and achieved a goal, like helping his uncle take down a dead tree or scoring a touchdown for the team, though he sometimes expressed contempt, or maybe it was just impatience, for school and the kinds of things we were expected to do there, sitting at desks, messing around with words and numbers. Charlie wore a bulky, black ski parka with green patches at the elbows, faded blue jeans, and work boots to school during the winter weather, looking like he was going to work at a construction site, which, in a way, he was, because everyone at school was busy constructing something, though Charlie didn't have to put any effort into his image. The first time he stayed over for dinner, Mom literally threw something together for the three of us, a frozen pizza, loaded with extra cheese and vegetables, which, when she pulled it out from the oven, fell to the floor in a splattering mess. She went at it with the green plastic spatula, cutting the pizza right there on the linoleum, throwing three sloppy pieces onto our plates. Charlie laughed. Desmond came in, barked, and started licking the floor where the pizza had been. We were all drinking white wine, which was unusual for me, drinking and getting tipsy around Mom. Charlie was encouraging and humoring her, free-associating with her about dogs and trees, topics he knew something about because his father bred Labradors as a hobby, and Charlie's uncle Sam ran a tree surgery business. Some man from the city noticed the Norwegian pine in front of our house, and he selected it to be "The World's Most Famous Christmas Tree," to be put on view in Rockefeller Center. He made Mom an offer she couldn't refuse. Part of Mom's logic for selling the tree was that it was getting too tall and had become a potential danger. What if it fell on the roof? A *New York Times* van and camera crew drove into our driveway one cold November morning, followed by Charlie and Sam in a truck. The snarling start of the chainsaw woke Mom, who drifted downstairs in her nightgown, opened the front door to the cold air, and shut the door as if we weren't there.

I lay flat on the floor with Mom's clipboard, and I could feel my heart beating on the fuzzy brown rug as I filled out the applications one warm Saturday morning in February, which soon became the early afternoon, and by the time I'd finished typing up my personal essay, it was late afternoon. During that last fall at New Canaan High, I'd forced myself to make a concerted effort, directing mental NRG into getting good grades and high test scores so that I might be assured of getting into Princeton. I remember studying, really studying for the upcoming Scholastic Aptitude Test. I had to compensate for my mediocre grades. I knew that my grades alone would not be good enough for Princeton, and I felt that even if Granddad pulled some strings, I would still have to get high test scores, at least where I could, in the verbal section, so I bought a spiral notebook and wrote on its cover "Vocabulary Laboratory," and I kept a list of new words in it, all of which I memorized. I got a high verbal SAT score, but my math score was low, and eventually I decided it would just be too much work to maintain the level of excellence required at Princeton, and anyway I didn't want to risk anyone's reputation, so I aimed my sights lower and applied to Rowanberry.

There was still some daylight left, enough to get on my bike and ride to Charlie's house and surprise him. One of my favorite ways to pass time and feel free was to hop on my bike and take off. I'd ride on roads I recognized from driving, years ago, with Dad, now on my bike, a gift from Aunt Pauline, with a steel frame and a small wicker basket attached at the back, right behind the seat, where she said I should always keep a hand pump and tools in case of a flat tire. Nobody wore helmets back then, and when I think of the way we— Marsha Brooks, Wendy Pembroke, and I—raced our bicycles up and down those roads, around the woods and pastures of New Canaan, out to the Pound Ridge Reservation, up to the Wilton Reservoir, and sometimes all the way down to Weed Beach in Darien, where groups of older, delinquent teenagers smoked marijuana, where we sat on the rocks and talked about boys, spinning our words like so many wheels, I am surprised nobody ever fell off a bike or collided with a car. No accidents, no unpleasant incidents, just a happy, free feeling, like swimming but on the road, with asphalt as my medium, and on that weirdly warm February afternoon, with just a little daylight left, I was on my own, riding solo, pleased with my speed as I flashed through the strangely snowless landscape.

Our last trip to The Ark occurred in the spring of my senior year, for a formal dinner for the immediate family, just Uncle Steve, Aunt Mary, and Ernie, their youngest who was still at home, and Mom, Tommy, and me. Gaga and Granddad were selling the apartment and moving into a kind of country club with medical facilities in a small town with the curious name of Onancock, somewhere in coastal Virginia, where some of their elderly friends were enjoying their waning years. They wanted to be both close to the ocean and closer to Baltimore, where Gaga still had family. It was the next-to-last time I saw her, her grey hair dyed an elegant bluish tinge, silver bracelets jangling, loudly out of sync with her shrunken, decrepit body. It was midspring, and I'd noticed bright tulips, red, yellow, and purple in new flowerbeds on Park Avenue. I was taking "General Semantics" that last term, an open-form, experimental English class that purported to teach us about literature, electronic media, and current events simultaneously, all in one place. Unlike almost all of my teachers, Dr. Hartkopft, who taught General Semantics, was interesting to be around and listen to because he'd traveled a lot, he listened to RPM, and he enjoyed painting pictures with words; it seemed to be his hobby. He'd suddenly wax eloquent, describing something for us, someplace he'd been, closing the textbook and going off on an extemporaneous tangent, deploying rich, descriptive language. He frequently used a slide projector to show us pictures of places he'd been. To make a point about life in medieval Europe, he once dressed up in a big brown bag, pretending that he was a monk. There was a portable stereo in the back of his classroom, and he'd sometimes play RPM to make a point, a statement. He once played The Beatles' "Back in the USSR" and said that they didn't sound convincingly sincere when they tried to imitate The Beach Boys, and then he quipped, in an aside to the boys in the classroom, that they didn't know how lucky they were to be in New Canaan. He talked about a "Consciousness Shift," a "Paradigm Shift"—those were the phrases he used—and he repeatedly cited a witty aphorism coined by a famous Canadian philosopher: "The medium is the massage"—not message but "massage"—and I still, to this day, repeat it to myself and try to "parse" its meaning. I guess we are moved or influenced by whatever medium we're in.

The air was incredibly fresh that evening, almost sweet, and when we arrived at The Ark, the usual elevator operator, the thin man in the red suit, who had given me orange lollipops, wasn't there, but there was someone new. Going up, Mom mentioned that Aunt Pauline had embarked on yet another crazy cause, fighting for elephants in central Africa, trying to save a dwindling population, exploited, being ruthlessly killed for their highly valued ivory, which struck me as ironic, insofar as Pauline played the piano, for I was beginning to see, thanks to General Semantics, how things that seemed unconnected were in fact deeply connected, such as pianos and elephants. Dennis, the butler, materialized; he happened to be right there at the door, holding an almost blind and invalid Crystal, who made a weak bark like a sneeze. "Come in, my friends. Come bid farewell," he said, in his deep, Teutonic intonation, with tainted resignation. There was a vase of huge white lilies on the table in the hallway. "Well, look who's here," Gaga said, as we entered the big room. "Look" had been a favorite verb. "Look at what you're doing" and "Look ahead" and "Look on the bright side of things" were favorite expressions of hers. Gaga rose from her chair by the fireplace and made a feeble expression of welcome, prompting Mom to go to the bar and pour herself a drink, and I worried about the drive back home, wondering whether I would have to drive us, illegally, because I didn't yet have my license, only a driver's permit. Tommy was distant during the visit, almost cold, as if he knew everything was falling apart, and he'd soon be moving down to Florida anyway, so he just went upstairs and disappeared into the room where Granddad kept a small television set. Dinner was a formal, subdued affair, with neither Pauline nor Dad there to brighten my experience of that dark apartment with its long hallways, old paintings, and rooms full of unused furniture. There was a chill, a hush.

The last time I saw Aunt Pauline, she had suffered what she referred to as "a sea change." It was just before I left for Rowanberry, and she had stopped in New York for the weekend, a brief visit, a stop en route to Paris from Mexico City, with a small entourage of bohemian friends. They'd encamped in a spacious suite at the Plaza Hotel. She invited me to come in for the day, a Saturday, for a late-afternoon cocktail party she was hosting, an informal fete—a "summer soiree," she said. I decided to keep Charlie out of it, so I took the train in alone, leaving Mom at home; she was already too soused to go. I was puzzled by her behavior. Walking to the station, I reflected on the wreck she'd managed to make of her life.

It felt strange, going into a large building alone on such a beautiful summer afternoon. The lobby was oddly quiet. I passed by the very large room where we'd once had afternoon tea, and it was empty. There wasn't much activity anywhere, but there was an aura of silent romance about the place, and I almost wondered whether that fact was or was not connected to the presence of Aunt Pauline and her entourage. I remember the elevator's purple carpet. There was a long hallway, and as I walked to the door at the end of it, I could hear waves of laughter and music grow louder. Since the door was unlocked, I just walked into a room filled with partying people. I remember feeling small, as though I were no one in that sea of faces. When I finally found Pauline, surrounded by friends in a corner, I understood in a flash why, maybe, Mom had decided to get smashed that morning. In any event, Pauline was in a wheelchair. Somewhere in Kenya, in her fight for animal rights, during an exploratory tour of wild habitat, she'd been charged by a stampeding elephant, and her spine had been seriously injured by the impact. Crippled by the powerful pachyderm, she operated the wheelchair with grace and moved around with startling ease, and her good spirits showed no limitation.

4

ROWANBERRY

ROWANBERRY COLLEGE WAS A GIANT STEP FOR ME, GOING UP ALONE on the train with my suitcases and expectations, and the thrill of my first day there was palpable, as I shared it with others, aware we were free to participate in a much more interesting world than the ones we were coming from. Nestled in the lowlands bordering Lake Champlain, the beauty of the campus was astounding. I'd seen the elegant, fanlike elm trees and brick buildings before, during a visit in late March, so I recognized the topography, but now the trees and surrounding mountains were deep green, signaling a fresh start with new parameters and rules. After swimming in an abandoned granite quarry, a remote pond at the end of a long, dusty road that warm, early September day with a group of fellow freshmen, part of an orientation routine, I felt free, as if I'd plunged upward into a deep, whirling pool of air.

Charlie visited during a color peak weekend in early October, arriving late on a Friday, driving his rusted green pickup truck. It was an unannounced visit, and I was hanging out with friends in the dining hall after dinner, when someone ran in and announced that there was a cute guy with a ponytail out there in a truck and that he was looking for Cindy Taine. I immediately thought, "Oh, Charlie." I walked outside, saw the truck, and continued walking toward it. There was Charlie's familiar silhouette, faintly illuminated by a cigarette's glow. I opened the door on the passenger's side and got an immediate whiff of weed, that aromatic, pungent smell I'd been glad to be away from. Charlie said, with a smile, "Surprise! Betcha didn't expect this." I hadn't expected it, of course, and I stood there facing the empty seat for an awkward moment, not knowing what to say. He'd left work early, driven for more than four hours, and here he was on a Friday evening at Rowanberry. I suppose he'd expected me to be happily surprised by his impromptu appearance, but it seemed rude and inconsiderate. It was an imposition to have to think, "Where is Charlie going to sleep tonight?" He couldn't stay in my dormitory room, so he slept on a sofa in the common room, after we'd walked around the campus, Charlie mostly talking about the future and how he'd begun to save money. He wanted to move out to Colorado, and he wanted me to come with him.

The next morning there was fog, almost opaque, that turned to a translucent mist that burned off by noon, revealing a perfect blue sky. We drove off together into the brilliant, flaring foliage after breakfast, where Charlie had exercised a voracious appetite, eating as though he hadn't eaten anything for days, putting a great stack of pancakes on his plate and smothering it with butter and syrup. I showed him the new gym and library building, and then we got into his truck. We'd planned to drive around, photograph foliage, and eventually go to Rutland to have lunch and see a movie starring Peter Sellers. Charlie said that his sister had said it was a movie he had to see.

Showing off his mastery of arboreal nomenclature, Charlie always knew what he was looking at, and I used to find his botanical knowledge fascinating, but by now I already knew what he knew about trees and their names, and all about the extraction of water and nutrients through the roots by capillary action, how the sap flows upward through the trunk, outward and forth through branches, into limbs and twigs, becoming green, leafy matter as the daylight hours grow longer, warmer, and stronger, photosynthesis peaking for a few summer weeks, and then how the chloroplasts fade as the temperature cools, and the shifts of autumn take over, in maples first, with red leaves falling over everything. There was a haunting, surreal, hallucinatory quality about the foliage. Charlie was intrigued by Carlos Castaneda's fantastic tales set in desert landscapes, featuring the Mexican shaman Don Juan, who, contacting chthonic powers, could transform himself, by a fiery NRG he harbored within, into an animal, an eagle, a raven, a fox, crossing boundaries, performing supernatural feats that defied physical law. Charlie had been introduced to Carlos Castaneda by his older sister, Carol, who went to Alfred College in upstate New York. "Alfred" had always seemed like a strange name for a school; it made me think of Alfred Hitchcock's *Psycho*, with the Bates Motel, the notorious shower curtain scene, the knife and the screaming, the car being pulled out of the swamp by a strained chain. Charlie prattled on about the astonishing, hidden powers of plants, postulating a realm of vegetal intelligence, the sentient souls dwelling inside of plants, bushes, and all kinds of trees, immaterial, slumbering spirits that still surround us today. We just had to tap into them.

Parting that summer, we'd agreed to let our relationship simmer, since I was starting something new, and we'd be so far away from each other. Charlie was working in the tree surgery business, so he spent a lot of time in physically dangerous situations, and he connected, I think, my being-at-Rowanberry with his sister's being-at-Alfred, a place that he had called, early in our relationship, an "ivory tower" where "dickheads on auto-stroke believe everything they read and write." I was then in the ESP (the Environmental Studies Program), taking an introductory course in zoology and finding it fun to be able to identify living creatures and learn about their behavior in the wild. The professor had published a book of photographs he'd taken at night in the forest with remote cameras positioned along a section of the Appalachian Trail: images of skunks, possums, foxes, and feral cats as they foraged for prey. Fieldwork for class involved several day hikes in local ecosystems, and we'd already done one up in the mountains, so I knew a bit about birds and other animals, such as the chattering red squirrels, and I was able to point out a red-tailed hawk to Charlie, who seemed to resent the fact that I knew and could explain the difference between a "hawk" and a "falcon." I was happy using new words for birds, but Charlie was on a mission, it seemed, to bring me back to New Canaan and eventually take me to Colorado with him. He became belligerent, and I didn't want to ride in his truck anymore. We were driving down Route 7 toward Rutland when he went berserk about my supposedly being condescending, making him feel uncomfortable the night before. "Here come the histrionics," I thought. He began to rant against "Deskism," arguing that the illusory forces of two-dimensional space, the flatland of reading and writing, had ruined my appreciation of nature's spontaneous happening. Charlie, if only by name alone, sometimes reminded me of "Charlie the Tuna," a fish out of water, the cartoon character in TV ads for canned tuna, who wore a beret, smoked a cigarette in a long holder, a token of the beatnik type, who wore hip glasses and struck a pose, standing on the tail of his body, but he always failed to attract the object of his efforts, the StarKist Tuna Company, whose disapproving voice boomed down from above, "Sorry, Charlie, StarKist wants tuna that tastes good, not tuna with good taste," a slogan that stayed with me, syntax suiting fancy. Charlie was good, as though he had a bit of immortality inside of him, and I cherished his physicality, his love for outdoor work, his kinetic knowledge of whatever he was working with. We'd go off on hikes in the woods around the Wilton Reservoir, and he'd look for trees to climb. He would throw down his jacket and climb up the trunk of a tall tree, like a cat or wolverine. He was compassionate about having a good time despite what he felt were the bad times we were living through. In his bedroom at home he had a poster of a photograph of an atomic bomb exploding. "All of the earth seems cloaked in a great cloud of blackness when I look into this," he said once, and I remember it because it was such a memorable thing for someone to say, both beautiful and horrible at once, but that day in the truck we had a bad fight, a real shouting match, which ended with my saying, "Sorry, Charlie, it's over."

Freed from Charlie's claims on my attention, I focused on what was going on, right there in front of me, at Rowanberry. I was participating in a new world, pursuing happiness and finding it in the constant train of structured days, my busy schedule of classes, athletics, meals, and social events. I became immediately friendly with my roommate, Patsy Fleming, a compact, pretty Irish gal from Boston—"Boss Town," she called it—a fine-haired brunette with laughing eyes, gay and sparkling like a Fra Angelico angel's. Getting to know her, I had the sensation of being with someone who never wasted time. Patsy was skilled at getting what she wanted, and she worked to get excellent grades. She was a superb student, fastidious about details, punctual about due dates, fanatical about the presentation of her academic work, and she spoke and wrote with a candor for content I hope someday to attain. She partied with an enthusiasm that I gradually became accustomed to, especially after that first spring semester, when I decided to drop out of the ESP. Patsy had graduated from a prestigious preparatory school, so she had a sophisticated air, an aura about her, as if she'd already been to college, and her actions showed an attitude that was more than a little bit proud. Even outside of the classroom, far from formality, even at dances and parties, she was distinctively accurate in her diction and use of speech, always at work on technique. She was into gymnastics, and I can still see her on the parallel bars she set up in our room, able to do exercises and read at the same time! Like all the smart students, Patsy was there for the ESP especially, and she mesmerized me with her ability to balance and manage the coursework, all the science and math that I found so difficult, with gymnastics and a busy social life. She had an older boyfriend at Dartmouth, thirty minutes down the interstate highway, and she seemed to have absorbed, by osmosis, a measure of his confidence and maturity. She radiated the ability to succeed. Rowanberry had gone coed only a few years before I attended, so the ratio of women to men was disproportionate, maybe six to one, and Patsy, with her nimble body's curvaceous athletic proportions, her optimistic smile, her infectious enthusiasm, her perfectly extroverted, convex face, a mirror in which men could read the future, played on the desires of many, I imagine, though she was always faithful to Duane, her Dartmouth boyfriend. After dinner, in our room during study hour, having made a tacit vow of silence, I could feel the vibrations produced by our separate realities, neither good nor bad in themselves, our attentions trained on reading assignments, printed matter keeping us busy, using up brains and eyeballs. Patsy, I think, had a more robust conception of the workings of the world than I, a vantage point from which she perceived the connectedness of things, people, cities, countries, and continents. She actually completed the ESP, fulfilling her initial intention while maintaining a busy social life, eventually doing important work on water treatment in El Salvador, of all places, where she settled, having married a colleague in the university there.

Everyone aspired to attain success, and some of us thought that we knew what it was, but Patsy seemed to already know, for herself, the essence of success, and her presence unspools through the play of my presentation, for she was an active participant, an agency of sorts, in the structure of my consciousness. The word "thinking" can be used to describe a kind of speaking in the head, a talking for a purpose, right? I'd read Sigmund Freud for a psychology class, and I'd decided that my superego, mediating the world, my id, and me, produced a constant flow of encouragement, pep talk, saying things such as "You can do it, Cindy. Stick with it, Cindy. Don't quit." "You can do anything you put your mind to," Granddad used to say, almost violently, as if it were moral law, and I'd try to follow through, but I just wasn't interested in being a scientist anymore. Whatever it was that the ESP required, some daring found within, the discipline needed to get something difficult done, certain kids just accumulated more of it or were born with it to begin with, like Patsy, but other kids, like me, who were not really academically inclined or motivated, were successful in other ways, in our gregarious, affable, and inconsequential ability to blend with the scene and go with the flow, a kind of charm I attribute to Dad—at least that's how it felt inside. I was blond, a blue-eyed girl, and pretty, so I automatically experienced my easy measure of popularity, and my real successes were spontaneous interactions with people, having fun, sometimes too much, so I had to force myself and use my superego to get any work done.

Although I'd been attracted to Rowanberry initially for the ESP, I discovered, while taking the biology and chemistry prerequisites during my second term, that an enviable career in something scientific was simply beyond me. The chemistry prerequisite involved a lot of math that I struggled with. Biology, with all its nomenclature, was tedious business, and the idea of finishing college to fulfill Granddad's expectations seemed more and more absurd. It had lost its grip on my imagination. It was easier to sit in the library on a snowy afternoon and become lost in a kind of reading that had less and less, almost nothing, to do with reality. I remember, my first winter there, breezing through one long novel in a mere two days, and I can still savor the gist of its opening paragraph, where the narrator remembers being taken into a jungle to discover ice, so I decided to ditch the ESP and switch to English Literature, so much easier and so much more fun! Science was hard work, and I just didn't feel like it. After dinner, in darkness, or in the peachy glow of a perishing sun, I'd walk on the pathway to the library to read where it was quiet. I took a course in nineteenth-century American literature that spring, discovering a whole universe of pleasant, diversionary reading that didn't tax my mental engine but let it spin, so that, as the snow thawed, as the solar force waxed and the streambeds filled with rushing water, I sat in a comfortable chair at the big window in the library, waiting for the warmer weather when the buds would pop open, when dogwoods and cherry trees blossomed with soft explosions, and I could sit in a portable chair outside and read, breathing in a veritable perfume factory. I'd refused to be dominated by my grandfather's plan. I would focus on what I was able to do with less effort, although it did take time: reading, scribbling in margins, giving voice and definition to inchoate thoughts, writing occasional essays on my electric typewriter, which I was finally learning to use. Happily for me, research papers were rarely required in literature courses; all you had to really do, aside from impromptu, handwritten paragraphs based on questions posed on the board, was read the assigned books and show up for class to discuss them. Our discussions often became lively debates, animated by an earnest theatricality, as if the whole class were leading itself along for some secret observer, some phantom agent's entertainment, so I just glided by.

I returned to New Canaan that fateful first summer home from college, having no alternative. The reality of Crozier Place was shocking, and I dealt with it by ignoring Mom and her drinking, now chronic; she'd stopped working at the real estate office, and she'd entered a phase of hedonistic nihilism. Tommy had moved to Florida, so she was able to do exactly what she wanted; there was no one to monitor her. I wanted to avoid any needless histrionics, so I spent a lot of time with my friends, out at the country club, down at the beach in Darien. Wendy Pembroke and I took a long trip by car to Cape Cod and Martha's Vineyard, where I worked briefly as a waitress. It was the summer of seemingly endless partying and fun, and when I returned home one sultry afternoon, late in August, to collect my things and pack for school, I was shocked to find Mom lying on the sofa downstairs, seminaked, in the arms of Mr. Van Warner, a wealthy widower and notorious womanizer. There was music on the stereo, Johnny Cash singing something about walking a line; I remember that distinctly because it seemed so out of place. Dreamy smiles played on their faces, and they were both smoking cigarettes. "Couple of kooks," I thought to myself. A half-full bottle of Jack Daniels dominated the cocktail table, and there were many smaller green bottles, all bearing the label of the expensive beer Mr. Van Warner's company imported from Germany, scattered around the room. They were inebriated and indifferent to my presence. I returned to Rowanberry, happy to leave home, rejuvenated, glad to be back, with my own room on the ground floor of the new dormitory, where I felt a small mirror inside of me fill, later that semester, one soundless, dull day in November, deeply aware of Mom.

There was an incredible snowfall one morning my second winter there, the day of my first trip to Jay Peak, and with silent anticipation I looked out into it, speculating on the day ahead. Karl was a year ahead of me. He was tall, dark, and athletic. The night before, not just because I happened to be there, returning books, ahead of him in line at the library, he asked me, out of the blue, out of nowhere, to go skiing with him. I'd seen him in places, and I guess he'd seen me in places too, so I said, "Sure. Where? When?" I remember responding with just those three words. "Jay Peak, tomorrow," he said. I went back into my room to gaze at my brand-new skis. I was all wound up, already making up memories. I'd learned some basic skiing skills, sidestepping up and snowplowing down a slope behind the dormitory, and I was determined to become a better skier. I wanted to ski like I could swim, in a rush of fluidity, fastened by flashy, sophisticated bindings to my red and white, sparkling-new fiberglass skis, a Christmas gift from Dad, who had now regained contact with us, sending presents to his kids. I wore a silvery, light-reflecting, goose-down-filled parka, which, although puffy, fit me perfectly; it made me feel like an expert when the sun was out and the snow was soft, and skiing turned into a water sport, wet and warm and white, which frequently happens late in the season.

Karl drove an old Volvo station wagon that seemed too long, like an antiquated school bus, its chassis creaking when he took it around turns too quickly. The drive to Jay Peak was harrowing; our equipment and skis, thrown into the back, rattled and shook as we careened around ascending turns. "Who is this madman at the wheel of this car?" I thought at first, but I eventually became accustomed to the way Karl drove, partly because of the way he talked about the process. Driving somewhere in the mountains, he'd sense my fear and say, "I know this road like the back of my hand. I can read it like a book." We parked in the already-crowded lot and stopped at the base lodge for a breakfast of scrambled eggs, and then we bought tickets, and I rode on a chairlift for the first time in my life, surveying the icy, hallucinatory beauty of the pine trees below, caked and glistening with freshly fallen snow. From the top of Jay Peak, as I looked out into the panorama, everything seemed suspended, a freshly painted mural of forests and faraway, snowy hills. Out on the slopes Karl exhibited his ability. He was a bit of a show-off, so he was always way out in front of me and had to wait at the bottom of the trail for me, but he was a patient instructor that first day, teaching me how to "wedel" and "schuss," and soon I could keep up with him. Next year he'd find a new arena for action, discovering cross-country skiing and vowing he'd never wait in line for another mechanical lift up a mountain again.

The club out on Route 7, the Chopping Block, was an old barn converted into a dance space with bar and grill, a hot spot, a student hangout, a place to party, and after I met Karl, I began to spend more time there. It was an amazing space, dominated by the huge, mirrored sphere with thousands of facets, all the same size, spinning over the center of the dance floor, shooting sequins of light out everywhere, and we danced to it, keeping up with the sound and the swirl. During the week, the music was recorded, lots of disco, but on Saturday nights, local acts, live bands of long-haired guys wearing flannel shirts and cowboy boots, played loud, raucous RPM, and we danced about to it, thrashing around like fish. I am not sure what self-consciousness is, but I'd have mature moments when I was there, but most of the time I wasn't there, looking over a small city of colorful bottles behind the bar, catching myself in the mirror at the Chopping Block, thinking, "I am filming this. I am watching ourselves as we truly behave," feeling both impersonal and remote, strangely in control. The lively material behind me surged and then went on without me, as though I had been stopped for a precious moment, a spot of suspended time. Finished with my scrutiny, I returned to my place and moved about on the crowded floor with everyone else, on a beach where it never ends, and I raised my voice to compete with the waves of music.

We drove down in the Volvo that spring to Karl's hometown in western Massachusetts, near Pittsfield, in the Berkshires, where I'd never been before. His parents were there, of course, and I can't remember anything about them, except that his father, a prosperous lawyer, wore a loud, plaid sports jacket, and he smoked little Brazilian cigars. The house, once the old manse of an extensive working farm, was a colossal white, three-floor colonial with several brick chimneys and many many-paned glass windows framed by dark green shutters. There were dormers on the top floor and a front portico with columns. I looked at it, and I first thought of Washington's Mount Vernon estate, and then I thought of the Tracy house in New Canaan. The yard was a beautifully modulated hill of recently cut grass, set off from the long driveway by a long, winding wall of expertly fitted stone, a veritable work of art. Out in back, there was a flagstone terrace, and it was intoxicating, getting up from our chairs, after meeting Karl's parents, sipping chilled white wine, and walking back into the orchard of fruit trees blossoming behind the terrace, pink against a powder-blue sky. There was a huge hedge of lilac, its arms of fluttering, green leaves waving, bearing purple flowers, attracting yellow bees.

Karl frequently referred to the planet as an "ark," and I thought this was a marvelous coincidence. Animals work, and they move to stay alive, especially the top carnivores in almost any ecosystem. Bears pause at streams. Fish swim after whatever in water. Bees fly from flower to flower and return to the hive to then move some more, doing the information-laden "waggle dance," prompting other bees into cooperation: do the distance, find the flower, gather pollen at its source, and return to serve the life of the hive. Birds move in accordance with environmental inputs, such as sunlight, starlight, insect populations, and temperature. The autonomous movements of living organisms became Karl's topic of general research and expertise. He spent long days at work in the fields and meadows, poring over flowers, studying insect behavior, entranced by traces of self-generated movement, the miracle of action, which, he argued, was the essence of work, for any species, and which necessarily implied an intentional mental state. He was preparing, he said, to write a paper on the intentional life of the common bumblebee, something he'd read about in one of the more speculative journals of entomology. Anyway, Karl began to carve out a region of theoretical concern, a research niche for himself, but he didn't stay with it, for he couldn't stay seated for very long. Like a repetition of Charlie, he sometimes mocked my bookishness; as I was smitten by the written, he was always going off somewhere, preferring territory to cartography. "The sedentary life is a sin against the Ecological Spirit!" he'd declare. He said he didn't want to have a career in an essentially bureaucratic culture founded on a vast, reflexive "paper mirror," the existence of the written word, and just like Charlie, he began ranting on about "Deskism," bringing up that word again, arguing that writing should be understood as a relatively recent technology, comparable to telephones, elevators, TVs, and washing machines, coincident and coextensive with the building of cities, the demise of ecosystems, and the general mismanagement of time. He'd harp on the etymology of the word "democracy," and he saw the power of people as a positive force that could change political institutions and establish a free, nonrepressive, nonhierarchical society, founded on direct democracy, pure hospitality, and easy exchange, all following the collapse of Capitalism, which was imminent. There was something fishy about Karl's argument, some logical loophole or contradiction, but I could never wrap my mind around it, and once, late one night at the Chopping Block, after a few too many beers with him, his talking away like that, his going on about walking through swamps and how his best ideas occurred to him while he was working his way through a dark, dismal swamp, I decided he was almost a complete idiot, and I didn't waste any more time with him.

Although I maintained my academic standing, getting good grades and all that, playing the part of literary critter, clawing my way through books, leaving tracks and traces, dragging the weight of my own interruptions and interpretations, I'd sometimes step into the recreation room to watch television, catch an episode of something funny, a situation comedy with interesting parts and plot twists, such as *My Favorite Martian*, or *Mary Hartman, Mary Hartman*, or a rerun of *The Mod Squad*, scripts with characters who just "feel real," and I'd be reeled in by the dialogue and action, pulled into some story unfolding. When I moved off campus, I bought a small color TV set, for my room alone, and I felt the power of the spectacle on its screen, as it operated on me, and I on it, begetting our symbiosis. Ostensibly studying LITTER A CHAIR, I soon discovered I was really more interested in a career in television, in mass media entertainment, where the electrons really go to work, unfolding between brain and screen, and the needle of my inner compass shifted profoundly.

Meanwhile, Mom found the courage and lucidity to telephone me a few times, and I endured her meandering monologues, her complaining about living in the house alone, the monotony of New Canaan, Desmond's declining health, boredom at work, the sometimes miserable weather, and how I had to "realize my potential," now a favorite phrase of hers, because she had fallen so short of realizing her own. She was beginning to exhibit sure signs of dementia. There were strange lacunae in her speech. Toward the end of that spring, she wrote me a long letter about Desmond "talking" to her, developing the idea she and the dog had developed some kind of telepathic bond. When I arrived home for my last summer there, her car was in the driveway. Desmond was sleeping on the back door mat. He woke, but he didn't seem able to see me, his eyes filled with a milky opaque liquid. I walked through the back door and yelled into the living room, "Mom, I'm home," but there was no response. I went into the living room and put on some music. I assumed she was somewhere nearby, maybe out in the backyard gardening, crouched over a flower, pruning a bush. I was elated, really, because it was the beginning of another summer vacation. I felt free. Many of my friends would be around. There'd be parties and dancing and day trips to beaches. I hadn't made any decision, really, about getting a summer job, and I wasn't tied down to any particular, steady boyfriend, so I said, aloud to myself, "I'm glad I'm glad I'm glad," repeating myself, speeding the words up until they made no sense. Then the phone rang. It was Uncle Steve, and he was wondering where Mom was. He didn't seem very interested in the fact that I'd just answered the phone, that I was home from college, and that, as her car was there, parked in the driveway, I was also wondering where she was. He told me to turn down the background music. A shift in the tone of Uncle Steve's voice suggested sorrow and exasperation. He told me that Mom had been shamelessly conducting a sloppy affair with Mr. Van Warner, something all the neighbors knew about, and that he was calling to check up on her, hoping to find her at home.

I was out of the house most of the time, with people to see and places to go to, but there was that television set down in the basement where I'd sometimes watch morning shows. Mom was seldom at home, and she'd take Desmond with her to Mr. Van Warner's house, so I had the place to myself. When I watched TV in the morning in the empty house, it was as if I were returning to an ANT CHANT scene of instruction, rekindling a forgotten relationship, being schooled by the spin of the "boob tube" again. I remembered faking being sick, artificially raising my temperature by holding the thermometer over a flame on the stove in Riverside, and I'd stay home from school, sink into the sofa to watch my favorite weekday morning shows, situation comedies, and daydreamed of someday working behind the scenes, helping make the dramatic magic happen, concocting playful narratives set with whimsical premises and plausible "denouements," providing a good model, I think, for anybody's story.

Uncle Steve arrived at the house one morning that summer and said to me, "I'm taking care of this." Mom had been out late, drinking with Mr. Van Warner. I heard her open the door downstairs in the very early morning. I'd come home and assumed she was out, but I was too tired, sunburned, and happy to worry much about her, so I'd fallen asleep immediately. I heard her open the door, climb up the stairs, and go into the bathroom, followed by the sound of rushing water. I came out into the hallway. She had a silly smile on her face, and her eyelids looked dopey, like welts dripping with water. "Mom, what's going on?" Her response was a dismissive laugh, and then she said, "What a drag it is, getting old! Don't ever get old, Cindy." "Where have you been?" I asked. She just waved me away with her hand, and I went back to sleep. At some point that night, she came into my room and asked, sobbing, if she could lie down between the sheets with me. "Don't you think there's a place for me between the sheets?" she asked. I yelled at her. She went out of the room, and I went back to sleep. When I finally woke and went downstairs, Uncle Steve was in the kitchen making coffee and talking on the phone about some incident at the country club involving shouting adults and a fistfight between men in the bar. Mom had played a causal role. She had really "blown it this time," Uncle Steve repeatedly remarked, and I thought that that was an odd expression for him to use. The smell of freshly made coffee lured Mom downstairs. Uncle Steve was determined to get her into some kind of rehabilitation program, but she didn't have the right kind of insurance, so he made arrangements that required, for some reason, that she be driven to a clinic in New Jersey. It was all his idea. "I'm not going," she said. I always maintained that Mom with her stubborn tenacity would never stop drinking unless she wanted to, for all true daring comes from within, and she didn't want to quit, she didn't dare; she didn't have the requisite courage and curiosity. Uncle Steve was really angry, and he yanked Mom by the wrist and took her into the dining room, and they sat down at the table, where he lectured her, overcoming her resistance, until he somehow convinced her, momentarily at least, that the change of scene would do her good, that she could make a new start. Suddenly, Uncle Steve, having won her agreement, didn't want to be around us anymore, so he left, and I was now the one who had to drive her to the rehabilitation facility in New Jersey. There she was, looking bad in the passenger seat, frowning at the sky. "It will be good for you. You'll be a new you," I suggested cheerfully. "Look, you'll go through detox safely there. You have to go through withdrawal safely first, and then it's just smooth sailing, a downhill glide," I offered hopefully, but she turned the radio on, losing herself in its unanticipated massage. It was that dopey Paul McCartney song about silly love songs, the kind of thing that made Mom cry, especially when her defenses were down. We stopped for more coffee. Mom looked into the distance, casting her eyes far away. She just sat there, stubborn, sullen, staring into the parking lot. We split a greasy grilled-cheese sandwich. I hadn't had enough sleep, and it was impossible to initiate and continue a conversation. I was filled with stifled rage at Uncle Steve. Back in the car again, succumbing to my disappointment at having to spend the day the way I was, I found myself suddenly lecturing her about all the problems her behavior was causing, how it was constricting me. Ashamed, shrugging a little, making sighs and miniscule, conciliatory motions with her fingers, tapping the upholstery, she reacted defensively, and I felt relieved when, over-coming her returned refusal to comply with the plan, I persuaded her to sign herself into the clinic, and I left her there, in the lap of professional care.

Soft fists of sunlight were hitting the beach where I was enjoy-ing spring break with Bob, my new boyfriend. Mom had been back home since Christmas, doing much better, staying sober, working again. Just before leaving for Daytona, however, I had phoned home to find her drunk, incapable of coherent speech, so I just tried to forget about her on the flight down. Bob spent the first day at the hotel by the pool, in an oblong, aluminum-foil-lined cardboard box, working on his tan, exhibiting an aspect of his personality I hadn't noticed before. He did a lot of surfing, taking on the big waves that sometimes turned up. I'd watch him from the shore, the beach, where bodysurfing was sufficient excitement for me, where salty water would get trapped in my ears, and I'd have to shake it out. I was drying my hair with a towel when Bob caught a wave, and there he was, gesturing at me with male bravado before he lost his bal-ance and fell into the turbulence. Later that day, swimming in the ocean, I tested and strained my endurance, and I stretched myself out on a line, going beyond the cresting waves to where the ocean water was level, taking my time doing a long, steady distance, paral-lel to the shore.

Suddenly, way out there, for some reason I remembered an es-say I'd written on Thomas Hardy's *Jude the Obscure* for a class that winter, somehow connecting the fictional, self-sacrificing hero of the novelist's picturesque imagination with The Beatles' injunction to take sad songs and make them better, all through the prism of a chapter starting with a paragraph beginning with a sentence containing the word "altruistic," which I didn't know at the time and had to look up. Toward the end of the essay, I'd said something about Hardy's use of snow as a symbol for death, and my professor was sympathetic to the notion that eraser fluid, "Wite-Out," could serve as a trope for the aim of all life, the inanimate state.

I realized how far out at sea I was, and I had to work hard, swimming against the current, to return to the shore. Reaching our place on the beach, I saw Bob was lying there, asleep on his back, face under a towel, with the inert surfboard at his side glittering in the sunlight like a huge, painted fish.

At some point past the equinox, when day and night attain a point of balance for a single instant and then fall out of it, I was finishing my senior thesis, "On the Place of Water in Wordsworth," taking my time with its composition, enjoying a newfound freedom and lassitude, watching TV, playing tennis, swimming in the indoor pool, having the time of my life, my senior spring, with lots of parties and celebrations, when on a Sunday evening the communal phone rang in the hallway, and somebody yelled in the direction of my room, "Cindy, it's for you!" I was living off campus, in a big, old house, a kind of commune-mansion, so people were always using the telephone. It was cool for early May, and I'd been on a day trip to Burlington, where Bob and I had hiked along the lake, stopping at Ben & Jerry's for some excellent ice cream. I think we had dinner at the Chopping Block. Anyway, it was well after dinnertime, and I was playing cards with some of my friends. We were fascinated with poker, and we'd play for small stakes. I think I once won twenty-two dollars. "Cindy, telephone!" someone yelled. I had just been dealt a hand with three aces, and I instantly knew it was bad news about Mom. It was a bolt of intuition. I put down my cards and said, "Wait." Then I got up to use the phone, and when I returned, the game had gone on without me.

I took the night train down from Burlington, and Uncle Steve met me the next morning at the station in Darien. He was right on time, sitting in his silver Mercedes-Benz, staring straight ahead. I opened the door and got in, and we drove to the hospital. A sad, icy silence reigned. I was trapped inside the signal he sent out, his wavelength squelching all speech. The familiar streets and houses seemed dull and predictable, and the space in the car was confining and uncomfortable, shrinking. I looked out and blinked, caught like a cat. Something about our mutual presence seemed only to perpetuate the silence. Finally, placing his right hand on the steering wheel, artfully guiding the car into the parking lot, he turned to me and said, "I guess you can't stop people from doing what they really want to do." Mom's last splurge had been very deliberate, apparently involving pills. "There were three empty vodka bottles. There were three empty bottles that once contained vodka on the table," he said.

Uncle Steve actually took my hand for a few seconds as we walked from the car through the bright sunlight to the hospital, a colossus of glass and brick. I was totally exhausted from a sleepless train ride down but also impressed by the lovely weather. It seemed like a beautiful day to die, and I think I detected a calm, accepting smile, just for a moment, from Uncle Steve, a sign that he, too, was too aware of natural beauty to ever be truly unhappy, which was probably just my own emotion projected onto him. We entered the building and walked down a long corridor. All was white, quiet, and clean, like a hospital, and when we reached the door and knocked, a nurse appeared to say, "It's too late."

Going through Mom's house that afternoon was like a peculiarly well-lit sequence in a horror movie: Everything was lurid, the colors too vivid to bear, with my lack of sleep, my frazzled nerves. The sun was out, and everything in the light of its presence glowed with eerie non-reality. Desmond was sleeping on the porch, oblivious to us, possibly expecting Mom to come home and feed him.

The grass had just been cut. Some squirrels ran along the fence out back, chattering like excited birds. The forsythia was in bloom, and the pink dogwood stood in full flower. Not much had changed, but then we stepped inside. A strange odor permeated the place, the pungent, sweet, synthetic strain of Pine-Sol cleanser. I walked upstairs. In my absence my room had become, in effect, a tomb, a depository for paperback and hardcover books, fiction and nonfiction, all of Mom's books arranged by the colors on their covers and spines. They were piled into three towers of predominantly red, yellow, and blue books, the primary colors serving as an organizing principle, orange being grouped with red, white with yellow, black and green with blue. Mom had always been an avid but never very comprehensive reader, though she aspired to be one, so maybe it all made some sort of sense. But it also seemed extravagant and mad, so I closed the door and sought sanctuary in the basement room, where the TV had been, our first and only color TV, which sat on the floor on four squat legs, encased in faux-wood paneling. It wasn't there, and I wondered what she'd done with it. The whole space seemed to have been recently cleaned. The blue shag rug had been rolled up, and the exposed white tiles, once scuffed with traces of black rubber, were clean, gleaming in the light coming in through the basement windows. It was as if everything had been prepared for someone's inspection, so I changed my mind and went back upstairs to Mom's room. There was no trace of sloppiness, no dirty glasses, no ashtrays. The bed was made, and the carpet had just been cleaned, its pattern present in a way I'd never seen. I opened a closet door and saw folded shirts carefully stacked on shelves. There were coats, shoes, and sweaters stored in ziplock plastic bags. "A place for each thing, and each thing in its place," she used to say. Uncle Steve had been checking up on something in the garage, and when I heard him feeding Desmond in the kitchen, I went back downstairs, through the living room, where the carpet and draperies were bright and spotless, emitting a sweet, artificial scent, suggesting that they'd been recently cleaned, where the furniture was arranged in an arc around the fireplace, as if waiting for someone to appear and speak. Walking into the kitchen, I felt my second shock. There were the bottles Uncle Steve had mentioned, three brown paper bags standing upright on the table, each one housing an empty vodka bottle. Uncle Steve was at the sink, washing Desmond's bowl, and without turning around, without looking at me, he said, "Take a look at Eudora's legacy, will you."

The funeral, several days later, was bleak and brief, though it was a chance to see relatives whom I hadn't seen in a long while; Uncle Edmund was there, as was Aunt Pauline, as were all of my cousins, but Tommy wasn't there, nor was Dad. What had I expected? The ceremony, held in the chapel of the church in Darien, seemed rushed through, as though nobody really wanted to be there. Mom hadn't been to church much recently. She had pursued and hastened her end with atheistic fury and determination, and she'd done virtually nothing to prepare for her death, so her brother took responsibility, dealing with the details, putting the service together, notifying family, pulling Mom's few friends together for a first and last time. Weak rays of daylight streamed through stained glass. Arrangements of white flowers, poised in gleaming porcelain vases, posed for the purposes of our collected grief. My grandparents, now attended by a pretty, young full-time caretaker, had flown up, by helicopter, from Onancock, and they were both visibly very, very old, full of forgetfulness and understandably uncommunicative, though Gaga, always the churchgoer, sang the opening hymn with a mournful expressiveness I found amazing for such an old woman, her silvery, blue hair thinned to a few final wisps. After some beautiful instrumental organ music that probably lasted too long, the eulogy seemed utterly unrelated to anything about anyone I'd known. What had I expected? Church is a place with an agenda; nevertheless, my indifference surprised me, because it bore no relation to anything I'd known before.

No stranger to train stations, I waited for nearly two hours for the train, because Uncle Steve had had business about Mom's will and financial affairs to attend to, and there was really only one convenient time to drop me off, so I found myself there, down at the station, early in the morning, after spending four consecutive nights at Uncle Steve's house, enduring the monotony of the dinner table, the polite, predictable conversation punctuated at points by Aunt Mary's inappropriate laughter. I remember her proposing a toast to Mom's memory, which really irked Uncle Steve. Two of their boys were there, Andy and Ernie, home for the funeral, and we went bowling one afternoon, just to get away from morose adults and entertain ourselves. While waiting for the train, I read from a book by Lawrence Durrell, thinking about my future, thinking about the Mediterranean topography Mom had encouraged me to think about as she read to me in my childhood about Greece and Rome, and the force of her diction, manipulating language, which she once had used so well and with such class, worked its way through me, playing around with the verbs and their tenses. Down at the station, thinking of Duracell batteries, I put my book aside and stood up in anticipation of more mundane topography ahead: New Haven, Hartford, Springfield, White River Junction. What could I make of it? It was raining heavily outside, so I couldn't go for a walk. Applying lipstick in the ladies' room mirror, I remembered Mom's enthusiasm for the alphabet song she'd sing to Tommy and me, concluding with, "Now I know my ABCs, tell me what you think of me," and I thought of bees seized by flowers. It was a wild, wet, and windy day, and I knew that the air was all that anyone knows, while Desmond, now in the care of Uncle Steve, possibly sniffed the air on the back terrace, thinking he might have a chance to do some actual duck hunting soon. The train arrived, and I hopped aboard, a rabbit in spirit, making partial adjustments for a change, settling into the headrest, and on the long ride back I slept.

With Mom's passing, soon to be followed by Granddad's, then Gaga's, then Aunt Pauline's several years later, it registered somewhere that I, too, would somehow eventually die and satisfy the built-in obsolescence that seems to be our only sure trait, something to refer me to the fact that I, too, was a self-scanning, epiphenomenal blip, my perceptions based in a conglomerate of living, organic material, seething with microscopic activity, a transient, arbitrary window of experience passing through, as though down a dark ladder into unmarked terrain. Just after Mom's funeral, Granddad bought me a bright cerulean blue Saab. It was a total surprise, and he had arranged to have it delivered right to the house in Rowanberry. There was a note on the dashboard that said something about an early graduation present and his deep, deep sorrow, but I was happy to have my own car, and I spent several happy days just driving around. I was driving it through Hartford, returning north after spending a weekend with my friend Allison Tyranny, who was at Yale, where she was already in graduate school, studying theater, when the tedium of the drive was interrupted, and my visual field presented, off to my left, a perfect dome of metal painted blue, a skin of pulverized cobalt atop an old brick building close to the highway, its curvature the shape of an onion, of seemingly celestial origin, with golden stars painted in its skin, topped with a gilded weathervane. As I passed, I thought, "How exemplary!" It was such a beautiful thing, at once surface and symbol, something to admire intensely, this architectural work, maybe a decorative flourish, some builder's whim, dating from the mid-1800s, before Mark Twain lived here and called Hartford "chief of the beautiful towns," before the town became a city and remained in fact for several years "the Wealthiest City in the United States," before it became "the Insurance Capital of the World." The dome on the building was close to the highway, as if it could be seen properly only by people in cars. What was the significance of the onion-shaped dome, and why did its presence inspire my inquiry? I thought of our actual stars, heavenly influences controlling destinies, particular densities, my own in a wave containing many others, other posts of consciousness, DENSE CITIES. I was wondering about causality when I was faced with the possibility of finding myself in an accident, caught in a contest for space, life interrupted, so I paid attention to what I was doing, driving, because if you don't pay attention, then it won't work for you, and, as I crossed the Connecticut River that sunny Sunday afternoon in early June, thinking ahead to the hours I still had to go on the road, the drive became tedious again.

NEW YORK CITY

JACK FLANAGAN, WHEN WE FIRST MET, WAS DOING PRODUCTION work at NBC, but that was after graduation, after I'd made my move, my secret return to New York City in early July, just after the Fourth, which, as I sit here and think of it now, I'd celebrated at a posh party on Long Island's North Shore, the old Gold Coast, GREAT GAS BUY territory. Something was emerging out of all that fiction I'd read in college, something more urgent, but before I moved in with Jack, I lived for three years in a cramped Upper East Side studio apartment, across from a busy post office that served as an early morning alarm clock with its fleet of trucks. It was all chance really, an arrangement through the friend of a friend, that led to my interview with William Rayburn, an executive producer at NBC, and I got the summer job of my dreams, working in the script department, a big room filled with electric typewriters, where I did revisions and prepared final drafts, routine secretarial experience that led, later that summer, to editorial work and a little light writing in the newsroom, where I found my true vocation. Watching the evening news anchorman read changes, usually light revisions with syntax and word choice, in texts I had been given to read for corrections, sometimes hearing words I'd conceived of on my own, audible there, was incredibly exciting, too fantastic not to tell, knowing my words were being heard, traveling in electromagnetic waves, by millions of people, and it sent a rush of happy molecules bubbling through me like an effervescence, and somehow I was singing with my xylophone stick on the back porch in Riverside all over again, jumping off the porch, running along Pasture Lane with the boys.

I was working in the real world, in the medium I found myself in: television. I ended up staying on for five years, soon working as a personal assistant to Mr. Rayburn, whose intelligent forehead would emphatically nod when he agreed with me on some contribution I'd made, some revision I'd suggested, an opinion or relevant viewpoint I'd expressed. There were rumors about his womanizing, but he was always perfectly polite around me, maintaining an appropriate distance. I was, I guess, too young and naïve, though he confided in me, and I in him, so it didn't feel like work. It was more like an informal party I was happy to attend, dress up for, and keep smiling through. My days involved showing up in a business outfit, making coffee and other adjustments while watching morning TV, and then sitting down to read scripts, going through piles of them, paper and more paper, printed matter that someone had to go through, and I was the designated reader. One morning in early April, after I'd been working intensely through the night, doing reedits for a serial that NBC felt was a sure winner, I literally bumped into Jack at the water cooler. I was filling the glass container for another batch of coffee. Jack had been in LA and had just returned, having flown in on the red eye, and he was reaching for a paper cup when he also happened to bump me on the shoulder, causing my hand to move, causing some water to spill on the carpet. His eyes locked into mine, and it was like being on a seesaw.

"Where have I seen your cunning comportment before?" he asked me, a fairly offbeat, even wired, opening line, but I could sense something click, as though there were no other way to appear, and I was struck, caught off guard by this candid question posed by this charming man. Like an athlete prepared for a major event, Jack could talk with calm intelligence about anything, especially in the entertainment world. We had a lot in common. We both enjoyed being outdoors. He was an early riser, a kinsman of the sun, and I recognized a candid, capacious mind, capable of containing multitudes. He seemed to learn as he went along, meaning: He improvised. We seemed to bring out the best in each other, and that's all that anyone really wants to do.

One radiant day, the air elastic and crystalline, Jack said, "Let's just do it and form a duet." We were married at a church in White Plains, with all of the Flanagan clan present. There was a bewildering number of brothers and sisters and cousins whose names I couldn't keep track of at the rehearsal dinner. The traditional Catholic ceremony was a chore, but I remember partying wildly at the reception. Jack's father congratulated us with an extravagant toast, shaking my shoulders, saying we made "a beautiful team."

Jack continued with production work at NBC, frequently flying off to Burbank Studios in LA, but then he began working with independent filmmakers, most of them based in the city. We bought a commodious, top-floor apartment in a landmark brownstone on the Upper West Side, just off the Park, a Victorian building with stained-glass windows and lovely ornamental brickwork. The backyard patio overlooked a garden, its round dirt beds besmirched by brilliant petals from a magnolia tree in the springtime, where I'd do some gardening, surrounded by forsythias, rhododendrons, and roses. The first few years of our lives were full and busy with predictable, job-related routines, though I stopped working at NBC soon after our only child, Susan, was born, creating more time for her and myself to spend together. I was free to do as I chose, so I enjoyed my leisure, taking pride in Susan's development, as we discovered the ability to divine and reach each other's thoughts through a nonverbal, almost musical mode of communication, the basis, I think, for her robust, trusting nature.

We'd always been close with Jack's family, especially his older brother Alan, the brain surgeon, and there'd be weekends of swimming and partying at his place, a striking structure of wood and glass in Amagansett, standing like a huge modern sculpture, right on the beach, set behind the dunes. Those were the summers of enormous sunsets, the moon in its phases a real treat to see; during the day, I'd slap sunblock all over my beached body and lie there like a whale, letting my mind go. And so, on the morning when Ted West phoned, I was probably looking forward to the weekend in Amagansett, for it was early August, and we were all packed up for an early getaway the next day, bringing Susan and her boyfriend, Chip, along. Alan was hosting a party for his forty-fourth birthday, a real bash with a live band, and we were all staying on through the week, so that Jack could go sailing, do an overnight with the kids on his brother's new boat. I was rushing out to do some errands. It was just another day.

My whole mood changed with a phone call. Granddad, at the end of his life, still owned a small piece of property in Belle Haven, an elegant stone outbuilding known as "the Stone Cottage," once part of a working farm, originally built as a carriage house, then becoming, as the old farm morphed into someone's country estate, a tea house, with a flower garden and stone gargoyles, a destination for afternoon strolls, all fitting into a mere acre of land enclosed by stone walls, with an almost three-hundred-year-old oak tree in the front yard, its arboreal brain dominating the green scene. Granddad had willed the property to my mysterious Aunt Alice, his not-so-secret mistress, "Cousin" Conrad's mom, and some clause in the will stipulated that if Alice at her death had not passed the deed of ownership on, then it would pass to me. Granddad's estate attorney, Ted West, phoned me that morning, and he launched into a description of the place, its three-foot-thick granite walls, built from native Belle Haven granite, rumored to be from the same quarry from which/where/whence the base of the Statue of Liberty had been built, the polished floors of quartz indoors, the copper trim along the gutters, the grey slate roof, the grand fireplace and chimney of red brick, painting a perfect picture for some buyer, though I'd be receiving it for free. "Are you sure? Can property just be passed on like that?" I asked, flummoxed by the news. I thought of the last time I saw Granddad, hooked up to tubes in a hospital bed, in Onancock. Now in New York, in the cramped kitchen of our otherwise spacious apartment, just about to rush out the door, I was poured through a temporal funnel, into a time when a golden section of coastal Connecticut imprinted itself somewhere on the container of this consciousness, though that was a time before language. I was elated, pinching myself.

Susan wasn't home, so there was no one there to share the good news with. I phoned my friend Sharon and filled her in. Back toward the middle of TLC, my grandfather, Arthur R. Prescott, had a mistress, a beautiful woman from Montreal, an indigenous Canadian, part Indian, with high cheeks, like an Eskimo's, with sparkling, laughing eyes, a dancer, a Broadway babe who dyed her black hair a bright metallic yellow, a glamour girl. Granddad adored Alice, eventually leaving her the Stone Cottage, the property down the road from his Belle Haven estate. It was a place she could call her own, later in life, property to chase rabbits on. I formulated an image of Aunt Alice in her dotage, grey-haired yet forever young and spry, retired from the theater, a wild woman of the woods, taking advice from caterpillars and blue jays, sometimes appearing at extravagant dinner parties in an elegant little black dress, but spending most of her days out of doors, exploring new territory, wandering on the bluffs or in the forest, culling wild mushrooms and berries with a laugh of inexpressible satisfaction, coming home late to her rustic cottage by the sea with a basket of simple gatherings, opening the thick, wooden door with a heavy iron key. There was a bookish silence at the other end. "Well?" Sharon said, after a stretch, "Are you going to take it? Are you going to go?"

The morning was foggy, but there we were, Jack impressed by the grandeur of the place. "I guess this is where you come from," he remarked, casting a glance at the mansion across the street from us. We walked from the car to the entrance of the cottage. "I'm not going to ask you if you're interested, because I know you are," Ted West chirped, unlocking the door and leading us through the narrow foyer into a large room with a smooth stone floor and walls, a space carved from rock, polished to a luminous emptiness. After Aunt Alice died at home, right in this room, all of the furniture, except the old piano, had been removed, and the place had been renovated, so everything was incredibly clean, the walls freshly scrubbed, and I felt a funny affinity, as if the spirit of Aunt Alice were here, hovering over my shoulder. It was all so easy and dreamlike, signing the papers, transferring the property rights then and there, and we moved in two weeks later.

PART TWO

· · ·

THE BOYS OF
BELLE HAVEN

1

CONSIDERING WHAT I'VE EXPERIENCED, I CAN'T HELP BUT FEEL, confined as I am to the poverty of my own point of view, that a larger activity shrouds mine, altering it and shaping me, so that I am a piece in a puzzle, tapping away, in a context that refuses to be saturated. The first time I saw Jerrold Draper was at a crowded cocktail party, on a flagstone terrace, shortly after we'd moved to Belle Haven; I recognized his face from a photograph in a magazine Jack had pointed out to me. It was on an unusually warm, almost buttery, late Saturday afternoon in the middle of October. The Bushwells were hosting their annual early OH TOMB HILL celebration, and everyone seemed especially lively and at ease, perhaps an effect of the house drink, gin and tonic, served from an enormous crystal bowl beneath the blue-and-white-striped awning. We were impressed by the park-like view, the wide, authoritative lawn, punctuated and bordered by magnificent flowering plants, hedges, and trees, rolling down to the Sound and the lighthouse on an island in the distance. I was taken by the size of the lawn, and then I noticed Jerrold, standing, in silhouette, for he cut a striking figure, bearing a kind of devilish grin. He certainly seemed to be enjoying himself. It was almost as if he did a little jig, entertaining the group of serious, well-dressed men gathered around him, peers presumably, his face flush with the pride he clearly experienced, flapping his peacock plumes, after he'd said something significant, and then his gaze turned to meet mine.

He moved his head like someone who was accustomed to being listened to, and the more I looked, the more I saw someone I wished to know better. I think I saw him wink, and I felt a fervor for fusion.

Earlier, days before the Bushwells' party, just after we'd made our move to the Stone Cottage, for two chaotic weeks before settling in, we'd been living out of boxes and suitcases, like college students—"just like real actors, gypsies on location," Jack had said—making the inert, lifeless walls seem almost human, almost an ear, glad to have us there. Our motive for moving was obscure to our city friends and neighbors, who shook their heads in amazement, dismay, and surprise, but to me it was perfectly clear, like directions scribbled on a map for a section of my soul, the one where I fold. We were tired of the temper of city life. Like any real decision, ours had a certain impulsive, impatient impetus behind it. Why do anything at all? Why not give it a chance? Jack, I think, was attracted to the upscale address, the posh, affluent suburb, set in the heart of "the super-affluent suburb," as he put it, where a part of him always was anyway, or had to be, given the way things work in this world of hours, and I wished to waken in a quiet neighborhood where I could hear a wide variety of birds right outside my window in the morning. We'd both, meanwhile, been bitten by what Jack referred to as the "Less Is More Bug," the "LIMB," as I sit here and think of it now, reducing the bulk of our cargo to a minimum, getting rid of excess furniture, books, and clothing. "Simplify, simplify," Jack would say to me, and so, with Susan finishing her degree at Colorado State, about to embark on a career in geology, we just decided to do it, make the move, and satisfy that craving for novelty buried inside of us all. There were other rationalizations. Jack argued that with the real estate market so good, we'd be silly not to sell the apartment and make a significant profit, and with Susan away, we didn't need all that space anymore anyway. The kitchen had always been too small, but the dining room and living area were huge, far too much for two. Packing, deciding what to keep, sell, throw or give away, I felt like a child preparing for a real-life adventure, and I was seized by my enthusiasm for new prospects.

The Bushwells were a fabulously wealthy family who'd lived in Belle Haven for years, and a phrase from out of nowhere, "the bush-iness of infinity," popped into mind as we looked at the orchard and vineyard, both in their stunning, autumnal beauty. The estate was set back on a large spread of property, undulant as a golf course, the huge, stone Tudor house rising in a unique amalgam of wealth and taste, its diamond-paned windows flashing light back to a setting sun, as we slowly drove up the driveway, our tires politely crunching pink pebbles, to park our modest Volvo among more expensive gaso-line sculptures: Mercedeses, BMWs, Jaguars, a silver Rolls Royce, and a black Bentley in the temporary parking lot set off to one side of the house on an area of lawn carefully mowed and marked out with festive yellow, red, and orange ribbons. It was a kind of harvest celebration, with a huge wicker cornucopia, filled with pumpkins and colorful squashes, set on the lawn in front of the monolithic house, and I felt dwarfed by palatial grandeur. Walking up the mar-ble steps, we heard the sounds of the party inside and out back, the decibels of music and talk creating a surge of unrestrained revelry, and I turned to Jack and said, "Isn't this grand?" We were ushered into a hallway and led through a space of mirrored walls and out to the terrace, where the other guests were mingling, milling about, drinking, and dancing, and I felt I'd been pushed back through time, squeezed into a sequence from TLC, a time when The Ark was the place for me. There was a small orchestra on a stage set up on the lawn, playing dance music, and I immediately noticed

Jerrold. He was dapper in his tuxedo; I noted his chiseled chin, strong forehead, and wavy, dark hair, greying elegantly at the edges. He spoke intently to the men gathered around him, and I think I heard numbers and the names of foreign countries mentioned, and it was then, when he finished speaking, that he seemed to look my way and wink, though it may have just been my imagination.

2

THE SECOND TIME I SAW JERROLD, JUST A WEEK OR SO LATER, WE spoke, albeit briefly. He shook my hand ceremoniously and penetrated my awareness with his sensitive eyes, marked with a self-assurance and smile that seemed both empathic and predatory, on my side but also outside of me, set against me, and I sensed a duplicity, an ever-working and scheming intelligence behind the façade of courteous restraint and decorum. He spoke clearly but in a strange accent I couldn't quite identify, maybe Bostonian, inviting Jack and me to attend a Halloween party, something he and Jessica were hosting, a masked ball, a masquerade bash, an annual event, all for the fun of it. He had walked down the road, informally attired in jeans and a light woolen jacket, looking dapper, clearly enjoying the bright afternoon, smoking a small cigar, its wisps of blue smoke disappearing into fresh blasts of Canadian air. The sugar maple across the street flared with bunches of red paper hearts, fluttering in the sunlight, and puffy white clouds flew by on a northwesterly breeze, putting a rapidly changing play of light and shadow on all things, spotting the lawn deep green in places, as I straightened up from my task of having bent down to pull up a weed, a dandelion probably, and I greeted him at the edge of our property. He was formal, even businesslike about the invitation, shaking my hand as if sealing a deal, saying how pleased he was to meet me, telling me, tersely, the time and place, reminding me that we should wear costumes and bring masks, and then he rushed off.

3

THE THIRD TIME I SAW JERROLD HE TOLD ME THE STORY, WHICH IS, IN a sense, the basis for this book, so I'd better switch gears, slow down, and remember as clearly as I can some of the sequence the events that evening took. Jack wanted to drive the Volvo, but I insisted on walking the mere quarter of a mile, past a wooded area on the edge of the Sound, to the entrance of the Drapers' estate, where an electric gate opened for us, as an expensive gasoline sculpture rushed past: a shiny, long, black limousine, RPM booming in its wake, trailing behind the dark, tinted windows, turning inaudible as the vehicle sped ahead. Jack muttered something underneath his breath, and I studied the lines of architecture looming ahead as we walked, slowly ascending a long, straight driveway of white pebbles. On its rise of lawn, the grand house rose, in Romanesque splendor, a magnificent structure, like a small palace with high terra-cotta walls and steeply sloping roofs fit with red clay tiles; there were stone towers and turrets, brick chimneys, and many large windows, some of them stained, all playing parts in the massive edifice, a whole so formidable it seemed incredible. I took a photograph of it, and then I looked away, seeking other registers. Festive shrieks, modulating into howls of laughter, resounded from behind the front façade, now absolutely brimming with electric light. There was a red carpet covering the front steps, and I found it odd there, so roofless, so vulnerable, open and exposed to the elements. A faintly malevolent wind tossed a handful of oak leaves into the air, just skimming by us, as we exchanged glances, wondering what was next.

We were greeted at the door by a tall man in all-black attire, looking something like an undertaker, who took our coats and steered us into the direction of the party, then in full swing, a sea of masks mixing, mingling, multiplying gestures and bursts of laughter, rushing about in outlandish outfits, talking and drinking, dancing and swaying while RPM played loudly, coming from sources I couldn't discern. One man, dressed as a grizzly bear, was careening wildly, colliding with people, falling into their arms, pawing at them with a blind, animal ferocity; he was obviously very drunk, or perhaps just deliciously happy with his anonymous role.

I noticed a long-haired, young teenage boy, peering through binoculars from a sequestered place at the top of the carpeted marble stairway, and I learned later that he was Jesse Draper, who was scanning the crowd in the ballroom below, searching for Jerrold, playing with the focus, trying to locate his dad in disguise, for he knew that his quarry would be wearing the black and purple cape, that he'd recognize the shape of his own father's head when he saw it. Jesse's inner conception of Jerrold, now keyed to context, partying, playing the forever-hospitable host, cast amid a throng of happy, irresponsible adults, failed to find its match, as Dad, unseen by his son, wielded his shield of hospitality.

A rainbow of floodlights suddenly illuminated an outdoor fountain beyond the French doors, and one guest, playing pirate, wearing an appropriate buccaneer's black hat and eye patch, ran through the ballroom like a madman, waving a gleaming sword, a cutlass, pointing its sharp tip at the spectrum-speckled shafts of water being driven up into the air outside. The already-low indoor lights went out, and the RPM stopped. There was a kind of hush all over the ballroom, as an infectious silence of surprise and expectation spread, and then, at an unexpected point on the dance floor, a small explosion occurred; a flash of sudden light filled the space, sending out yellow stars and sparks, the *whizz* of red rockets, and out of a swirling mass of white smoke a human form emerged, dressed as Count Dracula, donned in an elaborate black and purple cape. There was something lizardlike about its appearance, the velvet fabric gleaming. Removing his mask, Jerrold wished all of us a happy Halloween and grinned a benevolent grin, though it all seemed somehow feigned. He stretched his arms out, gesturing toward Jessica, putting the pronoun "we" to some use in a second expression of welcome. The music resumed playing, and he made his way, sometimes stopping, sometimes pushing guests aside with gestures suggesting a blunt urgency, toward the group of five or six people with whom I happened to be standing. Jack had gone off somewhere, distracted as he so often could be. Jerrold was, it almost seemed, rushing to my aid, not wanting to see his new neighbor lost in a crowd, adrift in a cloud.

He shook my hand, and I noticed his eyes, the knowing smile that seemed so engaged and kinetic, on my side but also outside of me, against me, and I sensed again a duplicity. I don't really remember what we talked about, but, very quickly, a small crowd of people gathered around us, around Jerrold, who now became especially alert, as he impatiently glanced at his watch, as if local time were of great importance, and he put his mask back on.

Jerrold was now playing guide, holding a candelabrum, and we followed him, out of the ballroom, off into another room, where he led us up a stairway, then down a long, narrow hallway, and then into a small, square room with plain white walls, adorned with painted images of fishes, fruits, and sheaves of grain, as if it were an Egyptian tomb; the space was lit with saucers of wax, with thick black wicks on fire, set on elaborate cast-iron stands, with several black cats milling about in the flickering light. In one corner, in an upright casket of glass, like a museum case, there was a human form bandaged in white gauze, a pseudo-mummy, its two arms and legs free to move. Meanwhile, downstairs, the dancing had begun again, and the RPM, now monster movie music, reached a kind of crescendo. I remember the sound of cymbals, and then the bound form sprang to life, smashing the glass case, stretching its arms out forward, marching forward as if under a spell, caught in a trance, walking into an adjacent room filled with dirt—a huge mound of dirt with actual gravestones embedded in it, the sites fastidiously decorated with hardy marigolds and roses. It was, I guess, a kind of masque, a form of courtly entertainment, distinctively Italian, Rococo. With deliberation, the quick of life returned, the mummy walked into the center of the mock burial ground, where it began to move to the music, unwrapping itself in a slow striptease act, swaying, undoing the muslin wrappings with its hands, keeping time with the music, revealing a young, buxom blonde, a real beauty, who stood there for a moment with her eyes closed, opened them, shrieked, and ran downstairs, screaming hysterically, playing a part in the performance. Jerrold, with his mask now off, gestured toward a table where a crystal punch bowl and glasses were set on an enormous silver tray, and he graciously served us a powerful punch, an amalgam of rum and something, which went straight to my head.

I drifted back downstairs, attracted to the music, where I began to dance the night away. Outside, seen through the French doors' windows, a great bonfire blazed, and the shapes of busy flames rose, as Jerrold played conductor, having come downstairs, the fire being—by synecdoche, I do believe—a sign of his enormous success. He had money to burn, and he was showing it, almost in the manner of an advertisement, to us and for us, as he moved through the celebration, playing the happy host, cape drawn up by hand above his head again, looking like a large, maniacal bat, and it all seemed plausible, the combinatorial product of a perilous, peerless experiment, inversely proportionate to all that wealth, taste, and power, the jewels and the gold, so that the funds would never run out, and nobody was sure who he or she was in the process, a mash of identities, a fluidity of personal pronouns, which was a good thing, as the party roared through its changes, bursts of self-aggrandizing applause, climaxes of RPM, coming from sources I couldn't discern. I saw him standing there, draped in a kind of terrible innocence, dressed in that outlandish costume of shimmering fabric, a strange new vehicle, as he recognized me, and I saw him, the financial wizard whose fame had recently brought a TV news crew, CNN, to Belle Haven, begin to walk in my direction. Jerrold looked dapper, almost hallucinatory in his Halloween garb, his handsome features enhanced by his bright white shirt setting a contrast to the black velvet cloak hanging loosely from his shoulders, its surface glistening with the sheen of an underground stream. In a sense he looked ridiculous, a grown man in that costume. I suppose he just wanted to entertain us, to take us away in the great, grand coach of his story. He was making a beeline for me, it seemed. "Do you want to know a secret?" he asked me, drawing his right arm over my head, playing the grand host, folds of webby fabric sticking out at perverse angles over my face right on cue. I guess he saw me as an appropriate vessel, right then and there, for the contents of his mind, and I nodded, encouraging him, and he spoke, so that something like an autobiographical synopsis emerged.

4

JERROLD DRAPER WAS BORN IN QUEENS, NEW YORK CITY, THE SON OF Joseph ("Joe") and Cecelia Draper, on the morning of the third day of January, exactly five years ahead of me. Can you believe it? Joe, an immigrant from Warsaw, wishing to assimilate quickly, had changed his name from "Drapenski," and he first worked in the Brooklyn shipyards, where he learned all about electrical wiring, and then as a repairman for Bell Telephone, where he put what he'd learned to good use. He impressed upon his young son the power of technology, the magic of telecommunications, the miracle of electromagnetism. Joe was part of a small Polish community, and he'd met Cecelia, also from Warsaw, while dropping his dirty clothes off at the local Laundromat, Snappy Sheets, the place of her employment and where, soon enough, she'd work again. Just after the wedding, they discovered, much to their surprise, that both their maternal grandmothers were from the same tiny hamlet in the Carpathian Mountains. Cecelia was a dark-haired beauty with a voice of gold, the star of Saint Basil's choir, and she gave birth to a daughter, Eloise, who died tragically young, and then a son. Joe and Cecelia saved enough money to move out of the cramped two-room apartment in Long Island City, and they bought a functional, two-story brick house on a quarter acre of land at the southernmost end of Utopia Parkway. Joe was always at work on home improvement projects, or in the basement, tinkering with his electric trains, boys' toys, really.

As soon as young Jerry was old enough to attend kindergarten, he showed an unusual knack for numbers; he was able to count and do subtraction all in his head, much to the surprise of his teachers and the chagrin of his peers. Cecelia went back to work; although getting there now involved a long bus trip, she enjoyed tucking up her sleeves two or three times a week, working part-time at Snappy Sheets, doing the washing and folding, falling into a familiar routine, singing along with the girls, snapping her fingers with what was on the radio.

Mom sometimes took young Jerry to work with her, where he'd watch, through the streaming portals of washing machines, the steady thoughtlessness of clothes churning in soap and hot water, sloshed around and around, then put on spin, then inundated with more soapy water. Sometimes he'd sit in the back room, where there were plastic buckets stacked in a tower, nestled within each other, like ornamental Russian dolls, each fitting neatly into the next. Small cardboard boxes of All, Cheer, and Tide detergent, fluorescently colored, were stacked on a long shelf behind the towering buckets, and young Jerry would sit and count them. He watched Cecelia fold the clothes, her body working with the material, bending in places, her hands making swift, expert motions, ordering the very fabric of time and space, and when she reached for the jars where she kept the gleaming quarters, dimes, and nickels, Jerry's eyes lit up with a special spark. He'd sometimes play with the coins all day, working with his hands, opening jars, running his fingers through the change, building towers with coins, discovering equivalencies, the logic of wholes and parts.

Young Jerry's uncle Ed, Joe's older brother, who had left Warsaw at an early age to study electrical engineering in Toronto, had an important job at an aircraft factory in Seattle, Washington. Uncle Ed was a big childhood presence, sending young Jerry expensive gifts for Christmas—chemistry sets, walkie-talkies, record players, and microscopes—and on the phone he'd say to Jerry, in an animated voice, "See yawl in Seattle," tantalizing Jerry, telling him that someday he'd fly to Washington State, way out west, and they'd actually see each other there, in Seattle, at the airport. Uncle Ed was, in Joe's own words, "a joker," "a card," and "a swinging bachelor to boot," and he'd sent a very young Jerry picture postcards of bathing beauties on beaches striking seductive poses. Joe, almost always busy working for Bell Telephone, would adopt a delaying stratagem, saying, "Someday, yes, we'll have to visit my older brother," but it never seemed like it would happen, until one day, it did, and they departed from Idlewild, the airport with the suggestive name, one sunny, warm April morning, flying in a huge, shiny TWA jet plane, wings speeding through the spacious skies to Seattle for a four-day visit, a surprise vacation. It was, probably, the most memorable event of Jerry's boyhood, his first trip on an airplane, and he had a marvelous time in Seattle, visiting its celebrated Space Needle, a tall, futuristic structure hovering over the parking lot, a column of gleaming metal sporting a saucer-shaped volume at its top, hovering over the parking lot. Uncle Ed had played an instrumental role in the engineering of its workings. Inside the saucer there was a restaurant with bright, modern decor, offering panoramic views of the scenery, the mountains and trees in the distance. Patrons sat at tables set on a revolving platform, a big, circular floor, rotating slowly, completing its cycle each hour. There were telephones on the tables, so that diners could place their orders for food and drink without having to interact with a waitress, but because of the motion of the platform, ordinary wire telephones couldn't be used, so a fancy, newfangled, closed-circuit, cordless telephone system was developed and installed, exclusively for the Cosmos Restaurant, and Uncle Ed had been part of the team behind its realization.

Jerry had the outgoing, extroverted disposition of a happy, healthy American boy growing up in TLC, his potential for optimistic play and work free to develop, though he sometimes felt unbidden pangs of terrifying wonder wander through his body, tingling his cortex, feeling as though he were somehow responsible for life on earth, the fate of the universe. Once, while playing football in Flushing Bay Park, shouting, running around in the mud, throwing a pass or scoring a touchdown, Jerry stopped, distracted, watching a jet plane passs overhead, a massive flying machine, the aircraft showing off the complicated mechanism of its undersides, its gleaming, metallic belly, and he was fascinated, amazed by the sight of all that mass up there, the realm of the inarticulate tightening its hold on him, as he attempted to estimate its weight, searching for a number that fit. It was apparent at an early age that Jerry had a mathematical gift, a calculative genius, a way with numerals that set him apart, enabling him to skip a grade in elementary school. He astounded his teachers and peers, seeming to learn the multiplication table in a single day, as if he'd grasped the whole web of relations between digits and products in a flash, the classroom experience only prompting a knowledge already within, ready to be sprung, but his being special didn't make him arrogant or aloof, and, unlike many children graced with preternatural intellectual abilities, Jerry enjoyed socializing, especially on the playground, where he could be fiercely competitive. A handsome boy endowed with a gift, he was the noticed one.

Encouraged, flattered, goaded on by teachers, parents, and peers, Jerry was soon able to multiply large numbers and do long division in his head with ease, speed, and accuracy. Fractions were a breeze, just like square roots, and he could recite primes extemporaneously, from memory. He was a whiz at algebra, intimate with integers and their variables. Suddenly, with calculus, any sense of mental effort ceased, so empowered by quantification was he when he performed with the sines, cosines, and tangents, his cogitations proceeding, becoming automatic, wired into his mental musculature. His mundane perceptions were enhanced through set theory, as he'd seize, with rapid mental manipulation, wholes from parts, casting his formative experience of the world into a rigorous, conceptual order, a broken palimpsest pieced and held together by the glue of logical necessity.

Jerrold won a scholarship to Exeter, the prestigious preparatory school, where many of his classmates were the sons of wealthy men, heirs to traditions of privilege, boys whose lives would be favored, inflected and tweaked by the power of money. He developed disdain for his working-class origins, and when he returned home for Christmas vacation that year, he felt a veiled alienation from his parents, the neighborhood, and the kids he'd known at public school, realizing that the circumstances he'd grown up in were far from ideal. Away from home he'd savored a sense of entitlement, something of a code, an air, a guarantor of real class and superiority. He graduated from Exeter with distinction, and, after a summer of golf, tennis, and sailboat racing in Maine, staying at the summer home of a new acquaintance from school, Jerrold enrolled at MIT to study advanced mathematics.

He soon became quite the Don Juan at MIT, where he met Wendy Hardwick, her blond hair and piercing green eyes, and her aristocratic, influential family. (Can you tell that I'm improvising here?) "I want to have fun in all the big cities on the planet," he once said to her father at a party at the family compound on

Martha's Vineyard. Jerrold aspired to achieve grand goals.

He seemed to sail through his mathematics courses at MIT, partying much of the time. Jerrold was jogging alongside the Charles River, unconsciously counting the numberless trees, pondering different levels of infinity, during which time the study of pure mathematics began to feel entirely too abstract, when it occurred to him that he should pursue a career in high finance, that putting numerals to work and making incredible amounts of money attracted him. It was exactly what he wanted to do. Just think of the profit! His ambition led him to the Wharton School, where he learned all about options, futures, interest rate swaps, and credit default policies. He became a staunch defender of deregulation, promoting open, competitive markets, a fervent believer in current growth indicators and a tireless champion of science and technology. He graduated from Wharton cum laude, beginning his career in global finance at Morgan Stanley, managing futures portfolios. The months swiftly passed into a few years, and he'd soon amassed a small fortune and a robust, confident knowledge of the market's intricate, complex workings, the secret ways of finance, enough to start his own hedge fund: EDGE, an acronym of his own device— Every Day Generates Excellence. He reminded himself of Uncle Ed, being quite the swinging bachelor, living out a James Bond fantasy, part of a new, young, wealthy elite, taking pride in his rapid rise on the rungs of monetary stature, driving fast, expensive cars and dressing in fine clothes, purchasing property in Scotland and a vacation home in the Hamptons, in addition to the townhouse on the Upper East Side, not far from where The Ark had been. He bought his parents a vacation home in Florida, in West Palm Beach, set on a canal, with a boat, a dock, and a pool. He moved in powerful circles, his associates being fellow champions in the arena of corporate competition, financial wizards, CEOs, Masters of the Money Verse, controlling the force that makes the world go. Romantically, he was profligate; he had innumerable relationships with women, picking and choosing partners of beauty and elegance for affairs that would last a few months, and it was at the end of a long stretch that he met Jessica Jensen, one sultry summer night at a party on a private beach near the Larchmont Yacht Club.

5

THERE WAS SOMETHING ABOUT JESSICA, PERHAPS HER SHEER, LITHE legs, her long blond hair, her slim, perfect figure, her excited eyes and personality; all of her attributes sparked a match, an animal attraction, and Jerry's initial attempts to rate it, her power over him, to quantify her and it, to assign a number to her being, to think of a number that fit the stunning package that she was, the rise and fall of her pert breasts just visible beneath the silk shirt, her perfectly blue eyes sparkling, were continually frustrated by indeterminacy, hovering somewhere between a "9" and a full "10." He was always rating women, determining suitable numbers, assigning exact values to the feelings they aroused, taking some care in the discriminations he made among the higher values. Jessica wasn't perfect; there was a disturbing dimple, almost a double-chin effect when she laughed, and she laughed too much and talked too loudly, almost like a man, when she drank too much, which was often, and to probe her autobiography, to attempt to engage her personal history, always led to the same end. She just didn't want to talk about it. In some ways there was nothing there. She'd simply materialized, coming to life, walking into his life at a beach party, beautiful and unattached, coming out of a difficult past that she didn't want to remember, a heroin habit and the collapse of a meteoric modeling career. Everything in her life was profoundly shattered, but that was something she'd passed through. "I'm finished with it. Let's drop it," she'd said, so he let it drop, and he appreciated Jessica in the bloom of her stunning youth.

It was the photographer phantom alive inside that watched her one morning lost in sleep, lips putting forth small puffs of sound, as she unconsciously scratched her arm with her hand, the crimson of her fingernails showing, and he, pulling away the sheet, looked down her long legs to her toes, painted an incandescent green. He saw a smile play on her face, and he pictured the pink streaks of cloud, the stir of yesterday's sunset, the swelling sea, the heat of their blending, eyes on each other, reaching each other, him with his sunglasses on, her blond hair bouncing in the surf, catching the light, as he ravished her, his whiskered chin digging into her collarbone's soft flesh flecked with sand, the lift of her perfect breasts. The power of her hold on him was almost hydraulic, coming in waves of pressure, release, and pleasure, producing his certainty: She was it, the real thing. There was a boisterous boldness about her, and Jerrold laughed more around her. She made him feel loose and decentralized, as if he were wearing a new suit, something to light a place up with, any time at all, and he provoked her witty repartee with an enthusiasm he had not known elsewhere. She made time polymorphous in her own inimitable way, and he found himself attracted to her, some element within her, able to unhinge time and relax its hold, taking him places he'd never been before, her smiling smile a spontaneous "yes" to the present, wherever it was, whatever it happened to be, her bold self a function of all that passed through. His eyes bumped into the wall of actuality: Jessica waking up. She took in the scene and made a little smile. "Wow, like I'm here."

"Right, and I've been watching you. I've been watching you for the past fifteen minutes, in fact," he whispered, embracing her, closing his eyes, taking her into his arms and under the covers, creating access, first with his fingers, then with his tongue. He opened his eyes and seized her again, one more time, and the wind kissed the curtains.

The earth on a tilt turned on its axis, and the remainder of that morning became a long, casual celebration of carnality at its best, refreshing flesh, eating fresh fruit, and by what Jessica referred to as "the time of four sticks," 11:11, she was down at the swimming pool, aircraft honing in above the splendid white city, the blue flash of the Mediterranean Sea in the distance, Jerrold nearby, reading in the sun, Jessica rolling up something to smoke before lunch, so that she might loaf the rest of the afternoon away, a little swimming and a lot of sunbathing, the skin of a babe in the sun. Jessica rolled the marijuana cigarette, then twirled it between her fingertips, as Jerrold extracted meaning from the financial pages, casting his right hand over the paper, gleaning information from a field of data, but it was impossible to focus on that cognition now. Roused from his accounts, shaken from the numbers by her graceful motion, he watched her seal the deal with her lips. She looked across from where she was sitting. "Let's get a buzz on, but first I want to take a dip," she chirped, and then she stood up, her lithe, perfect figure heading for the aquatic world, more cut off from numbers than a seal, as she dove, slipping in. She swam underwater for an unprecedented duration, proof of a sunny athleticism. Climbing out, she picked up the towel from the back of a chair and remarked, with a smile, "Oh, you're watching me."

"I sure am," Jerry chuckled as he focused on her.

"What is it with you guys?" she asked teasingly, spying his gaze now trained on her breasts.

"What is it about these?" she implored, cupping the tops of her swimsuit, then walking directly toward him, drawing the towel across the bottom half of her face, like a dancer, a gypsy, her blue eyes catching the light, and with no one else there in the midday glare, Jessica smiled; he undid the top of her bikini, revealing her perfect, firm breasts, all but the very tips tanned by the sun, and she curved into Jerry's open arms, resting her head on his shoulder, the delicate folds of her outer ear poised, like a sea shell, beneath his mouth. "I am unusually happy," he whispered. He produced a series of inarticulate, deeply appreciative sounds, satisfied animal sounds, expressing an almost brutish contentment, pushing his nose into the fleshy contours of her ear. She moved her face to catch a glimpse of his, awed by her beauty. Later, at dinner, picking at her fish, she picked up her knife and, drawing invisible figures on the tablecloth, talked about growing up in Douglaston, right at the city's limits, drawing a map of her old neighborhood, the house and its floor plan, giving an accurate description of the backyard, all those true tree names, babbling on, a little drunk, about her father's store, the Planter's Thumb, the plants and gardening equipment he sold from a quarter-acre plot of commercial property set on the Long Island Expressway, "the L-I-E," she called it, and Jerrold pictured these places, and he was filled with expectations of a smooth, fulfilling trajectory.

His right hand graced her slender left wrist, touching the band of her silver watch, studded with tiny diamonds. He believed in their present and future happiness. "It's just great to spend quality time with you like this," he said. The attractive thing about Jessica was her spontaneity, her openness, her readiness for fun, doing silly things on purpose, like mimicking the waiter's accent after he'd taken their orders, or miming some famous actor, watching television with the sound off, or spinning the ice cubes in her glass loudly and whistling, seductively, a kind of comedic act. In the afternoon they'd tossed a beach ball back and forth, blissfully stoned, just smiling with the pleasure of doing it, the two of them clicking, getting in tune for the narrow channel. The wine ameliorated an already mellow day. Jerrold was feeling very relaxed. He'd remember that evening's temperature.

"I'm feeling pretty comfortable now," he said, looking down at his large, competent hands and then into Jessica's eyes again. A sea breeze combed through the palm fronds, making a dry, faintly percussive sound, the nets hanging out to dry becoming a shimmering loom of silver. He took his Rolex watch off and brought it close to her face, moving it up and down her cheek, treating it as if it were a razor, now placing it on the table with a tender click. "I want to go places and do things with you, Jessica," he said. She seemed to rebuff his directness. Asserting control, honing his tone, he looked at her almost solemnly and held her wrist more firmly. "I want to go around the world with you. I'll take you places where you've never been," he said, pinning her with his eyes.

Jessica noticed the size of his watch, and she thought of the Planter's Thumb, intertwining the threads of past and present.

They spent a luxurious week in Portugal and Spain, staying in expensive hotels, exploring legendary cities, wining and dining at posh restaurants. Jerrold bought her clothes and jewelry. He took photographs of Jessica on the beach at Lisbon, where she posed, where he mixed business with pleasure, and it all felt like a dream, so taken, so intoxicated was he by the easygoing elasticity of her youth. They were sipping wine on a terrace overlooking a canal, toward the end of the trip, after shopping in Madrid, when he realized that he'd managed to spend more than a million dollars in just seven days, and although there was something hollow about all the excess, they both somehow knew this, and they reveled in that knowledge.

6

THERE WAS SOMETHING VAGUELY CONSPIRATORIAL ABOUT THE WEDding, a hushed event, with only a few of Jerrold's friends, close business associates, attending—with Joseph and Cecelia there, of course—and almost everyone in Jessica's family, dancing with wild abandonment at the alcohol-fueled reception. The service itself was short, but the celebratory dancing, drinking, and music went on for hours, the country club swarming with people from Jessica's circle of friends and family. The newlyweds honeymooned in Scotland, where Jerrold showed off some newly acquired property—another old castle—and it was during this rewarding phase, when EDGE was expanding investments, working with foreign economies, that Jerrold's net worth began to balloon into the tens of billions, giving him the purchasing power of a major player.

He bought the enormous duplex, with marble floors and a balustrade, a place with a lot of glass, class, and empty space, in a famous landmark building, right on Museum Mile, just a few blocks down from the Guggenheim. While Jessica led a busy social life, out with friends often, nightclubbing, attending events, sometimes partying until very early in the morning, Jerrold spent exorbitant amounts of time, or so it seemed to Jessica, downtown at EDGE headquarters, and during that first year of their marriage, she was continually demanding that they experience more quality weekend time together.

Having flown back from Paris on the Concorde the previous day, they were strolling along Madison Avenue, a little jet-lagged, one bright January afternoon, his arm around her waist, smitten with each other, stooping to inspect some attractive furniture in the gilded window of a local antiques shop, when Jessica suddenly broke from his embrace. She'd begun to feel real pain.

She knew she'd give birth to a boy, so she'd already picked out a name, short and to the point: Jesse. He was born very early in the morning, at some point during the proverbial "Hour of the Wolf," an allusion to her Nordic heritage, on a frigid February morning, and the hospital room window, in front of which Jessica held her baby in her arms, offered a picturesque view of the blue dancing river outside. He was the perfect picture of infancy, with blue eyes blinking, and she thought, "He has my eyes."

Jerrold, rushing down the hallway, tripped on an electrical cord, slipped, and fell to the floor. He'd spent the morning at the office, preoccupied with an uptick, the market's recent bullish surge requiring his supervision, his eyes fixed on cathode ray screens all morning, and he was already mentally exhausted. Composed like a flowchart oriented by a hierarchy whose crown is the nimbus of capital, Jerrold moved through the world with a pocket calculator, constantly quantifying, translating his experience of sensory phenomena into the fixed, numeric terms of dollars and cents, nickels and dimes, but there is a limit to what you can do with a game. He'd been studying the screens all day, discovering new investment opportunities, extrapolating potential gains, tracking incentives, and his imagination conjured a visual field of glowing digits, decimal points and numerals, the numbers when he closed his eyes. It was the only language he really knew, and the only one he would ever know with absolute exactitude.

He was in the middle of an important business transaction when the phone's call sounded, and a portable receiver, at the end of a long cord, was thrown into his hand. He was rushed by private car to the hospital, but there'd been midday traffic, and he'd had to wait for an elevator that didn't arrive, so he ran upstairs, but a stupid electrical cord sent him flying, hitting his head on some medical equipment left standing in the hallway, a machine with a curtain around it, something like a photo booth. Dazed and confused, he got up from the floor and felt for a bump on his head, but there didn't seem to be any, although his skull throbbed. He found Jessica's room, just as a camera flashed, and he felt a surge of contempt for the young man holding the apparatus, an intruder, now asking Jessica to strike another pose with Jesse at her side. Jerrold threw his coat into the chair with angry emphasis. "Get out of here!" he snapped. The young man, startled, collapsed into a kind of cringe, and he began to collect his equipment. Cringing even more, the startled young man packed his equipment, and then he walked out the door. Jerrold gazed into the baby's tiny black pupils providing access to currents that run through us all. "That was your father's idea," Jessica explained. She shook her head and continued, "Joe wanted photographs. Call the guy back. Let him take one of us, the three of us, so happy together." Jerrold went out into the hallway and caught the photographer by the arm at the elevator door, yanking him back for one more shot, and the proud parents posed with Jesse, with bright yellow tulips like living lemon lollipops. Jerrold teased Jessica about her obvious enjoyment of being-in-front-of-the-camera, her photogenic core, and she was laughing, clowning around, when the buzzer inside Jerrold's jacket pocket buzzed, calling him back to work. Jerrold kissed Jessica and clenched baby Jesse's tiny right hand in his fist, shook it playfully up and down, and then grabbed his coat from the chair and rushed out of the room. He ran downstairs and into the street, where he hailed a cab. Back at the office, he watched the numbers on the screens, the values assigned to the flows, finding rule, pattern, and meaning through the management of material in time.

With everyone gone, with Jesse lifted away from her side for the rest of the night by a pretty, young nurse, Jessica picked up the remote control and turned on the television, reflecting, with the sound off, on her experience, glad the ordeal was over. She was no longer hostage to another physiology thriving inside of her, whose motions she'd sensed acutely for weeks, and now she'd sleep soundly without the pushing and tumbling, as she put her fingers to her stomach and gently pressed down smiling, drifting off to sleep.

7

THE SEASONS PASS WITH CELERITY, SPREADING OVER MONTHS, TURN-ing into more than a year, and Jesse's in the kitchen with Jessica, who holds a spoonful of orange-colored baby food, a puree of carrots and sweet potato, up to his infant lips. She's humming a silly song, and Jesse gurgles and makes a face in the midst of it all, so much gorgeous raw material. There are no purposes at work here, just antecedent causes. He's learning that certain gestures and sounds "work," led by induction—as Mom makes a happy face in response to a certain strain in his guttural stammering, moving the spoon to his mouth—to act as he does, and they are corresponding, working together, coupling, uncoupling, doubling, silent except for these preverbal babblings, the auditory basis of a bond, as Jesse moves through infancy and works his way toward words.

Jerrold wasn't around much then. EDGE consumed the lion's share of his waking hours, and the glowing matrix of growing numbers that were his unique responsibility required continual care, feeding, and the focus of his acumen, but sometimes in the mornings he was at home, lingering over breakfast, exposed to the bond between mother and son. From a sofa upholstered in patterned silk, a flowery one, from the soft, cushioned surface where he sat, in the sunny, glassed-in patio off the breakfast nook, looking up Museum Mile, Jerrold could see the Guggenheim Museum—that colossal, white ceramic toilet bowl of a building expanding into space, a giant albino snail of monstrous curves, spiraling lines—and he looked into some trees surrounding the reservoir, the greens of summer anointed with a fine mist, though waves of blue broke through in places. Holding on to the back of his head with his hands, he mused on the upcoming weekend: trout fishing in Wyoming. Jessica appeared, moving surreptitiously from behind the sliding glass door, now pushing it open, the smooth sound announcing her presence, shimmering in yellow cotton fabric. In the glare of the light she'd put on her polarized dark glasses, picking them up from the table after she'd set the tray down. She was playing maid. She was pouring freshly brewed coffee, dark and savory, into his cup, when the sudden, loud crash occurred, and the forces of metal in conflict in space, right there on the street, the sound of glass breaking and metal fragments hitting the asphalt, skittering away, caused Jerrold to direct his line of vision downward and Jessica, startled, to jump with the coffee cup filled to its brim, so that some of it spilled on the marble top of the table, making a mess. She quickly walked into the kitchen and returned with a sponge to wipe it away. A siren of some kind sounded, as a car's alarm broke into a wacky fit of noise.

"What happened?" she asked.

"I don't know. Some kind of accident," Jerrold replied.

As the siren of the ambulance reached its crescendo, subsided, and ceased, the space below them filled with new, obtrusive noises, so that Jerrold followed Jessica back into the kitchen, seeking quiet in the quiet of the breakfast nook to look at her amid the kitchen appliances and announce affirmatively, almost out of the blue, "Look, sweetheart. I've got to do this, honey. It's just a long weekend, sugar, only three nights." Jesse was in his chair, seated at the table, playing with his Fruit Loops, picking out tiny, colorful frosted wheels of cereal with his fingers and grouping them into sets of primary and secondary colors on the table alongside his napkin. Jerrold looked at his son, part and parcel of himself, and he imagined proliferations of new neurons, new blossoms in burgeoning cortex, matter coming to terms with a world, becoming a point of view, Jesse's. Where did they ever get the name? Had Jerrold in his childhood admired Jesse James, the outlaw, as he had admired Daniel Boone, the adventurer? No, the idea had been from Jessica, who'd acquired, among her sisters and friends, back in Douglaston, the nickname "Jessie" during early adolescence, but it had never really caught on, and she liked to say she chose the name for its alliteration only, the three "jay" sounds creating a stable, easily spoken, phonetic-bonding element, the common consonant and syllable, something she'd made up for the fun of it. Her mind was always producing private, laudatory ideas and plans, such as gardening projects and things she'd do someday with "my Jay-Jay," her "little outlaw," her "little pal," taking him to the small zoo in Central Park, introducing him to picture books featuring favorite animals, turning the stereo on, singing songs along with him, dancing and clapping hands, but she sometimes spent most of the morning holding Jesse in her lap while she sat on the toilet and smoked weed, or lay alongside of him on the bed, watching TV while listlessly leafing through photographs in fashion magazines, or taking him in his stroller to an outdoor café on Madison Avenue, where she'd flirt with a particular waiter, drink too many glasses of wine, and find returning home difficult.

Jessica's dad had had a business associate and close friend, Jimmy Jespersen, a wiry man, a fishing fanatic with an easy laugh, nicknamed "Jay-Jay," who'd been part owner of the Planter's Thumb, who'd moved to Hollywood, Florida, and started a house-painting company there, which proved to be very lucrative, with houses going up like flares, new homes in the affluent gated communities. Once a year, every year, sometime after Christmas, in late January usually, Jimmy and his young wife, Elizabeth, the tall, athletic "Liz," would trek all the way up I-95 in their dark blue Ford station wagon with the faux-wooden sides, its back loaded with cartons of oranges and grapefruits from Florida and canned peanuts and pecans from Georgia. Jessica remembered Jimmy, the original "Jay-Jay," fondly, and the nickname caught on. She'd hoped that Jesse would bring them, in the middle of the winter, something like joy.

Finished with his Fruit Loops, Jesse threw his spoon into its bowl. Jessica had just sliced a pineapple into chunks, and the tangy fresh flesh, exposed to the sunlight, seemed almost alive.

"It's okay if Mr. Big Deal has to go fishing. We'll do our own thing. We don't need Big Daddy around. Go, really. Go!" Jessica exclaimed, in a tone that bordered on malice. She made a flippant gesture with her left hand, and Jerrold ventured forward to kiss her, but she moved out of range, as she pointed him in the direction of Jesse, changing the subject.

He looked at his son with a sustained, admiring gaze, lost in a moment of self-recognition, unaware that they'd soon enough become seemingly eternal enemies. "He's growing up fast," Jerrold reflected aloud, approaching Jessica, holding her in his arms, acting entrepreneurial, taking her eyes in the vise of his grey matter. "That's what he's going to be doing from now on: growing up quickly. Those neurons are proliferating, Jess, giving structure and birth to a whole new world. It's a stage he's going through. Oh, and by the

way, I'm buying that house in Larchmont, so we're moving to Larchmont soon, sugar." Jerrold, from where he stood, said, with added
emphasis, "Our Jay-Jay, Jess, he's going to grow up like a dignified
gentleman, a squire on an estate. We don't want a city brat." He
tightened the muscles in his legs and planted his feet more firmly
on the floor, crossing his arms, affirming his stance.

The declarative language was striking, and an almost physical
sensation of revulsion at the autocratic utterances spread through
Jessica's body. The shock of the house in Larchmont, the rhetoric of
Jerrold's mentioning it so casually, with almost mock presumption,
made her picture where she was going, and she wasn't sure that she
wanted to be there. It was an overly commodious white colonial on
prime property, right on the water, its borders surrounded by hemlocks and rhododendrons, something Jerrold had seen advertised
in a magazine. He'd always been especially keen on photographs
of houses, and now he was purchasing one that happened to catch
his eye. Jessica didn't want to leave the city. She really didn't want
to leave Manhattan, the sense of being at the center of things she
experienced at her upscale address, in her affluent neighborhood,
the museums, galleries, and shopping, her circle of friends, time
flying, the easy availability of good weed, or, at least, she certainly
didn't want to become another trophy wife in a huge house, stuck
in a wealthy suburb. Jessica felt a deep antipathy for the suburbs,
perhaps because Douglaston was essentially a suburb. Although
she sometimes imagined being happier in some rural location, such
as on a farm in Vermont, or on a remote island rimmed with white
beaches and palm trees, or living like that crazy lady in a jungle
with the chimpanzees, she was perfectly happy where she was.
She'd started jogging around the park in the mornings, guiding Jesse
around the Great Lawn on his tricycle, an infant vehicle—you know
the kind of thing I mean—giving his brain cells the velocity kick,
so that he would seek it on his own someday, and she was seeing
old friends from the fashion world again, renewing old connections.

And with Theresa, the new nanny, around all the time, she was free to go out whenever she wished. When Jerrold was working late, she frequently went to dance clubs. The idea of moving to Larchmont made her feel palpably sick.

Jerrold was going fishing with a pal, a business associate, a certain Donald Woodhouse from Darien, a gentleman of an older generation, a banker at Chase Manhattan, specializing in mergers, on the board of trustees at Wharton, who was also an avid fisherman and at one time a great yacht-racing buff, a real enthusiast, although too much enthusiasm, like too much avidity, isn't necessarily a good thing. Back when EDGE was just getting started, seeking investors from all sectors of the corporate spectrum, Don took a paternal shining to Jerrold, coaching him on the intricacies of high finance, and Jessica and Jerrold had gone out sailing with Don and his much younger wife, the pretty Maureen, several times aboard *Skimmer*, their sixty-six-foot ketch. Don would meet them at the train station, and they'd drive down Nearwater Lane to the Noroton Yacht Club in his big yellow convertible Cadillac, Don yacking away, possessed by a salty, old-school charm, being a real live wire, a rhymer, a rapper, a nutty fruitcake of an old man, chatting on about something nautical while turning into the parking lot of dirtied white pebbles in front of a huge, wooden, almost Gothic building that loomed up from the lot like a once-sunken, submerged ship. "The NO ROTTEN Yacht Club," he affectionately called it, waiting in the parking lot for Maureen to arrive in her little red car, provisions neatly packed into a canvas tote bag. She adored playing hostess, preparing delicate cucumber and crabmeat sandwiches, deviled eggs, and rum punch in a thermos, and it was beautiful out there on the water with a light breeze, when anchored in some comfortable cove, the smells of a shoreline ripe, slightly seasoned with salt, as they all gabbed happily on.

It was then, that sunny May morning when the automobiles collided, crashing beneath the patio overlooking Museum Mile, when Jerrold announced his weekend fishing plans and, as if to compound the effect, the decision to move to Larchmont, that Jessica remembered "Jay-Jay," the original one, Jimmy Jespersen, sitting in the red interior of his dark blue station wagon, waving a hand, getting out and opening the back to unload his cargo of edible comestibles, fruits and nuts, and the image of him running through her, the image she'd hatched of him now, floated forward like a giant white moth, landing on her, covering her face with powdery wings, occluding her mouth entirely.

8

SO JERROLD WENT FISHING THAT WEEKEND, AND THE DRAPERS SOON moved out of the city, first to Larchmont, into that absurdly large colonial mansion with myriad windows, right on the water, just down the road from the yacht club. EDGE, of course, prospered, generating endless success through excellence, making Jerrold and a select group of savvy investors multibillionaires very quickly. He was constantly at work, or play: flying off to Alaska to go bear hunting, or to Scotland for long weekends of fishing, visiting the single-malt distillery he'd bought, entertaining friends and business associates in his Highlands getaway, just an old castle. Jessica found a mother's helper, another Theresa, coincidently enough, who made excellent flan, who could basically raise Jesse for Jessica, be there in her place, so that she was free to come and go at whim, often driving her sleek, silver car into the city, sometimes disappearing for days and lost weekends. Jerrold bought his first yacht, a real racing machine, a fifty-foot yawl, which he named *Scimitar*, and he raced it. The scope of his summertime, home-base activities expanded beyond tennis and yacht racing; he became involved with a waitress at the club- house bar, became infatuated with her, initiating an affair that he'd conduct with her, off and on, for many years. He also became fascinated with an island off the northernmost coast of Maine, fifty acres of barren rock and heather bound by craggy cliffs, finally purchasing it and building a castle-like structure there, using stone imported from Scotland. He bought, for all of them, the black Bentley. He bought Jessica, for her driving delight, the silver Maserati. He bought for himself the blue Jaguar and the green Lamborghini. Somehow, despite Jerrold's flagrant philandering and Jessica's own form of absence, the marriage didn't fall apart. Jesse attended Larchmont Day School, and even in his elementary school days, he somehow got mixed up with a bunch of rebellious older boys.

Growing up on Museum Mile, sheltered by opulence and wealth, Jesse was prone to the convenient illusion that his parents were just like other parents, and he regarded them, at first, as warm, vague presences, wearing fabulously smelling clothes, speaking in cheerful tones, breaking the monotony of his frequently being cooped up alone in the nursery with Theresa, who could be so cold. Mom's laughter, when she was there, seemed grounds for instant levity, and she'd caress Jesse in her way, her voice like a flute, or a piccolo, or a humming of wings, while Dad's words suggested the register of a darker lesson he would someday have to absorb, and as Jesse's experience of the real world grew to include more than his immediate surroundings, he learned to view the surrounding world, whatever slice of it he chose, where the sights and sounds of other lives mixed and multiplied, with a clear sense of advantage and superiority, sensing that the order of things forms a great chain, or ladder, of beings, and he was, by happenstance and the mystery of the paternal bond, cast on an upper rung, a son and heir.

The move to Larchmont improved relations temporarily, as Jerrold and Jesse bonded during those few Saturday and Sunday afternoons when they'd busy themselves with yard work, raking leaves, devoting time to a common outdoor task, feeling any budding antipathy tempered, as anxiety melted away. Jessica, when she was home, would sometimes engage Jesse in a game of tennis, or a swim in the pool, or a walk through the neighborhood, and on one unusually warm Tuesday afternoon, he helped her with her gardening, tending to her treasured plants, the miniature fruit trees and medicinal herbs, this new hobby that she pursued with enthusiasm, soon insisting that a greenhouse/solarium be built.

Jesse seemed changed by the move, becoming a stranger, becoming hyperactive and unruly, having problems with school, showing a disturbing tendency to ignore boundaries, furtively sneaking into the master bedroom and the maze of rooms and large closets that surrounded it, messing around with Jerrold's clothes, expensive art books, and cameras, with Jessica's tools in the greenhouse, exploring his parents' private spaces and things, using the plasma screen in the library to play video games on without permission, breaking into the liquor cabinet, "borrowing" Jerrold's platinum golf clubs one notorious afternoon, behaving oddly, mumbling at the dinner table, dressing poorly, as if he couldn't afford good clothes, wearing torn T-shirts emblazoned with anarchist slogans, embellished with reckless images.

Shortly after the move to Larchmont, while sauntering, while strolling down Main Street one warm May afternoon, having parked the car, jewelry jangling, tentatively exploring the exclusive enclave to which she'd been exiled, peeping into shop windows and adjusting her hair and expectations, Jessica passed the local pet shop, from which she heard the sounds of barking dogs, squawking birds, and a wildly chattering monkey. She stopped in front of the glass, as if shaken, her motion arrested, her attention taken by a glimpse of the most adorable white kitten, a potential Persian cat. Looking at her, its narrow pupils seemed to widen into portals to contentment, bordered by pale green iris, portentous and pure, bringing the cat inside of her out. She named him Rex, the feline principal of the house, frequently waltzing beneath her knees in mute, hirsute elegance, his white tail a plume.

Sometimes, when conditions were right, as Jesse wandered through the rooms of the Larchmont house, empty except for himself and Rex, and Theresa, somewhere too far off to count, it seemed a place of brilliant beauty, thrown into a generous solution from which bright crystals grow, especially in autumn, so many manifestations of falling freely, especially with the passing of a particularly powerful shower one dull, grey, soundless afternoon, after an unusually long stretch of warm Indian summer weather, a chain of heavenly days, the sugar maples flaring, flashing multivalued ruby hues, with outbursts of orange and yellow: the oaks, elms, and beeches hidden in the proliferation of dark green hemlocks framing the backyard of the enormous house, set on its rise of manicured lawn. Jesse had been downstairs, playing the airplane game in his seclusion, where he stretched his arms out, careening around, as if flying, imitating the hum of engines on, high in the air, but in his socks, running, sliding, gliding on the polished wooden floors, while Rex slept on a cushion, and now Jesse was alone, upstairs in his room, as he watched the hired help rake leaves onto burlap tarps and carry them off on their backs, stooped like peasants. One was walking with a wheelbarrow, and some were using yard tools, and he wondered, looking through the window, what it was like to really work, what working out there was like, what it was like to be doing that.

Early one Saturday evening, just before the move to Belle Haven, Jesse was looking out from his bedroom window, anxiously waiting for a friend from school to ride his bicycle into the driveway. Sometimes at home with nothing to do, Jesse, now fourteen, was difficult, distant, and sullen, and he'd retreat into an introspection, an alienation from which no amount of artful vivacity could retrieve him, not RPM, not his new computer nor even his new aquarium, not before his friend rode in, prompting this action: Jesse ran downstairs in a hurry and a black sweater, swooped through the kitchen, and opened the refrigerator door to scoop up a can of beer, slipping it inside his back pants pocket, just as Jerrold arrived in the green Lamborghini, home from an undisclosed location, one of the places where he had his trysts, so that father and son passed through the pantry hallway simultaneously that evening, almost colliding, Jesse going out and Jerrold coming in, silent in their passages, separate ships, neither venturing any attempt to acknowledge the other, no questions asked.

Although his first years of fatherhood, years ago, had been fueled by the sense of a natural procreative impulse fulfilled, infused with genuine compassion and warmth for his new family, a sense of purpose, posing for photographs, feeling the promise of something unknown about to begin and give his life its higher order and new dimension, the magic of paternity was something for which Jerrold eventually felt very little, almost nothing, finding Jesse's presence, as he matured into a surly teenager, clearly acting out some form of oedipal rivalry, to be an irritant to the smooth, regulated flow of his own orderly thoughts. Jesse imposed a massive shift of his perspective. Jerrold still cherished Jessica, harboring pangs of lust for her body. He positively adored her Nordic beauty, her icy nonchalance, her cheeky sense of humor, her place as partner at important social events and dinner parties, his "sex buddy," as he referred to her, off the record, to business associates, but the reality of a baby, first an infant screaming for attention, then a bundle of centrifugal forces seeking satisfaction, a continual absence of attention requiring supervision and disciplinary action, now a sullen teenager with whom he had nothing in common, was all too much, and it made being married with one son somehow farcical. There seemed to be something wrong, something askew and dysfunctional, about Jesse from the start, this consequence of his seed and its conjunction with fertile soil, a buried strain of something from Jessica's side of the bargain, he thought, present since infancy, shown in his automatic resistance to instruction, whatever Jerrold might be trying to impress upon him, explain to him, Jesse seeming not to understand, which was why he was a wild child, howling into the night. He remembered how uncertain Jesse sometimes seemed, so tentative, seized by a strange hesitancy, even trepidation, as if what he was experiencing didn't make any sense, as if he couldn't make any sense of a situation, take charge of it, Jerrold having to help him tie his shoes, having to show him how to butter bread with a knife, having to hold his hand while taking the elevator down to the lobby, while walking out to the street, where a black limousine was parked. Once, before the move to Larchmont, he believed that Jesse would become a new, significant part in the project, the ongoing construct of his life, something beyond sex and finance to be concerned about, but it wasn't happening, as his thoughts became muddied, modulated, shifting to new content: a glimpse of a woman walking, her perfect legs, his thoughts finding diversion in finding her number, the right number for her, his constant lust for quantification dominating the operations of his mental life. He'd become enormously bored with Jessica, as they moved in different circles, Jerrold's busy and important life revolving around a dominant, dominating need for novelty, coming to terms with the world his way, which drove his behavior when he was away from home, so he stayed out of the house as much as possible, his attention consumed with EDGE, his passion for possession. He didn't really know what to do or say when he was with Jesse, hardly interacting, distancing himself from him, just as he distanced himself from Jessica, justifying his behavior by his own father's authoritative, autocratic, and remote approach to child-rearing, as he, when a very young boy, had felt estranged by the steadiness of Joseph's emasculating, enervating stare.

So the days went by, and Jerrold's father suddenly died, an event for which everyone was completely unprepared. Joe and Cecelia were enjoying their golden years in Florida. Joe had been out for an early round of golf one morning, at the club in Jupiter Beach, when he suffered a sudden, massive stroke, and it was one sunny Sunday afternoon in October, shortly after the funeral, Jerrold having just returned from the airport, having overseen the dispersal of his father's ashes into the surf of the Atlantic Ocean, the Gulf Stream. The three of them were alone in the Larchmont house, Jesse in his room upstairs, listening to music, Jessica watching TV in the bedroom, while Jerrold was sitting in his leather chair in the library, sipping from a glass of expensive Scotch, having just concluded a telephone conversation regarding his mother's relocation to a nursing home in West Palm Beach, leafing through the real estate section of a glossy magazine, looking for something to capture, to seize, when he saw the ad for the Romanesque villa, with its castle-like, crenellated walls, its impenetrable, steep expanses of stucco oriented by the cardinal points of the compass, its great, curving roofs of terra-cotta tile, its large glass windows, their casements wrought of stone, its megalithic masonry. As he sat in the leather chair, holding the magazine closer to his face, Jerrold studied the photograph in the ad with a magnifying glass. All of its essential attributes were visible. He wrote the relevant details down. There was no other way to explain it, and the days went by, and the Drapers moved to Belle Haven.

9

THE HOUSE IN LARCHMONT HAD BEEN LARGE, WITH FAR TOO MANY rooms, doors, and windows, but the new one was even larger, with a great, open breezeway leading to galleries with marble floors, a ballroom with a ceiling several stories high, an indoor swimming pool, a huge backyard, spread out like several football fields, with a meadow beyond it. At the very edge of their property there was a stone wall, and behind it stood the back of a tennis court, part of the estate next door, property of Randolph ("Rolf") Holt, who happened to have been a classmate of Jerrold's at Wharton. The Holt boys were four of a kind, a crew of rowdy extroverts, athletic boys for whom life was all about competition and glory, winning and having fun while doing so, because winning and having fun in some sort of organized way formed the measure of behavior. Rolf was a bigwig at Merrill Lynch, and during the weekends, when he was home, he seemed to be always driving his boys off to some athletic event in their shiny black Mercedes-Benz van, a vehicle with tinted windows and a secretive, governmental aura about it. The Holt boys appeared to laugh a lot, exuding the carefree attitude of those who are raised in an atmosphere of entitlement and privilege yet somehow unspoiled by the power it entails. All the sons, except one, had blond hair, wavy like their father's, and whatever they were doing, you felt they meant well, grinning with enthusiasm and high spirits. Before marrying Virginia, Rolf had briefly pursued a career in golf, traveling around the world and playing the professional circuit, not for the money but because he enjoyed the game so much, having learned, at an early age, all about swinging clubs and hitting balls from his own father, an illustrious industrialist, on the course at the Wee Burn Country Club in Darien. Rolf had been born into, as he liked to put it, "the lap of luxury," taking a great, rollicking pleasure in the very sounds of the phrase as he pronounced it, letting it roll for what it was worth. He'd grown up in a mansion on Long Neck Point Road, and he might have remained, after graduating from Harvard, a semipro and playboy, a wastrel and great embarrassment to his eminent, properly WASPy parents, had he not met and married Virginia, the bewitched and bewitching beauty from Vassar, an art history major, already becoming established in her field, for whom he gave up golf, for whom he felt indelible lust, to whom he was bound, with whom he then settled down in Belle Haven, buying the big house and property, a splendid Victorian mansion, strikingly reminiscent of his own childhood home, with its labyrinthine gardens, tall chimneys, stained-glass windows, and black iron fences. Virginia somehow managed, with hired help, to balance the harried experience of raising four boys with the demands of her busy career, co-ownership of a blue-chip gallery on 57th Street that dealt exclusively with contemporary painting and sculpture. She'd begun to collect art, paintings, during her year abroad, in Paris, and she maintained a sort of private small museum on the first floor of the house in Belle Haven, an important collection of painterly, early Abstract-Expressionist outbursts, like blazes on a mountain trail, contrasting effectively with the mute interiors, the almost medieval, monastic silence of the enormous space when nobody was home, which was often, with everyone usually out, Virginia at the gallery, Rolf at the office, the boys busy with school and athletics. During the summer months, all of the boys played tennis and raced fiberglass sailboats at the Yacht Club, though only one of them, Randy, the youngest, really excelled at sailing, having something of the sea in his genes. The eldest boy, Richard—"Ricky," as his parents affectionately nicknamed him—had the easy, disarming smile of a natural-born athlete, a winner and a charmer, distinguishing himself on the playing field at Sunswyck Academy by being the first student to captain three varsity teams for three consecutive terms: lacrosse, hockey, and tennis, and the other three boys all looked up to Ricky, who, being the eldest by more than three years, could, without much effort, simulate his powerful father's authoritative voice, of which his seemed a microcosm. Robert, their next boy, was more intellectually inclined, bookish, sometimes remote, but an excellent tennis and baseball player, showing an innate familiarity with the physics of balls in motion. Robert, like his older brother, was superbly coordinated, a star athlete and student, but, also like his older brother, he was but a mediocre sailor, just not that comfortable around saltwater, and he, like Ricky, was never really part of the Yacht Club scene. Ralph, the third born, the rebel of the bunch, the future tennis champion, wore his long blond hair tied up in a bandana, much to his father's consternation, as he ran about on the court, slicing the air with an aluminum racket, but

Randy, the only boy who wasn't blond, the one with Virginia's red hair, really excelled at sailing. He just loved being around boats, out on the water, eventually making a name for himself racing his fiberglass, single-sail racing craft, equipped with trapeze, competing in regattas, winning trophies. Randy was Jesse's age, just fifteen, when the Drapers first moved into the neighborhood, and he became for a short while Jesse's best friend, as Randy just happened to have Jesse as his lab partner in their Introduction to Physical Science class at Sunswyck, where Jesse was a new student; together they conducted experiments, some involving substances suspended in liquids, working with Bunsen burners, scrutinizing graduated cylinders, weighing precipitates on scales, measuring the results of their precise experiments, duly recording data on pages and pages of graph paper. Eventually they formed a friendship, based on their science class partnership and a shared, unexpected interest in a board game: chess, as Jesse had discovered, in a cabinet in the library of the new house, revealed in the process of moving, Jerrold's old board and pieces, a memento from his MIT days.

Jessica, Jesse, and Randy sometimes ate dinner together, when Jerrold was away and when Jessica was home, if Randy still happened to be hanging around after playing chess with Jesse, Jessica feeling obligated to have Theresa serve them all, set places for the three of them at the vast black table with a hard, shiny surface like an opaque sea of ebony lacquer, where the two boys seemed cast up on remote islands, each too intimate to explore. Jesse, watching the ice in his mother's glass melt, now that her "little pal" had matured into a complicated human being, trained inward, looked as if he were waiting for someone to start a conversation, and he saw Jessica's stony silence break, as she put her drink down. Mom—impatient, easy to please, sloppily sympathetic to Randy's side of the situation, it seemed—was super-soused again, her ability to control her emotions and facial expressions obliterated, so that whatever evening meal they shared, one like many others, an ordinary evening in Belle

Haven, overseen by the perpetually present Theresa, coming out of the kitchen, passed with the usual, banal confusion.

The two boys began to ride their bikes together, exploring the long, winding roads of northern Greenwich, as the bond between Randy and Jesse grew and was soon mirrored, paralleled, by the friendship that developed between Virginia and Jessica, back when Jessica was purchasing paintings and sculpture to decorate the new house, which had become her pet project, filling the floor and wall spaces, actually keeping her at home more, trapped in the principle of a great beyond she was just beginning to feel accustomed to. Jessica knew nothing about contemporary art, but Virginia was aware of Jessica, the celebrated model whose face and figure she'd immediately recognized from fashion magazines, and she envied her more than a little at first, but as they met and conversed, getting to know each other, first at crowded parties and later at more intimate gatherings, luncheons, and parties, as Jerrold and Rolf became friendly too, they became almost intimate equals, and it was as if the Drapers and the Holts had formed a temporary, kinetic bonding agreement, with Jesse and Randy, two boys the same age, teenagers with similar inclinations, pursuing the same ends, somehow being the foundation of it all. So Jessica sought Virginia for her expertise in contemporary art, urging her, asking her to accompany her, Jessica, to several important auctions, helping her decide what to buy, assuring Jerrold that Virginia's vast knowledge of contemporary art would enable her, Jessica, to make choices that could only appreciate in value. Speculating, putting her visual experience to work through verbalization, was her field of EXPERT TEASE, as she spoke of "passionate painterly passages" that, as she put it, "just worked," that made her eyes "feel satisfied," her discourse peppered with suggestive phrases, like "the integrity of the picture plane," which was "an arena in which to act" using "binding curves of NRG"—words that Jessica found somehow memorable as she learned about contemporary art and developed an eye of her own.

She discovered that she gravitated toward an austere, minimalist aesthetic, and she eventually made some important purchases: a floor sculpture of copper plates, an outdoor work of granite boulders arranged in a circle on the front lawn, and a suite of six large, almost electrically white paintings, not hanging but actually mounted to the wall with metal braces, nearly identical fields, five-by-five-foot squares of striking blankness, each one actually a shade of white, almost imperceptibly tinctured red, yellow, blue, orange, green, and purple, suggesting a rainbow that complemented the curves and complexities of Jessica's plants, riots of green growth that she kept in clay urns aesthetically positioned throughout the spacious gallery on the first floor, near where, in a room off the north wing, Randy and Jesse first played chess, teaching themselves the rules of the game on the carpet, an authentic weaving of talismanic value, just the two of them, using an old instruction manual they'd found on a shelf in Jerrold's study, something from his MIT days, back when he'd studied and mastered the game, the sixty-four-square looking glass.

The Holts were known for hosting fabulous Friday night parties, unselfconscious celebrations of the good life and its accoutrements, with live music and an abundance of alcohol acting as a catalyst for happy adult mayhem, breaking borders down, so that responsibilities were postponed and inhibitions overcome, and a mood of reckless affection prevailed, wherein Rolf, Jerrold, and Jack, a trio with the distinction of being able to drink and laugh a lot together, made plans for the upcoming weekend: sailing, tennis, golf, or fishing, sometimes flying off somewhere for a real adventure on Jerrold's private jet, or just hanging out at Rolf's, drinking Scotch and playing pool in the basement. At one point, the three of them all bought authentic handmade kayaks, the hulls fabricated from real seal skin, which they'd paddle around on weekend mornings, sometimes competitively, in the harbor, just the three of them, holding informal races when Jerrold was home, which wasn't often. So

Jack and Rolf spent the most time together, and I saw much less of Jerrold, who, when I did see him, always seemed to be experimenting with his hairstyle, challenging my memory of any clear, stable image I might form of it, finding it broken down into different characters from isolated episodes. Although the color was usually black, greying slightly at the edges, his hair began to appear, inexplicably, at different lengths; it would be short, in a crew cut, and then, just a month later, it would suddenly be long. One day he sported a quirky goatee, making him look devilish, scorpion-like, when he showed up at the door, looking for Jack, who was out back raking leaves. Another time I saw him in brown hair so long and lush I thought he was wearing a wig. Rolf's hairstyle never changed, always the same neat cut, an organized cap of black, no grey at the sides, each hair always in place, while Jack, with luxuriant blond hair like mine, let the length of his vary according to seasonal changes, temperature shifts. There was a brief period of time when Jerrold had had his head shaved, and that bold baldness characterizes, with all the preludes over and the curtain finally risen, my cinematic image of a very intoxicated Jerrold running off the dance floor and out into the Holts' backyard, all of the lights shining on him, as he leapt, fully clothed, into the swimming pool, making a climactic splash that only a few of us noticed, to return through the open French doors, dripping with water, as if he'd emerged from another planet's gravitational field, laughing with a morbid nonchalance, his wet clothes clinging to him, while the Holts' dog, Woofer, a black lab, barked at his side in excited, participatory appreciation.

Everyone knew about Jerrold's erotic exploits and excesses, his voracious sexual drive, but only in a vague and indistinct way. It was all by innuendo, something that was whispered about, hinted at, and intimately alluded to at crowded cocktail parties, where Jack and I mixed with our new neighbors, keeping, at first, our appropriate distance, listening and mingling, maintaining an aesthetic remove that has long since ceased to concern me. Jerrold had women all over the world, but somehow he never brought any of it, any of his compulsive womanizing, back home to the villa in Belle Haven, where a kind of mannered decorum reigned, a reflection of his wealth and taste, his mannerisms becoming increasingly reminiscent of a secret agent, some kind of James Bond. Somehow he kept the enormous house and the façade of a tiny, tightly knit, happy family dwelling within its fortress-like presence sacrosanct. It was through Virginia Holt, who'd been so close to Jessica, that I learned about his then-current mistress, Anna, an athletic beauty, a basketball player, her dark skin reflecting the steady rhythms of the sun, a chambermaid at the Hyatt Hotel on Grand Cayman, where Jerrold was always off to, "on business," he'd say, arranging for business to be mixed with the highest pleasure he knew, the one that convulsed his whole being. Bound to, and increasingly burdened by, a marriage that imposed the conventional role of a void on him, he felt deadened by the dire predictability of the motions he went through with Jessica. He was compelled by a desire to break away, which he did, finding what was, for him, the object of a compulsion, a material swelling reminding him every waking second of the day it sometimes seemed, that he was thinking with that fire in his loins again, possessed by the rage for something new, his pangs of perpetual lust, and he sought the eternal, erotic embrace, penetrating secret places, finding his ecstasy with his release. He developed a repertoire of seductive phrases with which to spike his lascivious banter. Jerrold's habitual haunts, at first, were bars and nightclubs, where he'd pick up beautiful women and take them back to a hotel room, but eventually he became more brazen, approaching women in open daylight and, as he liked to put it to his associates, "nailing them," clasping buttocks, breasts, and hips whenever the opportunity arose, on empty seats on jet planes, in closets and bathroom stalls, against a car in a parking lot, under an umbrella on a beach, in ditches alongside dirt roads: These were the sites of his conquests. Jerrold developed a special attachment to Anna, the chambermaid at the Hyatt, who was different in an earthy sort of way, her perspiration real and slightly antiseptic due to salt content, and they'd copulate on a foam mattress behind a tennis court at night.

10

MEANWHILE, SOMEWHERE OUT IN YES STIR DAY, SOMETIME NEAR the Pacific Ocean, deep in the hold of real time, geological time, the kind my daughter studied in Colorado, the kind the mind can't fathom easily, distant as DECAYED ANTS, before adopting "Omnibus" as an alternative moniker, a pen name, a pseudonym he found suitable one incredibly hot afternoon marooned amid thousands of vehicles, years after decidedly digging the sky and the weather, the density of his surroundings during those formative years in Bakersfield, part of a group set apart from the student body, picking up new vibrations from RPM in TLC, the electromagnetic ether, Oscar Topaz was not just another kid in Bakersfield, sitting in the front row of his Introduction to Physical Science class, the inertia and boredom of the first five minutes morphing into a mild, supple, periodic interest in what the teacher was attempting to plant in his head. He was a future page turner, a student of hydrodynamics and electricity, fond of fast, fluid guitar-work, an avid *Scientific American* reader, a whiz kid with a future in computers probably, though he'd originally favored audio production whenever he'd thought about a career, which he didn't do often, not until the end of his second year at Cal Tech, when he'd decided to major in electrical engineering, to focus on electron flow, but that was after his "experimental semester" at the Brie College of Art, sometimes called "the Last Art School," sometimes "the Marxist art school," once referred to as "the only place to study Conceptual Art," way off, way up in Halifax, Nova Scotia, a busy port city, where the public parks are commodious and well maintained, where the scents of tar, salt, and dead fish mix to pervade the downtown area with a distinctive aroma—Halifax, where Alexander Graham Bell stayed, with his young wife, Mabel, at the Victoria Hotel, during a summer trip to Sable Island—Halifax, once dubbed "the armpit of the provinces," where the harbor is famously deep.

Oscar, in the course of his high school years, had nurtured a lively interest in contemporary art, leafing through the flashy magazines, heavy books, and gallery catalogues in the Bakersfield Public Library. Inspired by what he saw and thought about, he decided that he'd someday make Kinetic Sculpture. He won a scholarship to Cal Tech, and he moved to LA, where, in tandem with his academic interests and responsibilities, he began to work his eye and brain in useless, imaginative ways. He made small sculptures with sharp, metal edges, assembling paper clips, razor blades, and long strands of copper wire into mobiles he'd hang from the ceiling of his dormitory room. He soon set up a makeshift studio in the basement. The demands of coursework contended with his ongoing aesthetic expeditions, Kinetic Sculpture becoming a destiny he felt he couldn't avoid. He explored a variety of mediums, soon constructing huge, balloon-like tents, made from black plastic bags, held together by insulated wire and strips of adhesive tape. Somewhere, in an art magazine, he'd read about "Conceptual Art," and he became fascinated with the idea that sculpture, itself, was an idea: a chair of air, a fiery spear, a vast stream of notions that harmonized strangely with strings already vibrating inside of him. Suddenly, by a trick of the mind, like a bell ringing up a curtain, he carried a new conviction. As he explored the vast mass of literature on which the existence of Conceptual Art was founded, a heady mixture of ideas, contexts, and issues, he became aware, as a submarine in motion, probing uncharted ocean floor, of grounds for a new reality, a rare terrain, easy to indicate, but not easily experienced and impossible to explain. It was Oscar's still-submerged vision of an expanded and unified sculptural field, steeling his heart with the certainty of whatever works, whatever prepares us for the shapes of things to come. In another magazine, he read about a distant art school, far away, on the other side of the continent, located in Halifax, Nova Scotia, of all places, an entirely different part of the planet, the Brie College of Art, named after that region in France that inspired both cheese makers and landscape painters. Conceptual Art was actually studied, taught, and practiced at Brie College, and he felt himself pulled into the direction of its enigma. A part of him just wanted to do something new in a small, foreign city. There was also the appeal of the maritime climate, so grey and cool, so unlike California, and so, having completed the academic requirements for his degree in electrical engineering, Oscar Topaz spent the spring semester of his senior year in Halifax, experimenting, goofing off in a sense, indulging his own precise whimsies, working with his brain and hands, making Kinetic Sculpture, studying Conceptual Art, not knowing that he, doing time at Brie, was being programmed to become "Omnibus," the nickname that caught on.

Oscar shared a bungalow with his girlfriend, Amy, somewhere near the center of Manhattan Beach, just a few blocks from the ocean. Computer data storage units, then, were cumbersome and large, requiring entire rooms, clean and well lit, and Oscar had found lucrative employment installing electrical lighting in corporate "safe rooms," spaces kept at a constant cool temperature of sixty degrees, special, lab-like environments, free of such external disturbances as dust and noise, where the storage units emitted a low hum. During the workweek he parked the company van in their small driveway and drove it to his job, which was, invariably, an installation site in downtown LA, at the heart of all the new construction. Amy worked at a public high school just a few blocks away from home, where she taught belligerent teenagers algebra. Blond and intelligent, she possessed the youthful ardor of a cheerleader, with a vivacious lift about her walk, as if she were always about to leap into the air and fly off.

One afternoon while driving home from work, after installing overhead electrical lighting in the safe room of a new corporation, Oscar was stuck in traffic, enduring useless information streaming from the radio, the plastic and metal smells of indoor lighting equipment and tools still clinging to him, weighing the wings of his nascent imagination, the late afternoon sun hanging oppressively low, a dollop of fat in a boiling sky, when he was struck by the audacity of his being immobilized, stranded there, contained by a carapace of metal, and he pondered the inanity of his situation, one he'd been in many times before, but somehow it was different this time, almost a hallucination.

Out on the road, where a new kind of emptiness prevailed, Oscar sat, thinking of what he'd do when he reached home—take a shower, turn on the stereo, open a bottle of wine. Oscar had always harbored ambivalent feelings about the van and its components: infant, mechanical things, now melding into each other, meddling with each other. It was a necessity, just like his job, but its ultimate purpose perplexed and eluded him. He saw himself there, catching his eyes in the rearview mirror, and he cast a sustained, questioning glance into the space beyond his pupils, peering into the runways of his brain, and something took flight that afternoon, soothing inside, his mirrored, multiplied eyes changing forever his understanding of past, present, and future, scrambling the shells of time, becoming diamonds the size of golf balls. Synapses snapped, a door in the wall of his cerebellum opened, and the alienating armor of his identity melted away, as if a higher neural form had completed its growth in his brain, now ushered into being, scanning itself, and he felt inexplicably elated and free and at the same inextricably bound to a context and its itinerary, as if he'd been selected, chosen, and his feet smiled with the chains wound above them, fastened at his ankles.

He reached a sort of tipping point behind the steering wheel that day. He was being held captive, caught between it and the black leather seat, stuck on concrete, one in a vast collection of gasoline sculptures, arrested, bound, marooned in a caravan of cars, trucks, vans, and buses, all stopped, feet useless with accelerators versus traffic, and everyone wanted to step on an accelerator, but they were all stalled, like parts in an installation. Oscar, nose now twitching, just sitting there, busy doing nothing, saw and received himself again, putting his pupils, putting his PEEPHOLES, more deeply into the rearview mirror. There was something he'd never been before: a rabbit, a fluffy white bunny with jet-black, beady eyes, perfected opacities. He was becoming Omnibus, the OMNISCIENT, OMINOUS BOSS, and it all seemed so arranged, to the point of his derangement, becoming animal. He looked around the van, sniffing for the significance of its interior, scanning door handles, dials, and buttons. He looked out again at all the stranded vehicles, remote, alien intelligences, forms charged with a new significance, as if there were something that had to be explained. "My mind's a cauldron," he thought, as he felt a sudden urge to get out and run. He pushed a button with his thumb, and the window automatically went down with an almost imperceptible rumbling, as a blast of hot air hit him, his nose and whiskers quivering, nostrils flaring, tweaking information out of the sultry mix. He was seized by a desire to be out in it, so he opened the door. He hopped right out of the van, happy to be free, and he stood up straight and paused. Paw held as visor shielding the sun, he looked out and saw gasoline sculptures, shapes in a thick paste of grey haze. With one last scan, he hatched the idea of hopping away forever, bouncing off into the distance, leaving the van's keys intact, its engine idling. With a final look at the seat belt undone in the place where he'd sat at the wheel, in a modality of consciousness I associate with a slap of water to the face, Oscar, becoming Omnibus, remembering the "rabbit ears" on the television set of his youth in

Bakersfield, the TV set in a corner of the living room, in front of the drapes, giving himself over to being a set of antennae, muttered, "Melt Along The Vertical," which he abbreviated as "MA-TV," a kind of slogan, chanting this mantra for himself and for everyone. "MA-TV," he said again and again, "MA-TV," "MA-TV," now fully morphing into Omnibus, although just the thought of it, a kind of televising of immediate sensory experience, a distancing of himself from the immediacy of his perceptions, a way of suspending his commitment to existence and its massive realities, stepping back to assess it, celebrating the miracle of veridical thinking itself, how so many thoughts can be true of the world as it is, as it appears to be, so that things are what they seem to be and one's steps simply fall where they will, which is sufficient, boggled his mind, pushing him close to and over an edge, passing into a permanent state of movement, making the pavement blur, with no way of knowing whether what he was doing made any sense, eluding the burden of mental content, and, as he hopped through the air, almost flying away from the van in a rabbit's trance, feet smiling, he tripped on an empty aluminum can, causing his fall, bringing his jaw down in an almost masochistic union with the sandy ground, where he noticed, there on the side of the highway, particles of green glass and black asphalt fragments lit by a waning sun. He raised his head to see myriad corkscrews of dark exhaust twirl upward from the gasoline sculptures. He set his head back down on the ground, letting it rest there, and he saw something alongside him, his lenses pressed closer, pushed into the details, something glimmering down there among the asphalt fragments and glass particles: a group of ants dressed in red robes, some wearing headgear, illuminated, like tiny iridescent antlers, some carrying miniature light bulbs, some carrying tufts of green plant material, parsley probably, between raised mandibles. Omnibus recalled a butterscotch candy wrapped in a silver wrapper in his back pocket, now melting, now sticky as he took it out and, with concentration and dexterity, peeled the thin metal paper away, placing the candy, after a quick taste test, there on the ground with his saliva on it, attracting racing ants, a rapidly arriving army of busy bodies, monsters in their own worlds, as a large truck shifted into gear and glided with a slow groan forward, honking its horn for emphasis. The spaces between the cars expanded, and the traffic became unjammed, but one vehicle remained stationary. People drove around it. Omnibus, oblivious to his van, was now engrossed with ants, focused on these tiny motors, ruby red, rushing around over what was left of the candy, soon devoured in a voracious swarm. The ants then disappeared into the spaces between the sand and pebbles, finally retreating into the tall grass on the highway's shoulder, and Omnibus, blinking in the delight of their relevance, stood up and melted along the vertical to practice MA-TV some more, chanting "MA-TV, MA-TV," finding it to be an effective form of meditation, a way of providing mediation, for form was all that mattered. He stood there like a steeple, a holy place to be, deciding that he'd quit his current job and become an entomologist, that he'd seek to know ants and their habitats.

He returned to the van, took the metal keys out of the ignition, and threw them on the plastic seat, slamming the door shut for the last time, its metal bulk illuminated by a fat, red sun cushioned on a bank of purple cloud, and he walked though a swath of tall, green grass peppered with wild flowers, buttercups, baby's breath, and yellow dandelions, up to an exit ramp, and he walked all the way home, seeing the earth move under his feet, arriving late, finding Amy out, finding a message on the machine; she was still at school, staying late to help students prepare for the upcoming SAT exams. He was able to walk around the kitchen table, staying in motion, just like an ant. He walked upstairs to the room where, typically, he'd sit and read, but he couldn't sit down. He didn't have the head for it. He thought about the chair, but he wouldn't have anything to do with it. He kept walking around, moving his hands in circular motions in front of him, placing his hands at the sides of his head, acting oddly, for now he had antennae; he was wearing head-gear, and although he was moving around in circles, he stopped in front of the bookshelf and took down an ancient, cumbersome, hardcover, clothbound atlas, something from his boyhood days in Bakersfield, and he pored with diamond eyes over maps, into pages and pages of maps, until he reached the back of the book, finding an appendix of pages depicting flags, and he noticed, listed under "Africa," Gabon's flag of three horizontal bands: blue, yellow, and green representing the sky, sun, and plant material, which works without any conscience and/or observable consciousness, by gas and osmosis, practically unconscious, which is how Omnibus works, which makes him feel small and free and organized, like a species of transparent, apolitical ant, indigenous to Gabon, known to form, in symbiotic synthesis with its peers, ribbons of a highly reactive, tar-like substance spreading through the Jungle in black, glistening tracks. "I will go to Gabon," he said to himself, closing the atlas.

11

A BREEZE CAME TO THE AID OF SOME WILTED ROSE PETALS SCATTERED on a brick walkway, and all things became more expansive, no longer inert, as I am pumping them up for show, pitting pink against red with a mere push of air, as Jessica, back in Belle Haven, in the master bedroom upstairs, sleepily opened her eyes to scrutinize the clock on her bedside table, bringing its digits into focus with a squint: 10:00 a.m., the time of a stick with three holes attached to it. She yawned and rubbed her eyes. Jerrold was away again, on business in Africa. She'd been rising, getting up late now for days. A boy rode by on a bicycle, wheels spinning with light, past the Drapers' gated entrance, and a brown UPS truck, shifting gears, began its slow ascent toward a gigantic Georgian mansion, then on the market, almost the size of a dormitory on a college campus, surrounded by acres of park-like, manicured landscape, obsessively formal, its decorative boxwood topiary complementing the main building's commanding bulk, echoing its contours, augmented by newly added pavilions, all set at the topographical center and high point of the peninsula that is Belle Haven. It was a mild, breezy morning, and the air was sweet with birdsong. Shrubbery, bushes, trees, and lawns, houses and gasoline sculptures sat contentedly in the lap of the always-accommodating "GREEN WITCH," Jack's expression popping into my mind again, while, down the road, Rolf Holt called out to Woofer, the big black lab, stooping to pick up a stick and throw it to be fetched. "Go get it, boy," he said with a hearty laugh.

Jerrold, the night before, had stood on the balcony of his hotel room in Gabon. Pieces of NRG flung out through space, the stars were glittering and remote, beautiful like airplane lights, myriad mysterious jewels, millions, billions bewildering Jerrold's calculative powers that balmy night in Libreville, an unseen tableau of cloud towering over his head, unfolding above the sweltering, simmering city below, this scene sewn quickly into place. The asphalt surface of a recently paved parking lot in the downtown area gleamed, its black space marked by yellow lines, lit, exposed, oddly apparent, the tar plateau suddenly there, as if put on display, illuminated by electric light. He savored the site, so that we might pass from this to the real subject of our concern, buried in the distance with some insistence. He heard the articulations of nocturnal Libreville rise from the busy streets below, the almost anarchistic sounds of people and music, a boisterous, communal surround. He rolled up his sleeves.

Jerrold could feel the potential, the pull of untallied resources, reserves out there in the Jungle, submerged, sunk in dark murk: first, there was silver and gold, then diamonds, rubies, sapphires, and emeralds, then the precious minerals, titanium and bauxite, key to producing aluminum, and now the rare earth metals, exceptional ores, especially Unobtainium, folded deeply and deeply folded inside the cold clay blanket of the lithosphere and the unchecked, primeval growth of life on its crust, the green machine of microbial circuitry, flourishing since the Carboniferous Period, when silent systems of vascular plants, teeming with life, the work of photosynthesis, first sprang toward its present, profuse abundance, no sentient consciousness anywhere to hear it unfold. It was like he was a child again, as his imagination took flight, moving through space, wearing a jet pilot's helmet. Titanium's a magic metal, light and incredibly durable, highly resistant to corrosion by saltwater, key to the construction of torpedoes and satellites, sought after by the aerospace and weapons industries, and bauxite is the main ore deployed in smelting aluminum, that ubiquitous stuff, but Jerrold felt most the pull of Unobtainium, king of the rare earth substances, a superconductor, able to contain an unprecedented density of electrons in an area the size of a pin's head.

A star from afar sent a steady beam of NRG, an intense wave of particles, a spirited ray, into the open, windy center of Jerry's capacious consciousness, and his spirits seemed to rise as he stood on the balcony, surveying the evening, busy with cars and lights, and he stretched his arms out, taking it all in, the nocturnal glow, conjuring prodigious distances, glad to be key to this new EDGE venture in Africa, which he knew to be true, because he himself was making it happen. The promise of a deal sealed always brought a light tremor of excitement to his lips, putting the tiny muscles of his face into play with the symmetry of contentment, creating a parallel world within, flashing like a great mirror to the sun, comparing, computing, bent inward to become invariable law, for he'd already made up in time what he'd experience soon enough in space, and a sign on a distant rooftop blinked its agreement.

Argent Rare Metals Ltd. ("Argent"), founded in the late nineteenth century by an enterprising group of London and Parisian businessmen, named for the abundant reserves of silver discovered at the original site, had owned and controlled a vast network of mines, some of them linked to naturally formed underground caves, all feeding covertly into one another beneath the dense, verdant, almost impenetrable rain forest canopy carpeting the southern slopes of Crystal Mountain, which were covered with mahogany, balsawood, and okua trees, with concentrated groves of zebrawood and African walnut flourishing in places. Argent, since the start of TLC, had dominated the market for silver, but by mid-century, after the rush on bauxite and titanium, the mines had been abandoned. A research team of geologists had, however, recently discovered Unobtainium in a particularly remote cave, property owned by Argent, before it was sold to/bought by EDGE. Mining Unobtainium required new technology and the implementation of a sophisticated infrastructure that Jerrold was there to review.

The next day, during a long meeting with Argent executives and legal advisors, sitting around a huge oval table in a conference room, signatures concurred, the deal was definitively sealed, and now the night air, the bright lights of Libreville, hummed with the promise of profit. Anonymously moving through the crowded streets, walking back to his hotel room, Jerrold, with his flair for financial wizardry, felt a robust optimism about new markets opening for Unobtainium, especially in the burgeoning telecommunications industry, when the prediction of worldwide cell phone use was still just a prospector's hunch, a prophecy. There were some birds he'd seen earlier that day, in the morning, while looking through the window of a black limousine, while being driven to the meeting place, while squinting through tinted glass at the white-feathered creatures with incredibly long wings, storks of some kind, fighting for the limited space on the corrugated tin roof of a decrepit building, making a horrific cackling and squawking, a rooftop he'd passed again hours ago on his way to the restaurant, riding in the black limousine, and the birds were still there, almost motionless, beaks buried in feathers, seemingly asleep, each in its place, standing on one leg. He was passing the building again, for the third time that day, now walking back to his hotel room, returning from a celebratory dinner with business associates, and he noticed the exposed sheet of corrugated tin, the empty roof, illuminated by a streetlamp, and the absence of the birds. He wondered where they'd flown off to, recollecting, vaguely, something he had heard somewhere about a local bird species that flew and hunted at night, using nocturnal vision. He and his associates had gourmandized on raw fish flown in from thousands of miles away, once refrigerated to an icy consistency, glistening pieces of pink salmon, creamy yellowtail, and red tuna piled on small, polished wooden blocks, like stages. The ceiling had been dominated by a large electric fan with wooden blades like kayak paddles, both functional and decorative, seven of them, each painted a single color of the spectrum, a fact he discerned when the fan was turned off and the blur above resolved itself into its constituent parts. He'd savored the slight kick of the rice wine, the feel of the ceramic cup in his hands, and now, just walking around, after stopping at a bar for a salutary gin and tonic, Jerrold was mildly, deliciously drunk, ostensibly heading back to the hotel room, feeling anonymous, safe, and powerful, secretly harboring an almost maniacal happiness, which made everything fit, as if the whole world had been thrown together for his benefit, much like what he'd experienced back when he'd foreseen a big sell-off in copper, his first billion-dollar deal.

Midnight passed, and Jerrold was still meandering through strange streets, moving with the loose, unbraided tread of a perfectly relaxed consciousness until he was eventually lost. Which way should he go? Moving along a main boulevard, taking an unexpected, thoughtless left turn, he strolled into a poor neighborhood. A beggar, a tall, funky-smelling man in a worn-out army uniform accosted him. Jerrold threw the man off, pushing him away with both hands. A screen of bright lights made the present reel. All around him the figures of an alien speech rose in patches, indigenous languages vying with French. A vast fragrance overwhelmed him, and there, in a vacant lot, he saw a collection of night-blooming flowers. He noticed a billboard, a Mercedes-Benz ad: "Imagine every aspect of a Mercedes-Benz automobile, and you'll find engineering genius." Reading it, thinking it through like an equation of some importance, he felt a sudden desire to be moving faster, and he wished he were driving the green Lamborghini, foot down to the floor. He sensed that he knew vaguely where the hotel was, having an imperfect impression of its general direction, but he didn't know which street to take, which way to go. The streets formed a confusing maze, and he wandered around in it, losing his body, going toward the hotel, it seemed, but actually walking in circles, counterproductive, until he noticed he had already passed the same neon sign twice.

It was way past midnight now, but there was laughter and music coming from the bar where people were carousing, drinking, enjoying themselves. Would anyone recognize him? Was Jerrold experiencing the anxiety of affluence and notoriety? He consulted the Roman numerals on the face of his new Cartier watch, comparing it with a clock on the wall. He was definitely in the mood for some more celebration. There comes a time when the moment is full of itself, so he walked into the bar, sat down, and ordered a drink. It was late, almost two, but still there was a lively crowd, mostly European businessmen and military people, dressed in brown, green, and beige uniforms. Everyone seemed lost in revelry, celebrating something. Looking up and around, he noticed a beautiful woman, seated at the bar, dark and alone, her emerald earrings glittering, picking up light, and her gaze, turning quickly, met his. She smiled and seemed to wink. Jerrold felt a rigid tingling spread up through his spine. Gallantly, he pushed himself off from the bar and, swirling the ice in his glass, sauntered over to where she was sitting. He stood, holding the back of the empty seat next to hers. "May I sit down? Can I buy you a drink?" he offered nonchalantly, flashing a boyish grin. She made a quick, affirmative motion, revealing the perfection of her chin, her perfectly symmetrical forehead, the bronze, burnished skin of her neck and shoulders, her short black hair, woven into a pattern, fitting her head tightly like a fur. "She is the daughter of some tribal king," Jerrold thought to himself, as their eyes met, contracting into an intimacy.

Later that morning, in the faint light, feeling anonymous and spent, Jerrold rolled into his room, almost stumbling into a chair that he had used to tie his shoes on many hours before. The air-conditioning was set on high, the ambience icy, and the sheets beneath the blanket seemed so tightly drawn over the bed that he couldn't take the time to take off his shirt and pants. He just dove onto the bed with his shoes and clothes on, spreading his body out like a swimmer's, quivering with delight on the blanket, smiling vaguely, warmed by his memory of spontaneous sex, remembering her firm, perfect breasts, their erotic embrace, the seizure of his release, as an image of some sword passed through his mind, quickly displaced by the fact that tomorrow was already today, and he had to be out at the airport by nine.

Flying into the Jungle by helicopter, Jerrold saw, as though through a window streaming with water, the dense tropical rain forest, its prodigious presence shrouded in layers of grey mist. He hoped the sun would eventually make an appearance, and it did, illuminating, as it emerged, at the end of the long flight in, the flashing green foliage below, the machine's shadow flying on the expanse of it, jumping about on the treetops. The pocket calculator of Jerrold's consciousness turned to an approximation of the number of trees he saw, as he bounced on the choppy sea of the ride, clinging to his seat, hanging on, sitting alongside the pilot, a tall, now taciturn black man in sunglasses, wearing an immaculate military uniform. He'd greeted Jerrold at the airport with an enthusiastic handshake. "*Bonjour*, Monsieur Draper," he'd said graciously, smiling with real cordiality, and then, the pilot grabbing Jerrold by the arm, they'd rushed out to the tarmac where the helicopter was waiting. They'd climbed in and strapped themselves into their seats.

The helicopter took a sudden turn, making a change in velocity, its blades shredding the air into fragments, creating a racket, an audible strain of human ingenuity, as they descended toward the slow, brown surface of the Wobongo River, its presence coming into view, the water ruffled by a breeze. Jerrold shifted in his seat, and he glanced out the window, up at Crystal Mountain, noting its amazingly still, icy top, remembering, for some reason, a scene from the recent past, some weeks before, in a motel room somewhere north of Greenwich, where he'd had spontaneous sex with a woman he'd never see again, someone he'd phoned on a whim, the bored, buxom wife of a business associate, late one wintry afternoon when he had nothing better to do, and he'd wanted something to bring his spirits up, something he couldn't make up. Wearing black panties and bra beneath a stunning fur coat, she had appeared and smiled demurely in the doorway, immediately exuding an awareness of what they were about to do, pouting her lips seductively, bringing the tip of her tongue into play. With a bulge in his pants, Jerrold approached her and, with a deep kiss, brought her down in a swoon on the bed, getting closer to her pupils, before getting up to lock the door. She took off her coat, and he ripped off her panties. With a kind of dreamy deliberateness, she undid his belt, smiled, and took his swelling member into her mouth, but quickly changed her mind, urging him to penetrate her from behind, which he did, in a sustained state of ferocity, swaying away into her, his eyes shut, her lips pursed with the pleasure of feeling him hard inside her, until he ejaculated and collapsed on her back, embracing her, cupping his hands under her breasts, and she felt his hot come inside her. Immediately, a speechless uneasiness prevailed, as Jerrold knew that she knew that he knew that both he and she had no interest in doing it again, and they retreated more deeply into the silences they'd emerged from. A few bitter words were spat out like pills. She marched to the door and flung it open, revealing the night, a blue one full of yellow stars.

12

Although Jesse's friendship with Randy had been competitive and intense, based on a heady board game, demanding mental mettle, and although Jessica thought Randy, who seemed bright, purposeful, and industrious, to be a positive influence on Jesse, whose moods could be so sullen, the two boys soon lost interest in each other, and they went their separate ways, Randy becoming more like his brothers, more outgoing and easy in the company of others, Jesse taking a further introspective turn, an almost sinister bend. It was around that time, in the throes of wayward inwardness, in retreat from the world, that Jesse first met Derek Bailey, an older boy who had grown up in Belle Haven, a Sunswyck Academy graduate, a Juilliard dropout, a son of Donald Bailey, the celebrated real estate developer, whose own house, the first distinctively modern one in the neighborhood, all glass, white walls, and open spaces, suggests, as I think of it now, something designed by Frank Lloyd Wright. Derek was something of a prodigy at the violin, or so I've been told, and although he'd attended Sunswyck Academy and seemed to be headed, like his two older brothers before him, to Harvard and a degree in government or business administration, his mother, a frustrated musician in her own right, encouraged and nurtured his musical ability. It flourished and was unleashed during his last year at Sunswyck, almost to the exclusion of everything else; at the last minute, he applied to Juilliard, and when he was accepted, there was a family squabble, turning into an actual fistfight, because Donald could not tolerate the idea of his son pursuing a musical career. Derek studied classical violin for a year at Juilliard, before he became interested in playing the electric guitar after buying a Gibson and amplifier at the Sam Ash store off Times Square, just on a whim, just something to spend his extra allowance money on, to fool around with, something he stashed away in the closet of his dormitory room, hiding it from his roommate, a piano prodigy from Germany. Derek was daunted by the prospect of a career in classical music, wary of the self-discipline it would require, and he was beginning to listen to RPM, becoming part of the downtown punk rock scene, insofar as he went to hear live bands at clubs, alone or with friends, so he dropped out during his second year at Juilliard, in early October 1991, complaining of chronic headaches and the need to take a break from consensual reality. He moved into a small ramshackle hut of a house near Banksville, way up at the state line, once an outbuilding of a large estate, bought for him by his father, given as a gift, a place of his own, because Donald didn't want his rebellious son in the house anymore, and although Derek was Jesse's senior by three years, they became friends, sharing dubious interests, introduced to each other by Joshua, a drug dealer from Port Chester.

13

JESSICA WAS A BLONDE BEAUTY STILL, AND THERE WAS SOMETHING about her body's racy talk, something about the way she moved her hair, something about that expensive, delicate wristwatch she wore, its tiny dial scintillating on her slender, tan wrist, and something about the unfolding, really a revelation, of her smile, clean like a cat's and open like a new, appealing magazine, something unspoken. Something about the white wallpaper, the crystal chandelier suspended above them, something about the light reminded him of falling for her so many years before, Jerrold thought, now back from Africa, looking across the room at Jessica through the smoke and chatter of another crowded cocktail party, where he had just boomed forth about extrapolations based on EDGE operations in Africa. And now Rolf Holt was speaking, holding forth, keeping a small audience captive with his description of hunting bear in Alaska, "You know it's something, Jerry, bringing a wild animal down." Rolf's vivid description of the way a grizzly would wait at the stream for just the right moment, dart its long-fingered paw in, and grab, by the prongs of its black nails, a fresh fish, provided Jerrold with a sense of focus, control after the chaos, after the angry chemicals he'd experienced upstairs earlier in an emotional exchange with Jesse. He'd been on his way to the gun room to get the rifle with long-range capability that Bob Thompson wanted to borrow for a hunting trip to Kenya, when he'd caught Jesse smoking marijuana by the open bathroom window again. It was totally inappropriate, way out of line, as he'd found him there the night before, at the same window. "Not in this house! Damn it!" he'd shouted, slamming the door. Jerrold now relaxed and let his marbles roll, settling back into the pace of an authentic adult conversation, as Rolf, animated by Jerrold's presence, rambled on about his last hunting trip to India, the dead tiger hanging upside down from its feet tied to a metal pole held by two grinning guides, the photograph he showed them. Jerrold held it up to his own gaze and squinted. He was planning to devote more time to hunting, feeling pleasantly buzzed, warmed by self-medicating slugs from his drink, which calmed him, secretly studying Jessica's cool, Nordic beauty from across the room in the light, statuesque, seeing its not-so-secret relation to the impish joy Bob displayed as he played with the gun, as he looked down its sights at her, as he played her for a target, as he brought other things into focus too, such as the seventeenth-century Dutch convex mirror, a precious antique, hanging above the Chinese chest, just before he, Bob, now really very drunk, decided to use it for target practice, not knowing the gun was loaded. And he fired it, the kind of loud and outrageous act he delighted in, making a sudden bang and crash, the bullet shattering glass, bringing Jesse downstairs to observe his parents and their boisterous friends, beautiful and damned. Yes, Jesse wanted to know what had happened, and he walked downstairs to find bits of broken glass scattered on the floor. Jessica, noticing Jesse, made an exaggerated fuss over his appearance, introducing him to Bob, saying that Bob had indeed authored the thunder of the blunderbuss. Jesse feigned intrigue, focusing on the fragments of glass, then closing in on the wallpaper, noticing, as if for the first time, its exotic floral pattern, the small, cursive petals swirling from ceiling to floor. Looking into the remains of the mirror still sticking inside of the frame, he shook his head; then he glanced at the adults and continued walking through the dining room, aloof and inarticulate, down the long hallway, through the kitchen, into the pantry, and out into the garage.

It was an ordinary Friday night in Belle Haven, but there was an extraordinary pool of black liquid, oil probably, spreading from underneath the black body of the Bentley. Jesse looked at the shining garbage cans, really digging the aluminum garb, hanging out with all four cars: the Bentley, the Maserati, the Jaguar, and the Lamborghini, their black, silver, blue, and green bodies shining in the glare from the fluorescent lighting above, as he, with the key, opened the driver's door of the Bentley and sat down, deep in the plush, leather seat, engaging in a little late-night reflection on John Lennon, on a book report he'd written on Lennon, way back in Larchmont, in the sixth grade, when the Beatles were his favorite band and he wanted to give peace a chance. "Drive" was a word Jerrold often used as a noun, a verb, an imperative, conceiving of steering the boat as an act, an instantiation, of driving. "Drive!" he'd order Jesse sometimes out on *Scimitar*. "Drive and hold her course," he'd bark out, going down below to fetch a chart. The adults were having a blast. The happy shouting and laughter was audible, even out there in the garage. "There are no adults here, only children and dead forms," Jesse thought to himself, entering one of his spells, wherein the world around him turned on his memory. One of his teachers at Larchmont Country Day, a certain Mrs. Gardener, who said such things as "Hay is for horses," loomed in his mind. She was incredibly dedicated to her charges, and she expended an inordinate amount of NRG on modal verbs, stressing the differences between "can" and "may," "would" and "could," "shall" and "should," and the differently charged "childish" and "childlike." She made these points, semantic distinctions, with the tips of her fingers, her fingernails painted bright crimson, stressing the difference between an "illusion" and an "allusion," and she'd focus on apostrophes and contractions too, showing the class how "its" can't be "it's," how "whose" can be heard as "who's," for she had a thing for homophones, warning the boys and girls about the ambiguities of the spoken word, how "burrow" can be mistaken for "borough," "rain" taken for "reign," "plain" for "plane," "pain" for "pane," and an "eye" for one's "I," and she once wrote this sentence: "They're out there" in chalk on the blackboard, to make a grammatical point, something Jesse remembered, just as he recollected, deep in the seat, her response to his book report on John Lennon. She just didn't get it: the concept of instant karma. He decided to change cars. Walking the short distance, just a few yards, to the green Lamborghini, he opened its door with another key, climbed in, grabbed the wheel, and pictured himself driving on roads north of Greenwich, late at night, headlights illuminating pavement, picking out turns, the wheels hugging a winding road, passing through an enchanted landscape, such as the one depicted in the tapestry that hung on a wall in the main building at the Sunswyck Academy. He sat there and mused, inserting the key, turning the battery, lights, and radio on.

Jesse's prolific and pointless doodling, a show of rebellion, a symptom of his chronic inattention, a refusal to follow, to participate within a larger whole, a logic of symbols and the rules for manipulating those symbols, had appeared in the margins of his algebra textbook—compulsive, repetitive geometric patterns wrought by some form of inner necessity: departures from classroom reality, fueling the illusion that he was experiencing the renewed originality of an absolutely primordial freedom, a grandiosity that, several years earlier, had generated concern at the Sunswyck Academy, specifically from Dr. Breakstone, Jesse's seventh-grade algebra teacher, who, serving as a sort of guidance counselor, made a phone call to contact and express concern to a parent. He just happened to catch Jerrold at home one weekday afternoon, back early from the office, unwinding with a gin and tonic in front of the new plasma TV, watching the numbers, enthralled by high definition on a big screen broadcasting a surge of just the right numbers. EDGE had recently purchased a diamond mine in Rwanda, and having renewed its infrastructure and attracted a whole cadre of excited, young investors, he was about to reap the rewards. The market conditions were right, the time was ripe, and the numbers were working. Jerrold was ebullient, his voice confident, pitch perfect, attuned to past performances and the promise of future gain, so that the doddering, elderly mathematics teacher, after some small talk regarding the market's volatility, a topic of mutual concern, implicitly acknowledging EDGE and the monumental wealth Jerrold had generated, starting tentatively, almost intimidated, his voice wavering, had spoken at some length with probity about Jesse's "dire situation," not just the doodling during algebra class—that was but one manifestation of a generally poor attitude—but also the moodiness, the repeated offenses, the quartet of sentences he'd scribbled in chalk on the blackboard in an empty classroom one afternoon—"Don't Get Fueled. Drop Out of School," "I Am

Bored of Education," and "We Are the Dead"—and the absences, the lack of team spirit, problems with the dress code. All of these factors were working against him, militating against him in the long run. Dr. Breakstone, assessing Jesse's situation, mounting the case he was building, feeling more relaxed and confident in his speech, yapping away on the phone, suggested that maybe Jesse would benefit, morally and academically, from a year spent someplace else, at another school, at a place such as Penfield Academy, the notorious all-boys boarding school in Delaware, boasting an almost military commitment and zeal to attaining excellence through the discipline of following rules. "That might straighten him out," Dr. Breakstone suggested, hopefully, rubbing his chin, leaning back in the chair in his office.

"Sounds like a plan," Jerrold remarked, scanning the numbers and planning to have a serious chat with his wayward son soon. Jerrold's experience of his own voice overwhelmed any opposition, and one month later, Jesse found himself talking to Jessica, complaining about the bad food from a pay phone inside a brick administration building on the dreary Penfield campus, where, for the remainder of the year, Jesse felt incarcerated. Detachment is caused by a slow, silent process, and the signs of its progress are difficult to detect, but Jesse, out of a weary sense of unease and desperation, learned to detach himself from the situation, duly attending a dull school, having no alternative, leaving him with very little free time, virtually no time to himself, almost always in the company of other boys, in the dining hall, in the classrooms, on playing fields surrounded by steel fencing, the smokestacks of a chemical processing plant in the distance, concrete columns rising above the reeds, belching billowing clouds of white and orange smoke into the air.

Penfield opened Jesse's presence to what was, for him, an at-first violent, hierarchical reality dominated by a sort of surrogate father figure, a self-described "benevolent despot," Penfield's head-master, a former U.S. Army colonel who inculcated his student troops with a zealous respect for authority and rule following. They were ordered around and told what to do. They were constantly being clocked, from the morning bell at six to lights out at ten: watched, monitored, and regulated by the schedule of a routine that was absolutely deadening in its predictability, and although Jesse was secretly contemptuous of the environment, which squelched all spontaneity, making him part of the machinery, although secretly sneering at the reality of his reform, he donned a mask of compli-ance, assuming, by means of detachment, the role of responsible student, one among others, actually studying to get good grades, applying himself in algebra and Latin, even showing some aptitude for school spirit, playing team sports, just to get through with it all in a hurry. Though he felt he'd been duped by a system he'd done his best to battle and resist, he now erred no more, and he savored the fruits of his apparent conformity.

With Jesse being home that year for the summer, prepared to return to Sunswyck in September, his attitude problem seemed to have been thoroughly solved, and any lingering discontent or resentment he felt dissolved in the simple joys of summer with all its outdoor activity, everything happening in its place. To Jerrold, whose perceptions of his son were always distorted anyway, Jesse had been rectified, transformed, and he deemed his son's general demeanor excellent, worthy of a high score indeed, an excellent grade, the pyramidal A, a full "10." That's what Jerrold was think-ing, that's how he saw it one fresh morning down at the Yacht Club docks, watching Jesse ably maneuver and pilot with expert ease the Boston Whaler into its place at the stern of *Scimitar*, then se-cure it with a yellow plastic line to the shiny brass cleat on her deck, and the animation of everything—people with people, peo-ple with things on, people with things on boats, everybody getting everything ready for the inaugural weekend cruise when Rolf Holt

donned his formal commodore suit and personally fired the ceremonial antique cannon on the front porch of the clubhouse—filled him with parental pride.

14

MEANWHILE, OFF IN AFRICA, CAST DEEPLY INTO THE INTERIOR OF the Jungle, where organisms proliferate like libraries, where chance can't cling to anything because everything's determined in this skin, where words necessarily give rise to birds and more birds, and there's no stopping the sun's fall down to its knees, driven by a totality of impressions, the close of another day, Omnibus was supervening a congregation of ants, attempting to do some MA-TV, to put theory into practice. "Perform, ants!" he shouted at a collection of unruly fire ants, as a ruby red, glistening throng of busyness gathered at his feet, evidently taken by his speech. "Perform against the vehicular madness that has brought me to this place!" he shouted again, with newfound conviction, shifting his feet, getting down on his knees, holding the magnifying glass over a particular instantiation of the species. He examined the mighty monitor of the red ant's dense head, its busy antennae and opaque, protuberant eye sockets, portals into nothingness, revealing some potential for socialization, but the performance wasn't happening, and Omnibus was becoming frustrated. Then a glimpse of something distracted him, a busy sparkling a few yards away: instantiations of Gabon's rare carpenter ant, a species with transparent, glassy skin, which, seen under magnification, bears an armor of air vents and ducts, clusters of tiny crystals, antennae combing the air, its legs and abdomen poised for action, in action. The gymnastics of its moving parts, like a group of boys throwing stones, derive from the peculiar elasticity of its sleepless body, constantly on the move, never closing its eyes, always animated.

Meanwhile, elsewhere in the Jungle, the Golden Cat crouched, safe in its giant gymnasium, dragging a beetle between its furry paws and toward its tawny spotted chest, just to toy with it, as an alligator might toy with a turtle, a bottle of light washed up on the shore. Pillow, a neighbor's gargantuan white dog, an Argentine Dogo, had played with a dead bird on the front lawn once, and Jesse watched it from his window, and when the dog went away, he walked downstairs, crept out on the grass like a snake in the sunlight, and saw it, the bird, all mangled, its pink, fleshy interior exposed. Birding up in the Babcock Preserve, I once saw a hawk catch a squirrel and carry it away in its talons, blood dripping through the cold air.

The Golden Cat then paused in its play, as the beetle sprung wings and flew off. Almost instantaneously, Omnibus stood up, holding his pad of paper and a felt-tip pen, ready to make an observation, and then, just as he was about to put pen to paper, the carpenter ant's performance stopped, and he looked down at the suddenly stationary insect, uncooperative, recalcitrant, deaf to his importations. "I'm the only president you've got," he said to the uncooperative ant, as he realized that successful communication with a carpenter ant was unlikely, given that shouted instructions were probably just old hat from its point of view, like private property, a concept that carpenter ants, like the indigenous people whom Omnibus saw from time to time, popping into view with their bows, arrows, and poisoned darts, didn't seem to have any grasp of, as they inhabited a different world, a world without hierarchy, a world without time, without bounds, and they never ordered themselves, nor anything else about them, around, and they always seemed to be traveling in circles, singing in cycles, forming alliances that would never be properly assimilated.

The Pygmy People (the "PP"), the indigenous denizens of the Jungle, have lived for tens of thousands of years in an always shrinking region of sultry, condensed rain forest, now smaller than Connecticut, a vast conglomerate of tropical biota, rampant green growth, where odors and colors predominate amid tall trees festooned with thick vines and lianas, African walnut trees towering over the scene, punctuated by the shrill calls and cries of wild creatures. The PP live and thrive in small nomadic tribes, with little or no knowledge of their neighbors. Fiercely independent, each clan functions on its own unique terms, hunting and gathering, its members participating in an idiosyncratic form of animism that exists through an oral tradition alone, active for millennia, shared with other clan members only, dead and alive, centered on the spirits of ancestors and prey: the antelope, the buffalo, and elephant, the monkeys, rodents, snakes, birds, lizards, and the wide array of insects that make the Jungle home. Anthropologists speculate that the PP are modern man's living ancestors, descendants of those early hominids who chose to remain in the rain forest, who never struck out for open grassland tens of thousands of years ago, who never developed a language with broad, referential properties, who dwelled in the Jungle, wrapped in its shades, merging with its organisms, coming into playful symbiosis with it, becoming part and parcel of its nature. The PP inhabit a world apart, where the plants and the weather and their primary prey are also projections of innermost, inarticulate wishes, and it is debatable whether they have a robust concept of a world external to consciousness.

Omnibus had been living in the Jungle for several months now, in a tent, not far from a PP village, pursuing entomological research. The hotel where he'd spent his first Friday night in Africa, alone in Libreville, the El Dorado, redundant insofar as it was reminiscent of certain locations he'd already been to and seen, set on a hillside of whistling goats, on the outskirts of the city, overlooked a busy marketplace, where bright-colored fabrics were hanging on lines. Old women's breasts sagged like empty athletic socks, and

younger women, some carrying clinging infants, some of them cry-
ing, mingled and danced in the dusty air. There was a wiry, bearded
man cooking meat on a small portable grill; old men were seated at
tables, playing cards and dice, and, as Omnibus watched the activity kindle below him, a slight pang of empathy, mixed with mild
envy, rushed through him, far above the street, his eyes on a scene
from which he was by choice excluded, a stranger in this land. "The
bus stops here," he thought to himself, attempting to practice some
MA-TV, chanting "MA-TV, MA-TV," making his consciousness
melt for as long as he could, and a radio somewhere far off played.
Already he missed Amy.

"Amy, what are you going to do? What am I going to do without you?" Omnibus had pleaded, begging her to join him, trying to
convince her to quit her job, sell the bungalow, and come to Gabon,
calling from a phone booth in downtown Libreville, having arrived
there by van. He parked it on Descartes Avenue, which runs along
the stretch of fine, white sandy beach bordering the city's growing
center, its new business district. He'd done some shopping at the
Science Store, purchasing glass jars, plastic containers, tweezers,
pins and glue, a magnifying glass, a microscope, slides and fixative,
a butterfly net for Amy, a can of kerosene, some funnels, felt-tip
pens, and pads of graph paper.

Amy, at first, was reluctant to go to Gabon, resistant to the
whole idea, despite intense pleading from Omnibus, for he truly
missed her, but as they discussed it more and more, as he pro-
moted with growing eloquence his case, the idea began to make
some sense to her, and it took root in the soil of her consciousness,
like a potato plant, flowering into sudden affirmation, for Omnibus proved to be a master of persuasive rhetoric, tantalizing her,
seducing her with his elaborate, glowing descriptions of the exotic,
indigenous butterflies, the airy, dancing denizens of the Jungle, the
workings of their colorful wings. Swayed by his use of language,
she agreed to make the move. She just dropped her job like a jar.

She sold the house and car. She booked a flight and went there. He met her at the airport. She flew into his arms excitedly, her face flush with the courage of her convictions.

15

A FEW MONTHS BEFORE THE KIDNAPPING, WHICH IS, FINALLY, WHERE the action of my story begins, but before that, on an evening in early December 1991, when a big bank of grey cloud hung oppressively low over the horizon, with the sun dropping slowly out of sight and into its sleeping place in a far corner of the sky, I received a telephone call from Conrad, my long lost "cousin," with whom I'd played at The Ark, and he filled me in with some relevant background information.

After almost four years of frivolous, fruitful, sometimes frantic, even fervid folly at the Brie College of Art, also known as "the Last Art School," referred to in some circles as "the only place to study Conceptual Art," located somewhere in Canada, in Halifax, Nova Scotia, of all places, its harbor a deep anchorage shrouded in frequent fog, the wooden docks, wharves, and warehouses of its downtown area dominated by the Citadel, a fortress carved into a massive hill, from where he'd view Point Pleasant Park at the southern tip of a terrain shaped like a heart, all pine trees, dirt roads, nautical monuments, and rocky shores, jutting out toward the constancy of the grey, indifferent ocean, its simple horizon always there, Conrad discovered that fly fishing, with its tactile rush of something on the line, was an art, a form of pure attention, and he said this to me, just for emphasis: "I just wanted to have some fun." Fishing was how he, as he put it, "came down to Earth," breaking with his privileged past, abandoning expectations, shedding the last vestiges of a former theatrical impulse, something he'd inherited from his mother, Aunt Alice, leaving that stage of his development far behind, a thing of the past, as if making useless objects, putting them on display, and plugging them into theatrical time were something there was no need for, because the very impetus to artifice, the drive toward psychic coherence, had dissolved into time per se, having finally become irrelevant, one with it, though he still retained a sense of a past. "Conceptual artists are mystics," he said to me, and the Brie College of Art was where he learned that, as his language became naïve and visionary, and he spoke with the cadence of a versifier, a tireless promoter. Everybody was experimenting with new possibilities in form, going beyond traditional painting, sculpture, and photography, developing new ways of carving out worlds, some of them immaterial, like radio waves, things at unseen frequencies, particles ripped from a wall, poured from a can, given the way things work in this complicated WHIRL OF HOURS, spinning on its axis, and when he spoke of TUBOTAC, I didn't know what he was talking about, and I asked him to backtrack.

One day, out for a walk, chilled and slightly dazed, after a long afternoon in the studio working with an electric saw, nails, and a hammer, after fabricating several waist-high, chair-sized plywood cubes, which he'd then painted a dull battleship grey, attaching protective metal brackets to the corners with screws, late one afternoon while strolling along down Water Street, just walking on, Conrad stopped and looked down where the white fragments of a dropped clamshell spread out before him, under his gaze, and the sun smiled like an old coin culled from a buried chest. Looking at the shattered shell, he suddenly and inexplicably experienced what he called "The Dematerialization of the Art Object," a kind of epiphany, ineffable in essence, realizing that things will, as he put it to me, "be what they are and what they seem, surviving the vicissitudes of gravity, time, and photons," that there was nothing for him to do about it, that there had never been anything to do about it, and he saw no need to make or add anything at all, because the world was perfect, just as it was, and this was a positive experience, giving rise, several seconds later, to "The Urgent Burning of the Art Concept," TUBOTAC, whereby his bodily form was, as he put it to me, "attacked by a kind of tubular fire, a cloak or shroud of flaming tubes," and the material of his body, stopped there on Water Street, burst into flakes and folds of flame. He saw no need to make sculpture anymore, as he slipped through his imagination into his fishing vest, found a tackle box, and grabbed a rod in its shiny container, already making the gestures that, in the wake of this genesis, would follow: the synchronized movements, spontaneously bending, angling away, skimming the super fluidities of streams, ponds, and lakes in a concentrated daze. Casting out, fetching his catch with spinning reel, putting hook, line, and fly to work, took him far beyond modern sculpture, and he reached his own conclusions. Capable of sustaining a fly's feigned flight by the trigger of a supple wrist, Conrad conceived of the fisherman's vocation as an ultimate act of synthesis, a sort of shamanism, joining realms, conjuring creatures of water, creatures of air, different respiratory systems, giving him, as he put it to me, "confidence in my offstage voice." "It was like finding the shortest distance between two points by folding the paper of their representations, proof that it's not a straight line"—that's how he described it to me. TUBOTAC produced an atmosphere of pulverized glass in which he could instantly recognize himself, moving, if he so chose, through a sort of constant synthesis or imaginative conjunction of sensory elements, something he called "Conjunctive Synthesis," whereby he became himself in the material situation of a swimming fish, water sliding BYE, inhabiting a distinct ecological niche, the base of his brain excited by its wet passage beyond the confines of personhood.

At one point, I queried him about "Conceptual Art." What was it? Isn't all art "conceptual" in some sense? Isn't reality itself a concept, if you really think about it, and doesn't the phrase "Conceptual Art" constitute a redundancy, an empty intuition, a mistake in categories, a needless multiplication of entities? Conrad paused, and I imagined him, in his silence, to be seriously pondering the implications of my queries, and then he spoke about TUBOTAC and the merging of content and form and the metaphor of a funnel, a model for pouring NRG. He began to ramble on about energy, liberty, and funnels. At one point, he launched into a promotional pitch for what he called "social sculpture," his thesis being that the world, just as it is, in the unfolding of its moments, in the mute distributions of its chemical and electrical exchanges, is a work of art, perfect at every moment, that every sentient consciousness is woven into this great complex of relations that forms the text of all creation.

When Granddad had died, Conrad received a generous, unexpected inheritance, and he was stunned, giddy with surprise, so overwhelmed with a new sense of freedom and the possibilities that money can buy, that he decided to drop out of art school and do his own thing, which was, of course, fly fishing. "It was just like that," as he explained it to me on the phone. Driven by TUBOTAC and a fresh sense of purpose, feeling a newly found unity with creatures that fly and swim, Conrad moved out to Colorado, where he bought some land and built on it, where his rallying cry, "ELF," was first conceived one sunny afternoon, sitting on the back porch of the log cabin he shared with Kate, his masseuse-girlfriend, while savoring an especially pungent cider in the soon-crimson sunset, a sense of warmth creeping, working away on his mental furniture like a cat or spider, as Kate tiptoed off to the kitchen to fry the rainbow trout he'd caught earlier that afternoon. "ELF," he said to himself, "just a SILLY BELL that rhymes exactly with 'pelf,'" just an idea out of nowhere, filling him with impetus. "This is ominous," he thought, as an elusive promise seemed to leak from the letters of the acronym. He reached for a pad, found a felt-tip pen, and scrawled the letters *E*, *L*, *F*, and then the words "ENERGY LIBERTY FOUNDATION," on paper, and he mused on these words and their meanings, going back and forth through them, like Hamlet pacing the ramparts. He

crossed out "FOUNDATION" and wrote the word "FUNNEL" under it, considering the abstractions of "ENERGY" and "LIBERTY,"
wanting to anchor them in something material, searching for something concrete, getting up from his chair to fetch the funnel kept
under the kitchen sink, bumping into Kate in the process, causing
oil and garlic to spatter from the hot pan, all for a fleeting, elfin idea
that soon became an organizing principle. He wondered what to do
with them, the letters and the acronym, holding the tin funnel in
one hand, returning to its consideration, pondering its shape and
purpose: pouring a substance—a liquid, water, molasses, salt, wine,
sugar granules, whatever—into a container, finding in its structure
again a metaphor for TUBOTAC, the funneling of attention, a
merging of content and form. He looked out through the window,
into a landscape of mountains and pine trees, and he remembered,
for no reason, the slew of mysterious, unused postcards he'd discovered, stuffed into an old shoebox, one grey afternoon while sifting
through a pile of trash. The images were, invariably, all of the Eiffel
Tower, prize of the City of Light, photographs taken from different
angles and perspectives at different, various times of day or night,
but they all showed the same familiar tower. He'd always wanted to
do something with the postcards, use them in some sort of epistolary
sculpture project, and now he knew what he'd do. He went upstairs
to get the box. It had been years since he'd seen these things; he sat
down at the table and counted twenty-two cards, reflecting on the
symmetry. Wondering what to write, he stared into space, reflecting
on chaos and its control, deciding to painstakingly inscribe each
blank, empty space with the imperative "Get Smart," signed with
the acronym ELF. The inscription on each was always the same,
though the scenes were all so different, a potpourri of Eiffel Tower
imagery, some taken in daylight, some in color, some in black and
white, others taken at night, some full of colored lights that made
the tower shine from within, but there seemed to be a sense, a
message running through them all, and it conceptually cohered,

circulating between the words and images, the suggestion, perhaps, of being a seer, as opposed to a mere student, or STEWED ANT, as he'd later say, under the sway of Omnibus, though he, Omnibus, was still Oscar Topaz, living in LA, working with electricity, the first addressee, the primary recipient of Conrad's epistolary efforts.

Oscar was at the height of his powers, a veritable tuning fork, held and ready to resonate, the current of his inner juices simmering, ready to reach a boiling point. Sometimes standing at the top of an aluminum ladder during an installation job, the electrician inside of him turned into space itself, and a vast, seething matrix of NRG was revealed on the screen behind his closed eyes, like an exclamation mark rising from the entrepreneurial grey matter trapped inside of his skull. What did these messages mean? The first cryptic postcard arrived on a Monday, the beginning of the workweek, and it was followed, erratically, sometimes for a few consecutive days, sometimes with gaps of three days or more, over the course of the next two months, by all the others, becoming a twenty-two-card suite of picture postcards, photographs, various views of the Eiffel Tower, with a simple, two-word message painstakingly inscribed in Gothic script in the space behind the image, an imperative: "Get Smart." He wondered what it meant and why he had been targeted. He noted, of course, the Boulder, Colorado, postmark, but he had no idea that Conrad was there.

Some weeks later, after the cards suddenly stopped appearing, Oscar was at home, recovering from an especially arduous day, sitting in his bathrobe, watching an episode of *I Love Lucy* when the phone rang, and he answered it. "What's black and white and red all over?" a distant voice asked, crackling, almost coming apart in the stormy static of the signal, a bad connection, cracking up like an adolescent boy in anticipation of the response. "Heck, that's easy," Oscar reflected. "It's either a newspaper or a nun falling down the stairs." It was Conrad calling, of course, who revealed his role in the postcard caper, and first they exchanged greetings and reminiscences of their art student days at Brie College, that spring when Oscar was there, and then they discussed, albeit haphazardly, in slapdash manner, the essence of ELF, Conrad unpacking the acronym, Oscar listening. The time passed quickly, but Amy would soon be home, and Oscar had to start cooking dinner, so he cut the conversation short. Collecting some cooking utensils, he cast a glance at the end of the kitchen counter, seeing Conrad's postcards piled in a heap.

As an accomplished angler, Conrad had been aware, even proud, of his casting and catching abilities, and he'd secretly harbored, deep within, even after TUBOTAC and all its existential implications, a yen for theatrical folly. Briefly, during his first year in the Boulder area, in a documentation/performance piece, he'd kept careful track of his catches, noting the length of each fish he'd caught, the foodstuffs he'd find in their stomachs, the colorations of the skins, the markings, the specks, spots, and freckles. He'd hunch over his drawing table, shoulders shifting while sketching on paper, moving his hand with care, concentrating his eyes on the fish, on the renderings he'd make with colored pencils. He had a small scale on which he weighed each one, and a measuring tape he'd unroll to take measurements with, but the purpose of the documentation had begun to feel pointless, like some form of otiose bragging, which was what led him to think, as he walked out the door one morning, "Forget the documentation. I'm just going to go out there and catch more fish."

About a year after the impromptu telephone conversation with Oscar, Conrad was in downtown Boulder, down at the Loon Saloon, sitting on a barstool, his moustache marked with hoppy froth, his right hand clutching a heavy mug of buxom brew. He'd been out on Lake Eagle ice fishing with Philip, a cohort, and they were celebrating a big catch, the two of them playing as one, flirting in the company of some bodacious vixen. There was something you could dance to playing in the air, but everyone sat on stools or in booths, yapping away in the vivacious, smoky atmosphere, RPM on the jukebox bringing them into focus under the influence of fermentation, the memory of casting whirling through him, within him, still bending, when the image flashed on the TV screen.

Compelled by the mystery of what he saw, like the blameless blue blanket of a sunny day's birth, all of its colors a miracle, Conrad felt himself turn spherical. It was a sudden break in the continuity of normal programming, like a test signal for the Emergency Broadcasting System. Three horizontal bands of color appeared: blue, yellow, and green, interrupting the evening news, the electronic image shimmering like a pattern in a pool of FIRM MENTATION, soon to be part of an incoming tide. "Turn off that music!" someone yelled out, and then the TV became audible, projecting the sounds of water, a river in a jungle, where small black men scantily clad in loincloths, almost naked, waded out into the slow-moving, waist-deep waters of the broad, brown flow, where they'd grab hold, bare-handed, of humungous bottom fish, huge flounder, engaging in a kind of mild wrestling match in the muddy water with the gargantuan raylike creatures. The grainy color footage, taken by a handheld video camera, accompanied by a muffled soundtrack of percussion instruments and human voices in the wind, chanting at high frequencies, lasted for about three minutes, enough time for Conrad to become motivated by the idea of fishing with his hands in Gabon, after catching the name of the country, a location that could be an imperative, as it sounded like one to him in his ears. In the middle of a close-up shot, the victorious grin of a man holding up in the air the fish he'd just caught, blew through the corridors of his attention, traveling down his spine, and then the footage ended, as all the fantastic imagery ceased, and the evening news began again, right where it had stopped, a talking head with a map of Afghanistan behind it, going on as if nothing unusual had happened. Conrad looked around him, and he noticed, first, that Philip was gone, no longer sitting on his barstool, and that nobody else seemed especially surprised by what they'd just seen on the screen. Was it a hallucination? Perhaps he alone had seen it? The Colorado winter dragged on, with more snow than usual, and Conrad reflected on the ontological status of the fishing footage, remembering that it had been filmed in Gabon. Was it simply a fantastic phantasm, a function of wish fulfillment, a product of his wild imagination, blinded by desire, feeding on warm, watery imagery, its essence reeling him into this small equatorial country on the coast of West Africa, where Omnibus was already established, performing experiments with ants and MA-TV? The Colorado winter continued to drag on, with even more snow, and although Conrad had always enjoyed downhill skiing, he found himself especially anxious for spring to arrive, and it did, buds bursting, and the biosphere filled with particles of sweetness, bringing back birds, fattening fish, as the aspen trees bloomed. Conrad, bored of fishing with rod and reel, tried catching trout with his hands in the pristine, sparkling streams, like a bear with its claws, consciously seeking something new, compelled by what he'd seen on the screen in the Loon Saloon, an excerpt from the Jungle—and I am calling attention to this word, capitalizing it constantly, suggesting an absolutely proper noun, perhaps a substantive wherein Omnibus and Amy presently perform experiments in ant and butterfly consciousness, in MA-TV, becoming friendly with the mysterious Pygmy People, learning something of their ways in a place where the funds never run out.

Thinking he'd been pulled there by the force of his two hands alone, as if climbing a ladder of water to where he'd soon be learning more about fish, how they extract oxygen from water in order to thrive and swim, and about birds, how many wings it takes to bring a flock up, Conrad, through the miracle of inscription and a place of destination, arrived in Libreville via an Air France flight from Paris, having stopped there to see the famous tower and to attend to some formal business, changing the initial letter of his first name from C to K, in homage to Karl Marx, a primary precursor. Leaving

Colorado, Konrad was ready to enter the Jungle, where Omnibus
was pondering ants primarily, while Amy was busy with butterflies,
the two of them living in a large tent, maintaining a sort of laboratory,
hidden under canvas cover, making observations, categorizing, creating a taxonomy of entomological reality, tokens of types, keeping
specimens in plastic containers. They were often found bent at the
impromptu jerry-rigged "table," a big piece of plywood set on metal
sawhorses, peering into microscopes. Solar panels powered the
overhead fan and the lighting Omnibus had ingeniously designed
and installed, having already absorbed some of the ways of the indigenous people, the mysterious PP, who pop into view now and then,
the children of the rain forest. With instruction from Kombolo, the
shaman, an important PP contact, Omnibus was just beginning to
practice telepathy without his being conscious of his being able to
do so—the only way to do it these days—exerting a kinetic influence
by the power of his mind alone, slowly pulling Konrad into its orbit,
attracting him, Omnibus realizing that thinking, the performance of
thought, forms a field of influence by intangible, seemingly immaterial means, bringing about Konrad's decision to fish with his hands
in the first place, bringing him here, colliding more or less at dusk
with Omnibus in a narrow street in Libreville, just outside a military
supply store where Omnibus was shopping for camping equipment,
as if he just happened to be there by chance, and they greeted each
other with expressions of instant recognition and genuine surprise.
"It's been a long, long time," Omnibus said, slapping Konrad on the
back, grinning a grin, as they stood in the street, absorbing the shock
of their sudden combination, strange to be thrown back together
again, sewn into the same time slot. They walked the short distance
to a local restaurant. Omnibus spoke first, explaining his presence
and change of name. "The postcards were a great motivator," he
remarked. Soon they were discussing their new identities, as Oscar
described his becoming Omnibus, the experience in the traffic jam,
MA-TV, leaving Amy to study ants, his arrival in Libreville, where

notions and ideas proliferated, leading him into the Jungle, then to the phone booth where he begged Amy to join him. And she had. Konrad in time explained his own fascination with funnels, speculating on marks, and how keys turned in locks, and the realm of a shared ignition roared, with Omnibus easily convincing Konrad to join Amy and him, deep in the Jungle, tangled within, where they'd form a triad, a secret cell, a trio of selves in the rain forest. And so they drove off, flying in the van on a newly constructed superhighway to a point where they parked it. They hiked farther in to where the canvas tent was pitched, not far from a PP camp, where Amy greeted them, her open arms morphing into fluttering wings, which she shook, releasing powdery blue particles. Konrad wandered off, looking for a funnel, which he found, unpacking his luggage, noting the shape of the thing, expanding on its exemplary function: the focusing of flow, the smooth channeling of content, forming "an endlessly mobile Moebius strip," he said with authority, and he assumed a meditative posture. The funnel routine was something new for Omnibus and Amy, who was especially amused by the example of this simple tool, frequently found in kitchens, garages, and laboratories.

"Perhaps ELF requires clarification," Konrad said, getting up from where he'd been sitting, holding the device in his right hand, making an attempt to explain his conception more fully. "Energy! Liberty! Funnel! This is not a compound noun modifying a singular noun, not a kind of funnel," he said, peering into the funnel, studying its structure, as if he were about to flow through it. "The funnel is simply a model for a possible course of action." Amy, as if responding to his utterance, fluttered about in her own inimitable way, as if she'd been through this before. Gifted with wings, she lifted off, flying slowly toward a profusion of brightness in the night, and she hovered at the edge of a flowering bush, landing on a singular phosphorescent flower, letting her delicate, long wings close over its glowing diameter of pink and yellow petals, her head bent in marvel, manipulating particles, her antennae and abdomen now glowing, illuminated by a special switch, and she, too, became a container of radical light, a bulb of bloom, linked by a language of tact to the sun, although it was late at night.

The tent, during the day, was a shady cocoon of camouflaged canvas, a cool and comfortable space, though Omnibus and Konrad were almost always out of doors, investigating ants and fish, lost in the definitive errand of whatever each one chose to pursue, while Amy, in butterfly guise, calmly collected particles, flying about, busy doing nothing. The tent was equipped with functional furniture: pneumatic mattresses and sleeping bags in one corner, cooking equipment, a propane stove, a few chairs, and a card table in another, but most of the space was dominated by the giant jerry-rigged worktable, two sawhorses supporting a large plywood plank, where she'd sit, in human form, working with the microscope and other instruments, measuring the particles she'd gleaned, making marks on pages of graph paper. Along with the one overhead, there was a huge, industrial-sized electric fan on the floor, hooked up to a car battery, which produced a constant spin of wind, cooling things down in the shade. There was mosquito netting hung over the tent's entrance and a deep pit outside for food storage. A nearby stream provided a constant source of water, and its liquid ditty played in the air, creating phrases of a capricious, idiosyncratic music that Amy wholly embraced, whistling while she worked.

16

MEANWHILE, SOMETIME BEFORE THAT, BACK IN BELLE HAVEN, having returned to Sunswyck Academy, Jesse never really distinguished himself, and he became but a mediocre student again, frequently alone and inarticulate about his feeling of not fitting in, unenthusiastic about it all, because he just couldn't see the point; he failed to muster any enthusiasm for any of the scrimmage. It was all a waste of time, a waste of NRG. Why study for tests and examinations, do research, write papers, strive to get good grades, play organized sports, work on a winning transcript, all so that he could go to college and compete with more peers, pursue a career, plant a house, build a tree, breed, and accumulate property, all while he was completely aware that he felt no need, no inner necessity, driving him, nothing pushing him to really do anything special with his life in the world after all? All that he wanted to really do was breathe, party, hang out with friends, drink beer, smoke pot, engage the pleasures of merely circulating, listen to RPM, ride his bike around, chase girls, have sex, and be at ease in his skin. How does one conduct a life amid such circumstances? School was just a drag, and the teachers who taught him weren't cool, so it all seemed so blatantly ridiculous, sitting at a desk, where he could neither lose himself in reading nor writing, nor in taking dictation, nor in the clear, linear thinking needed to solve math problems, as if life were one big math problem, as if he suffered a perpetual perceptual dysfunction, always distracted by his own vivid perceptions, a world too close for thought, closing in on him. But he was inventive, in a rebellious sort of way, and he developed notorious distancing techniques, ways of scrambling time, and this ability gave him access to a kind of cracked paradise, a power over his less advanced classmates, boys of comparable affluence and privilege, such as the Holts, boys who lacked an awareness of alternate realities, bound by the suffocating and stultifying influence money can have, if you let it get to you and go that way. Jesse, having grown up in Manhattan, was introduced to graffiti and carrying cans of spray paint in his backpack to school at an early age, and then, in Larchmont, he'd mixed with a crowd of older local boys, from whom he'd learned all about drugs and dropping out and how to get away with things, such as late nights out, because his parents were always so busy, caught up in dramas of their own making, pressing plans and pursuits, so Jesse had plenty of free time, time free for whimsy. By the time they'd moved to Larchmont, his weekday evenings were frequently without any parental supervision, except for Theresa. Dad was almost always away on business, and Mom was traveling again, seeing old friends from the fashion industry, spending a lot of time in Brazil, in Rio, so Jesse ate dinner alone, served by a silent Theresa, his maid, cook, and caretaker, with whom he shared an unspoken bond.

As every experienced tennis player knows, a serve of one's own plays a key role in the future of a game, bending into the ball, becoming part of the moving experiment. Jerrold's success on the tennis court was a function, in part, of how he moved, always throwing the full force of his verve into the ball, putting his whole cortex into it. "Keep your eye on the ball, Jesse. Make it be a part of you," he said, suggesting a different picture than the one unrolling before him, a disappointment. Jerrold was profoundly disappointed with his son's apparent inability or unwillingness to follow simple instructions, his failure to grasp the importance of being engaged in a game and really putting oneself into it, to see how it pays off, playing by the rules; Jerrold winced at Jesse's lassitude, his weak hold on the racket, the feigned force of his serve, his lame backhand, the bored grimace—all of this completely displeased Jerrold, who'd had such high hopes for his one son—and now Jerrold was disassociating, only performing, going through empty gestures, acting out a role, with his real thoughts coiled up somewhere far behind his eyes, deep in the entrepreneurial folds of his profligate grey matter, where, with high probability, he was thinking about EDGE, preoccupied with EDGE, while his body continued to automatically externalize a sort of promotion for the right stuff, the determination, and he'd tried, but he was tired, and Jesse just wasn't getting into the swing of things out there. Particles of red clay stuck to the rubber of Jesse's shoes' soles, and he ignored what his father was saying, turning the other way, blond hair falling into his eyelashes, his facial expression lapsing into a frown, an affectless, despondent shrug of his shoulders and an internal, interminable psychobabble. "How much wood would a woodchuck chuck if a woodchuck could chuck wood?" He pondered the question, for himself, by himself, holding the racket, about to throw it down, noticing sunlight splash the top of a car in the parking lot.

"Keep your eye on the ball," Jerrold barked.

Jesse threw the racket down. Jerrold worried about his son, because he never behaved like he really belonged anywhere, not on the tennis court, not on the boat. He was not one for the playing fields. He never seemed truly at ease, never able to engage with what anyone had to offer. He never seemed part of the party. Once, aboard *Scimitar*, on a Block Island Race many years ago, bringing Jesse along, thinking the adventure and interaction might do his sullen seed some good, Jerrold could see that Jesse proved to be inept at conversation, lazy at the winch handle, unable to tail a line, a poor helmsman, unable to hold the boat on course. He never was part of the Yacht Club scene. Almost pathologically shy, Jesse isolated himself, and his few friends tended to be fellow outsiders who gravitated toward deviant ideas and delinquent behavior, skipping school, sneaking out into the woods behind the gymnasium to smoke pot, taking no interest in their academic work, taking an extraordinary interest in aggressively deafening RPM, especially Heavy Metal, walking around with headphones on. Briefly, before becoming a Heavy Metal fan, Jesse had been fanatical about the Grateful Dead, becoming a "Deadhead" at the precocious age of thirteen, wearing rainbow-dyed T-shirts, his long hair in a red bandanna, becoming part of a tribe.

For some reason, ever since his first year at Sunswyck Academy, ever since he'd first stepped onto the polished, marmoreal floor of the main building's formal front foyer, the vestibule, the entranceway, where, over a long, wooden chest, seemingly carved from a single log of dark wood, the tapestry hung, where he'd deliberately, defiantly torn his tie off and flung his shirttails out, violating the dress code, a particular Grateful Dead song would run through the audio space of his head, and he'd tune it in, and the tapestry, a very beautiful object taking precedence, stunning, depicting a medieval landscape, a pastoral, a castle in the distance, a forest of incredible unlikeliness in the background, a unicorn somewhere, a present that was elsewhere, without equal in Jesse's experience, provided a suitable context for the RPM in his head. And the music just played through the hanging fabric: off of it, around it, out of it, swirling, and the braided colors of its weave burst into sonic truth, and he felt it was all for him, and he knew that something was gone for good, something the trees in the foreground had once embodied.

Jerrold's study, his spacious office at home, its walls painted a sumptuary, rich teal green, was exemplary in decor, notable for its steel and glass desk. There was a stunning chandelier hanging over some more classy furniture, a big leather sofa, mahogany book-shelves, a commodious fireplace, and an impressive collection of eighteenth-century foxhunting prints, lithographs, depicting a story of hunters, horses, some dogs, and a fox. Standing just outside the door, feet on the marble threshold, straining to hear his father's mind manifest itself on the telephone, Jesse was struck by a kind of infinite knowledge that everything he ever needed to know, every-place he'd ever wanted to go, every flash, forward or back, was but a function of his own choice, just as he was standing there, listening to the dread voice, spying, trying to make some sense of a room that would break like a bubble if he walked into it.

Late one afternoon in late February, with his parents away and Theresa out of the house, visiting family in Jamaica, just two weeks before the kidnapping, as a pale, moonlike sun was occluded by wispy banks of low, thinning cloud, Jesse felt like taking LSD, doing some blotter acid. Derek Bailey, having just secured a fresh supply of the powerful hallucinogen from a drug dealer in the city, was more than happy to oblige, and Jesse on LSD was Jesse indeed.

It was a Friday. "A good day to fly," Derek had said on the phone, and Jesse agreed, adding "a long, slow distance," to which Derek added, "into the night," to which Jesse cheerfully quipped, "of no return," but that was before the drug took effect and reality was doused with a luminous, silent paint, turning experience into a stunning sensorium that, at any point, could be tipped and collapse into anarchy, darkness, and terror. "I am a mess," he would later murmur into the mirror, dripping with water from the bathtub, leaving prismatic blobs of it on the floor, his thick blond mop obscuring his eyes, caught in a dream, his cortex saturated with color. Soon he'd be lost in a rush of fluidity, his gaze whizzing through pages and pages of reproductions of abstract paintings bound in an expensive art book he'd effectively stolen from the Sunswyck Library, a new building, all big plates of glass with stunning steel girders, polished wood, and carpeted floors, perched on its own bluff of lawn, overlooking the cluster of brick administration buildings—the new library, a space Jesse went down into the basement of often, skipping class to do what he was essentially doing again, watching the abstractions pass, the changes being wrung by the movements of his hands, his fingers working with paper, turning pages, flipping through reproductions of Kandinsky abstractions, the numerically titled *Compositions* painted early in TLC: warped checkerboards, hovering discs and oblongs, pyramids, grids and glyphs of some occult notation, broken packets of NRG, geometry flying apart into spirals, loops, and arcs, the parts of circles, all assuming sonic values, so that the brain properly named and designated "Jesse Draper" was hearing colors, seeing sounds, in a state of drug-induced synesthesia, enhanced by tracks from the hypnotic trumpet of Miles Davis sketching, resonating from magnetic tape unspooling on Jerrold's circa 1967 Sony reel-to-reel tape recorder, the electronic antique that he, Dad, had patiently shown Jesse how to use, back in the Larchmont house, his auditory module filled with the music that dominated the final hours of a long strange trip at home alone, a temporary "bummer" just after Derek departed, after they'd had some fun skipping stones on the water wavering with lines from the electric lights at the Yacht Club, watching the ducks, geese, and swans aloft, catching the movements of wings in oddly auditory flight, as waves of sound washed over him, bathing him, the acid coming over him, putting its amplified spin on things, pushing him into new lucidity. The inevitable change of awareness was fast and alienating, setting in with savage force, setting Jesse adrift alone, in a small boat on an enormous sea, tossed, like a piece of clothing in a washing machine, just as Derek, crouching, stood up like a mountain of sand and said, "I think I'm going to go."

Just a few hours before, alone at home, Jesse had been looking forward to something new, and now it was falling apart, the trip, as Derek walked away, and crimson spheres, tiny, intense dots, which at first dazzled him, were appearing everywhere, attacking things, dissolving distinctions and borders, eating the world up. He imagined he saw Derek again, picturing him present, a kind of projection of his own waking experience, something he'd been reading about in books about shamanism he'd taken out from the library, poring over certain sentences, highlighting them with the pink fluorescent Magic Marker he'd ceased using in his biology textbook.

His image of Derek dissolved.

Derek, always ready to drop and sell some acid, had driven down in a flash, and he cherished driving his new BMW motorcycle, a Christmas present, which he'd christened "Sid," having stenciled the letters S I D on the gas tank in bright red paint, the motorcycle's name being an advertisement for what he had to sell, though Jesse read it as homage to Sid Vicious and the future: gloom and doom and his own, private pact with sullen death. "I think I've died and gone to heaven," Jesse had said, with deliberation, trying to produce some kind of effect on Derek, without really considering the evident contradiction of his statement, for there he was, thinking, and didn't that mean he was on Earth, and didn't the capacity for thought necessarily entail his being alive, being there? So that the train of thought—"I have died, and I am not here, but in heaven because nothing is happening, and nothing can harm me, and it's beautiful and terrifying"—necessarily implied the contradiction of his beating heart, his private drummer sending tiny, bright spheres out to circulate through his blood, which made scenes beneath his eyelids, all directed by automatic mechanisms lodged deeply within the circuitry of his hallucinating brain, his central nervous system (CNS), which was where he was again. Whatever Jesse was thinking, he was alive, awake, and aware, through a global binding process bringing the details, all the phenomenal aspects and inputs of his senses, back home: the wavering lines of electric light, the traces of bird flight in his ears, the broken bells, the crimson spheres, the crunch of sand, the microphone suspended in front of his mouth.

"I think I've gone to heaven," Jesse said.

Derek, head turned toward the motorcycle, walking in its direction, stopped his forward motion. He looked at Jesse. "That's cool. Heaven's a cool place to hang, but I've just gotta get away and go out for a ride." Derek had a way with words that belied his privileged upbringing. He scanned the inertia around them, the huge, empty houses and lawns.

Jesse watched Derek walk off toward the motorcycle and climb on to it, fitting the helmet to his head, adjusting it, creating the impression of a giant ant-robot. He stood up higher and thrust his body down on the starting pedal, and the engine roared into action as plumes of blue exhaust streamed out from the departing vehicle, asphalt fragments flung into spirals, breaking the glass in Jesse's room again, as he entertained a prolonged, convincing hallucination, a sustained bout of watery delirium, during which he believed he was underwater, under the influence of that impression, and the roaring machine became some kind of vast, distantly vibrating vanishing point, cosmologically significant, much like the hum that was leading him back to the house, the big, empty house he could walk to if he wanted to, and he wanted to, and this amazed him, doing what he wanted to do. Just a few hours ago, home alone, everything was boringly ordinary, and now it had all changed profoundly, due to the friend who'd dropped by and vanished. Jesse was underwater, and he was walking home, just because he wanted to, toward the house, now a yellow spaceship of some kind, also submerged underwater. It took an enormous amount of time to reach the house, now a submarine. He walked around it, to the back, to the icy terrace skirting its monumental bulk. He studied a door, a large quantity of painted wood, gradually bringing about a reassessment of the situation. This was not a spaceship, not a yellow submarine. This was his palatial home. "This is not a submarine, not a spaceship," he thought to himself. He opened the door, knocking snow and slush from his boots on the stoop. Once inside the house, he veered toward its center, and then he turned into the great cavernous, curved space of the gallery, like the capacious interior of a dirigible. Feeling small and safe and free, he decided to build a fire in a fireplace so large he could practically walk into it. The big copper cauldron was filled with birch logs and kindling. Crossing some logs in a fireplace so huge he walked right into it, he constructed a celebratory pyre, placed some hastily crushed balls of newspaper beneath it, and then he telephoned the pizza place. But before that, standing there, he'd wondered, "I wonder where Rex is," and he'd wandered around the house, feeling as if it were all brand-new, startled, as if he had never been there before, never set foot through those rooms, amazed that he knew them, delighting in new perceptions, true memories telling him how and where to go, searching for Rex. He explored sunken chambers. He went into the game room and played a round of pool with an imaginary opponent, a pirate. He opened the liquor cabinet and poured some whiskey into a tall glass, quite a dose of it, and he carried it upstairs, trying to balance it on the palm of his right hand, to the bedroom mirror for a long, shallow chat with himself, making faces in its SIR FACE, remembering Derek becoming a vanishing point, a piece of improvisation, while he had walked back to the house, counting his steps, his circulation, taking his time in a slow trance underwater, back to the submarine, back to the door of the spaceship, to the fireplace, to the telephone, to the liquor cabinet, up the stairs and into the mirror, where he said to himself, "I am a mess . . . a messiah," an interesting proposition, a delusion with which to greet the delivery guy, who had been ringing the doorbell repeatedly in the cold air outside.

Roused from a dogmatic slumber, Rex trailed Jesse downstairs, who suddenly realized he had to find some money to pay for the food. It was just too weird thinking through the equivalence, money and food, being forced to think about money for food, where some cash might be, finding the thought difficult to manage, a cognitive challenge, a puzzlement, just finding some cash in a vast house filled with precious objects, expensive paintings and furniture. Rex retreated into an alcove off the dining room, where he curled up on a silk cushion, and Jesse, on his way to the kitchen drawer where Mom, he remembered, kept a roll, a billfold of twenty- and fifty-dollar bills, experienced a brief, intense exchange of NRG with the cat's porous image. Streams of radiant NRG poured from deep pools, the tinfoiled tar pits of its eyes, creating concentric circles, and Jesse was back underwater again, being addressed by furry white curls on a cushion, the fur of a cat beneath the waves. Rex paddled the air with his paws.

"Where do you think you are going?" he asked Jesse.

The library was, from one point of view, a sort of trophy room, dominated by a waist-high globe of pearl, onyx, multicolored minerals, and gemstones, and there was another commodious fireplace there, almost large enough to walk into, and over its marble mantel hung a taxidermy swordfish, a prize-sized catch from a deep-sea fishing contest Jerrold had competed in and won, just after meeting Jessica, the presence of its silvery-, blue-, and black-finned body catching Jesse's attention as he walked by the open door, though it hung there in darkness.

"I think I am going where I am going," Jesse shouted back to Rex, the cat, now following him, as Jesse navigated, dog-paddling, his way to the kitchen drawer.

The pizza guy was a local kid, a dropout, an educated derelict whom Jesse vaguely recognized, wearing a purple ski parka with a bright orange lift ticket attached to its zipper's tiny metal handle, a somehow salient, significant detail, like the mystery of the outdoor lights on the delivery car in the driveway, engine idling, breaking the icy silence. Without counting, without even looking, flaunting a certain indifference toward money, Jesse messed with the bills, giving far too many to the guy, who studied Jesse's face for a moment, noting the tinfoiled tar pits of his eyes. The guy looked down at the carpet and took the money quickly, pocketed it, and walked away into the night, as Jesse, walking the other way, back into the house, carrying a big flat box with both hands, confronted Rex, all-white cat, now standing erect at the kitchen's entrance, doing something with its eyes again, producing a hypnotic stare, pulling Jesse into it, the concentric circles of the cat's concentrated consciousness pulling him down the hallway, luring him into the library, where he switched the recessed lighting on, revealing an impressive battery of bookshelves stocked with volumes, like weaponry, ponderous leather bindings, paper cures for absentmindedness. Forgetting about food, unconsciously deciding to do nothing about eating, Jesse let the box drop to the floor, and he entered, as into a kind of trance, the silence of the library, where the form of the swordfish loomed large on one wall, its wide, surprised marble eye clearly accustomed to the science of being alone there, lording over space, being its sole inhabitant, caught unexpectedly, and then the creature's body moved, its taut skin twitched, soon trembling with the NRG of another environment, another world, from right to left, from the tip of its long, pointed sword, down the even longer, hydro-dynamic, razor-like edge of its body's long, quivering top fin, to the end of a single open parenthesis, the arc of its tail, taking Jesse underwater again, and bubbles began to rise, as the dead fish, its meek mouth open, started to speak.

He felt as though he were growing gills, diving into the un-recorded, delving through watery strata, permeating membranes, passing into a previous, prenatal state, entering new old dimen-sions, a time told somewhere a long time ago, where everything was wet and swift, and swimming was how he related to an essentially smooth environment, combing oxygen out of the water, coaxing its being into his brain, as if he were back in his body and in reality, his undulating spine bringing it all about again. It would be nice, wouldn't it, if all this were true, if my whimsical allusions to Beach Boys songs actually added up to something that went somewhere?

Jesse's mind went to Vivian, a moody girl with long, wavy hair, black as tar, as coal, like the night itself. She'd had a hearty, almost athletic laughter, which attracted him to her in the first place, the sound of her vivacious voice rising above the din at a party on the beach the previous summer, an emotional highpoint for Jesse. He slowed down and remembered some of the things she'd said. He was happy just to dance with her, happy with the way she stared at the ground, after she'd said whatever she said, looking as if she put the whole world down, which was often how he felt. He was drinking tequila and smoking marijuana, and he remembered how, inhibitions dissolved and turned into something else by the combi-nation of the two working together in him, he'd asked her to dance, initiating a series of actions that, rather ripped, led to their hectic embrace.

He walked to the door, flinging it open, and the smell of salt-water was exceedingly stirring, bringing him back from oblivion to where he was, where he found a match, one from a book buried deep in his pocket, and he walked back inside, toward the enormous

fireplace. He lit the match and flung it, a small, burning thing, raising flames in the space above the crossed logs.

The rest of the night was a party apart, attended by a group
of one, where Jesse was second to none, watching the sparks fly,
finding animals in the crazy irregularities of some of the trees outside with the floodlights on them, turning them into a scene. He
shared some pizza with Rex and what he believed were foxes in the
backyard before retreating upstairs and turning all the lights out,
to eventually go to the bathroom mirror, then fill the bathtub with
hot water and bathe beneath the electric lights, steaming the mirror, filling the space of the room with a tumescent vapor, so it now
seemed much like a car drowned in a dim film under the sea, and
he was looking through its windshield.

He went drifting downstairs through the free air in a bathrobe,
turning on the lights again, descending through more water to the
library, where he sank into the leather couch, and there, catching the wave of a dream, he closed his eyes and started levitating.
He was suspended in free, empty air, a great vault of space like a
cathedral's, flying above a scintillating forest, the color green gone
mad. Somehow, much to his surprise, the sensation of flying over
it wasn't unusual, and he felt compelled to go on. It wasn't fright-
ening, though the landscape below, a vast carpet of trees, seemed to
be painted on glass, with a bright light glowing beneath it, creating
the appearance of an apparition on unrolled parchment. Where was
he now, as he settled more deeply into the leather couch, enjoying
the view, watching various metals dance in the thin skin beneath
the closed lids of his eyes? Suddenly breaking the spell, he rose
and turned on the music again, more Miles Davis, whose trumpet was an incredible streak of gold, its impulse wildly beating,
and there was a long chain of musical moments and movements,
leading to Jesse's discovery, first, of the fire burning, crackling with
intensity, and then, in the alcove off the dining room, of Rex again,
circling his cushion until he settled on a spot to nap, the intrigue

of feline curvature engrossing him for what seemed like minutes, though nearly half an hour had passed. Jesse just stood there, posed over the white cat's PURR SUIT of sleep, fulfilled, curled up with composure while still being there, nominal king of the house, his accessible essence buried beneath snowy fur and myriad hairs, leading, eventually, to Jesse's fetal position alongside of Rex, the music on in the other room, and finally, bundling up and walking outside, into a chilly, predawn silence punctuated by the eerie, irregular clang of the bell buoy out in the harbor enveloped by an illuminated fog, a curtain of shimmering mist, dawn's early light, a place to catch his breath, which allowed him to see and think, as he walked toward the beach, of names for every natural fact, from the seaweed right up to the seagulls' wings in motion, a delicate cast of cloud, though his powers of discrimination were limited, not finding so many names for so many facts after all, making the beach an empty place to be, wondering about the structure of time, the importance of being on time, under its influence, the drug wearing off. Jesse in the wintry dawn, wrapped in his goose-down parka, playing the part of an Arctic explorer, should have been able to articulate more about his environment, the molecules of memory arranged a certain way. Ripples of clear water, miniscule instances of electrical NRG in the dawn's light, ran along the edge of the pebbly beach, breaking into a mild surf, making an incredibly busy, high-pitched music, and in the bubbly rush he noted the natural gas storage tank behind a tennis court. He began to walk back to the house. He looked back at the water, a band of cold steel beyond rocks half buried in ribbons of snow and sand. His ears appeared to be excessively large, and he felt like an elephant, wearing huge orchestral cymbals attached to the sides of his head.

On a cold, bright late Monday afternoon in the middle of February 1992, the year Portland, Oregon, began to recycle its garbage, just after Jesse's seventeenth birthday, shortly after Nirvana released the LP *Nevermind*, between classes and intramural hockey, in the liquid, golden glow, its light nearly splashing up against the sturdy wooden chest over which the tapestry hung, Jesse looked up, holding a can of spray paint. He sniffed the air, noticing a sweetness, and he saw, standing on a marble pedestal in a corner of the large room, a jade vase filled with white carnations and lilies, the assemblage of flowering plants visually enhanced, as if seen through a magnifying glass, giving the flowers an aura, something like a movie still. He was seized by a sudden imbalance, something in his genes, or he may have been acting out a forgotten memory, a buried impulse, trying to make a point, to stretch himself to a point he could reach, though he had no clear idea what it was, just the blind drive to register an impact somewhere, to be one amid other explosions of awareness, another bird that flies, another leaf that falls, one among many blades of grass. With the descent of winter, ever since his grades had begun to plummet again and the authorities had begun threatening him with reform school again, in Idaho this time, he'd felt condemned to failure, bound, locked into a dispirited space helmet, strapped to a meaningless chair, the trajectory of his time to be filled with the tedium of disequilibrium, downward to the bleak nadir of his consciousness. Yet an affirmative spirit from somewhere, like the other side of space itself, something wholly alien, totally unfamiliar, had been urging him to do something wrong, something egregiously wrong. As a boy, he'd urinate on a bathroom floor, just to see pee out on the tiles, for the simple pleasure of doing something wrong. It was as if he'd been placed under a spell, and here he was now. How would he entertain himself? He shook the spray paint in its can, feeling the little ball inside of it rattle, sensing the cold, volatile liquid inside, and he pointed the nozzle up to the colorful weave, marveling at its beauty. He stood there, transfixed, wondering what he'd write. He stood there for a protracted moment of indecision, not having really thought about it before. Fragments from a

Beastie Boys song lyric played on his radio briefly, then something by the Grateful Dead, before he pushed the plastic button and the red paint sprayed, directed by his swift hand and fevered brain, forming four capital letters, two of them being instantiations of the same type, spelling a simple word: "DEAD." It was audacious, right there in the foreground, in the woven splendor of the expensive, storied tapestry. He thought, for some reason, of adding another word, the word "PEST," but he decided to leave it at that, with "DEAD," and he ran away from the scene of the crime, stupidly tossing the can into a wastepaper basket, where it was later discovered. The police were called in. Fingerprints were taken, and, based on prints from a previous arrest for driving without a license, for which Jerrold's lawyer had managed to have all charges dropped, the match was made with Jesse's.

Two days later, Jesse was suspended from the Sunswyck Academy. Jessica flew up from Rio, where she'd been part of a promotional photo shoot with Madonna, and Jerrold phoned home from wherever he'd been, somewhere in Africa, suddenly caught up in an urgent conversation about what to do with his wayward son, again arranging for charges to be dropped, assuring the police that immediate and effective disciplinary action would be taken, that he, the famous and powerful parent, would assume responsibility, so he soon flew home. The whole family met for the first time together in several months, seated around the dining room table. Jerrold surveyed Jesse severely, but Jessica was preoccupied with the elegance of the new dress she was wearing. She really was, and her husband was impatient, demanding that she "get in touch with what's going on here" and "get in touch with those Idaho people." It all unfolded like so much meaningless drama in front of Jesse, who sat there in a daze, almost comatose, eyes glazed. Everything seemed to be painted on a glass pane with a host of burning candles set behind it, making everything less real and more real simultaneously. Theresa brought out dessert, flan and coffee, and Jesse excused himself from the table. Being around his parents, enduring after-dinner conversation, almost always brought on bouts of inner conflict for him, for which he'd already prepared his manic defense, going upstairs, putting his headphones on, and doodling to RPM.

17

Meanwhile, back in Africa, donning the mesmeric wings of a blue butterfly, Amy looked into the shimmering greens of the Jungle, her new location, and she felt a bath of benevolence surround her and pass through her skin. She felt her ego turn into impersonal particles, prismatic drops of water, and then she watched them hit the ground. She flapped her wings in a gesture toward flight, letting her nascent insect self leap into the air, a part of it arranged for her, as she kicked her legs wildly and flew on expansive wings into the open space, the great blue dome above.

The kidnapping was Amy's idea, springing from a seed planted in infancy, as if a part of her, in awe of all things vegetable, had been secretly thriving, growing, sending out shoots, subsisting through her childhood and adolescence on a potato farm in rural Idaho, just outside of Boise, where she'd labored in the flat, predominantly brown landscape, at work in the fields, sowing the furrows, hoeing soil, digging up tubers. The idea continued to foment within her, gaining clarity as she worked, in a different way, for her academic degrees at Idaho State University: a BA in adolescent psychology and an MA in mathematics, impressive credentials upon which she'd built her modest career, working as a high school algebra teacher, helping disadvantaged kids, so that she'd taken an interest in developing characters for whom number is eventually everything, for whom numbers are many things, so many lives, vast quantities of dream material, testimonial tales of perseverance and accomplishment, and Jerrold Draper's was one of these, the one she found out about, doing research in the library, between classes at Manhattan Beach High, finding diversion perusing glossy fashion and financial magazines, learning all about EDGE and Jerrold Draper, whose new investment strategies were making him very wealthy, a self-described "Master of the Money Verse." She sometimes felt, in an apocalyptic tone of mind, that our technological society is doomed, bound to fail; that mankind is a future eater, consuming his only environment like a plague animal; that the fate of our higher intelligence will be universal catastrophe—yet she was awed by him and men like him, by his preternatural mathematical gift, his meteoric rise to the pinnacle of power, his being consumed with the need to dominate and control, his wheeling and dealing on a global scale, and she also discovered details about his private life, his villa on Connecticut's "Gold Coast," his womanizing, his ex-model wife, her history of substance abuse, their emotionally and cognitively challenged son, and she cultivated a kind of perverse fascination for this wealthy family from Belle Haven, nurturing a plan, and she brought it with her to the Jungle, if only in the evanescence of a vague idea.

Amy was mounting a new pair of especially iridescent green butterfly wings to a panel, soon to be part of her collection, which hung on bits of colored thread from a complicated contraption of balsawood overhead, a kind of mobile aloft, setting the two wings into place with tweezers and dabs of glue, her activity lit by flaming torch, and the tropical night was abuzz with insects' expletives, when Omnibus, who had been gone for some time on an expedition, gathering data re: ants and bees, happened to stop by. He put down his backpack and walked over to where she sat, and he stooped, looking over her shoulder, admiring her manual dexterity.

He sat down on the stool next to hers, there at the worktable, and he listened to her plan.

Konrad, simultaneously seated at the other end of the tent, hunched over a portable word processor, was working on a particularly tricky thicket of theoretical prose, with a funnel on his head, something about ELF in the Jungle. He was consumed with inner, invisible weather, while Amy spoke, articulating her scheme, while Omnibus sat and listened. Far out in the Jungle, Omnibus had become someone acquainted with the territory, sometimes gone for days on exploratory treks, walking in rain or sunshine, wearing only a loincloth, carrying a spear and a backpack filled with provisions. He was accompanied by Kombolo, the shaman, his guide, who had shown him the location of a particular cave where a particular cat was going to be, if only they could make it happen. Spending most his time out of doors, feeling like he'd never land, becoming more and more in awe of nature, forming new and more interesting conceptions and demands, Omnibus had developed, as he explored the Jungle, impressive telepathic abilities, and he'd formulated a mental map of a conceptual possibility, dreaming with lucidity, and he focused on "Crystal Mountain." "It's the place," he said, "where there are indicative signs, automobile tracks, barbed wire, metal plaques on metal stakes, and all of the plaques are marked with four letters: *E-D-G-E*," and Amy made the connection.

An image of Crystal Mountain materialized, its green growth violated, torn open like a flayed animal, veins of gleaming metal exposed. "Edge," she said, letting the word dangle before them for a moment, before Omnibus nodded, tuned to her wavelength, in sync. It would be a bold act of retribution.

Konrad was on a mission now, roused from his musings, thrown into action, like a stone hurled. He was the designated kidnapper, and he drove the van into Libreville, stepping on it. He boarded a plane bound for JFK, flying into the city one cloudless afternoon in late February, when the sun hung impressively low on the horizon, like a coin on fire, and the western sky was a peculiar, homogeneous tint of pale aquamarine, that chalky teal, and there were waves, points of white surf on the face of the water. I was in the kitchen, tossing some salad together, preparing for a little dinner party, just Jack and I, when, suddenly out of nowhere, Konrad phoned again.

He asked me about the Drapers, the wealthiest family in Belle Haven, and I told him what I could. After our conversation, having hung up the phone, he first had to visit the men's room. "You're in me now, and I want you out," he muttered to himself or, more precisely, to his fluid-filled bladder, standing in front of a ceramic urinal, poised to pee, his posture just like in the rain forest, out on an exploratory trek, but now he was waiting for something to happen because it wasn't happening, and he found it to be an awkward experience. Eventually, something happened, in a stream of fresh, bright yellow. "However much you swing and dance, the last drop always remains in your pants," he mused to himself, zipping up, walking away with a swagger, remembering some graffiti he'd seen above a urinal somewhere, his concentrated glance into the mirror revealing a glimpse of his finite best.

18

SEVERAL DAYS LATER, UP IN BANKSVILLE, UP NEAR THE BORDER WITH Westchester County, Jesse was hanging out at Derek's place, not so merrily at home in the disheveled interior, waking up to a chilly, foggy Tuesday morning outside, with a raw wind rattling through the branches of some bare trees, making the sound of skeletons dancing, bones rattling in the wooded area behind the ramshackle house, a secluded piece of property, where Derek smoked pot, chopped wood, and played the electric guitar. "I know, it's only rock n' roll, but I like it," he'd said to his academic advisor, just before

quitting Juilliard. The walls of the front room were adorned with
travel posters, two of them for places in Greece, showing beautiful,
white ruins against the buff, blue planes of the Aegean Sea, another
one depicting a cathedral in southern France, a great structure
with stone spires rising above a field of sunflowers, and there were
a couple of lava lamps on an empty, wooden bookshelf, bubbles
percolating upward through bright purple and green jelly, vaguely
malevolent, and the pungent aroma of burning marijuana was hanging there still, like a psychotropic mist over the scattered playing
cards and dominos, the empty bottle of Bailey's Irish Cream. He'd
spent the night before partying, seeking oblivion with cohorts. A
vague wave crashed on the shores of Jesse's consciousness, as he
woke up on the sofa in the front room, light pouring over his body,
slowly coming to terms with consciousness, his awareness of the
fact that he wasn't in his own bed at home alone, that pebbles and
weeds filled his throat, that there was a wood-burning stove nearby,
that it spat out sounds and smoke, and then he remembered where
he was and how he'd been there, each fact exactly itself, the empty
beer bottles and ashtrays coming into focus, offending his eyes. It
seemed like one of the scariest places he'd ever seen.

Derek's snoring, coming from the room upstairs, resounded
through a partially closed door, and although Jesse couldn't see
him, he knew he was there, and he pictured himself as an Arctic
explorer, lying there in vigil under a sleeping walrus or sea elephant
that he'd captured out on the ice and now kept in a pen in the
room upstairs. The inanity of trying to sustain a wishful distortion
of reality, the hopelessness of the fiction, passed through him with
a shiver, as he got up and went to the bathroom. He splashed some
water on his face.

With nothing to really do but wait, he walked into Derek's
kitchen, a narrow space, cramped, like the galley aboard *Scimitar*,
defined by wooden panels and cupboards. Flinging one open, he
saw some instant coffee in a plastic jar, and, finding a cup and a

teaspoon, he unscrewed the lid and heaped three spoonfuls of the dark stuff, concentrated caffeine, into the cup, which he then put under the faucet, after adding brown sugar, turning it all, with hot water, into a black, bitter, stimulating paste. The chemicals excited him, making his awareness spin, as he paced the narrow kitchen's length, stooping to look out a window, facing Tuesday's prospects. The dull plumage of a common sparrow condensed into a grey profusion of feathers, coming close to the glass, and then it flew away, taking wing. Time passed more slowly, and Derek eventually woke, coming downstairs, waving his dirty black hair in a daze. He spoke a few curt words, coming out of a fog, having forgotten that he had a guest, with Jesse now sitting at the kitchen table, trying to celebrate whatever was going on.

It was a Tuesday morning, March 3, 1992, nine twenty-five to be exact, and no birds sang. The ruby red of a plastic taillight's casing glinted in the sun. The vehicle, a plain white van, had been secretly following Jesse around for the past day, since Monday morning, surreptitiously tracking him, trailing him from Belle Haven, through Greenwich, into Port Chester, up to Banksville, following Derek's Mercedes, going wherever it happened to go, and the van was now parked nearby, just down the road, around the bend, set alongside a stone wall. Konrad, sitting behind the wheel, was waiting for Jesse's next move. His neck was stiff from watching the rearview mirror.

Derek, as usual, didn't have anything planned for the day, and he didn't have much to say. They listened to the first side of Nirvana's *Nevermind* again, and Derek did an effective accompaniment to Kurt Cobain's solos, picking up his electric guitar, turning it on, and making its decibels scream, totally changing the mood of the room. They smoked some marijuana and ran out into the backyard, where Jesse picked up a football, and they passed it between themselves, laughing. Jesse noticed Sid, the motorcycle, attracted by its emerald green gas tank glowing, parked under a tin roof over stacks of firewood, and Derek went into a sudden spiel about the superiority of the experience of riding Sid, the motorcycle, to that of driving the Mercedes, but Jesse didn't have a helmet to wear, so they weren't going to risk getting into trouble with the police because of that. The sun warmed the morning, melting its shadows away, and they went back inside to smoke some more pot. Soon it was close to eleven, the time of two sticks. They both were feeling hungry, but there was nothing to eat. The confusions of idle youth taking license in the folds of leisure seemed the order of the day. Derek always ate out anyway, so they began to talk about a big breakfast, conjuring images of pancakes on ceramic plates, sausages, and pools of maple syrup. Derek's father had bought him the car to boost his sense of independence, and he enjoyed driving it around, so they decided to drive into Port Chester, eat breakfast at the diner there, and take a train into Manhattan, to avoid the hassle of parking in the city. Derek had a connection, somewhere in Spanish Harlem, someone from whom he sometimes bought cocaine, and he wanted to score some "snow" for the upcoming weekend, and Jesse, having no real alternative, nothing better to do, went along for the ride. They disembarked at 125th Street, with Derek running off to make his connection, leaving Jesse, who'd said he'd wanted to walk around on his own. He continued walking toward Central Park, going south, not knowing where he was going exactly, vaguely following the sun, knowing only that he had plans to meet Derek later that afternoon at a bar on St. Mark's Place, where Derek had other connections.

Rays of mounting daylight hit the hectic streets, crowded with human forms and faces, deliberate actions, unintended events, too many to keep track of. Jesse was trying to forget about Idaho, the place he might be going, unless something else happened. He stopped at a hot dog vendor's cart, where he bought one, washing the salty, undercooked pink meat down with a can of orange soda pop. Suddenly, he experienced a vivid flashback to his LSD trip, a sensation in his fingertips, frantically searching through his pockets for some money to pay for the food and drink. He found that he had more than enough, plenty of it, and he decided, remembering that there were Kandinsky paintings at the Guggenheim Museum, that he would walk down the avenue to the curving walls of world-famous architecture, go through the revolving doors, pay admission, and traipse up the ramp to seek them, find them, stand there and stare at them, but then he thought again, and he wandered more deeply into Central Park, continuing southward, eventually following a faint, flat stretch of brown horse manure, noticing flocks of dimwit sparrows and grey pigeons with iridescent highlights fluttering above the dull stones, feathers pulsing with light, as he walked down the drive toward the Plaza Hotel. Amazed that he'd walked so far in less than two hours, Jesse briefly wondered what kind of nourishment the small birds found in even more inhospitable circumstances—the wintry forests of Maine, for instance. What do the small birds survive on up there? The glittering glass of a broken green bottle, a pile of emerald fragments, caught fire in the waning March sun, and Jesse smiled in the weak light, as he gradually hatched the thought of going back to Belle Haven, sneaking into the house, and stealing one of Jerrold's credit cards to make an escape, purchase a ticket for a flight to anywhere—New Zealand, Tasmania, Iceland. "Here I am now, entertaining these places," he thought to himself, humming, sharpening the edge of a knife in the waters of his mind. Idaho: He couldn't conceive of the place; he had no idea about how time there would pass. He hatched an image of myriad ropes dangling down from the high ceiling of a large, well-lit space, a gymnasium with a shiny wooden floor, a basketball court, and he saw himself doing drills on those ropes, climbing them, being ordered around by men wearing military uniforms, holding whistles, holding stopwatches. He hatched the image of his body moving underwater through dreary hallways, swimming to his seat in a creepy room, his mind leaping with dull fins. He hatched the image of a subterranean library, a vast ship's hold full of books and publications, equipped with chairs and tables, cubicles and computer screens.

Huddled at the wheel of the white van, its bulbous sides now emblazoned with stickers espousing provocative sentiments, coated with slight sediments, thin films of dirt, oil, salt, and sand, Konrad, accompanied by Joshua, a hired hand, a temporary recruit, a tall, bearded young man in a trench coat, wearing dark glasses and a torn and frayed wool sweater, watched Jesse descend slowly down the drive and walk into that open area in front of the Plaza Hotel, right where I'd stood with Aunt Pauline, where he appeared stupefied, stumped, where the horse-drawn carriages congregate and wait for customers. He didn't know where he was going. He was watching what he was doing, conscious of his feet alone. He thought he was waiting for something, but he didn't know what. The kidnappers looked out through the van's stippled windshield, and although they almost bungled it, they didn't.

Konrad gestured to Joshua, putting his thumb up into the air. "There he is. That's the kid. Go, man. Get him!"

Joshua fumbled with something beneath his seat, producing a large, black plastic bag. He climbed out of the car and approached Jesse, who saw a strange, tall man in a trench coat, carrying something black in his left hand, plastic expanse billowing, who quickly threw the black opacity over Jesse's head. Bewildered and unable to breathe, Jesse panicked blindly, as Konrad drove up in the van, and he was shoved into the backseat by Joshua, bound by belt by his captor, who, taking the bag off his head, now produced a great wad of cotton, which was pushed into Jesse's mouth.

Konrad, turning around in the driver's seat, suggested that Jesse should relax and breathe through his nose.

Jesse at first resisted, but he gradually saw where they were going with this, as they drove across town, and he let them have their way. The kidnapping didn't happen in a void, like a random sneeze or yawn. It was the inexorable climax of a series of past events, an outcome with consequences, repercussions stretching into the future. There was no way of knowing what would happen

next, and although Jesse was frightened, there was something ex-
hilarating about the idea of being kidnapped, being forced into a
dangerous situation, thrown back upon his own resources, and he
suddenly felt possessed by a virile volatility.

"Preposterous" was the word Jerrold used, as he hung up the
telephone and spoke to nobody there in his office, convinced it was
a fraud, a prank call, reflecting on the grainy urgency of the voice,
thinking it that of someone he knew, some practical joker, gradually
realizing that this was maybe not a joke, allowing the possibility of
its truth to register, to sink in, causing him to reach for the telephone and push buttons in a frantic attempt to trace the call, but
it was too late. He was able only to feel a slow, sinking sense of
violation creep through him, an erratic awareness of the possibility that Jesse might have actually been kidnapped, so that a part
of himself was now captive, held somewhere against his will, and
his anger at the possibility mixed with his frustration at being, right
then and there, unable to do anything constructive about it. He
swiveled about in his chair, rose, and opened the door to call out
to his secretary, seated, tapping away on the computer keyboard
with pianistic expertise, totally absorbed in some task. "Something
outrageous has happened," Jerrold barked out, and she looked up,
startled. "Contact the police," he added, establishing eye contact,
then turning away, retreating into his office.

It was an enormous steel ship, a huge, floating warehouse, her
steep sides painted a dull, pale grey, as Jesse first saw it through a
chain-link fence, her wide deck piled high with more than a thousand metal containers, all filled with cars, over which a spheroid
control booth on a long metal stem rose. They were in the van, in
the parking lot, down at the docks, and soon, at dusk, they'd depart
from Perth Amboy, on a smooth trajectory.

To be afraid of doing something, yet to go through with doing it,
might be a criterion, a standard, a condition necessary for someone
to be attributed with, and applauded for, a sort of absolute, reckless

freedom. Konrad harbored grave doubts about what he was doing, fearful of the consequences if he were to be caught, knowing that he'd be found guilty of a serious crime, yet he persisted with the procedure. "If you need more air, you can open the portal. See?" And he leaned over the head of Jesse's bunk to manipulate a primitive, metal nut-and-bolt device that controlled the glass portal's lens. "It's standard procedure," he said in the time of its adjustment, "for a port of air," he added, with enigmatic emphasis. The reality of Jesse's imagination was better than the unreality of the situation, as he reminded himself of the exhilaration he'd felt with the very idea of being kidnapped, earlier, riding in the van. The experience of being alone in a room for the night wasn't really anything new; it happened all the time, although this time he was kidnapped, in a cabin on a ship, far out at sea.

The short chain of days soon passed, feeding into each other without striking incident, nearly identical, conduits of calm, consisting for Jesse of pleasant nautical hours spent in his air-conditioned cabinet of a stateroom, lying on his narrow bunk, listening to RPM on a Sony Walkman. His time alone was punctuated by meals, trips to the head, and significant stretches of recreation, playing ping-pong with Konrad, difficult at first, for the constant movement, the plunging of the vast hull, created distortions of spatial judgment down below, challenging Jesse, providing a chance to work on his sea legs and manual coordination. "It's all about the ball, so train your attention on the ball and focus on its motion," Konrad announced, handing Jesse a paddle.

Preparing to serve toward the end of one game, Konrad held the ball up and reiterated the score between them, noting his advantage, referring to it as an "immaterial thing," and he pressed the ball, slightly with his fingers, putting a certain pressure there. "Be subtle, be careful, Jesse, with immaterial things," he said with renewed intensity, "for there are such things, and one must be supple with them."

The ocean outside was a huge surround of shimmering sea and sky, dominated by the sun's ever-present, effervescent effects, the white caps of waves breaking as the ship approached the equator, passing through the notorious "horse latitudes," where captains of great sailing vessels in the past, becalmed on strange waters, ordered livestock, cattle, and horses overboard, to lighten their heavy loads. The sweltering ocean was exceedingly stirring. Jesse, holding the binoculars, looking out to see something on the horizon, at once felt as if he were the only one there, traveling, feeling the apparent wind caused by the motion of the massive ship, the impersonal play of charged particles at dusk, when the sky became an enormous show. Passing through the Sargasso Sea, he'd seen an impressive flotilla of aluminum cans and Styrofoam pellets—stretching for miles, it seemed—which slapped up against the sides of the ship. Reaching the Tropic of Cancer, standing alone on the stern deck, scanning the scene with binoculars, he saw a squadron of gulls flying, following the wake, and one morning he saw some porpoises Konrad had described earlier, the purpose of the description being to get Jesse outside, up on deck, while Konrad attended to whatever he was attending to, a mystery to Jesse, though he imagined him exploring the complicated interior of the ship with a flashlight.

The sea was calm and mirror-like, the hull hugging the long, low African shoreline, late that Friday night in March, passing by Dakar, its urban glow a faint halo to the east, when the rogue waves hit, a demonstration in unexpectedness itself, abnormal and extreme. Heaving heavily through a series of watery shocks, peaks and troughs, the hull veered one way and then the other, and the creaking of the metal containers above, the sound of all that weight shifting overhead, made high-pitched, inanimate screams, shrieking metal, as the great ship labored and the freak waves hit, coming from an unknown source, striking the sides, crashing through the rigging, causing metal cables and bolts to break as several large containers slipped off the deck and were lost.

"I guess it was," Konrad remarked, over coffee the next morning, "a random act of God, Nature, the Universal Mind, the display of a mean disposition, the soul of a bitch, whatever you want to call it. The sea is a vast, howling mother, and she plays without security, without any concern for our security. We are just dust in the wind, subject to her whim." Sometimes Konrad spoke this way, theatrical, bursting with elegant despair. He began to move his forefinger along the rim of his coffee cup.

Libreville emerged from the coastline that day, an impressive heap of white buildings and beautiful beach beneath a leaden sky the color of a television screen caught between channels, broadcasting a greyish blue monochrome of NRG, chaos made visible. "That's where the Europeans, the explorers and traders from Portugal, first made landfall, bringing fabrics, weapons, and germs, bringing salt to the Jungle," Konrad said, pointing out a monument. "The Portuguese maintained a lucrative slave trade here for over a hundred years, but in the complicated process of socioeconomic warfare that is the racing engine of human history, the French usurped power, on the very cusp of TLC, modernizing, creating infrastructure, building buildings, roads, and railways, discovering vast reserves of precious metals and jewels, constructing mines, extracting fuels. The lumber business flourished. Vast tracts of balsawood trees were cut down and used in aviation. There were rubber tree plantations."

Konrad handed Jesse the binoculars, and he looked through them, focusing in on where they'd soon be, studying the arrangement of the buildings, the streets, the white beach, and although he was bound for where he knew not, he felt perfectly pleased with his prospects, enjoying the experience of being held captive, treated like an important prisoner, though bereft of any princely status, now a mere pauper, a pawn in some elaborate game that he couldn't quite fathom. He felt as if he were on the brink of some stupendous discovery, as when the smelly canals of Venice showed a seamy side of life to him, long ago, when he was a boy: dirty water, soiled with refuse and floating debris, something he'd rarely seen and had never seen for any sustained duration until that long, hot week in Venice when he was ten, when he had immensely disliked being with his parents and the boundaries he had to endure in the city that sits on the sea. They'd visited the Bridge of Sighs one morning, gone shopping all afternoon, and dined at a chic restaurant, and he was alone in the hotel room at night, enjoying the air-conditioning, room service, and porn on television, eating chocolate cake on the sofa when his parents walked in. Dad glanced at the screen furiously, picked up the remote control, and immediately flicked the image off, while Mom kept laughing outrageously. And then Dad, who, unless he was drunk, almost always appeared to be under control, began bending at his middle, collapsing into Mom, waltzing her into the bedroom. They were obviously super-soused, the state of mind Jesse was beginning to hatch a clearer conception of, knowing how, when they were both super-soused, lit up with booze, with time blotted out, he could get away with things. As Mom's moans emerged from behind closed doors, he noticed the table where Dad had inadvertently, while taking off his jacket, thrown down his lizard-skin wallet, a recent Christmas gift from Mom, an item Jesse had had his eye on for some time now. This was his chance, and he took it. Pocketing the wallet, he slipped out the door. He whipped it out on the elevator down and tried counting the money, realizing he had no understanding of the denominations. Outside, he got lost in a throng of tourists, and then he wandered around the city all night, buying some pizza and cigarettes, doing something wrong for the sake of it, savoring the thrill of it, making paper balls of the money, throwing them downward into the dark canal water. What else could he do?

The impressive collection of buildings was larger now, a heap of man-made contours becoming distinct, and peering through binoculars, as the ship approached the dock, Jesse was overwhelmed with details. The sun was hot, and the air seemed washed clear, cleansed of, and by, the storm's rough stuff. Adjusting his lenses, Jesse brought something into focus: the stripes of a bright blue-and-white canvas awning flapping in the wind on a street brimming with people, many of them in bathing suits, some of them carrying colorful parasols through the marketplace. He fixed his focus on the wheels of a black limousine, ebony armor gleaming, parked alongside the beach, where the water broke in tremendous waves on the sand.

19

THE JUNGLE, FAR INLAND, WHERE THE PP THRIVE, WORKS THROUGH osmosis, waves of solvent molecules passing through permeable membranes in ceaseless recyclings of NRG. It is a matrix of biodegradable stuff, a reality where the PP have carved out, have been continually carving out, for tens of thousands of years, an inhabitable time slot, a sustainable way of life, a certain manner of thinking. The PP move from place to place, each clan nomadic in essence, setting up temporary camps, huts of mud and wood, in places providing resources, protein, edible plant life, a range of bugs and berries, instinctually sensing prey and avoiding predators, sensing resources and avoiding the presence of other, competing clans. A clan, consisting of twenty to forty individuals, will camp in one location for as many as six lunar cycles. The women gather edible plants, bugs, and berries. The men are scouts and hunters. Children, as soon as they are able to walk and talk, begin to mimic their elders, who guide them, sharing vast stores of relevant information. Hunting and gathering skills are passed down through the generations, first in the form of oral reports and then with demonstrations given on long instructional treks. Whenever a group of grown men or women is together with nothing particular to do, the conversation inevitably turns to hunting and gathering lore and the compendious mythology it entails, a comprehensive knowledge of the rain forest environment and its properties, a rich, narrative tradition, one that perpetuates a certain way of life, a certain rhythm of thought, so much to tell. The PP enjoy a seamless relation to their surroundings, for the animals and plants are interiorized, a part of them, a lineage linked forever within, and the PP make great mimics.

A party of four went out one day, three young men led by Kombolo, the shaman, hunting the timid, indigenous antelope, gentle, unsuspecting creatures, easy prey, protein for the PP, who hunt them with bows and poisoned arrows. They were tracking one now, imitating its cadence, racing, anticipating what was in view, soon creeping up, with cunning and stealth, in back of the animal's neck, their almost naked bodies bent toward a common goal, a young fawn licking the bark of a leafy balsawood tree. Suddenly, with the shuffle of several plants, Kombolo felt his attention shift, and he was struck by an unexpected sight, cast in a column of ghostly light, just to his left, a glimpse of the rarely seen Golden Cat. The shaman stopped and stared, eyes wide open, his pupils burnished to a mirrorlike daze, as the cat cleaned its whiskers, head bobbing away in busy concentration, paws making quick, angular movements. Acutely acoustical, the cat looked up at Kombolo, staring through the heat of contact, before the animal shot off, speeding through the forest with deliberately stiff, sharp bounds at first, eventually becoming a fluid identity, a melting entity, a blur, something golden in its fur, a blue shadow merging with plant life.

Led by Kombolo, the group followed the animal, shoving foliage aside, tracking its traces, pursuing its swift movements with stealth, but the Golden Cat increased the distance between them and itself, moving far out of range, soon dissolving into the impenetrable foliage, into a multidimensional labyrinth of leafy infinity. The cat was gone, its form lost in a curtain of green growth. The four men were stunned, and they shared the shock of surprise, which eventually dissipated, and the hunters returned to their routine task, hunting antelope tracks. When they hunt, they sometimes join hands and dance on either side of the path they make while moving through space, almost like swimming, as they move through what they see.

In the glow of the campfire, surrounded by a heady aroma of freshly cooked antelope meat, Kombolo recounted the encounter with the Golden Cat, and its image filled his audience and the frame of his expanding hands, as his high-pitched vocalizations penetrated the Jungle, and the surrounding foliage hummed, seethed with a pluralized, pulsing NRG. Simulating the Golden Cat's sinuous body, Kombolo danced before the fire, blending with serpentine flames, putting his whole body into it, carving ways through space with his hands.

20

DOWN AT THE STATION, EARLY IN THE MORNING, THE STEEL WHEELS on the steel tracks leading into the Jungle's dark heart glistened with lazy inertia in the morning sun, a harbinger of heat to come, as excited insects skimmed the air, dazzling it with irregular flight, and loud crowds of people rushed by in a hurry, some talking, some wearing sunglasses, all directed by motives ultimately discernable to and by themselves alone, for it is alone that each of us surveys the meaning of our footprints and feels light. Konrad paused and glanced nervously around him, scanning the station platform for secret agents, undercover detectives, policemen in plain clothes, anyone who might be following them, his attention drawn back, as he glanced with a nod of assurance to his keep, his charge: the kidnapped kid, reminding himself of their parallel, comparable backgrounds, remembering his own protected, protracted adolescence, growing up on Manhattan's Upper East Side in a sheltered world of high culture, fortune, fine furniture and clothes, theatrical afternoons. An only child, treated like a prince, showered with all the advantages and opportunities his proud biological father chose to empower him with, that father taking an interest in his secret seed and heir, my nominal "cousin," Granddad's "love child," prone to complex feelings of superiority as he stood in the opulent lobby of the building where he lived with his mother, my "aunt" Alice, where he'd wait for that private car to the private school where he, Conrad before his conversion, enjoyed playing roles, giving voice to dramatic dialogues, a participant in the fun of shifting locations and scales, the dreamy rites of theatrical time, staying late for rehearsals and reversals. There was the space of a year, before his interest in modern sculpture was sparked by an exhibition of primitive art at MOMA, when he'd been all wound up with the possibility of a real stage career, just like his mom's, with footlights, curtains, and bursts of applause, and then he changed tracks. He paused in thought. He was thinking of young Alice now, hailing a cab on Park Avenue, clutching her purse, the fur of her mink coat rippling. Suddenly, the chain of Konrad's memory broke, interrupted by a young hyena, practically a house cat, tawny and taut in a wooden cage, pacing back and forth, its eyes catching the free movements beyond the space of its confinement. He considered the purblind purview he supposed the animal was experiencing, as it seemed to be squinting through wooden bars, blinking into the busy glare of everything unwinding. A computerized, contrapuntal voice from a loudspeaker above announced their train's departure. Konrad grabbed Jesse's hand, and they ran down the platform and through the open door just before it closed.

The train's interior hummed with a mild, electrical, preparatory tremor, and then the engine started, and the wheels began to turn, and things were thrown into a state of rapid change. Jesse held on to his hat, and he looked out the window to see the platform slide by, stationary, secure in inertia. It was a flat, empty landscape at first, the poverty almost picturesque, and the ride toward the Jungle's border seemed interminable, so long and slow, brakes bringing all to a halt too often.

Looking out the window, appreciating the view, valorizing it with his sighs, milking it for all that he could, Konrad babbled on about time and the weather, marking the beginnings of a dialogue in which two minds, each on its course, might continue to merge, welded together by shady necessity and luminous chance. They looked out the window together and watched the landscape fly by. Fifty miles out, where the open land, crossed overhead by power lines and framed by small farms and irrigation ditches, suddenly yields to the density of the Jungle, the abrupt, thick curtain of foliage brought, with it, a sudden shift, as the train gained speed and its presence sped ahead unchecked. There was no more space to look into, just a green monotone rushing through the windows, the walls of a leafy tunnel showing an organic, vegetable indifference to the swift intruder, the metal fuselage perforating space with the ingenuity of man's hand, the power of two thousand horses bound by modern electrical and engineering wizardry.

Everything was running smoothly, the engine operating at full tilt, pistons moving, sparks flying, and the intensification of working parts was having its effect. Konrad was reading a comic book, while Jesse listened to RPM on the Sony Walkman, his body bent forward, his head hung down, long blond hair in his face, the music bringing him home, plugging him into musical motion, a loud, alluvial, raucous rush of guitar, bass, and drums providing a suitable soundtrack for the green, grinning spirits outside. He was on a train, and he couldn't complain. How had his thoughts once weighed him down? Why had sad days prevailed, threatening breakdown? He smiled sweetly, with felicity, feeling like a happy face, one of the yellow decals Mom used to attach to the refrigerator door, and he'd watch them ride there for months, swinging.

The air-conditioned interior seemed perfumed with an ancillary, sweet-and-spicy fragrance, a tingling immaterial thing, forming a striking contrast, surely immaterial, with the intense heat outside. Jesse let his attention waver over the warp and woof of his immediate sensations, resting his rubbery sea legs, all that below-deck ping-pong having temporarily altered his sense of balance and proprioception, deep in the limbic system, and it was really very amusing, settling back into his seat's headrest, feeling the train speed ahead.

The soporific powers of train travel are well known, though not very well understood by those on whom such powers operate, the regular vibrations of the turning wheels creating the effect of being asleep in a capsule, connected to other capsules, all speeding forward underground, oblongs traveling like coffins in a river, so that Konrad thought he must have nodded off, and when the train came to a sudden stop, the abrupt unexpectedness of it bringing him to awareness of the crash, he realized he'd been asleep. The shock of something hit, rippling all the way down the line from the engine, shook him out of it, and he saw that he hadn't been reading. He'd been dreaming, fly fishing in the temporal lobes of his past buried somewhere in Colorado, a fresh breeze filling a small copse of aspens, his line tightening, when the shock threw his head forward, and it bumped, slightly, on the seat in front of his.

"Yow! Wow!" he shouted, as Jesse took his headphones off and looked around.

A tiny, tinny voice from a small loudspeaker embedded in the ceiling above them announced: *"Olifant battre! Olifant battre!"* Shrill alarms sounded, and the train shook to a final stop. Jesse shot Konrad a troubled look, as a shared realization of what had just occurred crept over them, and they sat there. Collisions with young elephants were becoming a frequent problem. Bewildered calves, strays from the herd, wandered onto the tracks and were struck.

Sometimes sitting in the commodious lap of his paternal grandmother, Cecelia, addressed by Jesse as "Grammy," he'd felt trapped, flowering azaleas mixing with her perfume, a glue he couldn't break free from, bonding them together there, as they sat in the back garden of the house on Utopia Parkway, dogwoods in bloom, ornamental cedar trees standing behind the religious statuary and birdbath, and Grammy, iced tea at her side, had read aloud from a big picture book about Babar, King of the Elephants, the source of so much of Jesse's initial worldly knowledge, giving him some sense of geography, a world out there beyond his own, with oceans, a distant place named "France," another named "Africa," other ways of life. And in one peculiar two- or three-sentence episode, when Babar visits the U.S.A., he travels by car to Scarsdale, "where he discusses business with the good-looking men in their dapper suits, like your daddy's," Grammy had remarked. What had made her say that I cannot imagine, but Babar was a formidable presence, a uniform grey with great white tusks, his long, substantial trunk apparent, and he wore a green suit when in Paris. Jesse had an image of this in his mind, and he recalled the day Poppy had taken him to the barbershop for his first haircut in the high, throne-like chair, a massive white porcelain structure with red leather padding and the walls of mirroring surfaces behind him, in front of him, multiplying his head into a virtual infinity of personal dizziness, one all his own, and he'd told himself to remember that self-produced moment, which he was now experiencing again, the train speeding deeper into the interior.

Like many paternal grandmothers, Grammy had sometimes claimed to have eyes in the back of her head, and Jesse, like many young children, had believed what she said was true, though he couldn't understand how it was anatomically possible.

The train stopped for almost an hour, as the baby elephant's body was removed from the tracks with a mechanical forklift device, usually used to load and unload baggage, discovered to be effective for this purpose also, its twin blades sliding under the inert, dead bulk, lifting the body, the size of a horse, off the tracks. The train's interior hummed back to life again, and the overhead lights flashed on. Forward motion returned, the thrust of it sending Jesse back into the depths of his headrest, and he remembered a night in November, not so long before, at an outdoor party, when, in a drunken frenzy, he'd run directly into an oak tree, an obstacle in space.

They reached the station, the last outpost, a dilapidated building of cinder blocks, with an aluminum roof and a rickety wooden platform attached to its side. It was a drab structure, and nobody there spoke English. There was an unusual sleepiness about the few people they encountered, as if they'd made the wrong motion and taken a mind-altering potion, a CNS sedative, and the air was heavy, saturated with water. In a yard in front of a convenience store where they stopped to buy provisions, Gabon's green, yellow, and blue flag, representing foliage, sunshine, and water, wrapped itself around a sole pole, and the humidity palpably rose. Everything seemed enervated, drained of vitality, oppressed by the heat, the sky an orange glow before being swallowed by a massive, messy purple cloud, then the ink of total and abrupt darkness. Konrad handed Jesse a battery-powered flashlight and a tin of insect repellent, saying, "It's a long hike in, so hang in there, kid." He immediately disappeared into the forest foliage, his form sinking in, and Jesse duly followed.

21

THE LONG HIKE REQUIRED DETERMINATION AND CONTINUAL PERSISTENCE. Jesse had to force his feet into the challenges of a purely pedestrian dexterity, thinking with his knees for the first time since hiking the Appalachian Trail in the hills above Kent, Connecticut. The Jungle was a strange place, woven of silent paint at first, and here he was, walking through it, yielding to its abstractions and attractions, the immediate fascination of a small, fierce privacy fastening itself around him like a sheet, thinking himself the cause of its actions, a monkey with its tail, tall up there in the air. Space itself felt rich, pregnant with potential, the promise of intelligent movement springing up at their approach in a crowd of fluttering butterflies, rising wings. He felt enveloped by a rarely embodied intelligence, his skin broken by particles, changes in the external, sensory world, a spirit of innovation that Jesse sensed had always been there, though it had never taken place, never held sway, now sweeping through him, bathing him with chemistry. He was keeping pace with Konrad, who was also challenged by the terrain, perspiring, as the mist turned to a soft rain, and the foliage, under cover of the night, closed over them, and they were in it. Above them reeled the outraged chatter of an indignant monkey, invisible now, yet somehow grown to titanic proportions. Jesse slipped and slid on some sticky fungi, his fingers feeling its icky surface. He grinned and bore it.

Around midnight, following a path overgrown with foliage, with the aid of their flashlights, they finally reached ELF headquarters, the big canvas tent, where Konrad had expected to find Omnibus or Amy, but nobody was there. They dropped off their baggage and, although weary from the journey, ambled down a path that Konrad knew well, heading in the direction of the river, leading to the nearby PP camp, a circle of humble huts, small domes constructed from selected branches, leaves, and vines, providing amazingly waterproof shelter during the sudden afternoon downpours, when everything's seen through the blurred translucence of a wet shower curtain, and the whole environment feels redeemed. The huts circled a clearing in the forest, where a large group of short people sat around a big bonfire, their mostly hairless, dark bodies brilliant in the flames, which danced off their teeth and eyes when they smiled and laughed. Jesse followed Konrad into the clearing like a trained animal; dog-tired, he stood there, awestruck and dumb, looking on, bathed in perspiration. There were, for an instant, stinging tears in his eyes, as a thick smoke erupted from the crackling flames surrounded by a circle of caked mud where some men were playing instruments and some women sat with infants, rocking them to the music. A wiry old man, his feathery headdress bobbing excitedly, cradled in his arms an elephant tusk inscribed with strange symbols. Stifled by another belch of smoke, Jesse wiped his eyes and looked to one side and saw, squinting into the dark space, the delicate muscles around his eyeballs bringing wavy, vague outlines into existence, several large beehives in the darkness, and a busy buzzing sound began to increase its claim on him, like radio static exaggerated, like someone turning up the signal of a station broadcasting static only, as Jesse stepped forward, suddenly aided by a hand that gripped his own right hand with gusto. It was Omnibus, who'd materialized out of the night, wearing a suit of aluminum, grinning a grin.

Then everybody, all the PP at once, closed their eyes together and began chanting, most of them clapping their hands, some banging percussion instruments, some playing wind instruments, many making excited, high-pitched vocalizations, whistles and hoots, and a persuasive chorus was born, dreaming of where they were coming from. The wiry old man put the elephant tusk aside. Wearing nothing, cloaked in smoke, he stood up, and his elderly body began to sway to the music, as he broke into an exuberant, uncanny dance, his hand gestures directing the flow of the air around him, as if weaving, summoning invisible, inexhaustible powers, conjuring something from nothing: a key, a door, a resilient star, a new and different time slot. Jesse watched, fascinated by the performance, and he suddenly didn't feel tired anymore. He sensed a spontaneous, deep delight, feeling he was being carried off somewhere, borne again in the backpack of his mind. He felt the excitement of a brand-new adventure spread through him, coursing down his spine, like a fresh breeze rousing a restless sleeper aboard a ship, raising sails, promising movement and sustained flight ahead. The Jungle, this wild territory I am about to give some narrative shape to, was a new location to feel and communicate from, a place for people to ask about, originating somewhere, in a primordial, collective time, well before automatic dancing became associated with the parameters of pages.

Omnibus, for whom all was Oz-like anyway, like the green light at the end of a leafy tunnel, or a significant dock, stepped up on stage, his aluminum suit reflecting tiny tongues and pyramids of fire. He'd just completed a rewarding duration of research in the Jungle, investigating anthills and beehives, down on his knees collecting data, and he felt filled with secrets to share and find out about. First, he noticed the kidnapped kid, and then he glanced at Konrad, who nodded efficiently, putting his thumb into the air. Omnibus knew that something new had been set into motion, definitively launched, something that had started with Amy, who, simultaneously, seated among the women, looked on in a state of ponderous affection for her surroundings, as if she'd given birth to some important, difficult thought, just minutes ago, while flying around in a long, flowing take of insect moments, extracting sustenance from particles, fabricating scenes, realizing links for a language of tact, her almost singular cause and calling, like sunlight, oxygen, and the circulation of the blood, the basis of life in the Jungle, the inevitable race from the fire, the unavoidable, mad last scene, the constant contest continuing in Cindy Flanagan's consciousness, as I sit here and think of it now.

Working away in the air, turning on the wheels of wings, Amy postulated a cognitive medium, a subtle effluvium, a surrounding matrix of wholes and parts, through which the PP mind moves, guided by forces of a purely perceptual order, causing individual experience to dissolve into comprehension, all of them coming together now, melting, as the borders between things erased themselves, becoming a single, breathing membrane, a great solvent and solution. The process of assimilation was just beginning, though the cause of that process is timeless NRG, an immaterial thing. Amy was fond of pyrotechnics and speculative futurology, rising on butterfly wings. She liked to think she was deploying an alphabet of flames, burning a path, reflecting on the arc of life as she'd known it, looking ahead, beyond blackboards and screens, speculating on what a script rolled up and hidden inside a jacket pocket might yield, how it may play out. Jesse somehow intuited all this, and, stepping closer to the fire, an array of dark eyes greeting him, floating, like a sea of paper masks, he caught a glimpse of Amy. Some sort of audience was forming in waves at his knees, and he felt that he might collapse from the weight of the experience. He turned and scanned space, looking for Amy, but she had disappeared.

The PP, practicing telepathy, exhibit extreme sensitivity to subtle shifts of temperature and alterations of perspective, the multiple viewpoints of plants, insects, and animals playing essential roles in who they are, denizens of the Jungle, key to its warp and woof, adapting, bending, to the mundane reality of an immediate situation, whatever it is, even obstacles, through swiftly shared acts of mentation and comprehension: telepathy, an ability that has spread since the genesis of the species, born at a time when the borders between the human and the animal were porous, a time of blurred furs, honed over hundreds of decades, so that what seems a supernatural gift is actually an innate, hereditary trait, hardwired into the PP brain, and their speech, which is actually closer to song in spirit, is an adjunct, an extra, a supplement, something added on, a decorative appendage. Collectively, although they seem to communicate, like so many felicitous chatterboxes, through a vivid and melodious gift for gab, convivial in tongue, they are actually practicing telepathy, reaching each other without words in the Jungle, soon to be nicknamed "Hotel Green" by Amy, so attuned to its moods, its redundant furniture and hallways, an infinitely animated universe to which the PP adapt continually, usually smoothly, sometimes in fits and starts, and although they have no system of writing, although they cannot record anything at all, everything they think might be written down on the back of an enormous postcard, as they move with each other, in tandem through telepathy, swinging, practicing a fairly explicit set of conceptual techniques, modes of thinking honed through time, making each punctual PP mind an artist at ease in residence. The mellifluous, phonetic patterns, the melodic innovations, the sculptured airiness of their apparent speech, always inclined toward song, has fascinated musicologists, who compare their ways to those of the Australian Aboriginals, who also sing things into being.

The nocturnal excitement went on, drumming, dancing, singing, frantic hand flapping and celebration, a heady convocation, with convincing intimations of birdsong coming at its end, as the night dissolved into dawn. Kombolo, the shaman, danced with imagined snakes in his fists, undulating around the fire in sinewy motion. The chief, a vigorous man, short and muscular, whose body hair had been eliminated by applying special resins to the skin, wore elaborate headgear, a kind of glowing helmet fashioned from dried flowers, beeswax, and green feathers. There were streaks of yellow paint applied in patterns on his face, clear in the light, as he stepped out of the shadows, toward Kombolo, the shaman, who smiled, and the two of them shared a frequency, marking a knowing moment. The chief took off his headgear and ceremoniously placed it on the ground, after padding out, with one hand, an area for it to rest comfortably in, and then he began to dance, mimicking Kombolo, who was now stretching his arms out, spinning them swiftly, parallel to the ground, as if challenging the chief, who accepted the challenge, as the two did a dance, an accelerating duet.

22

LIKE A YOUNG SPONGE ABLE TO ABSORB NEW TRICKS FROM WATER, Jesse soon adapted to the relaxed, loose rhythms of life around ELF headquarters and the PP camp, where time passes slowly, at low decibels mostly, efficiently and effectively, like a truck carrying medical equipment through a hospital zone, the driver putting his foot down to the floor gently, and there was a curious clarity about the even motor drive of Jesse's first full day there, where life was a wakeful dream in which he was not responsible for any action. The unusually high humidity, alleviated by a brief morning downpour, brought sudden drafts of clear, cool air down from above, accentuating the proximity of all the living, breathing matter, membranes teeming with life, the dense, orgiastic dance of genetic drift, each change being exactly itself, playing a part, a role in a system of differences, and Jesse felt himself lifted, raised into the prolonged play of its novel and green machinery, a vast, vascular museum of arrangements and tints. Free of his charge, freed from playing kidnapper, Konrad displayed a remarkable capacity for idleness. "You are what you are, kid. Don't bother me anymore. It's Sunday," he'd flatly asserted, sending Jesse off alone. Relieved of responsibilities, Jesse's lackadaisical, erstwhile kidnapper spent most of his first full day back at headquarters playing cards with Amy in the tent, or in the shade of a tree, or lying about in a hammock, reviewing the mysteries of ant and bee consciousness in a haphazard way with Omnibus when he happened to drop by, letting Jesse do much as he pleased, wandering around in the green growth for hours with Amy, who repeatedly invoked Hotel Green, who harbored vast abilities and explanatory powers, who discoursed spontaneously on the miracles of photosynthesis, pointing out some leaf, flower, or mossy patch, while Jesse, not much interested in knowing much more than the fact that his forehead felt refreshed when he wiped it with a rag, enjoyed the new fragrances. It was a new way of being outside, being out of doors, purpose pouring in, and he was gradually gaining the perspective of where he was going, a participant in this new direction, with no way of knowing where he was going, but he could picture rich dirt and fresh scents. Looking up, he felt pliable and free, and the sky was a ceiling of blue and white, towering

clouds, and the obligatory ELF flag, a faded grey T-shirt, materialized, smeared with beeswax, so as to appear stiff in the wind,
though there wasn't any.

Falling water plays a role in Hotel Green, filling its bathtubs and
basins, and Jesse had enjoyed falling asleep to the complicated poly-
rhythms of rain, constant bits of water dropping, collapsing on the
canvas surface of his pup tent with gentle blips and plops, forming
trickles down the sides, coming into tiny vortices and streams, rivu-
lets in the dirt, and the sound of raindrops still flopping on the fabric
that Monday morning, as he lay on his pneumatic mattress, with all
of the weekend behind him, made him think, for a moment, that he
was back in Belle Haven, linked forever to the place, under that illusion until the lightning and thunder brought his consciousness back,
and he realized where and who he was. It was difficult to keep formation amid the constant saturation, as he lay there and wondered what
he'd be doing that day. Easy with the swing of things as they happened to unfold, he was startled by the presence of someone waiting
in the rainy ambience, crouching at the entrance of his tent. It was
Kombolo, unfazed by falling water, draping itself around him like a
great coat. He felt enchanted by its wet spread, for he had intimate
knowledge of water, of which he was a talking engine, and he could
see and seize things with his teeth, for his telepathic powers were
formidable. He was able to create a wide range of animal calls with
uncanny accuracy, and he chatted amiably with the rambunctious
monkeys that lowered themselves down on vines from the canopy.

Monday became Tuesday, and some more days went by, and
Kombolo took Jesse out on long, instructive treks through the wil-
derness, where Jesse learned, through osmosis and imitation, how
to run through the foliage furtively, fleet on his feet like a leopard,
or the ghost of one, without disturbing the green furniture, where
he learned, just by watching closely, all about hunting, how to mine
and mime the magnificence of the animals, how to see a scent,
visualize it, and see it through, how to catch a track and stick to it,

how to manipulate materials from a distance, to kill with arrows and poisoned darts.

Kombolo, one in a long lineage of shamans, had had the idea of the Golden Cat sown in the furrows of his brain, a seed implanted at conception, intact at his birth, filling its present vehicle, and he sought its instantiation in space. He knew he'd recognize it if, or when, he saw it, but he'd never seen it, not until now actually seeing it, so its potential presence had become a formal organizing principle behind all the preparatory dancing and dreams he'd entered at night by the force of his will, carving a cave from a mountain, a safe place for the image he sought, for he was keen on its being seen. Kombolo, so very adept at showmanship and visualization, was intent on catching another glimpse of that cat, perhaps even trapping it, bagging it, and bringing it back to camp, as he prowled on his hands and knees, his naked body smeared with honey, powdered with yellow pollen, attuning himself to another sensibility, passing through membranes, breaking borders and bounds, becoming cat, making its future capture pivotal.

23

MEANWHILE, BACK IN BELLE HAVEN, JERROLD AND JESSICA WERE, understandably, in a state of great distress and agitation. A week had passed without any sign of Jesse, and they were clueless about his location, without any lead as to where he might be. Jerrold had contacted the FBI and CIA almost immediately; both were on the case, but nothing had turned up, and the ineptitude of the police proved pitiful. It was an incredibly frigid early spring, with temperatures more like January, and the crisis of Jesse's kidnapping kept them both there, forced to be alone together in the big house for the first time in months.

Two weeks after his abduction, just another Tuesday, Jesse was out with Omnibus, Konrad, Kombolo, and Amy for a long, educational stroll, leading a large group of PP youngsters, whose emerging morals, manners, and telepathic abilities excited much curiosity and wonder in the mind of especially Amy now, sauntering along, morphing into a butterfly, hopping from flower to flower. They were hoping to catch a glimpse of the Golden Cat, when a big cloud above them burst into its constituent parts, the electrical flash scored by rumbling thunder, and suddenly there was water everywhere. Omnibus just stood there at first, dumbfounded, his mouth wide open, and he gestured toward the shelter of a huge flowering tree. Though an afternoon shower could cool things down with a misty conclusion, and the PP children played with joyous abandon in the sudden downpour, dancing around a lot, Jesse looked out at the rain and frowned, islanded by water, wishing he could rise above its turbulence. He held a broad leaf over his head to avoid the vast wetness crashing down around him. Last night, in the space of a dream, not subject to any form of logic, breaking the shackles of space and time, he'd been given wings and was suddenly gliding above sheer cliffs, stretching his arms out, putting new feathers to use, spreading fabulous wings over an expansive, silvery sea, and it was an airy feeling, looking down on the waves, then on a beach, where there were young people playing volleyball, and he was rising toward the sun, but here he was now, and it was raining, and they were all using leaves as hats. The situation was ridiculous, and he felt like an idiot, holding the bending plant material over his head.

Amy, morphed into a butterfly, was a flame in a world of slow water, and she fluttered around in an enthusiastic daze, ready to produce effects, amazed with how the flight she'd made, the wings that she'd brought into being, had taught her what she thought again, slipping through leafy passageways, wearing her bright orange wings.

It had been an ominous dawn, the ruby orb of its warning rising, presaging a day of storms, a billion of them behind it, yet Amy, casting a glow upon whatever her eyes alighted on, fluttered on through the Jungle alone, a star in the mystery of MY THICK time, as she hovered, to drop to the rain forest floor like a ball of pure fusion, picking up particles of dirt and organic debris, making contact with the microscopic stuff on the ground, sure of her pitch, before leaping back into the air. There was no time to lose and no time to think. It was just another dying moment inside the circumference of a dream, and she was just a little girl, back on the farm in Idaho, sneaking downstairs into the garden one night to flick the switch and observe the dance of the white moths over the potato plants.

"Today, any one of these days, you are going to see the Golden Cat," Amy had said over breakfast, making her prediction, almost flirting with Jesse, flashing her red fingernails, glistening in the light, and now he was waiting in a leafy corridor, like waiting in line anywhere, seeking shelter. Time passed, and they all became soaking wet, which the youngsters thoroughly enjoyed, and then the clouds disappeared, and bright sunlight poured down like honey through the trees, bringing fresh plumes of steam up from the saturated foliage. "I felt sure we'd catch a trace of the cat," Omnibus remarked, his low voice infused with regret, "but it may be impossible to pick up anything after a drenching like that."

A silent process was unfolding like a napkin in someone's lap, altering Jesse's consciousness, having its effect, making the rain move away, off in another direction, which was a good thing, as the process entailed the discovery of new certainties along the way. The rain ended, and an almost imperceptible trail led them downward through a foliage-covered hillside, into a valley where swampy shores, bordered by tremendous trees, gargantuan, green monsters of great variety and form, framed a large, inland lake. Amy, temporarily taking human form, stopped, stooped, and examined something carefully with her fingers, her voice turning to a low, barely intelligible murmur, with Omnibus now, also droning on, bending over the tip of a plant at his waist, breaking its bud open, tasting the purple pollen inside, identifying it, at last, with an exclamation, "Air Plant!" It was the sacred Air Plant, referred to, in the PP language, by/through/with a long, complicated, polysyllabic word of many phonetic components, the root of which, when boiled into a paste, becomes a mild stimulant, a staple in the diets of PP hunters and scouts, who consume large quantities of it, having to stay active for days, constantly on high alert, combing through new territory, but the youngsters were unimpressed, and they walked on, playing and shouting, teasing Omnibus now, making merry mimicry of his surprise, for the Air Plant was nothing new, just an ordinary facet of PP life, a nothingness, and they pronounce their word for it with a certain staccato inflection, stressing its penultimate SILLY BELL.

The sun showered the scene with photons, evaporating drops of water, and insects flew through the sultry space. Flocks of birds threw shadows down in places, as the process evolved into something new, Amy leading the way with her flight. Omnibus discovered a veritable city of green ants, uncovering it with a stick, while Jesse, meanwhile and very quickly, became aware of his own heartbeat and could picture and follow, in some detail, the course of his blood racing through him. He closed his eyes, and it was like an anatomy lesson under his eyelids, a vision of his body, displayed as if seen from above. He saw blood circulating, moving with fluidity, coursing through his fleshy limbs and organs, building new vessels in his head and chest, feeding his fingers, eyeballs, and hair.

They were combing through more territory when the squadron of PP scouts arrived. They had been sent out, by the chief's order, to locate the children and bring them back home. The squad leader, a short man with pointed ears and the face of an irate gargoyle, scolded Kombolo for taking the children so far away from camp for so long, his angry features showing no respect for the elderly shaman. Suddenly, with the children gone, the tenor of the whole expedition changed, becoming ominous. Omnibus wandered off, after liberally dousing himself with insect repellent, and Amy flew away in a dizzying series of widening arcs, vanishing in circles, leaving Konrad and Jesse, accompanied by Kombolo, the shaman, and three expert hunters who had arrived with the squadron, their backpacks filled with provisions, bottled water, and that special bread the PP women bake from a mixture of wildflowers, Air Plant root, and bat fat. They also carried some precious cans of Bumble Bee tuna, provided by an unknown source—"flown in for us by helicopter," Konrad remarked, and he formed a fist and shook its clenched form at the sky. Konrad was always getting caught up in real-time contradictions, and he'd try to clear the heavy mental weather through long, rambling monologues that eventually, like everything it seemed, led nowhere. The practical consequences of his theoretical enterprise required more thought, more planning, and it looked like a long trek ahead. Jesse turned to him, focusing a stare into Konrad's dark pupils, assuming the depths of inky question marks, two pregnant sites into which Jesse peered, pouring the rays of his gaze into these, now bringing, with expert ease, an image of the Golden Cat into focus: It was time to quest on. Konrad, stamping his feet on an imaginary doormat, felt a surreal intimacy with their surroundings take hold, and he was seized by a genuine optimism.

24

Meanwhile, back in Belle Haven, the moon was full, and the tide was high. Jerrold and Jessica were sitting downstairs, watching TV in the entertainment room, when the doorbell rang. The crisis had forced them to be at first at least cordial with each other, the parental unit. Now they were almost on intimate terms. The doorbell rang again, and Jessica looked at her husband, shooting him a distraught glance. Jerrold rose, maintaining contact with her eyes, until he disappeared, going up the stairs. Who was at the door? A third ring followed the second, a repetition, with insistence, of the deep, electronic gong. Jerrold opened the door and peered into the cold night air, sharp as a knife, not a cloud in the sky, the naked moon in orbit, shining above. There was nobody there.

"I don't know what's going on," he yelled back to Jessica, looking down to his feet, where he noticed a simple postcard, face up on the entrance mat. He stooped to pick it up and studied the image: a lighthouse amid some sand dunes, viewed through a frame of palm fronds, a bright blue sky, the ocean glittering in the distance. He flipped it over and read the print: "Discover Gabon: Vacation Here" and then the simple, two-word handwritten message, penned in turquoise ink, in painstaking, ornate Gothic script: "GET SMART," the imperative signed by blue ballpoint pen: "ELF (Energy Liberty Funnel)."

"Curious," he thought, for he'd seen that very same concatenation of three letters somewhere before, perhaps in a dream, not knowing what they had stood for, and he harbored a deep, inarticulate love for the very word "funnel," for Jerrold saw the world through an abstract ether of algorithms and extrapolations founded on a foreseeable future that guaranteed a continual flow, his kind of foundation. But what was this? It was then that he saw the numbers, tiny, carefully penned digits at the very bottom of the card, in the lower margin, geographical coordinates, degrees of longitude and latitude, the location of something or someone somewhere. He felt the cold night air. He looked up at the moon, and his voice cut out, like a knife, a place for his late echo and its empty elaboration, "Who's out there? Who's there?" Nobody was there, and the cold was pouring into the house. "Shut the door!" Jessica shouted, coming up the stairs. Jerrold sniffed the air and detected a scent of gasoline; he heard the sound of a car driving away. It sounded like a small machine. He shut the door and, walking into the front hall with an unusually haunted expression on his face, he smiled with determination as he handed Jessica the card. She was sitting on the couch now, nervously smoking a cigarette. He crouched down at her side, and they studied the postcard's inscriptions.

"There's no time to lose. I have to act fast," Jerrold said, standing up. Jessica nodded and nervously exhaled, blowing smoke rings.

"Don't you think we should first contact the authorities? The police? the FBI?" she asked.

"I've already done that, dummy . . . sweetheart," he replied, modulating his tone, surprised by her cogent suggestion. "No, the time to act's now, immediately. I have to take the logical step. Look, if you had the opportunity, a chance to seize everything you ever wanted, would you capture and capitalize on it, or would you just let it go? The authorities aren't going to be of any help, not now, not immediately, and I've got the jet. I've got the means. I'm just going to fly in and get him."

Jessica nodded again, saying, in that almost boyish way of hers, "Gosh, Jerrold! This is just too weird. Cindy Flanagan was telling me, just yesterday, about 'ELF peephole'—you know that funny way she talks—and she mentioned a relative of hers, some long-lost cousin who telephoned her recently, saying that he was one, an ELF peephole."

Jerrold, thinking again, realized that Jessica was probably just making something up, going off on a tangent, lost in the web of a messy fiction, but he couldn't tell, so he went to the phone and called me. We spoke briefly, and I denied any knowledge about what Jessica had said. I didn't want Jerrold to know that I was connected to any of it. I said that I wasn't involved.

He returned to the sofa, where Jessica sat, staring into space, laughing to herself softly, Rex at her side, purring. "What's going on?" he asked. "Why are you making up stories at a time like this?"

But Jessica was telling the truth, for I'd told her all about Conrad, how he'd inherited a small fortune, how he'd dropped out of art school and taken up fly fishing instead, moving far away, to remote Colorado, where he'd built a log cabin by the labor of his own two hands alone, how, casting through pristine streams, he'd discovered and squeezed himself into spaces where there were no clocks, where he'd become intrinsically, constitutionally incapable of any interest in time, intolerant of it, a quirk. He vowed that he'd never look at a clock, never wear a watch. The concept of knowing the time, of numbering what time it was, had been batted beyond the precincts of his mind. Why? Because Conrad had decided that he was asleep. He was waking up to sleep. He was awakening in the morning light and finding that he was located in an ever-deeper stratum of sleep, an experience where clocks and their numbers were useless, and he was exploring that timeless state like a slow-moving fish, a bottom-feeder, its undulant, internal combustion engine leading him back, like a fire underwater, to early, formative experiences, to the prelin-guistic template of his own bastard brain: fishing for flounder with worms off the pier in Belle Haven with his biological father, be-coming worm, later trout fishing in Maine and northern Vermont, becoming insect, becoming a flying bug, his feathered hook cast into increasingly wider arcs, fishing for trout in the clear waters of Colo-rado, finally fishing with his own hands in a muddy river in Gabon, the Wobongo. From the perspectives of all kinds of fish, time doesn't exist. Like lizards and rats, they see no need to track it. I told her all about ELF. I told her how Conrad had changed the first initial of his name from *C* to *K*, becoming Konrad, marking out new theoretical territory, remarking his irrepressible affection for the philosophy of Karl Marx, whose first published paper concerned dwindling timber reserves in the once plentiful forests surrounding Berlin.

"You're nuts, Jess, making up stories about that crazy Flanagan woman," Jerrold was about to say, but then he held his breath. He was about to speak again and say something derogatory about me—I just know it—but then he checked and stopped himself, forming a short ellipsis. The necessity of decisive action filled out his shoulders and upper torso, and he charged upstairs like a bull, finally convinced that this was for real. He sat down on the bed, and, opening the drawer of the bedside table, pulled out a small moleskin notebook and wrote some notes to himself. Then he made some important phone calls. He stood up and walked to his bureau, opening the top drawer, revealing a trove of male paraphernalia: sunglasses, a slim package of expensive cigars, his old Rolex watch, cuff links, small change, two miniature bottles of single-malt Scotch, condoms in tinfoil packets, bill clips with bills in them, his lizard-skin wallet filled with credit cards, his passport. He snapped up the wallet and passport and pushed the drawer. It went back on its little wheels and snapped shut. He made another quick phone call, and, minutes later, the black limousine was waiting in the driveway, ready to take him to the airport.

Kombolo, meanwhile, now dressed in feline garb, a smock of dried yellow flowers, wearing white feathers in his hair, his face smeared with golden resin, was leading the group, showing the way, acting the part of intrepid seer, taking them deeper into the Jungle. Jesse grinned with anticipation, flush with the wishful prospect of his participation in the hunt, although his role was purely passive, even ornamental, for he was there to continue to learn by osmosis. They walked alongside a stream, and he saw its waters rise, thinking of how glad he was, just to be alive, feeling as though he'd been born and raised in another country, in another land, where, although poor and primitive, he'd been happy and free-spirited, content with his lot. There were slow swirls of prismatic mist forming at the edges of some of the larger plants, and the green space looked safe, but the actual machinery behind it all seethed with a quiet, malignant NRG, waiting, crouched, ready to spring quickly into plurality. Sunlight filtered through the leaves, forming spots of light on his skin, and there was an unusually cool breeze wafting through the foliage, but Jesse felt tense with the sense that at any instant a poisonous snake might dart out, the Gabonese viper, or "swamp Jack" Konrad had warned him about, remembering to, first, upon eye contact, freeze, attempt zero movement. "The Jungle has eyes. The Jungle has eyes," Konrad had chanted in warning, suggesting lenses, the photosensitive membranes of breathing things, monitors in the trees.

With Kombolo leading, Konrad felt sure they were on the right track, and he was beginning to fill with expectation, when they unexpectedly encountered, bathing in a puddle of brown water, oblivious to their approach, an elephant, a male, with great white tusks glistening in a slanting shaft of sunlight. The encounter would alter the course of their day. Almost immediately, the PP hunters attacked the unsuspecting animal with their spears, striking the wooden implements on its grey hide, making a racket and a series of high-pitched staccato calls, before they began to pierce the animal directly, really break it down, as arrows and poisoned darts punctured its skin, and blood burst from its throat, soon torqued in a final bout of sound.

The quiet of the Jungle breeds a lush hush, an almost imperceptible field of busy, sonic differences, like chalk dust, but the cry of an elephant shatters it with the fall of an emotional powerhouse. Jesse watched the slowed, last movements of the heavy limbs, the final swinging of its trunk, the great grey body's collapse to the forest floor with a boom, and then, in silence, blood streaming from the quivering body, life seeping out. Jesse watched the last, sad flap of an enormous ear, and the dying elephant sent out one final message into the green machinery, the triumph of its collapse. The animal's sense of sight faded, becoming blurred and buried, closed within great folds of skin, and then it began to whimper and breathe heavily, the great concave chest heaving. Jesse noted the black powder the PP men had taken from small bags attached to their hips, setting it out in circles around the elephant, prized in part for the great proboscis of its head, its acute sense of smell, sound, and memory, the furrows of its brain impressed by local topography, flora, and fauna, the brain that has magical, medicinal properties. And the elephant, with its almost human awareness of death, its rituals of archaic mourning, occupies a key place in PP mythology, but the elephant is valued most for its meat, its molecular reality, its role as primary protein source, feeding the muscles of the clan in the great recycling scheme. The death of an elephant plays a fundamental role in PP behavior, for when an elephant is killed, then the entire clan will relocate, moving their camp to the site of the kill, it being easier to go to the elephant than to bring the elephant back home.

Everything now revolved around the elephant's death, the place where the body fell, marked with blood splattered on the plants and branches broken and crushed in the killing, flies beginning to coagulate above, forming clouds of teeming velocities. The elephant's skin, like the tough, grey bark of certain indigenous trees, trembled with small charges of electrical NRG as the life inside of it slowly dissipated, brain maintaining breathing still, a tenuous thread that finally went up with the rest of it in fire, carried by portable torch to the flesh, where it caught and poured over the body in hot sheets, great flashes of light, a colossal release of NRG. The hunters performed a routine ritual of song and dance to mark the hallowed animal's death, tossing more black powder out with their hands in wide arcs, particles forming dark bands on the ground. With their voices raised in unison, they broke into a lyric celebrating the powder's power over the animal's absence. They were waving their hands in the throes of pure heat. The elephant was returning to where it came from. Konrad sat apart from it all, quite out of it, busy watching them dance, letting Jesse saunter off in exploration, which was also a form of absorption, seeking spectacular flowers.

The bugs in some trees attracted aggressive birds, some shaking branches, which other marauders had already denuded of their fruit. A particular species of parrot, with striking yellow feathers at the tips of its purple wings, inclined to flock and forage in large groups, had found an abundance of bugs in a nearby treetop, and the brightly colored birds were chattering away in a noisy glory of rapacious delight, reminding Jesse that many animals make loud, expressive sounds, unaware of what they might mean. The sun here seemed closer, a ball of blood seen through gaps in the riot of green. He thought of the traffic light turning amber, then red, at the leafy intersection leading to Belle Haven, and a thought he hatched of his aluminum bicycle, like a flying cloud, crossed his mind, and he wished he were back in those familiar streets, on those familiar roads, and then he thought again. Some of the trees seemed to be sweeping themselves into existence, glad to stand there, wearing cloaks of photosynthesis. He thought of Jessica's gleaming kitchen, the marble floor and pans of bright copper, the shimmering solid surfaces, the hanging, innumerable long-handled spoons, strainers, ladles, and other cooking implements facing him when he came in the back way and flicked the switch, and how theatrical, growing large and becoming grand, his unique place in Belle Haven seemed, but he didn't want to go back there again. The trees, the green, growing, grinning plants, the apparent purposelessness of flowers, caused him to wander in wonder, stunned by the cause of it all.

Konrad called out, but Jesse was busy capturing the experience of an especially alluring bloom, a favorite flower. Konrad called again, breaking Jesse's spell, bringing him back to the scene of the kill. The PP were now tossing a crystalline powder, a kind of salty sand, throwing it around the dead animal's bulk, dancing around it, the white, sandy salt marking the vibrational field of the elephant's much revered heart. Konrad explained that an elephant's heart, a complicated motor the size of a baby's stroller, creates a force field, an invisible, dynamic doughnut of electromagnetic NRG, seemingly intangible stuff taking the form of a torus, that figure of solid geometry, its axis running the length of the elephant's large grey body, from furrowed forehead to thin, hairy tail, that the salt preserved the original NRG field of the heart, the torus, marking its place in space, which, as Konrad put it, "makes up all mentality," a space of spongy consistency, like sand suspended in water, like quicksand, where objects sink to the level at which the weight of the object is equal to the weight of the displaced sand, so that the object floats, due to internal buoyancy. Beginning to feel buoyant, tossed into a myriad of changes being wrung out for his benefit, like landing on another planet that is an endless amusement park, Jesse looked on with amazement, astonished, apparently tampered with. He was trying to fathom the significance of it all, and he turned to face the prospect of finding his place in it, when Konrad, in mock military manner, ordered him, out of the blue, to accompany the swiftest of hunters, the tallest one too, an excellent runner with dark marble legs, who was about to break context, run back to camp to tell of the kill, the site of a new location. The young man broke into a sudden, mad dash, as Konrad, pointing a finger in his direction, waved Jesse on.

Throwing tracks down with deft stealth, the runner ran with a dignified, conscious levity that's impossible to convey or simulate, so Jesse had to concentrate solely on his running, thinking with his knees again, the focus of so much attention, the heat swelling up inside him, but the duration of the trek, the insects and slippery footing, the distance and the difficult topography, the very real fact that he felt through his feet the surface of the floor, took root in him, like the bushy, green head of the largest tree nodding over the lawn of the house in Belle Haven. In the course of their rapid run back, the flora assumed aspects of a freshly prepared salad, the smells of its lettuces and diced vegetables calling attention to themselves, especially dressed for the unlikely event of their passage. Plunging through the Jungle, his knees crashing into green, waist-high foam, Jesse noticed how the soles of his feet seemed to be floating, like zeppelins gliding through the sky, engines emitting an almost imperceptible, friendly putter, as he panted on. They passed through a place where they both sneezed profusely.

When they arrived at camp, the news of the kill was received with a placidity of purpose, that same equanimity the PP reflect whenever they're about to do something deliberately, amazed there was something that they had to do. There was no undue emotion or rush. There was the sheer joy of making a decision and acting on it. Four portable torches were set from the main fire, which was quickly extinguished with water in a ritual dance, forming a circular site of sodden campfire ash, the area crushed into definition by the force of feet. The torches, like brooms, long bunches of dried plant material dipped into a flammable mix of bat fat and fermented honey, play an important role in the night rituals of the PP, bringing them all together, awake in flamboyant light, turning the night into sunrise. Some women bagged cooking implements into webs woven from vines, and some children helped men dismantle the huts, one by one, selecting certain structural parts to take to the new location. The gift of fire, the same vital flame, its origin buried in the abysmal depths of ancestral time, a time the PP still talk about, has been passed down by torch for tens of thousands of years, over thousands of generations, like a single telegraph signal heating the copper wire of its passage. The ultimate source of the gift is unknown, creating a topic of endless speculation in the oral tradition to which the PP are inevitably bound, as the flame has been burning, kept alive for generations, ever since life itself was first breathed into being, and its transformative power, the shock of the now, the miracle of existence, remains buried in the spaces behind appearances, in the deepest strata of reality. It had happened before, and it would happen again. They'd carry the flame to the place where the elephant's weight was thrown down, where the weight of the thing was brought down by human hands, arrows, and poisoned darts.

The clan moved with ineffable swiftness toward their goal, many of them becoming airborne, blithe spirits, eyes wide open and ears attuned, senses peeled, taking note of new territory, scanning the scene with anticipation, finding phenomena to explore and curl up with, places to sing into being, but they had to move on. Their exodus ended as the sun went down, sending its rays of orange light through the thick, green canopy. The distinct, heady smell of cooked elephant meat permeated the leafy corridors, and there were new modulations of song, for the PP always sang as they worked. The site of the kill was being transformed, cleansed, doused in water, swept clean with brushes, the elephant's blood diluted and distributed through the dirt, the sooty remains of the fire, the charcoal and salt now mixed with a glue of organic matter and grease, creating a smooth oil and beeswax-like surface, the children stomping it down.

Reaching the new site, some of the older men set about gathering building materials, combing through the primeval growth to see what they could find to use. It was an absolutely clear example of communal PP NRG at work, as they harvested fuel from an abundance of resources, finding more than enough. Amy found herself lost in a thicket of butterflies, but she soon found her way back to the group, joining them as they worked their way through a grove of hardwood trees, cutting and chopping, breaking branches with their hands and teeth, bringing it all back to camp, where several new huts were quickly constructed, and the main fire roared, its serpentine flames leaping. Soon the PP were busily engaged in evening activities and relaxation, some women dancing, some men playing drums, some other women cooking, mixing up medicines and foodstuffs, some weaving baskets, young people preening themselves, some painting their faces, preparing to break into dance as the tribal drums sounded and more songs were sung. Night fell, crashing through space with the weight of a featureless, futureless being.

25

THE NEXT MORNING, JUST ANOTHER WEDNESDAY, DENSE WITH THE experience of an experiment being realized in the present, where all contests end, Jesse woke to see the dark shapes of small beetles crawling on the canvas of his tent. Ever since childhood he'd harbored a fondness for insects, tiny, airy beings, a fascination and sympathy recently rekindled, sparked and set off by Amy. He remembered the flies in the apartment on Museum Mile, swirling beneath a chandelier. He remembered being a young boy in Larchmont, his bedroom faintly illuminated by the glow of the fireflies he'd kept in a jar. His visual cortex was exceedingly sensitive to the slightest motion, like a cat's, detecting, picking up, and tracking isolate flecks and flickers of movement.

It was already written somewhere that today would be one to remember, full of usable moments. The hold of sleep and its associations faded, evaporating like a mist, and Jesse moved with blind faith and renewed confidence from his tent, walking into the brash, busy light, the bright business of a whole day in a new location ahead of him, having folded his night thoughts up, having hidden them inside the pocket of his fishing vest, having been in the Jungle for some time now, just over two weeks, having settled into the rhythms of the sun, the moon, and the stars, having become accustomed to a certain morning routine: going down to the river to wash, greeting the water, slapping it with his hands. He'd lavished praise on an imaginary bathroom sink, greeting its water, slapping it with his hands, and then joined Amy, Omnibus, and Konrad at the picnic table outside their tent for a light breakfast of cornflakes and instant coffee, having concluded that his kidnappers were really just kidding, that they were playing parts in an elaborate charade, a caper, an escapade. It was like a loaded gun, a big shooter with one aim: to transform Jesse and change Jerrold's way of thinking, rearrange his mind for a realm where the heart beats—Jerrold, who had started it all to begin with, inviting Jack and me to that Halloween party so many years before.

Leaning a little into the day, letting its fingers hit his skin, sensing his full awakening, Jesse felt as if he'd passed through a strangely tangible membrane, a crystalline liquid coating all living organisms, like the boggy, soggy border of a vast, inland lake, a massive center of attraction. He saw yellow rays kiss the night dew

away, making him able to dance while lying down, and he thought of
the cemetery he'd seen, days before, departing by train from Libreville. It was like the difference between a living bird and a dead
one, and it puzzled him, this being alive, drawing his consciousness
further out onto limbs of idle speculation, the branches and twigs
of fuzzy thinking, like a broom hurled high to the top of a tree, already thick with telepathy. He remembered how, when a hunter's
provocative call elicited the response of a target animal, a kind of
seamlessness set in, merging predator and prey, a signal that binds
one to prints, and it was omnipresent, in the pulse he felt when
he paused, taking note of the tactical now. It was in every green
and growing thing, in the vine as it smothers another tree, in the
spindly antennae of ants, the lacy wings of flying insects, the red
drums in birds' breasts, inside the tubular musculatures of snakes,
the cobras, inside the breasts of chattering monkeys, in antelope,
in the arteries, veins, and vessels surrounding an elephant's heart,
taking the form of the Golden Cat for its apotheosis, and Jesse was
starting to see this, feel this, and he couldn't hide the pleasure he
took in the air that he breathed, part of a larger activity, a flow, plugging him into something new, though it all seemed so improbable.
He woke to the world like a part in a bundle of loose particles, his
consciousness rising, persisting like a calm cool collecting in the
shade. He saw his surroundings through a polished lens, just for
a few magical seconds, and he knew that something was about to
begin again. And he was following through with it, fulfilling it in a
way, and regaining the confidence of his steps through the process,
though difficulties still filled long stretches of time, his adapting to
the heat and humidity, adjusting to the outdoor lifestyle, attending
to cuts, bruises, and bites, setting up the insect netting, learning
to sleep on a pneumatic mattress, the constant perspiration, his
hair a greasy mass he had to wash every day, the upset stomach,
digesting strange foods, worms and grubs, struggling to sleep while
hearing the perpetual drumming and vocalizations of the PP in the

distance, careening away, carrying on, in dance and song, the real world of material processes being intrinsically incommensurate with language.

Life at a new pace proceeded, pushing time into space, filling it with rhythmic beings, Jesse quickly adapting to wherever he happened to be, as he walked toward the picnic table where Omnibus and Konrad were seated. Amy, wearing a skirt of leaves, appeared to announce there were more ants to fry. Sitting at the table, Omnibus and Konrad glanced at each other, not really surprised. The foliage glistened with morning dew, making the plants shine like emeralds. The bright sun burst out from behind a cloud so that Jesse blinked, ready for action, adjusting his channel of vision, his understanding of the situation gradually becoming something he'd be able to articulate.

The presence of some black ants figured, and he stared at them, and then he turned to Konrad, asking, looking his erstwhile kidnapper right in the eye, "So what's the plan for today?" Konrad looked at Amy, as if she should answer for him, but she quickly glanced down at the ground. Jesse was nonplussed and determined. Continuing the initiative of his thrust, ready to see where it might lead, he then turned to Omnibus and asked, "Are we going to search for that cat again?" A flock of white birds rose toward the canopy, and a mysterious breeze lifted some leaves. Omnibus remained silent, first making eye contact with Konrad, and then with Amy, and then he nodded to Jesse, letting the nonverbal communication work, as Amy crouched down to examine the ants more closely. Marching on dirt, the black ants felt with their feet, as sunlight entered the tiny monitor of each one's intelligence, directing the whole ribbon of busy asphalt fragments, animated, glistening in the sunlight. Do they know where they're going? Yes, in a sense, as a fine layer of ectoplasm forms over the traveling troop, and the magic of a shared medium connects a collectivity of quivering antennae. As a social organism of multiple, mobile monads, whose collective, orienting principle is an assemblage of molecules essential to its very movement, the ants exhibit sensitivity to sunlight, the smells in the heat giving them a sense of direction. Omnibus, turning his head, squinted at the busy, animated mass.

Meanwhile, in a festival of synchronicity, the PP were busy grooming themselves, and many of them were dancing and singing, but some were sharpening spears and arrowheads, and some were preparing poisoned darts. The hunters, who supply the camp with NRG, would be busy for several days now, engaged in strenuous activity, gathering new input, discovering hidden tracks, locating trails and lairs. A group of scouts would go out in search of edible plants and precious water sources. A select few, the most competent athletes, acrobats able to achieve remarkable velocities and ascend into the air with single, determined leaps, would search for honey, seeking beehives in the treetops.

"The Golden Cat," Omnibus explained, getting up from the bench, "will be the very basis of our actions today. You'll see. It's like a door that swings in both directions with such speed that it is virtually a revolving door, open and closed simultaneously." Something in the distance, a bright, brilliant bud on a bush, beckoned, and Amy reappeared, in butterfly garb, doing a dance, her wings in a state of absolutely frenzied enthusiasm. Working away, she became a gem of light, a tiny bell, an asterisk of petals, as Omnibus spoke, doing a sort of verbal performance for the cat, of the cat, imitating it in an ad, a pitch from this place of venomous snakes and brilliant butterflies, where the amateur entomologist delights in the innocent immaturity of everything, for everything was turning to gold, and the red rubber ball of the sun morphed into a distant orange, and the forest canopy dropped coins of fresh heat.

The currency glistened, and Jesse cocked his head like a dog, listening to Omnibus wax on, in praise of the cat, a centerpiece of ELF ideology and the subject of some exquisite murals in underground caves. Listening to Omnibus, thinking about what he'd said, he was fully playing the part of Jesse now, the designated passenger. The shrill, lazy whistle of an exotic bird ceased sounding, and from the ensuing silence something like a bubble hatched and spread through space, and Jesse was growing into it, going back, caught in the flow of a world he'd believed in. He was going backward now, traveling, returning to the mirror that always happens to fall into place, marking the spaces behind appearances, playing on the borders of actions that are actually vast collections of events, and he was at its center, where he carried the burden and responsibility of knowing that he was a slow learner.

He blinked at the fluorescent foliage, and he was drawn to the fragrance of the ants Amy was frying over a crackling fire, with bat fat in an iron pan, the flames in the sunlight being salient phenomena he'd been trying to assimilate for some time, and he blinked again, with dramatic persistence, as if some insect were provoking him to act. Just yesterday, after all that running around and finally settling into this new space, Jesse had been experiencing a heightening of his optical drive, the desire to seize things through his gaze and the pleasures of its immediate satisfaction, as he grabbed at the air, catching a colorful bug, a flying ant immediately, then closing it in his fist. Even as a young child, Jesse had shown an unusual sensitivity to colors, evidencing a lively receptivity to the synthetic chromatics of his plastic toys.

He opened his hand, and the bug flew off, free to go, to go free. Everyone acknowledged the accomplished performance, smiling with admiration, and then Omnibus recommended that Jesse put himself into the seat of an automobile, right at the dashboard, a purely heuristic device intended to hasten his transition, ease him into where he'd hold the wheel, becoming someone able to drive the car, hug the road, and he'd heed the suggestion, adopting it to his own purposes and ends. Before today Jesse had never really known what his own ideas had been, born of rebellion and truculence, a refusal to bear or be bored by whatever anyone else told him to do, anything that didn't have something to do with the clear, exact flow of his own ideas, the force that through the green hose drives the water, for it all came through him, by him, and that was his primary knowledge. Today the inner world of Jesse Draper revolved almost exclusively within the spaces behind appearances. The conspicuous absence of mirroring surfaces robbed him of any opportunity for the quick glances he'd give himself, catching himself, assessing his visage in a fixture. Without the familiar shape of his person there before him, without the pensive anchors of his eyes, he felt himself swimming through a sea of apparitions, a palace of paper masks, and he couldn't assess, consult, or modulate in any way the sense of being lost, because he saw no need. He was on an excursion, a trip outside himself. His last literally reflective experience was on the train, in the tiny, smeared mirror aboard that mass of moving steel, where he sensed that he'd seen himself for the last time. Konrad had purchased a big bag of disposable plastic razors, enough for the duration of the ordeal, and after a few days, in the absence of mirrors, Jesse had learned how to shave by the feel of his face alone.

While he was feeling the nodding pudding of his own proof present, breakfast ended, and the morning mist evaporated. The sun beamed down, so that when Jesse put his bare feet on the ground, he felt a certain burn. It was a good day, one full of sunshine and the possibility of laughter. Kombolo suddenly materialized, wearing a suit of yellow feathers, and the shaman excitedly gestured, his spine filled with feline spirit, as he sank to his knees, becoming horizontal with the ground, his arms becoming forelegs. The cat inside turned practical, and it was going to show them where it was going to be, somewhere out there ahead, leading them on, Kombolo's head bobbing up and down to unseen vibrations, cresting into presence, keen on the pursuit, having formed, through firm mentation, an image for the motion of its paws. He could almost see it run, the swift arrow of a strung and unrestrained consciousness, and, with his equally powerful olfactory sense, he picked up the piquant smell of scattered Golden Cat scat, leading them this way and that, sending them now on a sinuous path through the profligate Jungle, its syrupy flow coming eventually to rest with a full stop. Kombolo stood in a swampy area infested with carnivorous plants, sensing the Wobongo River nearby, meandering through the Jungle, its voluminous blue body undulating like a great snake, breaking into crests of white foam on moss-covered stones to form ripples, swirling off muddy banks, eddying into pools, places where water mixes with mud, its source an enigma, its sleepless head darting westward, toward the sea. Some birds were circling overhead, yellow parrots chattering, yapping away, and the shaman calmly combined their calls into his procedure.

A puzzling thought flashed through the theater of Kombolo's mind: "Cats seek fish, yet they fear water," and out of that thought an elongated trail of Golden Cat essence grew, particles hovering over the river in wisps of bright light, the TRANCE FORMATION plugging them into the current.

Kombolo was out there, ahead again, setting a sort of example, swimming in his skin, picking up signals and signs, looking for the point, the place where the path to the cave began, the Jungle line. He was concentrating on it now, imagining the line in an accelerated vision of future topography.

A mere tributary of oceanic PP consciousness, Kombolo maintained course with his hands in the water, simultaneously scanning the green curtain of growth, seeking the Jungle line, glancing back at Jesse and Konrad, following him in the flow. A spider spoke to baby snakes, a mass of slithering blackness, uncoiling and recoiling beneath its silvery web. A turtle's eyes blinked, retracting its head back into its helmet. Salamanders, frightened of intruders, slid into the water, leaving faint impressions of their basking places in the mud. Small, feisty arboreal rodents, eyes all startled pupil, rushed about on leafy branches, and a solitary antelope froze in a shaft of sunlight, unseen. Information, flowing through so many sensory receptors, flowed into the higher cortical regions of primates, some of them poised on the threshold of speech. Kombolo led, for the river was read in his head, the way it bent and turned at certain speeds, forging velocities, and they sped downstream to a point where they stopped, and the path to the cave was there.

The path, the Jungle line, was a moving target, and reaching its end required Kombolo's total concentration. He got down on his knees. They had stopped at a bend in the river, a narrow, twisted beach of white sand. He scooped up a handful and sniffed it, proving his nose was invented for odorous ardor, and he stood there transfixed, olfactory powers aroused, for a trace of Golden Cat scat had touched his consciousness, and it was producing new tracks. Kombolo peered into the rain forest, making it part of what he was trying to do. He sniffed for some more information, shifting his body with catty accuracy as he moved around, scooping up sand with both hands now, flinging it about him, creating sensations, before he returned to his knees again and, in a remarkable show of mimetic ability, became the Golden Cat, putting its sinewy motions into his body, insinuating them into his form.

They plunged into the foliage, dark and leafy, so dense it was almost black in places, almost obliterating the shaman's performance. Jesse savored the lush hush of Hotel Green, its hallways hypnotic. He wondered how much longer he'd be able to inhabit it. He saw, from under the shadow of his hat's wide brim, in a yellow splash, a small swarm of busy bees.

Sometimes it was so dark along the path that Jesse had to stay within a foot of Konrad's back in order to keep track of his position, sometimes reaching out and touching it to know he was still there, following Konrad, following Kombolo's feline form, setting the pace, running with expert ability, able to get around obstacles, dodge roots, avoid puddles, and plant his paws at moments in perfect places for a lift. He seemed to almost swim through the Jungle, and Jesse imagined himself up ahead, inhabiting Kombolo's body, moving in his place, swimming through this new environment, tilting his head from side to side, taking in great gulps of air, an instantiation of some rare fish, thriving on oxygen, and a strange fascination crept through him, making him think like a planet, though I played no part in any of it, and he found his fins alone.

They had stopped at one point to urinate and rehydrate, sharing Gatorade from Konrad's canteen. Kombolo rose from his feline position, grinning and walking toward them, his grin communicating an infectious certainty about the whole enterprise, when suddenly, momentarily walking into waist-high foliage, he irrupted into a vital dance, for he'd seen a hairy spider. It was a frantic punctuation mark, the rite of a racy expletive, as he gestured at the spider, an instantiation of the tarantula species that is easy prey for the giant sloths that live in the walnut trees, large arboreal mammals able to catch hairy spiders with their claws and deliver a deadly shot of venom, emerging from glands in the mouth, a poisonous, shining substance that paralyzes its prey, making it immediately edible. The presence of these spiders, for reasons best known by Kombolo alone, was a sure sign of the cave.

Suddenly, the cave's entrance materialized behind a mesh of rusted steel fencing, an old blasting blanket, a twisted curtain of oxidized weave, something left in the wake of a prosperous mining presence, a relic, a token of TLC. Other remnants of the presence soon came into view, a battered smelting machine, looming like a dilapidated roller coaster, its once functional components ravaged by indifferent forces: photons, gravity, water, and wind. The blanket had been there for years, wearing away. Kombolo looked up into the sky, and he saw a great vacancy glittering, and he felt a supernatural power seize his musculature, as though it were wired to our star. He tore away the fence, throwing it off nonchalantly to one side of the entrance, where it sat like the lungs of a beached whale, and he approached the darkness, moving his fingers rapidly, as if weaving something pliable from the invisible, conjuring, out of the air, a small yellow bird.

"Wow," remarked Jesse, "now we're really getting somewhere."

"Unfolding before our eyes," Konrad added.

The bird flew into the mouth of the cave. Kombolo, meanwhile and very quickly, continued to busy the air, appreciating it, directing it with seemingly meaningless gestures, praising its constituents, applauding its cordiality, its absolute hospitality, raising his hands, manufacturing a litany in the course of a eulogy. It was now or never. Attaching headlights to their heads, they prepared to go into the darkness. A bat flew out, then four, then more, then an entire horde, chased by the brazen, little yellow bird, as it flew at an incredible speed, flushing the mass of black bats out.

Jesse expressed his surprise, and Kombolo made a gesture, suggesting forward movement, and they walked in. The cave was a blinding, black pitch inside, and they were forced to focus on their balance, for there was a disturbing absence of visual cues. They heard the *click clack* of something in the stagnant air, like steps on a stairway. It was so dark, so suddenly disorienting that it was almost impossible to stand up straight, and Jesse thought he was going to fall, as though into a swoon, until his vision adjusted to the darkness, discerning a thin stream of light coming from somewhere ahead. He heard a sudden sound, like water splashing on a stone, like a fish jumping.

MEANWHILE, HAVING LANDED in Libreville early that morning, Jerrold Draper had had no time to waste. He had to rush to the location. The night flight had been a singular experience. He'd been the only passenger, and it was strange to be sprawled in a cramped, uncomfortable seat, trying to sleep in the vibrating volume of the fuselage. Although he'd closed his eyes, he hadn't slept at all, and when the jet landed, he felt disheveled and harried. All of his life converged to a point when he entered the terminal, his sense of a new vocation aroused by location. He was rushed in a cab to the hospital, where he was inoculated against parasitic diseases. The doctor was a talkative black man wearing a large green smock, who, bending over him, holding a gigantic syringe, its metal casing gleaming, posed an unexpected question: "Can you show me anyone who isn't a parasite, who isn't parasitic?"

Jerrold was rushed, driven to a military airport, where he boarded a helicopter piloted by a short man whose face seemed composed of black sponge. Jerrold needed sleep, feeling suddenly overwhelmed by the proportions of his venture. It was a gamble, going in alone, but he'd accepted it because, in part, he filled the role. He was moving into dangerous territory. How would it all pan out? The noise of the rotating blades above fortified his resolve. Clutching his seat as the machine took off, he felt a surge of strange NRG, a protective coating form, buffering him, and then he lay back and finally dozed off, the machine swirling upward and forward on course. He slept for more than two hours, and when he woke, he calmly shifted in his seat, glancing at Crystal Mountain, admiring the icy top, the vast canopy of green from which it rose. He felt an upsurge of volcanic proportions: An island was forming within him.

THE CAVE WAS resonant with dripping water, punctuating the silence of the scene. Through darkness, they followed the shaman's lead, deeper into the cave, until they reached an illuminated area. As though upon a throne of rock, the Golden Cat lay, asleep on a mat of yellow metal, as if floating on the surface of a shallow pool. The fires of torches flared, showing the sleeping animal, the end of their search, its naked nose tucked into the relaxed curve of its golden pelt, indifferent, unaware of any intrusion. There was a pile of small animal bones at its forepaws, bits of uneaten evidence, bony substance licked clean. Kombolo, the shaman, clapped his hands, and the resulting resounding decibels, with the echoes of those decibels, filled the cavernous space with invisible clapping hands. Roused from its slumber, startled out of a deep sleep, the cat stood up and arched its back, the curve of its spine ablaze with golden highlights. With a single swift push, it leapt off the mat and into the air, where it smiled and instantaneously dematerialized, becoming a particle cloud, a vapor of detached, miniscule Golden Cat parts, so tenuous that it almost vanished completely, but there it was, a golden cloud, a suspended mass of particles.

Kombolo, with an animated grin, walked forward and put his hands out into the cloud expertly, and the expression on his face turned taut, concentrated, as he did a dance with dexterity, beginning again to make weaving motions with his hands and fingers, almost playing the diaphanous cloud floating in front of him, working it like a loom or musical instrument. Jesse, unaccustomed to seeing animals lose their boundaries and turn into vortices of particles, shot Konrad an astonished, anxious expression, but Konrad only nodded, calm as a piece of fabric. Kombolo glanced back, grinning again, his hands at work with unseen threads, creating a container of some kind. He opened his mouth and produced a high-pitched howl, a piercing, hysterical cry, and the cloud of wandering particles began to swirl around a new center, reorganizing themselves into the contours of a cat, and that was that, as the animal reappeared on its mat, alert and awake in its skin, ready to talk.

"There is nothing grrrreater than to feel that one is never what one once was," it proclaimed, with a guttural "*grrrr*" for emphasis. Sensitive to location and set to a context, acutely aware of auditors, almost bending before an invisible taskmaster's presence, the Golden Cat spoke perfect English, as if it were now on the radio, its locution polished, speaking the language of international commerce and advertisement with the exact diction of an Oxford don. Its large, knowing eyes absorbed its audience, and its fuzzy tongue licked at the air. Talking more slowly, like a turtle now, its eyes absorbed the three of them there, and it spoke again, in slow, distinct SILLY BELLS: "There . . . is . . . no . . . thing . . . great . . . TAR . . . than . . . to . . . feel . . . ," altering words, putting the ellipses in, letting them work, putting a spin on its original utterance, and then it continued, gaining urgency, as if speaking to an oratory full of attentive students taking notes. "There is nothing stranger or stronger than . . . to feel, to feel, to feel," the cat spoke again, forcing its ellipsis to work, repeating the infinitive, making the words hang there, so that Jesse suddenly felt a tingling NRG throughout his body ring, a feeling he'd never felt before, a bell of some sort, and now he was present.

"The problem I see is, precisely, one of presentation," the Golden Cat remarked, as if summoning NRG from somewhere else, siphoning it. Instantaneously, from another point in the cavernous space, a loud gong resounded, producing coppery bubbles in the air. There was a slice of silence, a mere comma, its absence hanging for a moment there, for just a few seconds, and then a plethora of coppery bubbles, like bright, inflated pennies, began to invade space, and a resonant strumming, as of electric mandolins or guitars, all in synchrony, surged, irrupting into fresh waves of melody.

"What's that music?" Konrad asked.

Jesse had already recognized it, a sonic truth, and he was expecting a lyric to burst in on them, as a display of clumpy water filled the space ahead of him, and he looked through its bubbling, coppery mass.

"What solid geometric figure has only one edge?" the Golden Cat asked, posing the question to Jesse with a patient sigh, urging him to visualize it. "Visualize it! Work it out in your head!" the cat exclaimed with panache. Jesse, back in school, had never really tried to work much out in his head, but now he realized he could produce the correct answer immediately. "A cone," he said effortlessly, as all of it was coming true when he thought about it, with the force of an incredible charge, and a golden material showered down to accumulate, forming at his feet.

The cat, in an instant, disappeared, as all of the lights went out. Moving his line of vision around in the dark, Jesse found himself holding a long stick marked with numbers, a ruler, and he took that tool from geometry class, and the vast cave became perfectly suited with whatever moment of his attention he chose to fill it with, this underground world, parts of a road revealed by the headlights of his own measuring. The cat was now an invisible cloud of purring particles, sounding like a loud, humming hive of bees, the pulse of its acoustics forcing Jesse back into a corner of the cave, where he saw a spear of gold appear, a fire at its pointed tip.

"To raise that spear, you'll have to use your brain and hands," the cat remarked, and the challenge of the music, as a switch was flicked, filled the cavernous space with accumulating decibels, an ascending intensity of amplified sound, as the darkness turned into photographs, images of all the things Jesse had seen, places he'd been, and things he'd done. Chained to a chair in a theater, he saw, in a movement of insight, that he was swimming through flashes from the past, holding the pan they presented themselves in, as he saw himself in Venice wandering, throwing money away, crumpled balls falling into the canal. He saw the coastline of Belle Haven in the wintertime, snow silently falling into the water, the waves on the rocks. He saw the red carpet on the front porch. He saw himself playing tennis. He saw himself skating, taking a puck out on the ice on the rink at Sunswyck Academy. He saw himself aboard *Scimitar*, tacking upwind, his face filled with spray as they reached the marked buoy and swiftly turned around it, heading downwind. He saw the yellow spinnaker bloom into its arc, trapping the breeze, putting it all to work. He saw the water rushing by. He saw himself visiting a bridge of some size, and he saw himself unleashed, shot like a missile through the sky, something amazing, and then, as on a train brought to a stop, the imagery ended. There seemed to be mirthless laughter, incommunicative and full of malicious intent, coming from somewhere deep in the cave, partaking of grim infallibility, somehow related to the cold, anonymous certainty of geological processes. The air felt like a wet shell, and each drop of water seemed full of storms.

"There is nothing outside of the Membrane," Konrad said, as if in summary, filling the silence that followed, the experience intensified by breathing.

"There is nothing outside of the Membrane," he said again, the mechanism of his mind engaged, impregnating the impenetrable. Jesse's heart beat rapidly now, as he lay back on a rock surface, head swimming, having caught a wave of his own, its peak unleashed through the cavernous place, its darkness illuminated by phosphorescence. Suddenly, there was a strong wind, and Jesse was whirled, as all of his surroundings were obliterated, as if driven into him, and he felt himself becoming reduced, returned to a tiny shape by the necessity of some strange chance, and he was conveyed downstream on a great floating leaf, which issued into a lake, where he morphed into a fish and swam, and it seemed like a million golden arrows were streaming down from the ceiling above through a big blue brush of living organisms, heavy with infinity. Darting about in the rush until dizzy, he saw himself as a particle, driven and diluted, and he floated in a sensation that was elusive, like the import of that outward peace attained at any price, that we seek in the prints of others, as they do in our own.

It was all just an act, but the animal had performed brilliantly, and the idea of its behavior resonated inside of Jesse's body now, running along through the worn grooves of his consciousness, a concatenated collection of connected parts.

Konrad grinned, and Kombolo clapped his hands, making a syncopated rhythm bounce off the walls, and then he produced a mesmerizing chant, creating, at the top of his voice, a sequence of excited shrieks, a tremendous stretch of sounds so bleak, so real, that Jesse, shivering in the darkness, imagined a horde of black bats hurrying behind him, hurtling though space, rushing him through this experience more quickly, be it real or hallucinatory, as they ran out of the cave and stood there, shaking in the morning light, stunned. It was like coming out of a movie theater in the middle of the afternoon, but now it was Thursday morning. Jesse blinked his eyes at the bright air around him, suddenly alive with insects, so that his surprise became apparent, as he maintained his balance in a surfeit of impressions, catching one wave cresting after another. What had happened? Something had happened, and it was still present, latent in its hidden happening, though he couldn't remember the exact contours of it, and trying to figure it out, trying to make it happen again through rational reconstruction, was impossible; he found his will was useless. He breathed, and he experienced a pleasant, easily obtainable hum, pumping the air with expectancy, thinking of changes to come. He had a world within him, and it was beginning to take place. He felt like he wanted to perpetuate incessant spiritual exercises, expressions of thanks, prayers without ceasing, but he couldn't determine what form to take, fluctuating, rapidly oscillating between possibilities. He felt seized by the desire to be a revolving door, do an authentic dance, and Kombolo, the shaman, sensitive to these sudden shifts of human mood and atmosphere, swayed by subtle indications, broke into one, its movements illustrating Jesse's own desire accurately enough, as he looked on, amazed that so much flimsy stuff was becoming endurable.

The Golden Cat created a separate, special bonding experience for everyone involved, making reality cling to their notions of it more closely, especially for Jesse, the neophyte, the one being inducted into this matrix of changes for the very first time, and he saw the air that Thursday morning as though infused with miniscule charges of electricity, charging his batteries, making him feel invulnerable, indefatigable, fueling the scope of his burgeoning telepathic powers, bringing Amy back, a freely flying flower, a blue morpho butterfly, weaving her wings to produce an effect, sprinkling crystals and flakes of blue frost on the ground, reminding Jesse of the image he'd taken of the totem animal, an impression of its mass trapped in the cage of his mind.

The group was back on the path again, Kombolo showing off his multitasking ability, simultaneously thinking with his knees and navigating by voice, singing a fast line into being, a more rapid route back, a quick one this time, and they all experienced an amazing increase of muscle power and resilience in their feet and legs, as small wings sprouted at their ankles, and they shot through space with incredible speed, like rockets, giving Jesse the sensation of a power he'd never known before.

26

EVERYONE HAS TO MOVE, AND EVERYONE MOVES IN ACCORDANCE with curtains and a certain amount of light, so I must rush to end my song, to finish this drama of silly boys, heads full of curls and putty, an illusion from which I've already awoken, here in the Stone Cottage, staring at the floor.

Meanwhile, in another part of the Jungle, a group of ingenious PP men, the carpenters of the clan, had constructed a large cage, shaped like a gigantic igloo, on the outskirts of camp, from the branches of walnut and balsawood trees, using shower curtains, tarpaulins, and ropes to bind the structure more firmly together, giving it a mostly translucent border or skin, suitable for framing a context for an event of some importance, a ready, waiting, theatrical space. A tall pile of glossy American, British, and French business and fashion magazines sat in one place, bound up with string, and near it there was a bed of straw, and the floor was compressed clay and dirt mixed with beeswax, almost polished, a shining ground of dark chocolate, and the curving ceiling was adorned with purple Air Plant blossoms. There were aluminum bowls full of tuna fish and water, and in the approximate center of the space there was a very large chair, like a throne, wrought of splendid hardwood, where Jerrold would sit, if he chose to.

Jerrold had already arrived by helicopter, in a rude display of hovering that is key to TLC, common to airports, cities, and war zones, metal blades shredding the air, a whirling disc of flying dirt and plant material raised by the giant mechanical, aerial dragon, causing the PP to run off in fear, finding engines that draw birds to their deaths to be something to seek haven from. He was enormously pleased with the course of his calculations. Using the new, sophisticated Global Positioning System, using satellite technology, he'd located the exact point that the two coordinates on the back of the postcard had designated, all by the rigidity of numbers, suggesting a system of labyrinthine causality. The machine hovered, holding the clearing in a rude cone of loud noise, site squelched by decibels. Omnibus, just back from the cave, appeared at the entrance of the canvas tent, professionally attired in a tight-fitting snakeskin suit, "ELF" brashly painted in red on his front and back, distinguished amid all the ado. In the ferocious sunlight, capable of destroying the nuances of vision, his eyes were bold, convex lenses reflecting the long metal blades of the hovering machine, piloted by the short, taciturn man with a face of black sponge, who had gestured to Jerrold, urging him to jump. Suitcase strapped to his back with a belt, wearing a safari hat and sunglasses, dressed in flashy, light flannel clothes, Jerrold flung open the door of the cabin compartment and jumped, his shiny black combat boots landing with an impact on the dirt, as his left knee gave way, and he fell down to the ground. Omnibus ran up to him, helped him up to his feet, and, brushing dirt from his clothing, directly facing Jerrold Draper, Master of the Money Verse, welcomed him, doing a ceremonial jig, as a nearby group of PP men and women began to sing and play percussion instruments. Jerrold nervously glanced around, evaluating his new parameters, and he was aware that his left knee hurt, and he hoped that it hadn't been injured badly, as he noticed a whole cast of characters emerging from the Jungle's green growth, small, chocolate bodies, more men and women, the PP appearing, popping into view, some of them waving their hands through the air, some drumming and singing, some holding spears, some of the women clutching infants to their breasts, most of them staring at Jerrold, eyes focused on the form this new white man took, as Jerrold looked around him, perplexed, wondering what would happen next. Omnibus exercised formidable telekinetic powers, as he examined the bruise on Jerrold's left knee, treating it with a natural antibiotic, an ointment he produced by simply snapping his fingers, and the bruise and the pain disappeared, producing an even more significant effect. Jerrold was struck by the unusual sensation of a soft cloth netting, like tender white gauze, falling over his head and shoulders, draping over him, and it turned into a kind of frothy fabric, like a pulp, a foam whipped up around him, effectively binding and blindfolding his upper parts, his throat and head encased by the soft, wet, amorphous material.

The cries of excited monkeys pierced the sultry atmosphere, and the sun glowed, its presence distorted behind a tall, towering mechanism of cloud, as Jerrold lay there, prostrate on the ground, waking from sleep, surrounded by lush foliage, wondering where he was that significant Thursday afternoon, feeling fused, sensing the influence of solar rays infiltrate the base of his brain, the chassis of his consciousness. The concentric circles of baffling foam that had covered his head for several hours were melting away, leaving him feeling fresh and pliable. He could hear the PP singing softly, almost whispering, providing the context for a relevant event. While Jerrold had lain unconscious, Jesse and Konrad, bringing the Golden Cat with them, returned, stopping first at ELF headquarters, where Konrad picked up an important document, a site for future signatures, and they finally deposited the Golden Cat, still under heavy sedation, into its new cage and home, the dome.

Up from the ground where he had been sleeping, spurred by what a shout's about when it happens in a dream, Jerrold assessed his awareness of the scene. The PP women were singing loudly now, almost shouting, as if announcing something imminent and new. Cast as an object that's been lost and found and lost again, the purpose of his being there returned to him like a pulsar's signal, coming from somewhere far away, and the thought of Jesse filled the corridors of his consciousness.

Konrad suddenly materialized, bearing a silver tray upon which an expensive ballpoint pen and the important document, rolled up and bound by yellow ribbon, lay crossed. It was a legally binding agreement of exchange. Konrad handed the document to Jerrold, and it unrolled like a small carpet in his hands. He scanned the lettered paper, and in a flutter of rapid movement his eyes devoured its content, immediately incorporating the logic of an agreement, clearly spelled out in meticulous Gothic script, and in the oblivion of a present, incantatory tense, he was persuaded to succumb to newly formulated demands. Jerrold proceeded, as if in a directed daze. Yes, he would spend a day, twenty-four hours, from sunset to sunset, in a cage with a wild animal, the Golden Cat, an infrequently fierce feline, a potentially benign, shy, and even harmless creature, if and only if, in return, he could leave, free to go home with Jesse, his son. He felt an objection form from within, and he wanted to see Jesse immediately, in the living present of his skin, but the desire dissolved. Now he was under the sway of the document's terms. It was a small, temporary sacrifice. Picking up the pen, hovering over the parchment, stalled for a moment of ceremonial indecision, he finally scribbled his signature, however improbable, without drama, binding himself to the ordeal. It was his signature, and it meant all things real, and the document rolled up automatically, as he tossed the expensive pen away, letting it slip into foliage.

Jesse, meanwhile, was off with Omnibus, studying the big mirror outside, in the form of an enormous anthill, a vertiginous

awareness of the NRG at work underground building within, and
he was just about ready to break into it with his hands, feed a tree,
plant a house, praise his incessant good fortune, when he stopped
in his tracks. The dread voice had returned, and he knew it; he felt,
in a flash of telepathy, Jerrold nearby, just around the corner, and
this new item of information tempted him with the possibility of being shipwrecked on an island with his father, trapped in a fishbowl
with him forever. It was as if he had grown gills again. Tentatively,
Jesse approached the anthill, sensing the pressure of his father's
voice hurtling nearer. Suddenly, in a mode of manic escape, he was
swimming underwater toward the drain at the bottom of a pool, and
there were bubbles of air, and the voice lost its hold as he swam
down deeper, spreading the water with his hands, allowing something new to pervade his field of awareness, a persisting, seething
substance, prompting implosions in his ears, as a subtle body of
crystalline liquid enveloped him, and he went into a telekinetic
state. Jesse entered the cocoon-like, vertical casing of his own making when a familiar human voice broke through.

"I thought I'd lost you. Now it seems we're together, here again.
It's funny how things work out," it said, almost soothingly comic,
coming through the air to him.

"Only for a while, Dad," Jesse replied ominously.

Jerrold, meanwhile, blindfolded again, this time by a grey handkerchief, was led to the place where he would be, for the duration
of a day, a twenty-four-hour adventure, detained by the terms of the
agreement, constrained by his signature, locked into the deal, alone
in space with a wild animal, and he tripped on a rude root, sticking out at the threshold of the enclosure. He teetered and regained
his balance, and Konrad guided him to the chair, fastening a huge
straitjacket-like belt around Jerrold solemnly, securing him there.
Konrad undid the blindfold, in a rush to get the ordeal over, as
Jerrold surveyed his new surroundings, a veritable cage, a sort of
enormous igloo, a dome constructed from sheets of translucent

plastic spread out on a curving wooden lattice, with tarpaulins and ropes binding its form, surrounded by green growth outside, visible in a blurry way through the translucence. There was a dirt floor, made bright with some kind of resin, parts of it bearing paw prints. There was a bed of straw. Jerrold immediately noticed the waist-high stack of magazines, admiring the knot in the string that bound them together. Suddenly, his face expressed surprise at the presence of the cat, sleek and compact, glistening. Konrad turned to go, and soon he was gone, outside locking the door. The cat was there, and they stared at each other with the indifference of unrelated species, alone and inarticulate, as Jerrold considered his ignorance; he usually took the life around him for granted, but this was not one of those times. He noted the afterglow of the sun, seen through the translucent membrane. There was still enough light to see clearly. The pupils of the animal's eyes seemed to narrow, as if in concentration, evaluating Jerrold, scrutinizing him, the large white man bound to a chair. The animal then closed its eyes.

Jerrold warily eyed the animal, and the intricate muscles around his mouth relaxed, allowing it to make an inadvertent, momentary "oh" in an expression of dignified ease. The cat's eyes had scanned Jerrold for the animal that he was, an auspicious aura in the air between things, and it had swished its long tail in contentment. Taken by the many burnished hairs of its thin fur coat, Jerrold pondered the flame within its mortal frame, the sleeping beauty of the animal, and in a flash he suddenly understood something, but he didn't know what it was. He only knew that it was something he couldn't understand, life in a cat, the feline mind in principle, something without measure, a vast ocean without bounds, and he was becoming part of it. There was a canteen of water placed on the ground some distance from the prisoner's feet; it almost resembled a tambourine, and acting as if it were one for an imaginative moment, he picked it up and shook it, all in his mind, and then he opened the cap and put the opening to his mouth and let the cool water quench his thirst, his imagination running away. Suddenly, Konrad materialized in the doorway, facing Jerrold, and he looked at the prisoner quizzically, shaking his head in dismay. Konrad was grinning a grin. "Hey, man, I'm just kidding. You're not going to have to stay in that chair, strapped to that seat, for a whole day's duration. We're not into cruel and unusual punishment here."

Konrad undid the straitjacket, shaking his head, muttering to himself with suppressed mirth, while Jerrold stared straight ahead, a portrait of stoic indifference, unruffled, maintaining a posture of conscious control, though a strange, new passivity was sweeping through him like a broom, ever since he'd signed his name on the line, binding him to the agreement, and it seemed he was blending with things. Was he being taken for a ride, and if so, where to? "We're not going to confine you. We're not going to deny you your freedom to move within certain bounds," Konrad said cheerfully, as he walked out, locking the door for the last time.

Jerrold, now free to get up, rose from the chair, quickly and quietly picking up the canteen, keeping one eye on the sleeping cat, as he unscrewed the cap and cocked his head back to open his mouth and consume the cool, clear water, noticing the animal fidgeting in its sleep, its whiskers quivering, its eyes closed, yet somehow appearing occupied with mental content. The sun went to rest in a sea of grey cloud, while Jerrold sat patiently in the dusk, waiting to see what price he'd have to pay for going through with this. There was really nothing else to do. He was waiting to see what the animal did first. The cat did nothing. It slept. The night was a moist mass, saturated in places with fragrant molecules from invisible flowering plants, and Jerrold's head felt strange, as if it were a funnel, with all kinds of influences pouring into him, through him.

The night wore on, and Jerrold dozed off. It was a surprisingly eventless night until the animal, roused from its slumber at one point, rose on its paws, arched its back, and opened its fleshy, pink mouth, like a nocturnal flower, noticing Jerrold sitting there asleep, only to yawn, blink, and settle back into its feline slumber.

Sometime toward dawn, as the new day's light began to seep through the translucent membrane, revealing the green furniture outside, slowly linking things up, bringing the calls of early birds out, forming audible causal chains, Jerrold regained consciousness, amazed that he'd actually fallen asleep in a chair in a cage that he shared with the Golden Cat. He got up from the chair and walked with stealth toward the stack of magazines, thinking about breaking it open, undoing the string and taking one, just for something to read, without disturbing the animal's slumber. Suddenly, the cat's eyes opened, and its pupils turned into large black orbs, each suspended in a glistening emerald iris, expressing its potential for dangerous behavior. Stopped in his steps, Jerrold felt a tremor of fear fill his spine. He had tapped into a primal response, prompting an immediate knowledge of what the animal's claws and teeth could do, as he saw how they might rip him apart, and the animal stood in its golden coat, holding its ground, producing the contented purr of an efficient feline engine. Jerrold raced back toward a space behind the chair, crouching, now clutching the heavy chair in front of him by its legs, holding it like a protective device. The panic of these first impressions passed, and he regained composure, remembering the peace of last night, daring to put the chair down and sit in it, to simply stare into the vacuum of the animal's eyes, where he discerned something unobtainable, the light a finger points to, and it made him tremble, and the surface of his experience was like water being heated in a pot, water just about to boil, trembling, about to erupt into bubbles of gas, as it occurred to him, with more force again, that the Golden Cat was a finite, contingent, living being, breathing, consuming precious oxygen, a piece of furred nature, forming a container bound to appear physiological, psychological, organized, sharing the same slot as he, the here and now, the dimension they were alone together in, bonded by true glue. The production of an awareness of the miracle of existence takes time, and Jerrold stood stunned for some seconds, admiring the animal's cunning comportment, before it sneezed and yawned, showing its teeth, but the cat proved finally disinterested, declining interaction, almost completely indifferent to the human presence, licking itself, putting tongue to furry flank, picking at its whiskers with one claw, as it sat back on its hind legs and became sleepy, supine on the straw, but not before exchanging an emotionless look of pure animal lassitude with Jerrold, then turning away, resting its chin on its forelegs and closing its eyes. Jerrold became attentive, his eyebrows taut, as he stared at the ways of the cat, an enhanced hearing allowing him to listen more closely to the beating of its heart, as though heard through a stethoscope. Lying down, with his head on his hand like a thin pillow, copying the cat's relation to the ground, Jerrold gazed at its slumber, feeling a new, feline knowledge of reality, feeling as if his chest held a glittering ball of light, seeing wheels of color spin.

Jerrold was soon sitting in the chair again, relaxed, sipping water from the canteen, noting the shape of its fit in his hand, assessing the situation, sensing the tuna fish in the aluminum bowls, seeing the head of the animal there, now eating, then watching its attention taken by something new, a butterfly, as the creature took off with a leap, losing its shape in the chase.

The cat was now obviously male, its testicles bound tightly to its lower abdomen by the contracting lace of a delicate pouch of pink skin, revealed as it flew, its dense, golden thighs giving a forceful grace to its leap, flight in the fuzziness of perfect pajamas, long sleeves spread out, becoming great wings, now making arcs in the air. The miracle of the arrangement worked, and the flying creatures appeared to cavort through the space, playing in a kind of dance, the insect somehow eluding the grasp of the mammal. They gamboled about in parabolas. Jerrold was transfigured and transformed by the magical "aura," if you will. At the peak of a particularly highly charged moment in the spell of an exchange, Jerrold's attention, burning with hard fire, a flickering ace of flame on a wick, called himself outside of himself in a thousand forms, so that he might gather up what otherwise might have passed unnoticed: the power to be deeply moved by the dynamic mystery of another living being, and he saw, as though rising in renaissance, in resonance with the feline within, that he was only a child of this world, where he discerned the inklings of a permanently new condition. The creature had acted with secret agency, changing the space he was in.

By the turn of its glance, by the intensity of its sheer eyes, now two green, glowing marbles, the flying animal sent waves of NRG through Jerrold, his mind tuned to an unassigned frequency, as though he'd been slipped a powerful hallucinogen, inducing these visions, as the cat began to move into his body, inhabiting him for several swift seconds, before it turned and ran back into standard form and state, purring loudly, but intermittently, as if to take a point of view, but how does life become a point of view? The creature rolled on its back.

Amazed by the cat's acrobatics, Jerrold did a slow scan of the caged space, and the movement the animal made in it, a smooth, unhurried lope, returning to its straw bed, after nibbling at some tuna fish and lapping up some water, then settling into a curled position and purring softly, but consistently, ready for the conduction of sleep.

"I am just flabbergasted by what's going on here. What's going on here?" Jerrold posed the question to the empty air. The cat, taking this as its cue, promptly began to speak in a clear, distinct voice: "You are just an instantiation, though an exemplary one, of a new world rising from the ashes of the old," it said, and then the talking animal went through some profound changes in its material coloration, from yellow to red and then to black, and then back again, from black through red to yellow, as if being painted by invisible brushes, emerging, through the process, after the six layers of paint had been applied and allowed to mix with each other, in a new brown suit, and it stood there, poised on its hind legs, its fur becoming a burnished copper, its shimmering form a show of mettle.

The cat conducted a change of Jerrold's neural chemistry, shaking up circuits, building new fires, causing waves on the surface of his consciousness, rearranging the uppermost few millimeters of formidable cortex, his grey, entrepreneurial matter, altering the tiny brain trees thriving there, the actions of axons on dendrites, binding them in new ways, bringing him into an awareness of the essence of his own experience, the MISSED TREE of a turning mind, letting the grand mechanics of random currents run through him, his capacity for orderly thought now fading, melting away in the time. He could feel its absence. He looked for it, and he found it was no longer there, and with it had vanished a kind of tyranny. He was completely incapable of forming any objective judgments about reality, overwhelmed by the breathing body before him, not him, yet alive and somehow part of him. What was the animal doing to him, and how was it happening?

The Golden Cat spoke again, commencing to rant, consumed with the conviction of a position based in raw temporality, venting the pent, as it went into a ferocious tirade, tied to inner weather, speaking for all cats and dogs, deer, squirrels, raccoons, possums, mice, toads, turtles, and other roadkill on Earth, forming a sustained invective against gasoline sculpture, cursing car culture, the relentless burning of fossil fuels, speaking as president of a political party for animals, condemning the vehicular madness that has brought us here—to end where, Mars? It was an exercise in self-accompaniment, a contrapuntal contrast to be played by the other hand. The cat then spoke, in deeply appreciative tones, about the aesthetic beauty of their surroundings, a confluence of many factors, underlying kinetic things that aren't even things, and Jerrold experienced the sensation of being a funnel again, open to fluidity, without a clear sense of who he was or what he was going to be or do in the future, experiencing a disorienting duration of radical uncertainty, undermining his sense of personal identity, during which he began to definitely turn into a gas. He endured bouts of doubt about his heartbeat, wondering how it was caused, how it happened outside his control, without his willing it, and he was perfectly perplexed about his place in the scheme of things. He was going through a narrow passageway it seemed, like an astronaut on a spaceship, wearing a thick suit and glass mask, unsure of his steps, beclouded, befuddled, going he knew not where, yet imbued with courageous curiosity, wary of nothing in his way. He was processing signals from a distant source, moving in accordance with it, a beacon outside of his consciousness, beyond the scope of his ego and prosperous personal history. He was going underground, inside a deep tunnel, his body diminished by the length of it, yet paradoxically emboldened, dissolving into a mode of comprehension that bore no relation to his actions anymore. The illusion of his separate solidity ceased, and he felt himself rise. Everything was turning to gas, and then with a great flash of light, a vision rolled across the contours of his brain, changing its innermost structure forever, as he grasped the primacy of fluidity, a perpetual fountain of flame.

He was reduced to a small cinder, a dust mote, a dot in a large drop of water, and this drop was full of storms, and his experience was evaporating all around him, having fallen upward, into the sun, having been swallowed by an immense sphere of burning gas. Helium and hydrogen atoms sped busily about him, like express trains, too fast to be seen, and he rode on a single, intense, steady beam of unbroken light. The immersion taught him to see again, as waves of insight rocked him, and his thought found its crust, cresting in the shapes of distant, remote mountaintops. Confused, in a daze, he gradually regained his earthly, ordinary consciousness, with its discrete and linear webs of belief, the advantages of anthropological feeling padding him like fellow fabric. The experience with the magical cat had heightened his sensations, and it made him feel as if he were connecting with something that he hadn't felt since before his formal education, before the dawn of his vocation, as though reality were changing its directions, creating a joyful roar from afar. Previously, his consciousness had been consumed with numbers for things. He'd thought them through with numbers. His thinking had consisted essentially of trying to make numbers come into existence, and he was always finding ways, and his trying triumphed repeatedly, so that he wasn't ever truly trying, just putting numbers to work, generating a way of life, the commerce that constitutes luxury, for the ways of our world are numbered.

The cat took off like an eagle, flying around in the cage, executing circles through the air, astonishing Jerrold, and then it settled down for a period of recuperation, afternoon stasis, a nap on its mat, and the day went on.

"What am I doing here, sitting in a cage, soiled burlap on the floor, a pile of magazines in one corner and a mattress of straw in another, where a cat of gold sleeps? What am I doing in this place?" Jerry wondered, watching the animal sleep, its whiskers quivering like the gills of a caught fish plopped on a wooden dock. The sisterly morphemes of its constituent parts did a little dance, even in its sleep. He drew his head back as far as he could, his eyes scanning the cat's composure, for it seemed to be suspended there, almost levitating, like an instrument of many strings, a potential source of music, a lute, waiting to be played. Somewhere at that instant, a distant drum sounded, and melodious sounds from hidden birds emerged, bewildering causality, so that Jerrold entered another mental state entirely. What do you know when you know you don't know? He was rendered inarticulate, thrown like a stone down a hole, descending into the microbial wheels of his own awareness, his circuitry charged, looking for cover and finding nowhere to go, caught in a downward spiral, but he was certain that that's where he was, and it was a place of free air, in the sense that he'd ceased to think of a number of things, like numbers for things.

The Golden Cat sat, nonplussed, its eyes closed, shut in meditative concentration, its limbs neatly tucked under its coppery body, its pose hieratic, showing off links to hallowed ancestors, the image of the Great Sphinx rising over the sand. It commenced to purr with contentment, oblivious to Jerrold, who was now taking off his shirt, captivated by the fur on his own body, touching his chest, caressing it as if he'd never noticed hair there before, this trait he shared with the animal.

The cat opened its eyes, engaging in a little conscious play on the straw, twisting its flexible back on its spine, teasing Jerrold, paws put into the air in a rite of facile feline felicity. Jerrold noticed a small pile of fabric and copper wire behind where the cat had been sleeping, something that hadn't been there before, something that had just materialized, and he knew that he didn't know enough. Holding on to the chair, hands clutching the edges of its seat, he watched the animal's face change, framing a fey smile and laughing eyes. The eye contact startled Jerrold, now open to the cat within, as he felt the borders of his skin being broken, perforated in vital places, allowing an alien essence to enter him again, instinctively focused, the sinews of its intentionality gathering around the shape of another butterfly aloft, homing in on it, leaping up, and trapping it between its paws, bringing it down, batting it about for more play, like a child performing complicated piano music spontaneously, before it was distracted again by some new thing, the feel of its fuzzy tongue running along golden, furred contours, sealing its hairs, and the cat yawned because it realized there was nothing more to do, stopping and, staring at Jerrold for a last time until, sufficiently tired of the routine, the animal lay down, closed its eyes, and seemed to fall asleep. Jerrold, compelled to feel the role of the creature, slid down from the chair and curled up on the warm dirt floor alongside it, assuming a fetal position, letting what's coming to him unfold.

The sun was headed for its knees, seen through the translucence of the dome, all crimson and mottled purple with the day's end and the appearance of brief Jungle twilight, and the animal roused itself, kicking the golden filigree of one leg up into the air, licking it in a show against inertia, then jumping up on all fours, a gymnast tumbling out of catatonic slumber, as it suddenly went through incredible changes, morphing into a black leopard, slinking about for seconds, before shrinking into the body of a rat, compact and busy, and then into a flying bat, its leathery wings rapidly beating a way out, its escape a black, formal gesture.

Cat, rat, bat—what could these changes mean? The question of the meaning of the transformations reverberated, echoing through Jerrold, sending him into a torpor, a deep stupor, a bottomlessness, and he began to feel himself becoming broken into pieces, sinking again, like gravel tossed at sea. The bat then flew back, circling space, executing a series of promotional arcs, making elegant banks and turns before it dropped to the floor and flattened itself out like a black handkerchief, and then, in a cloud of smoke it had ushered into existence, transformed back into rat, right there on the floor, soon running about wildly before becoming the Golden Cat, asleep again.

A desultory breeze agitated some straw, and bits of shredded paper, coming from somewhere, began to move upward, the matter lifted into the air. Something was coming to its end, savoring the miracle of script and a role to play in it. The last rays of a setting sun passed through the translucent membrane of the dome, through the thin, pink skin of the cat's erect ears, alert, its hearing now trained on Jerrold, who consequently morphed, for a moment, into a mouse. The gigantic specter of the animal towered over him, and he quivered in its perfectly outrageous shadow, cowering with fear. The cat relaxed its focus, allowing its force to wane, pass, and Jerrold returned to human form, just as Konrad materialized, and the cat paced through space one more time, stopping to nibble at some more tuna fish from one of the aluminum bowls, and then, with a final leap, it took off, breaking context forever. Like an old god grown shaggy with lichen, a chthonic spirit revived on its rock, Jerrold looked around, feeling humbled, peering into a space that, only a day before, had seemed ordinary and plain and calculable; he licked the back of his right hand, concluding the performance with the shape of things to come.

"How did it go?" Konrad asked. Jerrod was puzzled. He wasn't sure if he believed that what had happened had actually happened. He didn't know what to say. Had he really turned into a mouse, a gas, a dot in a huge drop of water? The experiences had been unsettling and demeaning; they'd devastated his ability to form sentences about the world around him, to make sense of appearances, and he couldn't control it, this inability, this new unaccountability that overwhelmed him, I think, as I look at the worn, stone floor and wonder where I am going with these changes he was happy to champion, giving them all he had.

"I'm not sure where I am, what I am, or what I am going to do about the long conjunction of seeming certainties that has been my life, my past experience and personal history up to this point in time, but everything has changed," Jerrold said portentously to Konrad, who had already been through this kind of thing before. Jerrold was suddenly possessed by the sensation of something new, a fresh breeze, and the pleasure of simply being there, merely circulating, sensing his bodily processes, produced the pleasant rush of a slight inflation, a push of wind up from his intestines into the more remote parts of his lungs, into the throat and nasal cavities, finally reaching the ethereal folds of his upper brain, the topmost layers of cortex, and fine jets of air streamed forth through his scalp, ears, and nostrils. Spontaneously, he lifted his hands up, letting Konrad join them with his, and they raised their four hands in fusion, unison, making some sort of earthy oath, for Jerrold had had an experience.

Amy appeared, surrounded by a cloud of colorful purple butterflies, bejeweled pairs of fluttering wings becoming a unified field, as she slipped into it, her form shifting to an invisible frequency of the spectrum, until she disappeared entirely, transparency in motion. Jerrold peered into the moment of her absence and took his directions from it. He'd been given a new lens with which to seize a world of invisible radiances, the speech of ultimate forces at work, like the voice of a special day. Suddenly, in a rush of fluidity, his thoughts were running ahead of him, as if they'd been there before, like a comet with its tail thrown out in front of it, and that was the end of it.

It was soon time for real celebration, commemorating Jerrold's realization of his true nature, his gassy essence. Jesse was becoming slowly cognizant of his father's presence, making telepathic contact, and everyone was preparing for their reunion. There was a tremendous amount of excitement amid the PP, empowered and protean, changing forms with incredible ease, the slender, central stems of their collective waking consciousness slipping into plant material, then changing into insects, birds, and animals, breaking bounds through the power of song and dance. Konrad took Jesse aside, explaining to him the presence he'd already sensed for himself, and to Jesse's lips a low hum came, and out of it a live song grew. Suddenly, Jerrold was standing there, in a scene in a play, a seed in soil, holding an incandescent stick, a boomerang of sorts. Seeing Jesse standing there, as if on neutral ground for the first time, an autonomous bundle of biological facts, the changed terrain giving him the quality of being absolutely himself, a flash of recognition sped through Jerrold's consciousness, kindling his metabolism with the empathic power of parental love. Kombolo, the shaman, stood behind him, manipulating the magic stick, showing him how to aim and throw it, helping him with his hands, like a lesson in physical education, and the bright stick sailed through the air with a smooth, swinging motion, out in an elongated ellipsis, like a bird on a tether, returning to land near where they stood, amid bouts of clapping and gentle laughter one Friday night in the Jungle of Gabon.

27

Something was burning the very next morning, but nobody knew exactly how the great conflagration began, for the point of its origin was impossible to locate, to find any name or number for, just a tendency to end in a blaze of sparks, an irruption of infinity. What set it off? Nobody knew how to look for it because it was everywhere, ready to strike, catch, and be caught, a viral fire clinging to the other side of space itself, consuming everything, feeding on life, flamboyance turning it to ash, like Vesuvius exploding, destroyer of cities. It happened in flashes wherever you went, with a force so great that vines burst like grapes, and trees exploded into enormous brooms of flame. Invisible waves of heat carried molecules into the air, as invisible gases billowed upward, and a thick black carpet of heavy, toxin-rich smoke spread.

Jesse rolled over on his pneumatic mattress, his sense of smell aroused. The air was thick with acrid smoke. He was awakening from a strange dream in which Rex, the white cat, had been swimming in the pool back home in Belle Haven, oddly in love with the water, his hairs slicked back like a seal's, diving down under the surface, taking Jesse with him, leading him down to the drain. Jesse yelled out, "Dad!" and a shared awareness of what was happening passed between them, went through them, each in his own tent of air. The fire was making its way forward, as the whole PP camp woke. The flames moved swiftly. They were moving with velocity, feeding on fauna and flora.

"I had tremendous plans for further theoretical work," Omnibus confided to a nearby tree, "but the fire's raging, and there's no time to think." Its branches burst into flames, while Konrad seemed secretly pleased that it was all ending in waves of intense, senseless combustion, the explosions sending billowing columns of smoke upward, like signals in a cartoon. He could sense the rising temperature, and he breathed deeply, smiling, for he felt akin to its aim at work in him. Amy, meanwhile, had assembled a new set of wings. With just a quick flutter, she'd leap into the air and soar, setting an example for Omnibus and Konrad, now following behind her, themselves turned into butterflies (like all of the PP, too), and they'd move through space and vanish, leaving the fire behind them, leaving Jerrold and Jesse to carry on.

Moving in a display of selfhood and determination that wasn't surprising, given the circumstances, Jerrold, for a moment, wished to be inside a camera, having never been exposed to this kind of thing before. There was no space to step back into, no way to get a perspective, no place to look out from, as he grabbed Jesse's hand and panned the burning foliage with manly and terrified eyes, beyond bemusement, wondering which direction was their best bet. What was there to do? Where was there to go? What happens next? The temperature made his face sweat.

The fire raged, an inferno towering over them, as Jerrold and Jesse ran, breathlessly, running without rest for miles, thinking with their knees, hearts pumping furiously. Jesse tripped on an exposed root, which took on the aspect of a cog in a machine, a secret door in Hotel Green, functioning as a kind of latch or trigger, unleashing latent, chthonic forces, and the Pool of Quicksand materialized, its murky, brown surface bubbling with methane and carbonic gases, a toxic cover of hovering ectoplasm. Hearing him trip and fall, Jerrold looked back and saw Jesse there, getting up, struggling with the sandy stuff coalescing over his body in a burdensome, useless coat, standing in the expanding pool, an expression of terror on his face in disbelief at what was happening, as the quicksand performed its silent work, its powers of conjunctive synthesis sucking him up, pulling him down, a substantial wetness grasping his feet, rushing up to his knees, pooling around his waist like so many wet, busy, tan ants, particles of spongy sand taking him down, the end of the incarnate engine. The sheets of wet sand collapsed over his head in layers, and his trapped mass sank to a level where he attained equilibrium with the ambient medium, a thick, suffocating substance filling his esophagus and lungs.

The glue of wet sand filled him, bound him, wrapping itself up quickly inside the remainder of his body, stuffing heart and stomach, filling internal organs and the gaps between them, the hidden cavities, tiny conduits and vessels, channeled into the intimate, curved interiors, the micro-tubes of his mystery, its alliances and history, the movements of his limbs, now useless against the constant current of invading sand, pulling him down, obliterating consciousness in a kind of swan's swoon. Swallowed by the opacity of the experience, Jesse felt himself secluded, isolated, cut off with a final, bewildering blow to the candle of his being, his last atom of awareness overwhelmed by the driving force behind everything in the universe, seeking fusion.

He expired, and his breath entered the gigantic incubator of Earth's atmosphere, and he couldn't deceive himself with beliefs anymore.

Frantic from a distance, Jerrold ran to the edge of the pool and stopped. He crouched down, elbows on his knees, and pondered the busy quicksand, now a percolating putrescence of brown liquid, bubbles of gas breaking out on its surface, its metabolic activity quickened by a new source of NRG. Burdened with disbelief, as if the bubbling monochrome were all a mirage, as if nothing had happened at all and the pool were some sort of optical trick, Jerrold was stunned. "Jesse, where are you?" he called out in desperation. He stood up and looked around, scanning the pool and the vegetation. It was then that he gradually acknowledged the reality of what had happened. The quicksand had swallowed his son. There was a slight variation of color, a lighter shade of brown, suggesting bodily borders in a sea of hungry ampersands. It was there, like chalk on asphalt, an outline at a crime scene, the effect of initial impact, a trace of the catastrophe. Crouched down again, searching for clues, he scrutinized the riddle of the roiling sands, and the liquid began to percolate more quickly with the rising temperature, the approaching fire, like a gaseous clay releasing bubbles, so that Jerrold, holding his nose, sprung up and, in the heat, a great sob rose from his chest, up through his throat, and into his opened mouth and eyes, as if he'd been incubating this catharsis, a final expression of grief, as the surface of sand seemed alive with purpose, pooling its way toward him, extension flattened by gravity. Jerrold stared at the anomalous, animated substance, as if taking a stand, and suddenly, in a kind of sudden reversal, the Pool of Quicksand began to shrink, with accelerating speed, becoming smaller and smaller, reducing itself, turning into a puddle, and then just a drop, and the image of Jesse's impact became remote, and the remaining spot of quicksand percolated itself away into air.

The wall of fire flared forward in waves, feeding its metabolism with plant material, speeding on Jungle spirits.

Jerrold shook with grief and terror, his face made stiff against the burning trees, and then, looking up, he saw a huge sphere of incandescent purple gas hovering over him, the size of an ordinary two-story house, like a baby planet, and a long, flexible tube, like a giant, green garden hose, dropped down, and then the tube bifurcated into two growing tendrils of pale green, like giant bean vines, and these reached his ears, like the tubing of a stethoscope, plugging him into a voice, bearing a whimsical lightness to one he'd heard before, in a reign of little sentences, riddling him. It was Jesse, in an altered, gaseous state, in exhalation, whispering, assuring his father that there was nothing to fear, that it would all work out in the end.

Jerrold ran through the Jungle, his body at odds with circumstance, gorging on adrenaline, heading west, powered by forces he could not understand, attaining an inhuman speed on his feet, which seemed to have wings attached at their ankles, generating flight. He considered the Jungle's density and the distances he'd accomplished, stopping like a piece of statuary every few miles, standing on a pedestal, suddenly able to decode a wide variety of bird calls and animal vocalizations. He was reading veiled instructions, directions to places where he found sustenance, nutrition, and sources of cool, clear water. Finally, after hours of automatic motion, he arrived at a busy highway. He jumped over the guardrail and hitched a ride in a truck to the nearest town, where he rented a jeep, a dependable vehicle.

He'd be able to catch the last train to Libreville, reach the airport, and find a seat on a flight to Paris, from where he'd fly home, finally to Belle Haven, if he was able to drive fast enough. He had run through the Jungle on instinct, directed by forces he could not understand, though he'd trusted them, and now he was approaching a return to civilized life, the one where numbers mean everything, although he felt no need to exercise his mathematical gift, though he sensed its returning. He preferred to divert himself with mild occupations, useless games, adding up the numbers on license plates, finding some odd, some even, with the occasional prime granting him access to a veritable mental romper room of parts and wholes, a space to play around in, altruistically, preferring to share it for the benefit of the planet now, to shine a light on indisputable, necessary truths that all minds could access if given the chance. And then he thought of Jesse, and he was filled with a deep awareness that an entire way of life would soon be passing out of existence.

Jerrold raced forward, gripping the steering wheel, remembering running, slipping on the moss-covered stones, exhausted and overwhelmed by the distances, the trauma he'd endured, watching Jesse drown in the monstrous Pool of Quicksand, so much so that he almost couldn't handle the wheel and keep the jeep on the road, but he did, assuring himself with a visual image of the incandescent Purple Sphere and an acoustic image of Jesse's voice. The road, turning from dirt to cement, morphed into the smooth, broad span of a steady river, its debris speeding up, rushing in the same surge. Everyone was aware of the impending fiery curtain coming, the blaze, the flaming balls of flying pitch, and almost everyone was rushing into Libreville that Saturday afternoon, funneling into Libreville in a great wave of racing gasoline sculptures, all headed for the airport, leaving long trails of dirty exhaust hanging in the air like sheets, chiefly carbon dioxide, hovering in noxious ribbons of particles. Foot down to the floor, he drove and drove, finally reaching the low-lying, forsaken shantytowns on the outskirts of Libreville, where gangs of homeless children roam like packs of wild dogs, where two new superhighways merge, forming a lovely cloverleaf pattern, and there's an enormous BP gas station there. As the highway filled with vehicles, Jerrold was forced to slow down, the jammed traffic bringing the jeep to a standstill. Deciding to abandon it, he put the keys on the vinyl seat, jumped out, slammed the door, and ran the rest of his way to the crowded train station. There were crowds of anonymous people, a sweltering sea of faces, and he was surprised to find himself alone and unnoticed, as a voice from an overhead speaker announced, "Last train to Libreville." He ran toward the final departing car, boarding it just before the doors closed, grabbing them, forcing them open with both hands. The train to the airport was efficient and fast, but the airport was mobbed with people, a rat race of bodies, swarming like flies, seemingly millions milling about, everyone seeking escape, a way out. The wall of fire, its flames now grown to mythic proportions, was sweeping toward them, escalating, defying gravity, fire vying in the sun, and there was just too much confusion, so that nobody knew what to do. Jerrold never traveled without identification, but he hadn't made a reservation. Showing the authorities his passport and some money to make a handsome bribe, he was able to finagle a seat on an Air France flight to Paris.

The late-afternoon flight was strange, a departure from fundamental reality, as time itself seemed to freeze and reach a stasis, becoming a crystalline liquid of instantaneous images of all the things he had already seen, giving the whole day a cinematic density from which there was no awakening, although he could count his heartbeats, as he summoned an image of the voice again,

and he marveled at the miracle of modern air travel, watching
the waves of the ocean below, myriad whitecaps unfurling upon
a section of the great sphere, before sinking into the headrest,
where he closed his eyes and heard the muffled vibration of the jet
engines working, somehow soothing and reminiscent of simpler,
easier times. He thought some more, and then he leaned forward.
There Jerrold sat, at twenty thousand feet, opening his eyes again,
in awe of clouds resting like lily pads on a vast lake of air below
him, noting some particles of sugar on the plastic tray that fell,
jolted unintentionally, out in front of him, which he stared into for
an instant. He put the tray back up, securing the latch. Hunched
at the scratchy portal, peering out, he was struck by the mass of
the aircraft, the extensive, aerodynamic structure of its left wing,
calculating the speed at which it flew, almost impossible to detect, but he was able to imagine it, finding the usually routine
experience of flight changed, altered to suit his thoughts. He was
enthralled. Everything was registering in a new key. The shiny
engines on their wings were working by magic, it seemed, one
winking at him, and his imagination was playing with the scales
of his experience, investing it all with a new sense of purpose that
he couldn't yet identify because he didn't want to, not yet, but
he knew it had something to do with Jesse and the incandescent
Purple Sphere, the mysterious consolation of the voice he had
heard, still reverberating after all these hours, coming down like a
hand from the sky.

Briefly, he fell asleep, awakening to the busy, bright lights of Paris
below. They were making an unusual approach to the airport, flying
in from the north, flying directly over the city. He could identify
Notre Dame, the cathedral's bulk of Gothic intricacy all lit up along
the rim of the dark river. There were boats and barges, illuminations
of electric lights, and then the endless suburbs, labyrinths of streets
and highways, the rhythm of modern civilization returning as the
lights came on overhead, and they were told to fasten their seat belts

for landing. The comforting confusion of a loud crowd at Orly only cheered him on, as he waited for his suitcase, soon making its unexplainable appearance on the carousel of gleaming luggage. Through the tinted glass window of a black limousine speeding toward the city's center, he studied the brightly illuminated Eiffel Tower. He saw a plastic garbage bag in the branches of a dead tree, and he wondered how that could be on the boulevard. He stayed at the Paris Marriott, right on Avenue des Champs-Elysées, where Jessica and he had spent a memorable weekend, when they were taking Jesse on his first and only whirlwind tour of the major Mediterranean cities.

Out on the hotel balcony, Jerrold was carried away by the wind coming in from Africa, if only in his mind, looking down, somehow taken by the sinuous flows of traffic around the Arc de Triomphe, all of it speeding on wheels, the sounds of late-night entertainment rising from the street in pleasant bursts of polite applause—some kind of performance going on, with street musicians making him smile in this festive environment—as he fixed his attention on the palatial room behind him, the high ceiling, the splendidly papered walls, the ornate entablature, the crystal chandelier, the great big mirror in a gold frame, the elegant, antique writing desk, standing upright, as if at attention, the redundant furniture, silk upholstery, and cushions, the big brass bed with its long, weirdly cylindrical pillow. He looked out into the skyline, savoring the city's ashy silhouette in the warm spring air, and the figuration of a slight erotic *ping* passed through him as he thought, briefly, of phoning an old flame, Anne-Marie Barry, a fashion editor at *Paris Match*, an old friend of Jessica's who'd become a regular hookup during his first few years of frequent travel. But the thrill was gone.

He thought back on what had been, and the details congealed into something like a story, something to tell, but he had no time to think, realizing that thought, or what is called thinking, is only the play of words, and he gazed at some vapors in the sky. There seemed to be a sudden abundance of light, as a neon sign outside flashed on. It had been a long day, and it all seemed too incredible, creeping up on him, the journey at its end, culminating in horrified shock, as he realized and relived a spontaneous materialization of the brown pool of ampersands, the graphic collapse of Jesse, his body immured in wet sand, walled in forever, a flashback to all of the loss. He looked at his hands, and he thought of feathered birds flying. The Golden Cat's preposterous presence popped into place, modulating Jerrold's mechanism, rearranging the delicate bones and membranes of his inner ear and related cortical regions to the point where he vividly heard that voice again, settling in his ear, assuaging his fear, assuring him that Jesse would return, like a form of heroic sculpture, although nothing was certain. But there was some sort of certainty there, and the fact that there was some provoked a sensation of change, making anything possible. "I am unlimited. I have reached the summit of my experience," he chanted to himself, as a glow spread through his bones. The whole man was becoming a planet again. Before he turned and walked back into the room, he noticed the French flag, its three colors unfurling from a pole, hung from a nearby building, mixing the colors in his mind, merging into a purple sign of permanent victory. He curved into his hotel room, lifting a magazine up from a table, and as he sank into the cushioned surround of a plush sofa, eyes wide open, he flipped through that month's *National Geographic*, stopping at a lavishly illustrated article about, of all things, the Apollo 11 moon landing, featuring a photograph of Earth viewed from space, the face of this blue sphere, this house of ours, dominated by Africa, all beige and green, the sandy Sahara bordered by the Jungle below it. He squinted at what seemed to be a smile there, suggested by the shape of the desert, and he was struck by that sense of distance again, playing with the scales of things, as he scrutinized Earth, a ball of geology bound to space, as if it had floated away from him, an independent balloon connected by the thin umbilical cord of his own stream of light, which had brought him where he was, at the center of it all, for there he was, sitting on the voluptuous sofa, looking at where he'd just been. Being became the sole topic of his meditation, and he was filled with the impulse to pass beyond limits, into the other side of truth, startled with astonishment over existence, and it felt like a very spatial song, a new knowledge of reality, incorporating changes.

With a surge of NRG, he rose from the sofa, feeling like a free man, unfettered and alive. Something was flowing like honey, slowly draping the lens he was looking through, and everything was turning to gold, glittering with the promise of renewal and change. He rifled through the contents of his suitcase, finding, much to his surprise, a navy blue blazer, a plain pair of pants, and a white cotton shirt. He went to the mirror and made himself feel presentable. He picked up his wallet, put on some shoes he found in the closet, and went out into the night, walking without destination, gradually recollecting broken pieces from the Jungle, his time in a cage with the Golden Cat—a cat, rat, and bat—gradually letting the experience wash through the machinery of his memory, preoccupied with moving motor vehicles, the gasoline sculptures gathering, as he walked along Avenue des Champs-Elysées, open, he felt, to whole regions of consciousness no one before him had ever even begun to explore, headlights on everywhere. There was the mystery of each automobile being exactly itself, identical to itself, caught in its own mirroring case, and this was cause for wonder, calling the Mercedes a "Mercedes," the Porsche a "Porsche," the fender a "fender," the wheel a "wheel," until the question of the meaning of these beings became moot. He could feel the pulse of excitement creeping over him, the thrill of the night. He was walking toward a bright configuration of whirling identities, and he could grasp them all, all of these splitting off into attributes, as a circle of predicates formed around him, a flowering of his experience, so that each and every thing he thought was actually a particle, a point of light, a bubble in a rush of fluidity, a feeling in his knees, the foundation of all he now knew, which didn't seem to be such a big deal anymore. He shrugged his shoulders and buttoned his jacket. Sometimes he had to take liberties. He continued walking, down along the boulevard, to the front entrance of another luxury hotel, where he witnessed another display of ostentatious, useless beauty, another gorgeous automobile, and he was engaged for a moment with its being there, stopped on four wheels, as he passed, stopped, took a photograph of it, and eventually continued walking on. And then he stopped again and looked at his feet, noticing tiny, glittering crystals of light caught in the pavement. He looked up from his place in the street, glancing back at the parked car, noticing the steps he'd taken, feeling he was late for an important date.

Suddenly, it was playtime, and it wasn't too late, and Jerrold was playing basketball around a utility pole with a backboard and hoop bolted to it, back in Flushing again, back in Queens, the sun going down, painting the sky red, helping himself to some memory there, and the river accompanied him. They played so that their bodies glowed, but now there were adjustments to be made. Suddenly, a cloud of charred material fell down from above, falling out of nowhere, and Jerrold entered a senseless present tense, a sequence of absolute synchrony, as a cloud of turbulent water washed over him like a great wave of many particles, eventually solidifying, wrapping itself around him in an exoskeleton, an external carapace, a shell, covering him from head to toe, surrounding him, encasing him in a thick suit, a dull, elemental cloak. He was stuck inside of a body, and there was the gravity of matter filling the space around him, mummifying, and although this was at first a disturbing, surprising phenomenon, he began to appreciate it, for he'd been granted the license to walk, to saunter on, and watch the grim scrimmage unfold, as he melted into anonymity, a number on a piece of plastic film.

Seized by an ideal insomnia, Jerrold walked through the night, wired with the reality of what he'd been and was still going through, simultaneously harboring an attitude of complete disbelief, and thus an indifference, and yet he continued to experience it, a kind of trial by alienation. The city streets, the very pavement stones, were especially clear and distinct, each one an individual yet part of a group of pavement stones. Some ordinary bricks in a wall, exposed where plaster had fallen, made a show of brute inertia, material animation, particles passing through his skin by osmosis, the singularity of an irreversible process. He tried to walk with total randomness, unguided by any intention, letting his body in its restless mobility become subject to structures over his head, as he found himself in a swarm of vehicular madness, his calculating capacity crushed by a chaos of suns. Beyond a jewelry shop window, near a row of yew trees, Jerrold, standing in the shadows, turned into a gas definitively, a steamy white cloud with bluish borders, becoming larger than he had ever been before, expanding, but at the same time shrinking, becoming smaller than he would be in the future, as his gaseous essence flew, becoming a field of external relevance whose main trait and key characteristic, aside from not stopping, was to elude the present forever. He became a connoisseur of cordiality, the secret curator of this vast museum of strangeness that was Paris that night. Walking alongside the Seine, he was becoming a river also, the great breast of Being nursing its latest lost cause into existence, and he, a pensive man, picked up something physical with his hand, a piece of chalk, shining in the luminous clarity of a general idea, a short, broken cylinder of pale blue chalk.

He walked for almost five hours, all around Paris, up to the high point in Montmartre, taking the steps to see the white church, light showing up on it there. He passed a famous cemetery, its presence cresting into a series of retreating waves. Every thing he passed was a matter of waves in space, scattered, startled like hidden birds.

The new order of the things around him figured as he thought about his former life and the weight of its alienating armor, knowing he would never lift it, never fit his mind into it again, for the facts of the recent past had revealed an ardor submerged beneath appearances, now at the center of it all, as he thought of Jesse and the Purple Sphere, of the voice he'd heard, and he felt, with his hand, for the back of his head, now a single, intricate nest.

Finally, the flood of ideas flowing through him while just walking around subsided, as the first faint glow of dawn began to paint the night away. He sat on a park bench, and a medium of early morning sounds, mostly crickets and pigeons, reached Jerrold's very sensitive ears, however small they appear to me, when I think of his face, conjuring it more carefully. Exhausted, he made the decision to go back to the hotel and try to sleep. He wandered out of the park, finding a surprisingly busy street, where he saw a fleet of sanitation trucks and men standing around, preparing for a day of work. He hailed a cab and returned to the hotel, using the staircase, walking the five floors up to his room, where he stretched out and lost consciousness.

Later that Sunday morning, sometime near noon, Jerrold woke, feeling rested, amazed at the depths of his seemingly timeless sleep, from which he emerged to face a clear, blue sky, and then he thought of Jesse, and the question of what had happened began to rattle him. Yesterday's contents returned, in all of their vivid detail, changing the view through the window he looked through. It all seemed too fantastic, as he thought of the voice of the Purple Sphere, but he made a conscious decision to suspend all doubt about it, just go with the flow. Jerrold felt certain that things would work out, and he soon sat in a restaurant, eating a spinach and feta cheese omelette, his appetite for life brought back by the simple experience of nourishment and the sight of the waitress's legs. He nibbled at a croissant, sipped some espresso, and looked with intense excitement at the activity kindling into real action around him. He eyed the screen of a portable electronic device on a nearby table, and he realized, as more of his ordinary, past personality returned, that he had to phone Jessica, and for a moment he felt as if he were hovering again, a gas again, looking down on an environment, dizzy with vertigo.

In a mild repetition of the night before, in another blaze of insight, he saw his essence, and it was a gas, startling him, seizing him, and he felt as if he were about to drop permanently out of sight. Constantly thwarting oblivion, he struggled to retain his identity while dealing with the bill. After breakfast he made the important phone call, using a secluded phone booth, letting Jessica know that he was safe, although he felt like a phantom, and that Jesse was going to be safe too. He told her about the Golden Cat, the Pool of Quicksand, and the Purple Sphere. He assured her, again, that Jesse was safe, that he would return, and of course she didn't know what to think; she thought he was crazy, delusional, under some spell, plain psychotic. He told her that the deal in Gabon was called off, canceled, rescinded; that EDGE would soon no longer be, for something new was in the works, something that would change their lives together forever. He arranged to have a late lunch with an old friend, Dick Hundt, a classmate from Wharton, an expert in corporate litigation, living in Paris, working with the International Monetary Fund. Having lost his computational powers, Jerrold needed some immediate practical pointers, some good advice, and Dick, joining in with the fun, was able to offer some input.

So Jerrold flew home from Paris later that day, after lunching with Dick, with whom he'd plotted an itinerary, a financial future, after he'd spent the rest of that lazy afternoon in a state of excited contentment, casually strolling about, sauntering through the Louvre for hours, doing something he'd never done before, visiting a museum alone, finding himself suddenly enthralled, a fan of Renaissance art. He was thrilled now, grinning like an overgrown child, by the experience of flight again, considering the magic wings. Looking out the window, another scratchy portal, looking down from up above, he saw a vast, green plane of some kind in the growing dark, and later, looking down to where he'd expected to find empty ocean, he saw the lights of human habitation, and he recollected the great arcs transatlantic flights make, and he first thought it might be Dublin, Ireland. There were interesting people living down there, and he was busy imagining himself becoming part and parcel of a local economy based upon a plentiful harvest from the sea, dairy farming, brewing beer, some limited agriculture, soybeans and potatoes maybe, when a voice from a tiny speaker above him informed them that they were flying over St. John's, Newfoundland, and he began to discern, in the very early light, a barren landscape of rugged, rocky shores. He must have fallen asleep for some time. Looking down from above, sure of his gassy essence, Jerrold was filled with a new, central, organizing vision of the one thing that could save the world.

Possessed by a penchant for theatricality, he filled the remainder of the flight with sleep and dreams of inspired actions. After landing, after picking up his suitcase, he made another important phone call, this time to a hospital, arranging for an ambulance to drive him back home. The car had long, classic lines, with thick glass windows and heavy doors, shiny chrome fixtures, and an aerodynamic, creamy carapace of dense metal; its shrill siren would sound and its red lights flash, rushing Jerrold through the leafy intersection, past the gatehouse, up the hill, and into the great, relaxed curve of his pebbled driveway, amid much media fanfare and hullabaloo.

When Jerrold arrived home in Belle Haven, he was met by TV camera crews. Someone had telephoned ahead to the local networks. People were interested in the Draper kidnapping, which had been in the news. A small crowd of curious neighbors, Jack and I included, gathered on the lawn in front of the house, at the base of the marble steps and portico. A man with a microphone approached him, and Jerrold seemed to welcome the chance to speak. Nobody knew what he'd say. Suddenly, he unleashed a litany of scientific truths about the air around us, what was happening in the air. Jerrold's understanding of the physics, chemistry, and thermodynamics of the troposphere was practically instantaneous and incredibly formidable, lucid, and pertinent. The information positively poured out of him, and I experienced a wonderful consciousness of my own complicity in his way of speech, as he spoke about emissions from gasoline sculptures creating small, incremental increases of temperature, warming the atmosphere and oceans. He used the phrase "carbon footprint," a new concept at the time. At one point, as if possessed by some visionary power, he stared at the camera with widened eyes and simply said, like an overly cerebral performance artist, "Look, the universe is going to continue without us, without you, me, everyone eventually, so we're all potentially dead, already spirits, ghosts, and how seriously you decide to take yourself in the face of that, you decide for yourself, and I'll decide for myself." And he pointed the forefinger of his right hand into his mouth, revealing gold fillings, finally waving the cameras away while walking up the steps to join Jessica, who had been standing there all along.

She looked troubled and confused by all the fanfare, though she would eventually accommodate her husband's desire, agreeing to stand by her man. The events of the past five days, or what she knew of them, had sapped her strength, taking a toll on her health. She looked strangely spectral, standing there with Jerrold, as they kissed for a photographer, and then they rushed inside, he taking her by her left elbow, and the door slammed shut.

Sitting together on the sofa, Jerrold assured her again that Jesse was safe and would return home, that these experiences in the Jungle were fantastic but true. She was bewildered by his speech and mannerisms. Inside the house, he displayed a fear of reflective surfaces, exhibiting phobic behavior around mirrors and screens. He went up into the attic to find the antique hurdy-gurdy, something his mother had owned, something Cecelia's mother had brought over with her from the Carpathian Mountains, and he came downstairs to play it for Jessica, turning the crank to turn the wheel rubbing against rubberized strings, doing steps in his little trance and dance. He stopped playing and looked directly at Jessica, and he shook his head, noting, for the first time really, a nasty scratch on the back of his left hand. "Cars scar," he said in succinct summary of something that had happened. He looked at both of his hands, turning them over to meet the lines in his palms. He broke down here, and he burst into strange, adult tears.

28

FOR THE NEXT FOUR WEEKS JERROLD WAS POSSESSED BY THE MONO-maniac's sense of purpose and urgency, absolutely bursting with plans. He was sure of the truth of the Purple Sphere, certain of Jesse's return, and none of the people working with him, under him, and for him at EDGE had any idea what he was talking about. Jerrold had, for all intents and purposes, cracked, so he couldn't be held responsible for his actions, and there was some formal, reasonable resistance to the liquidation process, resulting in a lawsuit and claims of duress, but he emerged with roughly enough assets to finance his pet projects: funding homes for stray cats and dogs; providing financing for independent farmers all over the world; purchasing a pea-canning operation in Mississippi, potato fields in Idaho, and a number of apiaries in Maine; making risky investments—basically repudiating everything he'd once stood for, putting him at a tremendous remove from the world of big business, a world that had once been so real. He purchased a large tract of land in northern Westchester, a former horse-raising operation, up near Peach Lake, acres and acres of rolling meadows, woods, and open fields, comprising innumerable ponds and streams within its borders, with an old fieldstone farmhouse and a group of enormous old barns huddled in a small vale. He renamed the property "Stay Still Farm," and he planned to set up some sort of independent think tank up there, a free university, a progressive, open forum, hosting colloquia and symposia devoted to finding real solutions for real problems: global warming, environmental destruction, wars and fires, floods and famines, water and food shortages, issues requiring immediate philanthropic action. Within a few weeks, he'd been able to divest himself of billions by giving to animal rights groups, to such organizations as Greenpeace, Doctors Without Borders, and the newly formed Earth Liberation Front. He poured capital into humanitarian agencies working for the health, the education, and the welfare of the planet's poor, in a rush to be rid of so much money as quickly as possible.

The house in Belle Haven, with all of its contents, the tennis courts, the lawns, and the flower beds, was put on the market immediately, all at a ridiculously low price, so that a buyer was quickly found, and Jerrold and Jessica, by early May, were all packed up and ready to move to Stay Still Farm.

One morning before the move, Jerrold was sleeping upstairs. The snow didn't know it was going to happen, but there it was, like a jarring anachronism, lying in great white, illuminated sheets in the landscape of Jerrold's dream. He seemed to be off on a polar expedition, trekking through silent, white waste, the cold making his fingers numb, and then, with a sensation of inner necessity, he felt a cellular shift, finding himself a much younger Jerrold, in the basement of the house on Utopia Parkway, working on a model airplane with patient, adolescent attention, using printed instructions to construct it, then suddenly seeing himself looking into a kind of diorama, onto a theater stage, then down to a tennis court. He was playing tennis with Jesse, or a version of him, a figure fierce and fragile. Jerrold was trying to keep up with the rate at which the tennis balls were bouncing into his court, accumulating there like small white grapefruits. He only wanted to move his feet freely. Feeling his feet tingle awake, he was struck by his suddenly increased olfactory powers. At first he thought he smelled pancakes.

Jesse was in the kitchen, cooking scrambled eggs. He'd been gone for almost four weeks, and he'd been through a real ordeal. Taken by quicksand, pulled into earth, sucked through layers of lithosphere, his then molten spirit coalesced and cooled into a dense iron sphere, the size of a beach ball, busting crust, penetrating the mantle as though he were a professional, swift geologist, his voice expanding into explanations of the genesis of the various rock and mineral strata he passed through until he reached the Earth's fiery core, where, under pressure, he obtained equilibrium, and in a sudden burst of rising NRG, he entered a fit with an environment, an instantaneous state of contentment. "You can't cheat nature, so don't cheat nature," he said to no one in particular, holding up his hands, as if in complete terror of knowing what this world is about, indicating surrender, although there was nobody there. He shook himself like a wet dog, scattering off traces of his impossible passage underground, his body becoming human, sinewy again. He'd materialized, flushed from the crust, emerging behind a rhododendron bush, as if from an oven, flung beyond some rosebushes in the backyard at Belle Haven, and he noticed he was naked. The temper of a light breeze worked the nearby water, its blue surface full of sky communicating calm, and Jesse could feel the heat he held dissipating through his fully exposed skin, evaporating into threads of steam, as his body slipped back toward homeostasis. It was then that the sensation of seamlessness set in, the sense that the cause of his actions was no longer located within him, lodged in some hidden interior, any more than it was simply the world around him, though this wasn't easy to comprehend. A crow flew by, there at the head of the driveway, as he shook himself again and began walking.

Jesse enjoyed feeling the white pebbles with his bare feet, his eyes scanning the house with its turrets and large windows, the red tiled roofs, the trees in their sage, silent ministry. He wandered the lawn, eventually going around to the back, to look at Jessica's flower garden, all the plants wet with morning dew. He saw a Japanese beetle on a peony blossom show its iridescent shell. Scenes from the interior of the earth, flashbacks to that ordeal below were becoming less frequent, as continuous streams of real blood filled his head with friendly feelings. He felt himself being pulled, reeled into the door at the back entrance that Theresa and the other staff used. It was rarely locked, and he opened it, stopping inside to quietly listen for the sounds of someone awake, up and moving about, but as he continued through the pantry and into the kitchen, noting all of its shiny metal and plastic surfaces, he realized no one was up, remembering that Theresa didn't usually start breakfast until sometime around eight.

Reminded of his nakedness, Jesse withdrew from the increasingly bright light, furtively sneaking upstairs, although there was no cause for secrecy, to his room, where he put on some clothes. Suddenly famished, he thought of going downstairs to the kitchen and getting something to eat, cooking a real breakfast, but then he thought again. Everything had changed, yet things were somehow still the same, as he felt, through his cotton socks, the fuzziness of the carpeted stairway. Singing a song, he descended, now walking through the galleries on the first floor, where he stopped to admire all the white paintings, and then he went into the front room with a large glass window. He stood there, looking at Long Island Sound. It occurred to him that his parents, especially Dad, might actually enjoy some scrambled eggs for breakfast. He could cook some for Theresa too. It was a thought that just popped into mind, dizzy with all of the things he could do if he chose to. He had a hunch about the action: cracking the eggshells against the rim of a ceramic bowl, feeling the plop of the slimy yolk in the bowl, adding a little water and salt, stirring it into a protein-rich froth. The more he thought about it, the more he knew it was something he'd do, though he felt the insistence of something outside of him pulling him away.

On his way to the kitchen, he noticed Rex sleeping on a cushion in an alcove, feline face buried in a fluffy white tail. Rex was an elderly animal now, but he purred with excitement when Jesse bent down and picked him up, partly to examine the tiny white hairs inside of his ears, where dirt and wax sometimes collected, but they were clean today, though his eyes were clearly clouded. The cat was sixteen years old, and the now ancient bond between them was palpable. Rex expressed the desire to be put down, so Jesse gently returned him to his cushion, kissing the animal's forehead, knowing he'd probably never see Rex again.

He slipped through the formal dining room, the one they never used, just to look at the chandelier hanging there. The antique clock on the wall, with large, easy-to-read Roman numerals, numbered his place in space, its brass pendulum swinging behind glass, its minute hand about to tick into a new place. Reaching the kitchen, he opened one of the refrigerators, the only one they really used, the storage ledge of its inner door holding a dozen eggs. There was a neat little oblong of yellow butter, untouched, sitting in a glass dish, and he was seized by a sudden desire to consume it, the butter, for instant nourishment, as if he could aim for no other thing, but also remembering his parents, thinking of them and Theresa, thinking of them all, remembering that they might enjoy some scrambled eggs this morning. Jesse had never scrambled eggs before, but he had an inkling of the procedure, having watched Theresa, having drawn a diagram of her gestures for this purpose, fetching a bowl from the cupboard, a large spoon from the utensil drawer, and the special copper and zinc pan she used, hanging among other implements. With the felicitous NRG of a bright child, he set to work, cracking the shells, beating yolks and whites into a homogeneous consistency, seasoning it all with a pinch of salt. He lit a burner on the stove, turning a knob, where the wave function of his organism was most dense.

When Theresa appeared, too early in her morning, she was pleasantly shocked to find Jesse there. She'd smelled something cooking, something burning, and she'd thought it was Jerrold, who sometimes, very rarely, when in a rush, made his own breakfast. Theresa smiled sweetly and walked toward Jesse; he was wearing her apron, and she embraced him with a warm hug, wrapping her arms around his back, the spatula dangling from his hand. The surge creates its own edges as I picture them there, Jesse pouring orange juice into glasses, soon joined by Jerrold and Jessica, amid this show of properties, the whole room strewn with small rainbows thrown by a prism hanging from a thread above a collection of seashells and pieces of coral Jessica kept in a glass bowl. "We're here too," Jerrold chortled cheerfully, appearing in the doorway, having put on a plaid bathrobe and come downstairs, along with Jessica, still in her nightgown. Seeing Jesse standing there, she was overwhelmed with powerful emotions, breaking into tears of joy, while Jerrold was not so surprised, really, at seeing his son there, his fatherly expectations finally fulfilled amid the shimmering, seemingly solid surfaces of the kitchen. There was something completely compelling about Jesse standing there at the stove, acting the part of provider. Urged by their son, his parents sat down at the table in the breakfast nook, and he persuaded Theresa to be seated with them, and he served them there, transporting scrambled eggs from platter to each plate with the spatula. While the three adults ate, Jesse did his intense best, cleaning up some, managing his mood, thinking about the near future, then running upstairs to his room to pack a knapsack, blood pumping oxygen into his cells.

Lit up by lights in the water, the colorful shapes of the tropical fish in the aquarium surprised him; he'd been in such a rush, he hadn't noticed them the first time. He'd forgotten all about the fish and assumed that someone had been feeding them, judging by the way they darted about, a healthy, finny tribe. He opened a closet door, and he found an old knapsack on the top shelf. Theresa probably, or maybe Mom, or even Dad, had been feeding the fish. He was amazed by how much unnecessary clothing he owned: shirts, coats, sweaters, jackets, and parkas, most of which he never used. His wardrobe had always been a mystery to him, as he never did any shopping for himself; everything was provided by someone else—not Mom, but someone on the household staff who knew his taste and sizes, maybe Theresa. He took three shirts off of their hangers and he grabbed a sweater and a floppy hat. He found some pants, socks, and underwear in his bureau, and he packed all these items into his knapsack, along with a toothbrush, comb, and shaving kit, thinking of the future. He felt, again, the strange insistence of something outside of him, pulling him away.

He whispered goodbye to his old, familiar room. He saw the posters on the walls, and he shot a last piercing glance into the aquarium, a purely perceptual experience. Knapsack on his back, he gamboled downstairs and was soon helping Theresa finish the dishes, while Jerrold and Jessica had both walked off, retreating to the patio to sit outside in the sun, nursing cups of coffee. There was something decidedly unusual about Jesse's being there, his head bent at the sink, below the array of gleaming pots and pans. Feeling like he wanted to leave immediately, he had to control his impulse and focus on the present task, blocking out anything that would disrupt his ability to perform.

Finishing the dishes, he walked out to the patio to communicate with his parents. There was a bounce about Jerrold as he stood up, and he hugged Jesse, not in the modest, formal way he'd hugged him a few times before, but with a warmth and confidence that affirmed the strength of the bond grown between them, two boys burying the hatchet of ignorance and foolishness they'd based their mutual misunderstandings of each other on in a previous lifetime, before they'd discovered that everything is permeated by love, penetrated by this form of NRG, a gold that glitters everywhere, what the whole world needs, something that money can't buy, the ability to renounce and reject anything that prevents one from seeing that everything is connected, like the "freak" in "Africa," like "pore," "poor," and "pour," by a thin thread's glimmer, by the bubbles inside of our speech. In a language of sheer gesture, Jerrold and Jesse reached each other spontaneously, not as a self-imposed duty, but by authentic action done with benevolent detachment, enjoying no sense of separation between them.

"Dad," Jesse said as they parted, "I want to be a nomad. I think I'm going to walk across the country."

He had put down his knapsack and had spoken partly to explain its being there. Jerrold's ears pricked up and seemed to twitch with this new bit of information. After a second or two of thoughtful reflection, he smiled and responded with one simple word, "Okay," and that was that. Jesse sat down and talked about his experiences underground. Jessica, transfixed by her son's fantastic story, held his hands in hers, and she sympathized with his earnest restlessness. Absorbing Jesse, she comprehended his choice of vocation. She was ready to let him rise and go, and although he was wearing loosely fitting clothes, he felt like a knight embarking on a crusade, leaving the realm of his upbringing, the subject of one long, circular sentence, bringing him back to Belle Haven.

Leaving the house, now at the end of the pebbles and the driveway, at approximately the time of four sticks, Jesse stopped and turned to see a ruby-throated hummingbird hover over a branch of pale purple wisteria. Its stationary flight was a thing of absolute wonder. The abilities of bodies moving through space, his own including all he saw, was a source of constant awe.

Green blades of cut grass sprinkled some pavement as he passed, a wandering spirit. Where was he going? He had a vague yearning to see the Blue Ridge Mountains in Virginia, as he started out, feeling himself oriented, walking westward, down Route 1, the Post Road, and then he thought of Texas, the Lone Star State. The whole of his experience was bathed in a yellow light toward noon, as a bright black BMW, a car he'd seen before, a car from the area, appeared at an intersection, and it seemed like the driver's window was rolling down, but the automobile just drove off when the light turned green. Jesse, with what I can glean from the look of rapture on his face, felt a joyous fanaticism for the open road. He belonged where it was going.

29

JACK AND I VISITED JERROLD AND JESSICA AT THE FARM, JUST ONCE, early in the summer, after their first full year there, and I recall how the plush foliage undulated in fabulous green, wavy forms around the haphazard cluster of dilapidated buildings—barns, sheds, a garage, and the modest fieldstone house, a two-floor structure. There were great beams of hardwood inside. Jerrold was visibly pleased with all the renovation work he'd done, showing off the newly finished upstairs to Jack, while Jessica was present in a new light too. She had just rediscovered her lost green thumb, her passion for growing things, her "botanical madness," as she put it to me. The kale yard then was just a small plot of land, but it would soon expand into acres, becoming a viable business enterprise. They both seemed happy with rural life, doing the chores and all that, both moving with a new, alert sensibility, as if they'd rediscovered the joys of being embodied, the voluptuousness of just seeing things. I don't know what happened to Theresa. There weren't any people around to do things for them anymore. The only other people we saw were some local farmers who were using the land for free, planting fields of corn and soybeans.

Jerrold took us on a walking tour of the property, stopping to deliver spontaneous accounts, detailed, content-laden explanations for all kinds of natural phenomena we happened on; he'd become a veritable encyclopedia of scientific knowledge. He led us down a dirt road where there was a fruit tree orchard, and he spoke in excited, exacting terms about making jellies and preserves from his harvest. He showed us the silo he'd recently reinforced with concrete, covering its cylindrical interior with copper, the place where he'd practice telepathy, giving full rein to the reality of an already perfect, peaceful world, "PURR FACT," he said.

A colony of feral cats had made one of the abandoned barns into a communal lair, a hangout where the furry felines lounged about, busy doing nothing, sleeping on the rafters, playing in the straw, eating, mating, tending to their young, getting up to stretch bones and muscles on padded paws, going out to hunt mice and moles, birds and caterpillars, anything alive to pounce on. It was like their hotel, a place for the cats to stay. Jerrold had posted a "No Trespassing" sign over the entrance. Nobody, not even he himself, was allowed inside; he said it was an installation piece, a monumental sculpture commemorating the mysterious felinity inside everything.

Jerrold's last publicized cause was something called "biochar," a possible form of future fuel, one of his great enthusiasms during that first decade back from Gabon, when Stay Still Farm was thriving. We still saw the Drapers then, mostly at other people's parties. I remember one unseasonably warm evening toward the end of October, on the Holts' terrace, comfortably sipping gin and tonics in the lively glow of the jack-o'-lanterns Jerrold had carved, performing for us with a knife, from some pumpkins they'd brought down with them from the farm. His plan was clear. He was going to usher in a New Age of clean, balanced, eco-friendly NRG. A mouse or chipmunk skittered across the flagstones, its tiny claws picking out a fragile soundtrack.

"There," Jerrold pointed, excited like a child by the serendipity of it all. "Yes, that little critter is a container of all kinds of microbial processes that depend on the atmosphere, our air—inhaling, exhaling, pulling in oxygen, and pushing out CO_2—and that's the source of its awareness, to be a tiny mammal on the prowl, but it doesn't have a clue as to how it all works, just as you guys don't really understand the chemical turnings, all the fine tuning, that makes the troposphere turn. But it's simple chemistry, in a sense, and a balance should prevail, and with this technology, called 'bio-char,' it just might start to happen: peaceful coexistence through AGREE CULTURE. The pyrolysis of biomass, the burning of vege-table matter in a little- or no-oxygen environment, releases chemical nutrients that increase soil productivity, and its noxious gas effects are negligible, actually able to reverse current trends by produc-ing negative carbon dioxide emissions." We all shook our heads, as Jerrold rambled on.

With Jack away on business, finishing production on a docu-mentary film for PBS, for almost sixth months now, I've had the time to reconstruct, from ME-MORE-ME, the story of my boys, and I am struck by how Jerrold's and Jesse's lives mesh with mine, for it all blends together in the end. Soon I'll blow this candle out, and I'll go back and discover where I've been, and what this has all been about. Jack's current film project, *The Lesson of the Turtle and the Bat*, takes place in the Yap Islands, a remote, gorgeous jewel of an archipelago in the South Pacific, part of Micronesia, several hun-dred miles east of the Philippines, and it takes that place and makes it, the topography of the islands and the plethora of flora and fauna that thrive there, its subject. With Jack away for so long now, it's as if he's gone off from home to boarding school for the first time. He phones me, full of excitement about the project, explaining under-water camera techniques used in a scuba-diving sequence, yapping on about the exotic fish and birds, and he sounds like an excited child from another planet, so far from my sphere, for I know noth-ing, really, about lights, cameras, recording equipment, and action, how to organize groups of people and get them to do things for you, as I sit here, fiddling with keys.

Thinking, what was it? It's related to anticipation, a mental state allowing meaningful interactions to occur between mobile creatures and their environments. The rain, like a wild wish come true, is lashing wet whips of wind-driven water against the windows, creating undulations and distortions of the lights on inside, streaming through my medium. I hear the waves curl and the fresh surf crash on the beach. According to the television, which has been on, more or less constantly, mostly with the sound off, while I've been writing, a hurricane is approaching, expected to hit the south shore of Long Island sometime tomorrow morning, the origins of its course embedded in its eye, now gathering force, still far off shore, but the storm's surge is building as I sit, fiddling some more, polishing this reflection of a gilded cage, my puzzled look a kind of counter to the gravity of water falling outside, having closed the heavy, wooden shutters over our storm windows and locked all the doors, having spoken on the phone with Jack (it seems he's never coming home) about how to turn on the backup generator and basement pump.

EPILOGUE

SOMETIME AFTER 9/11, WE LOST TOUCH WITH THE DRAPERS. I'D heard rumors about hard times up on Stay Still Farm, where Jerrold had tried to grow grapes and establish a winery, building beautiful arbors, hoping to produce a fine Westchester merlot, but that endeavor failed due to uncooperative weather and poor soil, and his extensive network of agricultural projects became problematic because of mismanaged funds. It was odd, thinking of Jerrold Draper, once "Master of the Money Verse," in dire financial straits, living off the generosity of friends, but something like that is what happened.

The last time I spoke with Jerrold, he was sitting in a deck chair on the porch of the Yacht Club, more than five years ago, sipping a gin and tonic, with the wind coming in from Long Island, bringing with it a preponderance of fresh, lively whitecaps. Jessica had left him by then, running off with a coworker, someone from the farm. It was a perfect day, a late September afternoon, filled with that mellow richness, that depth of resonance and tone that only the promise of winter brings, rousing us to our fate. Jerrold was immersed in a book, something about the state of the Earth. He looked up, seeing I was surprised to see him. "Guess who's back in town?" he asked me, rolling his eyeballs dramatically, informing me by pointing to himself, with all that old velocity, and he shook his head in bewilderment. The Sound seemed to glitter, and the waves broke into a fine, white spray, lifted up from the rocks. Jerrold was dressed in a blue-and-white-striped shirt, a yellow sweater, a fine cotton knit, draped over his shoulders, and khaki pants, his usual formal outfit. Somehow, whenever I saw him in Belle Haven, down at the Yacht Club or at some party, he was always dressed appropriately. I think he would stay with the Holts, and Rolf would lend him some clothes. If Jack had been around more, I am sure we would have seen more of him, and he would have stayed with us, in the guestroom, but it just seemed uncomfortable, with Jack away so often, so I never made any forward gesture of invitation, though we were still on friendly terms. Tempted to make some small talk work, I felt a wave of familiar sentiment sweep through me, for it's hard not to smile when it's a beautiful day. He said, at first, he had nothing to talk about. "I have nothing to say, and I am saying it," he said, though he seemed, as usual, cheerful, an innocence at play in his placid eyes and the lines around his mouth. I remembered what small ears he had, and I noticed how carefully he was listening to me as I spoke, taking a great interest, it seemed, in Jack's cinematic adventures. I didn't mention Jessica, but I asked about Jesse. He said that the last postcard he'd received had been postmarked Anchorage, Alaska, of all places, where Jesse had been working for an animal shelter, caring for stray cats and dogs, but that was several years ago.

We spoke, for about fifty minutes, about the future and the fatal character of the present. "It's all too sad, and it's all pretty lies," he said, toward the end, and he began to talk, in a rambling way, about a brilliant idea for a miraculous paint containing microscopic transducing mechanisms, stuff fit for pinheads and razors' edges, to be applied to gasoline sculptures, a magic coat of paint that takes NRG directly from the sun, absorbing photons by capillary action, like a plant, milking them for all they can give, putting them to work. He said it would run through osmosis. There was the highly informed sense of the genuine inventor about him, radiating accomplishment, and, although I found some of his wordplay both bothersome and fatuous, I thought the general tenor of his ideas was good, like a working railroad bridge or a breezeway, and the way he expressed himself seemed genuinely planetary.

The last time I saw Jerrold, just last spring, on a rainy Monday morning, he was scavenging through the trash in an alleyway off the main drag through Greenwich, Route 1. His hair was grey, like wild steel wool, and he looked physically wet and wasted, dressed in a long, dark coat, tattered and stained with spills, a felt hat on his head, dripping in the rain. It was just past the entrance to Starbucks, and I was on my way to The Darning Egg, to do some last-minute Easter shopping, trying to find a fabric with a specific floral pattern. I slowed down and stopped, and then I rolled down the window, "Jerrold! Jerrold Draper!!" I yelled out. He looked up, startled, like he'd just seen a ghost. "You look like you've just seen a ghost," I said, wagging my forefinger playfully, gently reminding him of my presence, jogging his memory, reprimanding him, taunting him for his obliviousness, his lack of social tact, but it was a futile exercise. He seemed unobtainable, off on a mission. He just looked up, turned his gaze toward me, and eventually shook his head and smiled. He searched through the garbage right in front of him, sifting through it with his hands, digging deeper, foraging like a wild animal. He forced himself to search, and he searched until he pulled up from the trash a pretty pineapple, a whole fruit, crown intact. He smiled again, nodded, and put a finger to his lips. Then he just walked away from the car, moving into the distance, counting every step of the way, for that was how his mind worked.

CPSIA information can be obtained
at www.ICGtesting.com
Printed in the USA
BVHW08*0533100718

520933BV00001B/2/P